ANOTHER ROADSIDE ATTRACTION

ANOTHER ROADSIDE ATTRACTION

TOM ROBBINS

BANTAM BOOKS
NEW YORK • TORONTO • LONDON • SYDNEY • AUCKLAND

The characters in this book are fictitious,
and any resemblance to actual persons,
living or dead, is purely coincidental.

This edition contains the complete text
of the original hardcover edition.
Not one word has been omitted.

ANOTHER ROADSIDE ATTRACTION
Bantam trade edition/May 1990
Bantam rack edition/April 1991

ISBN 0-553-29205-6

Published simultaneously in the United States and Canada

Bantam Books are published by Bantam Books, a division of Bantam
Doubleday Dell Publishing Group, Inc. Its trademark, consisting of the
words "Bantam Books" and the portrayal of a rooster, is Registered in
U.S. Patent and Trademark Office and in other countries. Marca Regis-
trada. Bantam Books, 1540 Broadway, New York, New York 10036.

Printed in the United States of America

OPM 0 9 8 7 6 5 4

This book is dedicated to the Kendrick boys—
Capt. John (deceased) and Billy (kicking); to
Shazam, to tiny Terrie, and to the "fantastic
foolybear" wherever she may be.

"And there are also many other things which Jesus did, the which, if they should be written every one, I suppose that even the world itself could not contain the books that should be written."

JOHN 21:25

"Incidentally, Reggie Fox, who runs the Dalai Lama's 16-mm. projector, said that 16-mm. Tarzan films or Marx Brothers films would make a big hit with the Dalai Lama and those around him. They most certainly don't want to see any pictures where human or animal life is taken; amusement and adventure are the things that they are interested in."

> Lowell Thomas, Jr., *Out of This World* (Appendix, "What to Take When You Go to Tibet")

Part I

The magician's underwear has just been found in a cardboard suitcase floating in a stagnant pond on the outskirts of Miami. However significant that discovery may be—and there is the possibility that it could alter the destiny of each and every one of us—it is not the incident with which to begin this report.

In the suitcase with the mystic unmentionables were pages and fragments torn from a journal which John Paul Ziller had kept on one of his trips through Africa. Or was it India? The journal began thusly: "At midnight, the Arab boy brings me a bowl of white figs. His skin is very golden and I try it on for size. It doesn't keep out mosquitoes. Nor stars. The rodent of ecstasy sings by my bedside." And it goes on: "In the morning there are signs of magic everywhere. Some archaeologists from the British Museum discover a curse. The natives are restless. A maiden in a nearby village has been carried off by a rhinoceros. Unpopular pygmies gnaw at the foot of the enigma." That was the beginning of the journal. But not the beginning of this report.

Neither the FBI nor the CIA will postively identify the contents of the suitcase as the property of John Paul Ziller. But their reluctance to specify is either a bureaucratic formality or a tactical deceit. Who else but Ziller, for God's sake, wore jockey shorts made from the skins of tree frogs?

At any rate, let us not loiter in the arena of hot events. Despite the agents of crisis who dictate the drafting of this report, despite the spiraling zeitgeist that underscores its urgency, despite the worldwide moral structure that may hang in the balance, despite that, the writer of this document is no journalist, nor is he a scholar, and while he is quite aware of the potential historical importance of his

3

words, still he is not likely to allow objectivity to nudge him off the pillar of his own perspective. And his perspective has as its central focus, the enormity of public events notwithstanding, the girl: the girl, Amanda.

"There are three things that I like," Amanda exclaimed upon awakening from her first long trance. "These are: the butterfly, the cactus and the Infinite Goof."

Later, she amended the list to include mushrooms and motorcycles.

While strolling through her cactus gardens one warmish June morning, Amanda came upon an old Navajo man painting pictures in the sand.

"What is the function of the artist?" Amanda demanded of the talented trespasser.

"The function of the artist," the Navajo answered, "is to provide what life does not."

Amanda became pregnant during a fierce thunderstorm. "Was it the lightning or the lover?" she was sometimes heard to muse.

When her son was born with electrical eyes, people no longer thought her foolish.

Wearing a yellow velvet toga gathered at the waist with green scarabs, a garland of blue Japanese iris about her neck, her bubbling baby strapped to her back, Amanda would charge her motorcycle through the meadows searching for rare moths. One lingering afternoon in spring she chanced upon a small band of gypsies camped beneath a willow tree.

Suspecting them to be skilled in such arts, Amanda asked, "Will you not reveal to me something of the nature of my true being?"

"What will you do for us in return?" the gypsies asked.

Amanda lowered her long lashes and smiled sweetly. "I will suck you off," she said.

It was agreed. After she had thoroughly pleased the four men and two girls, the gypsies told Amanda, "You are by nature a very curious woman," and sent her on her way.

For her birthday, Amanda's father (who was enormously fat) gave her a performing bear. The bear understood only Russian while Amanda spoke only English and Romani (although she was familiar with several of the North American Indian dialects, she never spoke them publicly). There could be no performance. What to do?

Amanda made friends with the bear. She baked for him delicious meat loaves. She scratched his ears and fed him oranges, Oreo cream sandwiches and Dr. Pepper. Gradually, the bear began to do tricks on his own accord. He danced when Amanda played her concertina, he rode her silver bicycle, he balanced three croquet balls on his nose and smoked fine cigars.

One day a man from the Moscow Circus visited the city near Amanda's town. At the request of her father, he came to see the bear. He barked commands at the bear in Russian but the bear paid no heed and eventually rolled over on his rug and went to sleep.

"That damn bear never would take orders," the circus man complained. "Frankly, that's why we sold him."

That summer, Amanda's big project was the establishment of a Butterfly Conservatory. Since many moths have a very short life-span, there was a big turnover among the inhabitants of her institution.

Down by the waterfall, Amanda pitched her tent—it was made of willow sticks and the wool of black goats. Having filled the tent with her largest and softest paisley cushions, Amanda stripped down to her beads and panties and fell into a trance. "I shall determine how to prolong the lives of butterflies," she had previously announced.

However, an hour later when she awoke, she smiled mysteriously. "The life-span of the butterfly is precisely the right length," she said.

It was one of those mellow October days that seem concocted from a mixture of sage, polished brass and peach brandy. Amanda's father hiked (puffing) through fallen leaves, nut burrs and squirrel tracks all the way to Bow Wow Mountain. There he found his daughter in the mouth of a bat cave talking softly with the Idiot.

The father was both relieved and perplexed. "You have a terrible cold, Amanda," he scolded. "I thought you had gone into town to see Dr. Champion but someone said they'd seen your motorcycle zoom into the forest."

"I came to visit Ba Ba," Amanda answered. "He has revealed to me the hidden meanings of my fever and the deeper significances of my sneezes."

"When one is ill it is much more logical to see a physician," her father insisted.

Amanda bestowed loving smiles upon her father and silently continued to embroider her dragon cloak.

Blushing, the Idiot rose to his feet. He removed, with respect, his battered gray tam and stared down at his boots. "Logic only gives man what he needs," he stammered. "Magic gives him what he wants."

One morning after a wild electrical storm, Amanda woke to find a strange inscription on the palm of her hand: a single "word" written in some obscure alphabet.

All during her yoga exercises; during her garden-pagoda breakfast of poached salmon, strawberries and cream; during her astrological plottings down on the creek bank, she puzzled over it. She considered it as she and her baby rolled and giggled in the yard grass, she pondered it during her lunch of frog legs and coconut milk—even that afternoon as she circled the lake in her orange and purple sailboat, a choir of eight peyote buttons singing in her head, she probed its enigma—though, in truth, the inscription seemed less mysterious than funny to her then.

The following day—the inscription would not wash off —she researched it in the Library of Anthropological Yearnings. To no avail. She sent photostats of it to young Jewish scholars who had loved her. She tried twelve times to decipher it during trance. Pleading letters she wrote to the Ministry of Esoteric Knowledge, Division of Archaic Titillations.

She never did learn what it meant, although one night years later in an Armenian restaurant, a very old musician took one glance at it, handed Amanda a heavy iron key and ran down the fire escape.

"And what do you believe in?" the parish priest asked Amanda sternly.

Amanda looked up from the beetle shell upon which she was painting a miniature scene in watercolors. "I believe in birth, copulation and death," she answered. "Although copulation embodies the other two, and death is only a form of borning. At any rate, I was born nineteen years ago. Someday I shall die. Today, I think I'll copulate."

And indeed she did.

Birth, copulation and death. Fine. In truth, however, there were at least two other things in which Amanda strongly believed. Namely: magic and freedom.

Only a belief in magic could explain the nature of her tattoos. And had she not been a very free woman she never would have consented, in the first place, to being tattooed in that manner and in that area of her anatomy.

"Although there are more than one hundred and fifty thousand species of butterflies and moths in the world, only about twelve thousand are found in the United States. That is far too few."

Down by the creek, Amanda was speaking gravely to an audience composed of Madame Lincoln Rose Goody, the librarian and naturalist; Smokestack Lightning, an aged Apache medicine man; Ba Ba, the toadstool visionary (townspeople called him the Idiot); her infant son; two dogs; her bear; a turtle; and Stanislaw, seventeen-year-old exiled prince of Poland and rock-and-roll singer who was currently Amanda's suitor.

Having fed her friends a picnic lunch of acorn-flour biscuits, goat cheese, gooseberry preserves and iced mint tea, Amanda was seated in the lotus position atop a stump with the others on the turf at her feet. She was wearing a peasant blouse, lace knickers and Blackfoot beads, and, as earlier mentioned, was talking in a serious manner.

"Unless they have been to Colombia, down near the emerald mines of Muzzo, no American has even seen the blue phantom," Amanda complained.

"That would be *Morpho cypris,*" Madame Goody chimed in cheerfully.

"Yes," nodded Amanda. "We have nothing on this continent to equal the metallic azure luminescence of that superb creature. And think of the death's-head hawk moth with its banded moon-gold body actually robbing honey from the hives of southern Europe; and think, too, my friends, of the gorgeous silky swallowtail brightening the treetops of New Guinea, and think—"

"That's *Acherontia atropos* and *Papilio codrus medon,*" interrupted Madame Goody.

Amanda gave the plump little librarian a long piercing look and was about to say, "Madame Goody, I do not give a rusty goddamn what these butterflies are called in Greek," when she relaxed and smiled. She thought to herself, "So, the scholars are tedious, the experts never see the whole truth of things, still they have their role to play." But although she said nothing, she made it clear to the others that it was the beauty and mystery of butterflies that interested her and not scientific nomenclature.

"Did you know that Brooke's birdwing is so huge that in Sumatra it is often mistaken for a bird in flight? How grand it would be if in our own meadows we could be startled by the beat of its black-velvet and spinach-green wings."

"The *Ornithopteria brookiana*—er, that is, Brooke's birdwing," said Madame Goody, "frequents paths that have been fouled by urine. Your baby"—she pointed to Amanda's son—"is already doing his best to make the birdwing feel at home here."

Amanda giggled. "I would also like to see the tropical castnid—"

"The males of that species are very quarrelsome," Madame Goody warned.

". . . living among my father's orchids," said Amanada.
"And in all our parks and gardens."

So, Amanda outlined her plan. Stainslaw's band, the
Capitalist Pig, would soon be making a world tour. Amanda
would contact foreign naturalists and collectors who, in midnight rendezvous in secret groves or rowdy waterfront bars,
would supply Stanislaw and his fellow musicians with the
eggs or larvae of many an exotic moth. The band members would hide these specimens inside their instruments:
taped within the bells of guitars, concealed inside the hol-
lows of drums, snug among the tubes of amplifiers. The
ancient occupation of smuggling would be embraced in
order to enrich the entomological resources of America.

And so it came to pass. Alas, however, customs agents
at Kennedy International Airport discovered and seized this
noble contraband. The entire membership of the Capitalist
Pig was imprisoned. And almost immediately a rumor swept
the land that butterfly eggs would get you high. The woods
and fields were overrun by unlikely-looking entomologists,
and a sudden demand arose for nets, tweezers, magnifying
glasses and the other trappings of zoology's most vast and
gentle branch.

"My dear Amanda," intoned the family lawyer, "it has
come to my attention that you are increasingly seen in the
company of extremely weird individuals."

Brushing a cigar ash from the attorney's somber necktie,
Amanda corrected him. "There is no such thing as a weird
human being. It's just that some people require more understanding than others."

"My dear Amanda," ventured her father (he was enormously fat), "while I do not subscribe to the old saw that 'a woman's place is in the kitchen,' still I think it a salubrious thing when a young female undertakes to become expert in the culinary arts. However, it gives me little pleasure to learn that you have acquired a surprisingly wide reputation for the quality of your marijuana breads. In fact, I understand that you are sometimes called 'the Betty Crocker of the underground.' What am I to tell our relatives and friends?"

"Let them eat cake," said Amanda, gesturing benevolently.

Amanda signed on as a clairvoyant with the Indo-Tibetan Circus and Giant Panda Gypsy Blues Band, then touring the Pacific seaboard. The fetus, at that time, was no bigger than a pocket watch but already it huffed against Amanda's bladder, and as the troupers motored up Highway 101 they stopped frequently at gas stations where their intentions most certainly were not to "fill 'er up."

This did not annoy Amanda for it had long been her theory that human beings were invented by water as a device for transporting itself from one place to another.

Amanda read the future in tarot cards. She consulted the *I Ching*. She even practiced a spot of palmistry. Her principal duty with the traveling show, however, was to give consultations while in the wakeful sleep of self-induced trance. For the privilege of her psychic readings, customers paid a $4.98 fee.

But mediumship—for Amanda, at least—was not as cut-and-dried and businesslike as the foregoing might imply.

From the time of her puberty, she felt herself able to register the subtle and delicate vibrations of that area of collective consciousness we call the "spirit world." As she grew older and more practiced, she found it easier to enter trance, and the trances themselves became more substantial and were of longer duration. In short, she assumed a certain amount of control. However, mediumship is never an exact science, and for Amanda it was a clear risk. There were occasions when the vibratory phenomena did not register, other occasions when they registered erratically—or got completely out of hand.

For example, one muggy evening in Santa Barbara—just before a shattering electrical storm—Amanda suddenly broke contact with the "voices" who were speaking through her about the marital problems of a well-dressed female customer. After a minute of static and babble, she launched into what might properly be described as a philosophical discourse.

"The most important thing in life is style. That is, the style of one's existence—the characteristic mode of one's actions—is basically, ultimately what matters. For if man defines himself by doing, then style is doubly definitive because style describes the doing."

Amanda expounded upon this at some length. "The point is this," she said eventually. "*Happiness is a learned condition.* And since it is learned and self-generating, it does not depend upon external circumstances for its perpetuation. This throws a very ironic light on content. And underscores the primacy of style."

After nearly an hour's monologue, she summed up by remarking, "It is content, or rather the consciousness of content, that fills the void. But the mere presence of content is not enough. It is style that gives content the capacity to absorb us, to move us; it is style that makes us care."

Whereupon the customer, who had waited patiently throughout the speech, clouted Amanda on the head with her handbag and demanded her $4.98 back.

About thirteen months ago, John Paul Ziller married a pregnant gypsy, bought two garter snakes and a tsetse fly and, on the Seattle-Vancouver Freeway, opened a roadside zoo.

The garter snakes were quite ordinary specimens. The tsetse fly was not even alive. The "gypsy" turned out to be half Irish and half Puerto Rican and was not pregnant long: she suffered a miscarriage after falling in a hole one night while out in the brush with an army-surplus flashlight catching mice to feed the snakes.

Eventually, however, both the marriage—Ziller's second —and the business venture—his first—did, in a curious way, succeed. Even before the Corpse arrived, he had in wife and zoo a very definite roadside attraction.

As the reader must have guessed, the "gypsy" whom Mr. Ziller took to wife was Amanda, then twenty years of age and swelling with her second indiscretion. For those who savor the usually suspect "facts" of romantic love, an attempt will be made to render the details of the meeting, the courtship and the wedding. But first, in the interest of exposition—

A BIOGRAPHICAL NOTE

John Paul Ziller was born in the Congo. That was all. Born there. When he was one year old, his missionary parents returned to America and John Paul spent the rest of his childhood in a Lutheran parsonage in Olympia, Washington. But he was born in Africa. That made a difference.

When a Tarzan film would come to Olympia, John Paul would be at every screening—in the front row with his little friends, telling them loudly, "I was born in that jungle there. I used to swing on them vines." No kid in his neighborhood could play Jungle Jim or Tim Tyler without hiring (for gum balls) John Paul as technical adviser. He could describe the poisons with which certain pygmies smeared their arrows, he knew that *simba* was the Swahili word for lion. The fact that he gathered that information from the library books which he devoured like cookies was of no consequence. He had been born in the jungle, he really had.

By high school, most of the children of Olympia had outgrown games of Tarzan. Ostensibly, John Paul had, too. Maybe he was not quite like the others, but he was no freak. He was the best drummer the school dance band had ever had, and he made good grades, especially in art (those masks he carved were terrific). Although he was well over six feet tall, he did not play basketball, and sometimes his obvious disdain for competitive sports elicited physical attacks from some jock who doubted John Paul's "patriotism." His virility, however, was never questioned. After all, he had been the first male in his set to have the courage to visit Big Ruth's in Aberdeen (where he was said to have gotten all to which his five dollars entitled him) and he was the first boy to "go the limit" with Elizabeth Lee Franklin, thereby launching her long and dedicated career. Such feats insured his popularity with the boys, and with the girls? well, John Paul was lean and mysterious and sophisticated and "Golly, mom, he's better than any drummer I ever heard on the radio or *any*where."

If one accepted his devotion to music and sculpture as normal, then John Paul's only peculiarity seemed to be a kind of exaggerated romanticism in which he sat as a deity in an aura. He was a dreamer who entertained exotic visions of himself, visions related to what he obviously regarded as his ties to another zone, perhaps to another time. When a chaperon caught him drinking beer at the junior prom, he asked, "John Paul, what makes you so darn wild? Is it because your dad's a preacher?" And John Paul got that funny smug look in his eyes and said, "It's in my blood, Mr. Yarber. When I was born, the drums of Kivu beat all night long, the hyenas ate my afterbirth."

Soon after graduation, John Paul took his late father's insurance money (fortunately, the old parson had not taken his "God will provide" sermons so literally as to ignore the man from Fidelity Life) and was off to Paris "to study art."

The next that Olympia saw of him was three years later when he showed up with a fantastic mustache and a young baboon on a leash.

The Indo-Tibetan Circus & Giant Panda Gypsy Blues Band, being a somewhat unorthodox troupe, often aroused the ire of policemen, pastors and pursed-lipped ladies: those vigilant citizens who saw in the exotic trappings of traveling show folk a manifestation of some unnamed conspiracy to subvert their politico-moral prerogatives. Generally, however, as a result of the manager's buttery tongue, rustic diplomacy and thoughtful monetary "donations," the show was allowed to go on (as they say), and by and large those community elders who reviewed the performance would agree that while some of it was weirdly incomprehensible, it had entertaining and even educational features and was unlikely to turn their children into Communists, desperadoes or fiends.

So, while the troupe frequently was sideswiped by the machinery of law and righteousness it deftly avoided a head-on collision—until one mid-August dawn in Sacramento. Some say the orders came from California's glamorous governor himself, although there was scant proof to genuinely involve the guv. No matter. The raid, at whoever's instigation, did occur. And after each member of the circus had been harassed, intimidated and thoroughly searched (the girls' vaginas were explored for hidden vials), eight of the troupers were hauled into jail on charges of possession of narcotics—although the substance found by police was not a narcotic but merely the mild euphoric marijuana, the law being somewhat remiss in making the proper pharmacological distinctions.

Those forty or so troupers not arrested—this group included Amanda and her baby son—moved to an isolated spot on the Sacramento River some miles out of town. There, they arranged their silver milk wagons, star-spangled VW microbuses, motorcycles and mystery-emblemmed '50

Dodge panel trucks in a circle, camping inside its circum-
ference in the manner of early American pioneers. For two
weeks, they feasted, danced, swam, fished, read, rested,
practiced their acts and awaited the trial of their companions. When Justice came, she was not quite as predatory
as some had feared. Two troupers had their cases dismissed
for lack of evidence, four were released with fines and
suspended sentences. The remaining two, however, were
second offenders and they received prison terms of five years
each. One of these had been a roustabout and the circus
manager replaced him easily with one of the young unem-
ployed cowboys who had taken to hanging around the
Sacramento River campsite. For the other, unfortunately, a
substitute could not so quickly be found. He was Palumbo
the drummer (whose prior conviction had been for smuggling butterfly eggs in the hollow of his bass), and in order
to drum with the Giant Panda one had not only to be versed
in the blues-rock tradition but had to have musicological
knowledge and polyrhythmic aptitudes so as to help weave
those esoteric and eclectic textures in which the Giant Panda
specialized.

Since there were several weeks of good bookings awaiting
the circus in Oregon and Washington—dates that must be
kept if the show was to finish the season in the black—the
manager and the bandleader pulled the most roadworthy
vehicle out of the encampment and sped down to San
Francisco in search of a suitable drummer. Days passed. An
occasional northbound traveler would stop by the encampment to deliver the message, "No chops yet." On the tenth
day, in the midst of a late communal breakfast of toasted
puffball mushrooms (*Lycoperdon gemmatum*, Madame Lincoln Rose Goody would have called them), yogurt and
fresh pine needle tea, the missing van squealed into camp,
smiles hanging out of both windows.

"We got us a drummer."

"God almighty yes, we do have us a drummer."

"And do you know what drummer we got?"

"Ringo Starr?" asked a mouth full of puffball.

"We got John Paul Ziller," the manager cheered. "He's
gonna join us here in two or three days."

Around the breakfast fire there rose a loud buzzing. Many
troupers were excited, others clearly puzzled. Amanda, for

example, was certain she'd heard of the new drummer but she could not readily identify him.

Well, by this time next week every man, woman and child in the civilized world may know the name Ziller and for whom it stands. But for the present it must be assumed Ziller is, to the general public, a nonentity. Therefore, the writer calls for additional

BIOGRAPHICAL NOTES

I

Occupation _____. On the billions of varied (yet somehow identical) forms in whose linear receptacles (_____) Western man deposits the salient data of his being, upon whose tiny empty lots (_____) he erects the established facts of his identity; on those forms—tax statements, credit applications, mortgage papers, divorce papers, Social Security forms, insurance policies, Selective Service examinations, job applications, census surveys, police blotters, rental leases, passports, medical records, ad infinitum, near the tops of those forms not far from the open spaces provided for such cardinal intelligence as Name _____, Address _____, Sex _____ and Marital Status _____, there is an area of perhaps an inch in length and one-eighth of an inch in height for the confession of one's Occupation _____. Even John Paul Ziller, although more loosely rooted in the hardpan of traditional behavior than most men, was forced from time to time to fill in forms. And when Ziller would come to Occupation _____, he always wrote "magician."

Now as the reader shall soon learn, whatever compensation Ziller earned (prior to the opening of the roadside zoo) came from his artistic endeavors: visual and/or musical. And while there is no little magic in the arts, particularly the way that Ziller practiced them, it must be assumed that in calling himself a magician John Paul was speaking figuratively and, face it, pretentiously. Yet, in reviewing Ziller's life—as some have been wont to do these past few days—one concludes that "magician" probably covers his activities as well as any other occupational description. After all, it is indicative of some kind of appropriateness when a CIA agent says of a fugitive as one said yesterday of Ziller, "We'll tear this country apart if necessary to get our hands on that fucking magician."

II

Never prolific as a sculptor, it has been several years now since Ziller has exhibited at all. Yet few articles on avant-garde art are published that do not refer to his contribution. That the authors seldom are in agreement as to the nature of his contribution only supports the general notion of its significance.

The Non-Vibrating Astrological Dodo Dome Spectacular was his masterpiece, about that there is no quarrel. When it was unveiled at the Whitney Museum of American Art it brought to its obscure young creator the art-world equivalent of the kind of instant notoriety a starlet achieves when she successfully pulls a film out from under the weight of a veteran and venerated actress. It was saluted as a tour de force and cursed as a scandal. Some critics were afraid to acknowledge it, others afraid not to. When a representative of the *New York Times* called at Ziller's studio for an interview, she was received by a near-naked, savage-looking man who stopped playing his clay flute only long enough to insist that the complex electrochemical sculpture in question actually had been executed by his pet baboon.

III

The prominent Janstelli Gallery presented Ziller's first one-man show of Cosmos Mystique Apparati. These were fiber glass pyramids and cones (volcano-like) about five feet tall. Some were covered with the skins of poisonous reptiles, others with the feathers of small gray birds. Others were painted in translucent whites and pinks, often with a bulb of weak light bulging in the bowels of the fiber glass like some frosty hemorrhoid or mathematical pun. Near the base of each piece was riveted a small brass plate which read: "Upon proper viewing, the external surface heat of this apparatus may reach 2000 degrees Fahrenheit. At that temperature, Old Master techniques are known to fail."

IV

"The Jansfelli Gallery is proud to present an exhibition of Ready Made Fossils, created by John Paul Ziller who has recently returned from travels in Africa (or was it India?)."

The artist had carved from ivory, alabaster and onyx replicas of important archaeological tidbits: the jawbone of Java man, skull fragments of Marmes man, telltale arm sockets from Tanganyika. Ziller chose to display these half concealed in mounds of sand or mud which he had dumped on the gallery floor. Upon two of the more striking pieces (embossed with gold), vats of fresh garbage had been poured. And the largest piece was buried beneath a pile of offal Ziller had gathered along the bridle paths of Central Park. Naturally, as the days wore on, the exhibition began to engage senses other than sight and touch, offering somewhat of a challenge to olfactory aesthetics.

V

At the same time that Ziller was itching the visual art world with his fossils, apparati, post-lunar illuminated Buddha turds and magnetic jade divining rods (helpful in locating the lost city of Mu), his reputation as a drummer was running like a vine along the invisible walls of the musical underground.

In those days he blew jazz, chiefly of the Afro-Cuban variety. Such was his ability that he was welcomed at jam sessions of the top jazzmen in New York, and on occasion he sat in during gigs at famous clubs such as the Half Note, the Five Spot and the Village Gate, drumming in the *bata* fashion while using an African thumb harp for orchestral effect. Since it was rumored that he had turned down chairs in some very fine combos, there was an eddy of interest in the musical undercurrent when word flashed around that Ziller was about to organize his own band. Zollie Abraham, who both promoted jazz and wrote books about it, visited Ziller with a twofold plan: (1) he would contract Ziller's group for a New England campus tour and (2) he would write an article on the aims of the new band for *Downbeat* magazine. It was a warm autumn day and Ziller and his baboon were seated on a Nigerian cotton cushion in front of an open window, eating plums and listening to the sounds that bounced in off the streets. There was a smell of carbon in the air. Upon hearing Abraham's proposal, Ziller, yellow berries of plum juice hanging from the hairs of his mustache, replied, "The jazz was the very same shape as the keyhole so that went through, the blues was lean and conditioned to suffering so it snugged through, but the rock was big like a sausage and got stuck in the middle ear to the ground."

Pretty pissed, Abraham went away and informed all the jazzheads that Ziller was insane and an opportunist to boot. He had sold out to rock-and-roll.

In the mashed banana sunlight of Labor Day morning, Amanda basked on a log in the Sacramento River, talking to her two closest friends in the Indo-Tibetan Circus: Nearly Normal Jimmy and Smokestack Lightning. A burly redhead whose walrus nose and oxblood mustache both drooped wearily as if overpowered by the weight of his ice-cube-thick spectacles, Nearly Normal Jimmy was manager and ringmaster of the circus. An administrative genius, Nearly Normal had been a childhood playmate of Amanda's and had befriended her again after he dropped out of the University of Arizona Business School to manage and produce the Capitalist Pig. It had been this myopic red pug who introduced Amanda to Stanislaw. And it was the same Nearly Normal who recruited her for the circus. It was he, too, who found a job for Palumbo, the ill-fated drummer, after Stanislaw had been deported and the Capitalist Pig disbanded.

At seventy-three, Smokestack Lightning could still do a dance that lowered the blood temperature of the most urbane and confident white American. In the circus arena, lit only by a dry twig fire, the old Apache would don his

Ghost shirt, its blue-dyed buckskin adorned with thunderbirds and fat white stars (a design that had been revealed to the shirt's original owner in a vision). Then he would commence a performance of calculated frenzy, identifying his bodily rhythms with the historical migrations of his people, recalling both their triumphs and their tribulations, insinuating their glories and humiliations, howling myths in the shadows like a coyote, clacking his peyote-stained teeth like a beaver, arching his back like a mesa, planting his toes like the dawn of agriculture, weeping like a long winter, laughing like the mouth of a river, stalking with his arrowed eyes some unlicensed prey in the faces of the audience. And the audience would sit chilled, bound to the stake of congenital guilt, its thoughts paddling along some quiet piney lake or spurring a pony around the bend of a canyon, all trails however clean and simple leading to the scene of slaughter; the woodsmoke ribboning from the dancer's tiny fire filtered through Cinemascope and dime novels and TV tubes and Jungian memory to sting spectators' eyes with metaphors of barbaric lust, as if it were the gunsmoke and torchsmoke still lingering from some old wounded knee meadow of battle, cooking their hearts over the embers of once-bright genocide. And when the drums suddenly froze and the hard mahogany Indian stilled his dance at the summit of its demonic power to shriek in perfect magpie Trickster, to scream in flawless American, *"Hi'niswa'-vita' ki'-ni"*—"We shall live again!"—the stoutest of mechanics coughed nervously and children and women were known to pee in their pants.

Smokestack Lightning also executed an expurgated version of the Hopi rain dance, using live rattlesnakes when he could get away with it: the deputy sheriffs in some towns forced him to substitute nonpoisonous serpents in the interest of public safety. Incidentally, it was a couple of those garter-snake substitutes that the newlywed Zillers purchased to stock their roadside zoo, although the reader doesn't have to be burdened with all these details, now does he?

Amanda plopped her feet in the cool water. "What truly mystifies me," she confided to her friends, "is the way things are always happening to me during thunderstorms. My oddest experiences, the ones that are most occult or that seem to seep out of the deepest cracks in my psyche, in-

variably happen just before or in the middle of some storm.
I mean it's spooky. As if there's some connection between
my innermost karmic structure and violent electrical dis-
turbances. Why do you suppose that is?"

All squinty-eyed, Nearly Normal Jimmy was wiping river
spray from his glasses with a brakeman's bandanna. "People's
heads are always affected by thunderstorms," he allowed.
"It's the negative particles released in the atmosphere.
Ozone gas is released, too. It activates the mind. Makes
you feel kinda high, haven't you ever noticed feeling kinda
high just before a storm? People dream more, dream more
vividly when there's a heavy concentration of ozone in the
air. They've proved this in scientific experiments. Did you
know that if you take an IQ test during a thunderstorm, or
just before one hits, you'll make a higher score than you
normally would? That's a fact. Activates the brain. Shit,
baby, you're like everybody else, just more sensitive, that's
all."

"Thunder is sky power," said Smokestack Lightning.
"Very different from powers of earth or underearth. Much
war come between power above and power below. Maybe
war between head of Amanda and body of Amanda? No,
maybe not so. Thunder is season power. Always come before
spring season. Make corn grow, make trees catch flower.
Thunder friendly spirit but big, clumsy, sometimes break
things. Maybe Amanda have big spirit in her. Big power.
Sky power. But she cannot understand. Because she woman.
Also have earth power. Earth is woman. Woman is earth.
What so big sky power doing in woman . . . ?" The Indian's
voice faded. It was nearly noon. The day had an edge of
real heat now. Amanda was wearing a little shift of off-white
organdy which she had picked up at the Sears store in San
Luis Obispo and to the neckline of which she had sewn
peacock feathers and beads of black glass. It was a thin tex-
tile and she wore no bra. The sun warmed her chest like a
VapoRub. Very relaxed, she had mulled over her companions' explanations of the thunderstorm syndrome for just a
minute or two when she became aware of a fourth person, a
stranger, in their midst.

Smokestack had noticed the intruder first, but said nothing.
Finally, Nearly Normal turned to see him, too. The man was
Caucasian but the color of a good cigar. He was quite tall,

maybe six four or five, and slender. Two pounds of Fiji hair sat upon his head like the barbed-wire nest of a mechanical bird. His face was long and gaunt and wild; his eyes piercing, his mouth fierce, his mustache mockingly extravagant. He wore a sorcerer's cape—yellowed celestial secrets on a field of sidereal blue—over a vest shirt of some reddish leather which Amanda could not identify; trousers, he wore none but rather a parrot-green loincloth; his feet were sandaled; about his forehead was tied a narrow band of giraffe skin; in one bejeweled hand he held a primitive clay flute. Towering above the trio on the river log, he was an imposing figure—a bit like an ancient Egyptian ruler, especially Egyptian because of his strange tomb-wall eyes: his pupils seemed to remain in the center even when his face was in profile.

Nearly Normal was so startled by the presence of the man that it was a moment before he recognized him. Of course, it wasn't the man's attire that surprised the ringmaster: among Nearly Normal's troupers eccentricity was the uniform of the day. No, it was his stealth, the manner in which he suddenly had materialized on the log without a warning sound. (Like a magician, eh?) But shock speedily gave way to pleasure.

"Amanda. Smokestack Lightning. Let me present the legendary John Paul Ziller. I've been telling you about him. Self-exiled from the international art scene. Leader and drummer of the Hoodoo Meat Bucket. Until he split for Africa. Or was it India?"

The lean man stared only at Amanda. He was pensive. When finally he spoke, the voice that fell from his ferocious lips was both jarring and vulnerable: like a bloodshot eye. There was something of the Negro bluesman in it and something of the Shakespearian stage. No one recalls his exact language but they remember that it was spicy with portent. He awakened in Amanda's consciousness the image of the monarch, the far-ranging, high-flying black-and-orange butterfly that is one of our most familiar insects. He reminded her that the monarch's nickname is "storm king." That it is always most active before a storm. She had seen them, hadn't she? Sailing in the electrified air, beating head-on into the gusty thunderclouds, reveling in the boisterous winds. And did she not know that monarchs usually emerge

from their cocoons just prior to thundershowers? The first
sound they hear is likely the rumble of thunder. They are
literally born of the storm. No other creature is so susceptible to the tense vibrations of a summer squall. A butterfly. Somewhere in its minute mechanism is a device that
responds to and perhaps assimilates the gestalt of storm. If
there were some psychological or physiological link between
Amanda and this butterfly, some unusual rapport . . .

Amanda's mouth eased into a long slow smile. Her eyes
grew as bright as violet silk. "Yes. Yes," she muttered. "The
monarch." She stared at Ziller. He at her. They modified
each other by their looking. Something almost angelic
danced on the abrasive surfaces of his face. She carried her
excitement lightly, the way a hunter carries a loaded shotgun over a fence. Warm chemical yokes burst in their
throats. Ziller had the stink of Pan about him. Amanda
heard the phone ring in her womb. In the magnetized space
between them they flew their thoughts like kites. At last he
reached out for her. She took his hand. As they disappeared
far down the riverbank, the ringmaster and the Apache sat,
stunned, in the kind of vacuum that forms in the immediate
wake of an historic turn.

For all his courtly title, the monarch (*Danaus plexippus,*
thank you, Madame Goody) is the most down-home of butterflies. That is, before they were virtually extirpated by air
pollution and pesticides, monarchs were familiar figures in
most American neighborhoods. They fluttered their zigzag
course (as if under the orders of some secret navigator
whose logic was as fanciful as true) across backyards and
vacant lots and swimming holes and fairgrounds and streets
of towns and cities: they have been spotted from the observation deck of the Empire State Building by surprised
tourists from Indiana who thought they had left such creatures down by the barn. Indeed, wherever there is access
to milkweed (*Asclepias syriaca:* let's not carry this too far,
Madame G.) there you will find monarchs, for the larvae of

this species is as addicted to milkweed juice as the most strung-out junky to smack. His appetite is awesome in its singularity for he would rather starve than switch.

But if the monarch is (or was) a common domestic, as old shoe as the folks next door, he is by no means a stay-at-home. Monarchs, in fact, constitute the jet set of the insect world. These butterflies, stronger fliers than many birds, are spectacularly migratory. In the first autumn chills they gather—having cruised about individually all summer—in enormous flocks. Millions of them in good years, literally millions, mass for the journey south. On four-inch wings they may trek for more than a thousand miles. Monarchs have migrated, in all kinds of weather, from Canada to Florida, from California to Hawaii, from the Pacific Northwest to the Gulf of Mexico. At twenty miles an hour it has taken some monarch movements five hours to pass a given point. Tides of them; miles-wide galaxies; vast flowing rivers of insects staining the wind with their moody hues; force fields of haphazardly modulated entities; notes in a numerical narrative; syllables of equal inflection, rhythmically pulsating, decreasing in optic tempo only on their peripheries where instensity and density finally slacken—as at the edge of a Jackson Pollock painting or the frayed ends of a patchwork quilt.

To science, the migratory flights of the monarch remain a mystery. An enigma of tactics if not of strategy. There are certain channels of communication that operate outside the frequencies of the most prying investigators. A hundred blackbirds will evacuate a tree at precisely the same second—without a discernible signal of any kind. A variety of orchid, lacking nectar as an enticement but needing to be pollinated, attracts male bees by emitting odors like that of the female bee. A wasp will bore for an hour into the hard wood of a tree at the exact spot where hides the tiny grub in whose body she lays her eggs: there is no outward sign that the grub is there, yet the wasp never misses. At the disposal of the "lower" animals are invisible clocks and computers about which science can only speculate. Similarly, scientists have discovered and recorded "laws" to which electricity, gravity and magnetism adhere—but they have practically no understanding of *what* these forces are or *why*. It would seem that there exists in the time-space grid a system of natural order, a mathematics of energy whose "numbers" are even more a riddle to us than their progressions. It is this arithmetic of consciousness that more simple men call the "supernatural." The mystery of migrating butterflies, the mystery of gravity and dreams are but operating arms of the Great Mystery, the perpetuation of which sustains us all. If that declaration has a taste of corn about it, so be it. Language grows a bit sticky in areas such as these. However, concerns of this nature can be quite practical and concrete, as we shall see. It is in the realm of High Mystery that certain men and women are destined to act out their lives.

For several hours, the couple walked in the landscape. They held hands but did not speak. They dared not speak. Vast energies flowed between them. With the sun, they formed the points of a radiant triangle. Bloodpools sang in their temples, their hot breath was dispersed in the fields.

Toward midafternoon, one of the pangs in Amanda's belly became gradually familiar. For her, it was the recognition of a single instrument in a symphonic crescendo. Assuming Ziller was hungry, too, she broke his hold at last and began to forage. She gathered acorns and puffballs in the skirt of her dress, she dug dandelion roots with her nails. These items, with cloves of wild garlic, she skewered on slivers and toasted over a fire that Ziller made without matches. A farmwife approached cautiously and offered them peaches and almonds. Amanda presented her her Madame Blavatsky wristwatch in return. The country woman declined but accepted a peacock plume. It was the first time Amanda saw Ziller smile. She detected filed teeth and a reserve of joy.

"I am told you are somewhat of a wanderer," she said. Her tongue was thick with peach juice. It turned in his ear like a key.

"That is not correct," he answered. "I travel a great deal but I never wander."

"Then I assume that you move about with direction. What is your usual destination?"

"The source. I am always voyaging back to the source."

"You must initiate me in the science of origins. I suspect your travels are soaked with adventure."

Ziller drew from a hidden pocket in his cape a journal (Yes! *The* journal.) and began to read random passages aloud:

"At a cruel souvenir stand beside a dry water hole, we check our maps against the extended umbilicus of a shaman. He reveals to us the hidden meanings of our moles and the deeper significances of our snoring."

"From the vines upon which he travels first class in the free space between heaven and earth, the Lord of the Jungle dives into the translucent river. Disappears with her beneath the giant lily pads. Quiet. A few bright birds throw themselves against the cheek of the humidity. Silence. A hippopotamus slumps like a lobotomy in the vegetating stream. Not a sound. The hippo yawns, disclosing his marshmallow gums. Peace. The bubbling of Jane's orgasm."

"We breakfast at the All-Night Sanskrit Clinic and Sunshine Post. Phosphorescent toadstools illuminate the musicians. Ghost cookies sparkle with opium. We learn the language of the Dream Wheel."

"Forward the march. The burden and the glow. We are approaching our destination. The sky is filled with messages the color of spires. Butterflies as big as tennis rackets flap around the base of the volcano. We stop long enough to synchronize our religions. A white hunter shows up and fills our pockets with omens. And terrible trophies of Felix the Cat."

Fragments. They had Amanda bubbling like her baby. First she wanted to inquire about those big butterflies. Larger than Brooke's birdwing? Surely she would have read of them. But before she could blurt out one thrilled question, Ziller said to her, "I am told that you are a gypsy, and a clairvoyant in the bargain. Does that mean that you, too, are a traveler?"

"I'm a gypsy in spirit only," she confessed. "I travel in gardens and bedrooms, basements and attics, around corners, through doorways and windows, along sidewalks, up stairs, over carpets, down drainpipes, in the sky, with friends, lovers, children and heroes; perceived, remembered, imagined, distorted and clarified."

Ziller was pleased. He played his flute for her, gave her a ring whose ruby setting had been chipped from the Great Eye of Deli, whispered his secret name to her, stood guard each time she went behind a bush (the day's excitement added to the pressures on her bladder) and asked her to become his wife.

Amanda sang for him the seven peyote hymns of the Arapaho, gave him the scarab out of her navel, told him *her* secret name and said, "Of course."

Flushed with sun and passion, they floated back to camp and into the flailing arms of a celebration.

When she was a small girl, Amanda hid a ticking clock in an old rotten tree trunk. It drove woodpeckers crazy. Ignoring tasty bugs all around them, they just about beat their brains out trying to get at the clock. Years later, Amanda used the woodpecker experiment as a model for understanding capitalism, Communism, Christianity and all other systems that traffic in future rewards rather than in present realities.

Obviously, Nearly Normal Jimmy had sensed the union for he had driven into Sacramento and procured gallons of Eleven Cellars sauterne. The new roustabout contributed a quarter kilo of locally grown grass ("Rio Linda green"), a portion of which Takamichi, the tiny Zen tea master, had boiled, whisked and steeped into a most expressive brew. Under the direction of Nuclear Phyllis, motor-scooter daredevil (and granddaughter of a U.S. senator), the women had concocted an immense stew of potatoes, onions, burdock tubers and frsehly netted trout. Having served its culinary functions, the cookfire had subsequently been built into a roaring, spitting, leaping blaze that rouged the evening sky with foxy hues and made the river canyon seem a caldron not unwitchlike in character. Near the fire, the band—with Smokestack Lightning sitting in on Palumbo's abandoned drums—was into something ornamental and ceremonious: an adaptation of a rare hours-long Tantric raga which the ancients had reserved exclusively for lunar eclipses and the nuptials of important personages.

Amanda and John Paul were seated on a painted log and garlanded with chrysanthemums that had been recently liberated from a suburban lawn. The lovers refused stew and wine but accepted bowls of tea. After toasts, Amanda's son—dressed in a tunic of rabbit fur and yellow brocade—was fetched from the nursery van to meet his new father and to kiss his mother good night. (Ziller could scarcely believe the child's eyes: they seemed almost electric.) Ten or fifteen minutes of silence followed the climax of the band's special selection—the players were exhausted and the listeners transfixed. Then Nearly Normal, sweet with wine and giggly with grass, delivered a short address in which he attributed the events of the day to Tibetan intervention, although exactly how that far-off nation interposed itself he did not say. "Up is up, down is down, and Tibet is Tibet," said Jimmy, reasonably. "You may scoff but I know what I know." He introduced Ziller to the musicians and troupers, for most of them had encountered him only in myth and innuendo. And he announced officially this time—the union. In word and smile and kiss, the performers paid their respects: it was apparent that Amanda was sharply loved by all.

When the band began again to play, it worked into an impromptu arrangement of "Barbie Doll's Hysterectomy," a little number from the repertoire of the Hoodoo Meat Bucket. This, of course, in honor of Ziller, who, toward the end of the piece, was persuaded to relieve the old Apache on drums. Oh my. Yes, yes. Everything they'd heard was true. In and out of the melody, crossing the beat like a jaywalker dodging taxicabs, accentuating the offbeats, creating counterbeats, he drummed like a thousand-handed deity: Kwan Yin, all arms and bliss.

Next, a raga-rock rendition (sans Ziller) of "Back Door Man," the rhythms of which pulled dancers, singularly or in pairs, into the reeling wheel of firelight. Most of the troupers were rolling their own ectasy now. Dancing. Singing. Climbing trees. Moonwatching (it was mango orange and as thin as a tortilla). Eating. Drinking. Necking. Dreaming. Goofing. Groping. Trephinating: frescoing their pineal glands with the cardinal brush. Takamichi swaying in an American flag hammock intoning his great wooden beads. Nuclear Phyllis and the new roustabout skinny-dipping in the stream. Only Amanda and Ziller, arm in arm on the log-of-honor, seemed restless. Noticing this, although his spectacles were sticky with wine, Nearly Normal led them away.

Now Amanda, who traveled in the nursery truck, owned a lovely little goat-wool tipi, and on the rear of his motorcycle John Paul carried an Arabian tent. But believing that honeymooners should engage on neutral territory, Nearly Normal and some other troupers had taken the liberty of constructing a hasty hut of sticks and boughs. It sat the length of a spaghetti dinner outside the laager (as Ziller, with his knowledge of South African wagon trains, called the circular camp), protected by an outcropping of rock. Inside, the ground was covered with Amanda's own Persian carpet. In a corner sat a small wedding-gift table of carved quartz, on the top of which were carefully arranged Ziller's compass, sextant, charts, telescope, French ticklers and other navigational instruments. From the ceiling hung a brass saucer in which Nearly Normal had thought to burn incense until he remembered Amanda having once told him that smell was 80 per cent of love.

Here, the couple was left—the sounds of the festivities seeping through the walls like some disjointed Musak of Mars. Moonlight pressed in on them like a hungry ghost, feeding on the wholeness of their hearts and brains. But as they sat undressing on the edge of the bedroll, each trying to please the other with gesture and look, a spike of tension suddenly drove between them, prying them apart.

"It appears that the gypsy traveler has taken on a passenger," Ziller said dryly, observing her through his antique spyglass.

"Yes. I'm afraid I have been outfitted as a vessel."

Amanda lowered her lashes and crossed her arms in front of her slightly bulging belly.

"Was it someone in the circus or band?"

"No. No, it was a lonely writer I met one stormy day in Laguna Beach. He had a poem about Theolonius Monk that he sealed in a tin can and labeled Campbell's Cream of Piano Soup. Later, I heard he killed himself to avoid the draft."

A moment of fidgety silence. A tentative embrace. Then, Amanda's turn.

"I've heard that you were married before, John Paul. What happened? Where is she now? And so forth."

"She was the daughter of a Kansas City meat-packer. A frail debutante sopping up culture while working as a secretary for my gallery in New York. On our wedding trip we went to Ceylon to hunt flying foxes, a species of bat. One became entangled in my bride's hair and I awoke to find her squeaking like a dying bat while hanging naked upside down from a rafter. Soon afterward, she entered an asylum. Her daddy had everything efficiently annulled. Now I understand she's one of the leading socialites in Kansas City. Though subject to embarrassing attacks. One night at the opera . . ."

Another sickening silence. Both were ashamed of their indulgences. They could sense a taint on their karmas. Gradually, however, Ziller climbed into a smile. From Amanda, a diffident giggle. In a moment, the two of them were laughing—freely and deliriously, like children tickled in their cribs by a roguish uncle. Their mouths mashed together, hotly, moistly. His gentle hand kneaded her breasts, then slid down her belly and into her panties. Her clitoris perked like a bud, buzzed like a cicada. He grew masculine to an improper degree.

Most of the night they did it, laughing and biting. Waking in the morning with rhinestone crustations on their eyelids and the butt end of a rainbow filling their tiny room.

The Pelican, in Bryte, California, is one of those taverns that function as a neighborhood social club. There is a coin-operated pool table of less-than-regulation size. There is a shuffleboard table that seems as much too long as the pool table seems too short: it looks like a landing strip. There is a bowling machine and two pinballs. There is a library of punchboards: Black Cat, Texas Charley, Lucky Dollar. There is a jukebox stuffed with country-and-western hits and the kind of tin pan alley laments that sound poignant to the jilted and juiced. There are revolving wire Christmas trees laden with beef jerky and beer nuts; there are jars of boiled eggs and hot sausages and a larger jar in which pickles lounge like green Japanese in a bath. There is an animated plastic trout stream advertising Olympia beer (It's the Water"). There is a friendly middle-aged couple behind the bar.

A lot of brewy laughter and first-name calling jostles the smoke bank that hangs in the Pelican almost from ceiling to floor: the Pelican is in a shuffleboard league and competition is keen and boisterous when its team is matched against a tavern from Sacramento. But on that particular September evening, at a table near the bar, three men in their mid-twenties were in conversation grave and angry.

"They've got a big fire of some kind going," said Bubba. "Canyon's lit up like the streets of Hell."

"Yeah, and you can hear that stupid music all the way over by Ritchy's dairy," complained Fred.

"Hell, I heard it right out here in the parking lot," said Bubba. Andy grunted and nodded.

"Well look," said Fred, "if a bunch of queers and niggers and sluts want to have an orgy that's their business. But let 'em have it in San Francisco or L.A. or wherever they come from. Don't let 'em come around here and spread their filth. Folks around here don't want that shit. We've got sisters out on dates tonight, Andy and I have, out with decent boys. Those weirdos get full of that LDS, God knows what they might do. Got no morals, no respect for property—"

"There, you said it," Bubba jumped in hotly. "No respect. No respect for authority, no respect for law and order, no damned respect for nothing. That's what the trouble is in this country today. Bunch of niggers and weirdos trying to tear down everything this country stands for. Falling right into the hands of the Commies. Uncle Sam's in a bind overseas, you think they'll help? Shit no. They want to dress up like cowboys and Indians. Go pick flowers. Make a bunch of loud noise and call it music. Want everybody to work and support 'em. While they take a bunch of drugs and attack innocent people and God knows what all."

Andy's big blond head was bobbing like it was on the end of a pole. The other two took long pulls from their schooners. Wiping his mouth, Fred said, "Ain't there something the sheriff can do about that riffraff? Let's go have a talk with the deputy. Those scum been around for three weeks now. What are we paying the cops for?"

"Already talked to Dick," said Bubba, belching. "They already nailed 'em once, you know. Searched 'em took 'bout eight of 'em off to jail. Rest of 'em hid their dope and needles somewhere. God, you shoulda heard what Dick said about those broads. None of 'em wears any underwear. Anyway, they can't bother 'em for a while, I guess. Unless they get some complaints. The queers got permission to be on that land. And the Cleevers who own the closest ranch, they ain't gonna complain. Liberal Democrats and Unitarians to boot. Hell, their oldest boy Billy's joined up with 'em."

"Maybe we can go talk Ritchy into filing a complaint," said Fred. "That music will curdle his milk. Or maybe we oughta do a little complaining ourselves."

"Now you're getting an idea," hissed Bubba. "Now you talking, son. The three of us, we go pick up Spud and Joe. And Dick Wilding, he's off duty now; hell, Dick'll go. Six of us be plenty. We'll get us some ax handles and ball bats and go over there. I mean clean house. Put the fear of God in 'em. They're just germs, you know, no more than germs or flies or rats. People that sink to that level ain't fit to live in a country like this. Let's do Uncle Sam a favor and clean out that rat nest."

"Right, boy, right," said Fred. "I didn't risk my life overseas to come home to something like this. I don't want my folks living around trash and traitors that'd sell their own country to the Reds for a bottle of pills. I say run 'em right out of the country. Better than that, hang 'em."

Andy was nodding and grunting and thinking of his baby sister. The trio finished its beer. "Well, what are we waiting for?" asked Bubba.

"You're waiting for somebody to turn your heads around straight," said a clear calm voice from the bar. The three men looked up to find the stranger who had been sitting with his back to them, on the nearest stool, now looking into their faces—smiling. "The ladies and gentlemen whom you desire to assault are showmen—jugglers, fire walkers and yogic acrobats—whose mission it is to entertain and enrapture children of all ages. They bring into the lives of ordinary Americans the color and splendor of the Orient, especially of those Asian cultures whose folkways have been abolished by Communist invaders. They are no threat to your freedom for it is in the name of freedom that they perform their magical feats."

Fred cocked his right arm and Andy growled. Both made a move to rise, but were restrained by Bubba. Bubba was more observant than his drinking companions, perhaps that was why he was an auto parts salesman and they laborers on the river docks. While the stranger had been talking, Bubba had been sizing him up. He was dressed in jeans and a black sweatshirt and although his hair was fairly long, he was clean-shaven and did not have the weirdo look. More importantly, he was *built*. Shoulders wide, hips narrow, biceps like eggplants shoved up his sleeves. He had moved very little on his barstool but the slightest turn of his head suggested a superb athletic grace. He was a few years older than they and looked as if he'd caught a few punches, although not enough to scar his face. "This joker would go through Andy or Fred like thin shit through a tall Swede," mused Bubba. "He wouldn't be a push-over even for me." Bubba was discreet. "You from around here, buddy?" he asked in his best no-nonsense John Wayne baritone.

"No, I work for a logging outfit up near Aberdeen, Washington," the stranger explained in his willowy drawl. "Been whoring around San Francisco for a few days, and now I'm about to deliver a bab—a pet, to a friend of mine near here. My name is Plucky Purcell."

There was activity in the front of Bubba's brain. He looked the stranger over well, his eyes squinting, his mind wrestling with the uncomfortableness of associations. The frayed ends of his thought patterns seemed to bleed into the stranger's space, merging with him in some sweep of self-canceling perception. And then he hit upon it, or rather, tripped over it, fell on top of it, held it down like a farm boy trapping a pig. "Purcell," Bubba purred slowly. "Plucky Purcell. Say, you ain't the Purcell who played ball, the one who stole . . . ? Yeah. You are him, ain't you, huh?" Bubba's teeth showed big and yellow inside a heavy timber-cat grin. His jowls were candy red.

"Well," said Purcell with hesitation, "all that happened a long time ago."

"Oh shit. Oh shit." Bubba was squealing, laughing, jumping up and down in his chair like a baby. "Hey, guys, this is Plucky Purcell. Remember? About ten years ago? Hey, Purcell, come over here and let me buy you a brew. How about telling us about that mess, huh? Tell me what really happened. Oh shit, boys, wait'll you hear this. Oh my."

"Gentlemen, I don't really relish heating up those old cold chestnuts. But I'll make a deal with you. I'll tell you about my little escapade if you'll come—peacefully—with me out to where that circus is camped. I want you to meet those folks and get to know them a bit so you won't have to fear and hate them as you do."

Fred and Andy were not sure what was transpiring and they were less sure that they liked it. Bubba, however, was spastic with delight. "Look, boys," he whispered, "I just remembered, Spud and Joe are at the stag movies over to the Legion hall; we couldn't get them to go anyway. Now just listen to this story. This Purcell's okay."

So, over a couple of beers, Purcell told them a carefully rehearsed version of an event from his past. Then they left the Pelican and after securing a pint of Seagram's 7 from the glove compartment of Bubba's Mustang, they boarded Plucky's VW microbus for a visit to the campsite. They had traveled only a half-mile or so, passed the bottle only once, when Fred yelled, "Hey, who's this in the back of the wagon? You got a kid back there?"

Bubba whirled around and studied the shadowy figure in the rear. "Kid, hell," he roared. "That's an ape! Purcell's got a friggin ape in here!"

"Calm yourselves, gentlemen. And be humble." Purcell spoke with the hermetic theatricality of John Paul Ziller. "You are in the presence of Mon Cul, prince of baboons. Mon Cul has been around the world eight times and met everybody twice. He is better educated than you or I, and is the only creature on earth, man or beast, who knows an English word that rhymes with orange."

"Oh crap," said Bubba. "It's just a dumb ape. Come here, monkey. God, it's funny-looking. Look at that big red ass. Come here, monkey, come here and let me— Yeoowwww! Jesus Christ! It bit me. Look! The son of a bitch nearly bit my finger off." Bubba thrust his arm over the driver's seat between Purcell and Andy. Indeed, blood was gushing.

"Just relax," Purcell told him. "We'll make a bandage. I've got some clean white socks in the glove compartment."

"Bullshit," hollered Bubba. "You turn this damn bus around right now. We're going to see the sheriff. I mean it. Turn around. That goddamn monkey's gonna get a bullet in its head. It's probably got rabies and I don't know what all. Come on now, buddy, I mean it. Turn around and head this zoo on wheels to the sheriff's office. Hauling wild animals around without no cage. You probably connected with that freak show yourself. There's gonna be hell to pay over this. . . ." He was livid.

Purcell pulled the bus into a small private road as if to turn around. Instead, he killed the engine, got out, opened the back door and pulled Bubba out by his collar. He coldcocked him with one swooshing Joe Palooka uppercut.

Frank and Andy jumped him, one of them momentarily blinding him with a thudding blow to the temple. But, using a combination of judo, jujitsu, karate, kung fu and aikido, Purcell gradually chopped them into gory unconsciousness. He felt a wee dizzy himself. He lay down on his back in the ditch. Sucked the remainder of the Seagram's into his head. Giggled at the moon. And sunk into an honest sleep, dreamless but sweet as clover.

So the Sacramento celebration of the Indo-Tibetan Circus & Giant Panda Gypsy Blues Band transpired without interference. For one participant, however, the aftermath of the revelry was not the least benign. The ringmaster was afflicted with a hangover of near-terminal vileness. While the troupers prepared their belongings and equipment for the caravan to Eugene, Oregon, where they had three performances scheduled, Nearly Normal spent the morning vomiting self-portraits and farting looney tunes and merry melodies.

Now, in the curious medical treatise of Marcellus, who hung out his shingle in Bordeaux in the fourth century A.D., there is a treatment for post-intoxicant malady that prescribes certain white stones found in the stomachs of young swallows. Amanda just happened to have some such stones in her centaur-carved lemonwood herb cabinet (all dried plant material in the cabinet had been confiscated by the Sacramento police), so she led Nearly Normal to a grassy spot by the river where he lay with the stones on his forehead and midsection. First, however, he ingested three aspirins which were not unlike the stones in color and size. "Medicine change very little," Smokestack Lightning was heard to observe.

About ten o'clock—the September sun was just starting to tickle the bare backs of the roustabouts—Plucky Purcell chugged into camp, whistling "Try a Little Tenderness" through a muffler of dried blood and whiskey phlegm. "Ran into some old navy buddies. Bit of boyish horseplay," he explained to Ziller. John Paul and the baboon had a restrained but joyous reunion.

"Amanda," said Ziller, "permit me to present Plucky Purcell, great transcendent eagle of crime. And Mon Cul of the genus *Papio,* my trusted friend and brother through all weathers, frictions and sublimes." Whereupon the baboon bowed deeply, catching a ray of sunlight upon his scarlet buttocks. "Amanda and I were married yesterday, Dugoobie fashion, sun officiating; and this is Thor, aged two and one-half, who has graciously allowed me to be his pa-pa." Purcell shook the boy's hand, then kissed Amanda's cheek in the manner of Leonard Bernstein, executing a baggy shuffle all the while so as to conceal the erection the bride has immediately inspired.

Ziller explained to Amanda that California had recently enacted a law requiring motorcyclists, passengers as well as operators, to wear helmets. A policeman had pulled Ziller over in Golden Gate Park and insisted that if Mon Cul were going to ride on a cycle like a human, he'd damn well better wear a helmet, too. Naturally, the baboon refused to submit to that indignity. Although John Paul was aware that state patrolmen were generally a more intelligent breed than their muncipal counterparts, he nevertheless did not wish to chance penalty and/or delay while biking up to Sacramento. Hence, he had requested that old friend Plucky give Mon Cul a lift.

"Now isn't that the shits," exclaimed Nuclear Phyllis, who, being a two-wheeler herself, had been drawn to the conversation. "It's bad enough a person's head isn't his own any more—the cops want to control what goes in it and what goes on it—but now they want to tell animals what to wear. I mean, seriously, does the helmet law protect the public health, safety or welfare? Hell no. It's designed to protect the bike-rider from himself. A person's got a right to break his own head if he wants to. It's his head. It's his decision."

"That's not the point, baby," said Purcell, appraising the girl with a greasy butcher's eye, apportioning her into loin chops and rump roasts and nippled filets. "Granted, the helmet law is unconstitutional, like a good fourth of the new laws today, but safety, health and welfare were never a consideration. The pigs wouldn't care if every biker in the nation split his melon. Huh-uh. 'Duly constituted authority' would sigh with relief. Think for a minute. What motivates the Man to act? Bread, right? Like everything else, it's really a question of economics. The majority of motorcycle accidents are caused by automobile drivers. They aren't conditioned to looking out for bikes so they're always slamming into them. A cat gets knocked off his scooter, cracks his headbone, who has to pay? The auto insurance companies, that's who. Now the insurance gangsters got one of the most powerful lobbies around. When they say 'shit' the Man says 'what color?' " So it's the insurance companies who pushed that helmet law through to save themselves some bread. Everything that happens in this society sooner or later boils down to a matter of a buck."

"Are you truly convinced that our culture is that monetary, Plucky?" Amanda asked.

"Look, sweetie, you got your own reality going," Purcell replied. "But that isn't the reality of the United States of America. Huh-uh! After the doctors and scientific experts testified in Congress that cigarettes cause or compound not only cancer but a number of other diseases and are responsible for hundreds of thousands of deaths annually, the senior senator from Kentucky stood up just shaking with anger and moaned, 'You're trying to wreck our economy.' And what did Henry Ford II say when the government began insisting on safety devices in cars? 'The American people don't want anything that's going to upset the economy.' And what's more, Ford was right. Fifty thousand a year dead on the highways, but don't rock the economy. Look, America is no more a democracy than Russia is a Communist state. The governments of the U.S. and Russia are practically the same. There's only a difference of *degree*. We both have the same basic *form* of government: economic totalitarianism. In other words, the settlement to all questions, the solutions to all issues are determined not by what will make the people most healthy and happy in their bodies and their minds but by economics. Dollars or rubles. Economy *über alles*. Let nothing interfere with economic growth, even though that growth is castrating truth, poisoning beauty, turning a continent into a shit-heap and driving an entire civilization insane. Don't spill the Coca-Cola, boys, and keep those monthly payments coming."

"Shee-it. That American eagle needs a feather job, don't it?" grumbled Nuclear Phyllis, staring at her own helmet in disgust.

"Well, now, honey, that old helmet law might not be so bad," said Purcell. "I know this cat down near L.A., got stopped by the heat for wearing his helmet strapped to his knee. He told them, 'The law says you gotta wear a helmet, it doesn't say *where* you gotta wear it.' Well, the cops wrote him a ticket anyway and made him put the helmet on his head. So what happens? Five miles down the road he flipped the bike—and broke his kneecap."

Evidently, either the aspirin or the bird stones had

worked a cure, for Nearly Normal walked up and en-
joined the rapping troupers to return to their labors. Purcell
climbed back in his bus. He had to get on to Aberdeen.
He was already a day late and the logging foreman
cracked an even smarter whip than Nearly Normal. He
promised to catch up with the show in Washington, however, and spend a weekend or two with the troupers.

Alas, that never came to pass. For within a month,
Plucky Purcell was to unwittingly instigate the chain of
events which was to put Amanda and John Paul Ziller in
their present jeopardy, which was to threaten the well-
being of millions, which was to lead to the drafting of this
very report.

In the manner that is common among newlyweds,
Amanda and John Paul exchanged many confidences during the early days of their marriage. The magician showed
his bride how one could alter reality by rubbing mercury on
one's feet or by sniffing uranium. The bride, her tattoos
resplendent as never before, showed the magician how one
could chew wintergreen Life Savers in a dark room and
make sparks with one's teeth.

Peppermint won't work.

L. Westminster "Plucky" Purcell is the youngest son of
an old Virginia family, a once-aristocratic clan which, instead
of floundering in Faulknerian funk when it ran out of money,
simply blended with good-natured resignation into the lower
middle class. Unlike the desperate daughters of those unfortunate Virginia families that have sold their pottage for a
mess of birthright, Plucky's sisters made no attempt to
marry the clan back into wealth and society, but settled

instead for a barber and a civil engineer, whom, presumably, they loved. Plucky's brother, rather than scrambling to rescue a bit of family prestige by entering the medical or legal professions or, preferably, the Episcopalian clergy, played and later coached pro football.

In fact, the elder Purcell son was a three-time All-American halfback at Duke University. Plucky received an athletic scholarship to the same institution, for scouts who'd seen him in action at Culpeper High were of the opinion that he would develop into a harder runner if not a more accurate passer than his big brother. That is, scouts who'd seen Plucky in action on the gridiron. Had they seen him in action on the back roads of Culpeper County, they might have more accurately forecast his future.

After a mediocre start his sophomore year at Duke, Plucky blossomed toward the end of the season. In the last three games he scored ten touchdowns, four of them on carries of more than fifty yards. Sportswriters from all corners predicted confidently that Plucky Purcell would run off with national scoring honors the following season. Who among them could have guessed that a week before the season opened, Plucky Purcell would run off to Mexico with the backfield coach's wife?

It was decided that Mon Cul would travel in the nursery truck. Although he was well past the age when his peers were said to grow cantankerous, and although he was a chacma—the largest of the baboon families—Mon Cul was considered a fit companion for the circus tots. "My friend has shared private amusements with children on five continents," Ziller assured the parents. "He has romped with heirs to a hundred fortunes and a dozen thrones. There will be no unpleasantries."

In a canvas jump suit decorated with watercolor landscapes and embroidered Indonesian butterflies, Amanda mounted the BMW behind her husband, who was in loincloth and leather. She had been warned by Nearly Nor-

mal that the harsh bouncing of the motorcycle might jar
the embryo loose from its moorage, but rather than be
separated from Ziller, she elected to assume the risk.

The day was an Indian summer showpiece. In the
sunny calm, the canyon seemed a gallery of bronzes and
jades. High overhead a hawk traced a helix on un-
blemished newsprint blue. A frictional vitality burnished
the guts of everyone in the caravan. It quickened when
Nearly Normal sounded the move-out command on the
Tibetan devil horn. The show was back on the road! As
Ziller was about to kick the BMW into action, little Pammie, the goat and yak girl, ran up to his side.

"Mr. Ziller," she cried, "Mr. Ziller, I just wanted to
tell you how much I dug the Hoodoo Meat Bucket.
Oh, it was super groovy. All my friends have your record
album. Got it on the black market. My mother wouldn't
allow it in the house. Said it was the sickest thing she'd
ever heard. But I love it. So beautiful and funny. Why
did you break up? I mean just when you were getting
accepted? What led you to take off to Africa?"

The sun gleamed on Ziller's opal-studded helmet. He
stood erect over his motorcycle as though he were about
to bend it to his will. To Pammie he handed a page that
had been ripped from some kind of journal. And as the
BMW roared to the front of the motorcade, she read:

> *The invitation to*
> *Tarzan's bar mitzvah,*
> *written in nut juice*
> *and wrapped in a leaf*
>
> *Arrived in my mailbox*
> *with an organic rustle,*
> *smelling of camel dung*
> *but promising a feast*
>
> *And evoking immediate*
> *black jungle visions:*
> *The hair of the cannibal*
> *and the sweet of the beast*

A rather anxious football coach flew to Mexico in pursuit of his wife and her famous athlete lover. While the sporting world reeled from the delicious blow of the scandal, the lovers ate mangoes and fondled one another in the streets of Guadalajara; and that is where he, the husband, caught up with them—in the plaza of the city. Officials had taken his Colt from him at the border, but he had purchased a cleaver from a native butcher and upon spotting the fugitives, sought to put it to grim use.

His wife was so weak from love and diarrhea she could neither fight nor flee. "I'm like a cream puff with the cream squeezed out," she sighed, and slumped on a bench to accept her fate. "I'll take care of you later," said her husband and he made a move for Plucky Purcell. Plucky, too, was experiencing a touch of Montezuma's revenge but he nevertheless gave the greatest broken-field running performance of his career. Now, the coach, though a bit out of shape, was no lead-footed mover himself, yet after sixteen wild minutes through the narrow streets of old Guadalajara he fell to his knees panting frantically and watched Purcell stiff-arm an orange-juice vendor and disappear down an alley.

That midnight, as he nervously checked out of his hotel, Purcell paused to share a short tequila with the desk clerk. He gave the Mexican a true account of the day's adventure. "You are preety lucky, señor," the clerk confided. "Not lucky," said Plucky. "Plucky."

As the careful reader might have supposed, Amanda has been a bit distraught of late. In fact, so preoccupied has she been with the fate of her husband—and the Corpse that accompanied him in his flight—that she just this hour noticed the writer's efforts at reportage, although all afternoon his typewriter has been bobbing before him like a rubber duck in a tub. At her belatedly expressed curiosity, the writer disclosed that he was attempting to record the bizarre and momentous events in which they seemed so irredeemably entangled. He did not, of course, tell her that it was *she* who was the substance of his accounting. To reveal that would be to reveal the breadth of his esteem for her—which she would consider excessively misplaced in light of the Corpse, who, dead as it was, was the true and important protagonist in this drama.

The extent of the author's regard for Amanda is a bagged cat to which he cannot grant amnesty at this time. There are too many unknown quantities. Not just the matter of the Corpse, which is scary enough, but personal considerations. What is to be Ziller's lot? What, for that matter, is to be the writer's lot? One does not sit at ease with one's future when one is trapped in a roadside zoo by agents of an unfriendly government, even when that government is one's own.

At any rate, it was admitted to Amanda that the report was only in its preliminary stages (otherwise, how can the writer explain his planned return to the keyboard in the morning?). She inquired if might not the report one day be of interest to historians and such. "Yes," replied the author, "that's a possiblity—providing it is not suppressed." Silently, he added, "But if it's history they want, they'll have to accept it on my terms. I'm not without a sense of duty in this matter—but duty to whom is quite another business."

It was then asked of Amanda if there was not some comment she might like to insert here at the onset of the account: no, it wouldn't interrupt continuity, no, not at all. In cutoff jeans that hung below her belly button and a gypsy cape that barely concealed her breasts, she was paler than the writer had ever seen her; a moistly gleaming ivory like the neck of a clam.

"Well," she said brightly, "do you notice anything odd about these crackers?" She held them out in the woven Haida basket from which she was snacking.

"No, they look like ordinary sesame crackers to me."

"If you were more perceptive," she said, "you would have noticed that they have seeds on only one side."

"That's true. Why don't sesame crackers have seeds on both sides?"

"They do at the Equator," she said. "But in the Southern Hemisphere, all the seeds are on the *other* side."

Sailing a lighter-than-air kiss at the author, Amanda vanished into her meditation room to try once more to induce a husband-locating trance. "How do you suppose the seeds are distributed at the poles?" she called through the perfumed curtains. Then the writer heard no more. Except a gentle fanning. Like the passage of a moth.

Part II

Part II

Along their migratory routes, monarch butterflies stay nights
in certain trees. The "butterfly trees," as they are called,
are carefully chosen—although the criteria exercised in
their selection are not known. Species is unimportant, obviously, for at one stopover the roosting tree may be a
eucalyptus, at another a cedar or an elm. But, and this is
what is interesting, they are always the same trees. Year
after year, whether moving south or returning north, monarchs will paper with their myriad wings at twilight a single
tree that has served as a monarch motel a thousand times
before.

Memory? If so, it is genetic. For you see, the butterflies who journey south are not the ones who come back.
Monarchs lay their eggs in sunny climes. Then they die.
The hordes who flutter northward in spring are a succeed-
ing generation. Yet, without hesitation, they roost in the
same trees as did their ancestors.

Scientists have examined butterfly trees and found
them chemically and physically identical to the trees surrounding them. Yet no other tree will do. Investigators
have camouflaged a tree's color, altered its scent. The
monarchs were not fooled. Another of nature's mysterious
constants. A butterfly always knows when it is *there*.

They found the zoo site on an October Sunday: a
soft burpy day on which they crossed many bridges. Bridges
over rivers and bridges over sloughs. The sky sagged like

an udder. The air had a feel of heavy birds. Their motorcycle was a flash of overheated color in the damp green
landscapes. At seventy miles an hour, it whined like a spinning top—and rattled Amanda's kidneys like dice in a box.

Amanda had peed in Seattle, she had peed in
Everett. And now as they sped through the Skagit River
Valley, she had to pee again. Already, she and John Paul
were far behind the caravan that motored to Bellingham
(near the Canadian border) where, on the campus of
Western Washington State College, the circus was to un-
furl its canvases for the last time. But when she rapped her
code on Ziller's ribs, he dutifully braked the BMW and
turned into the big fir-ringed parking lot of Mom's Little
Dixie Bar-B-Cue. Luckily, Amanda's biological urgency became manifest on that rare stretch of Interstate 5 where
the limited access rule had, for some reason, been suspended. Along that one fifteen-mile section of the Seattle-
Vancouver Freeway (between Everett and Mount Vernon), there were scattered gas stations, general stores and
restaurants. Not many, however, for this was farming country of almost unequaled lushness and the black juicy soil
was far too valuable to be relegated to commerce.

The motorcycle engine died with a prolonged series of
soft smoky gasps—like a dwarf choking on a burning rag.
The couple dismounted. Only to discover that Mom's was
closed. Not shuttered for the Sabbath but permanently
shut down. Padlocked. Vacant. In a cobweb-frosted window corner a faded FOR RENT sign hung by one ear from
a snipping of tape. So, while his young bride went around
back to water the ferns, Ziller scrutinized the roadhouse—
noted its spaciousness, its quaint but sturdy construction,
the broad fields behind it, the grove in which it sat—
and surmised that it was a likely edifice in which to house a
zoo, a family and secret world headquarters.

"I am always voyaging back to the source," Ziller
had said. He was a source-rer. Internally, he pursued
the bright waters of his origins with whatever vehicles he
could command. "In our human cells are recorded every
single impulse of energy that has occurred since the beginning of time," Amanda had said. "The DNA genetic
system is the one library in which it is really worthwhile to
browse." Although *he* never said as much, Ziller seemed to

find the key to that library in various mental disciplines, in capsules, powders, symbols, songs, rituals and vials. Externally, the source-search proceeded on a more obvious level. Ziller had pilgrimaged several times to Africa, place of his birth. Now, it was time to reassimilate the Pacific Northwest, the rained-on, clam-chawed land where he had lived his childhood. (Although it *could* be said that considering his books and films and daydreams and maps he was "in Africa" all those child-years, too. Or was it India?)

When Amanda returned, John Paul clasped her suspiciously moist fingers and led her across the Freeway —traffic was sparse and there was little danger of their being struck—to the edge of a lemonade-colored slough. Clotted with eelgrass and driftwood, the slough curled forlornly through the cropland like a moat that had been abandoned by its castle. The newlyweds stood with their backs to the water, stood on the muddy shoulder and gazed across four lanes of asphalt at the cafe, its two-story Cowboy Gothic facade silhouetted against the god's-belly clouds like the fortifications of a forbidden city. Amanda squeezed her husband's hand. She knew that they were there.

In the wash of the afternoon they perceived dimly that once, before the paint began to flake, the wood-frame facade of Mom's Little Dixie had been festooned with cartoon pigs, all wearing chef's hats and carrying steaming platters of barbecue and buns. Which caused Amanda to announce that she could never trust a pig that sold pork sandwiches. Which prompted Ziller to point out to her the parallels between such swine and businessmen everywhere.

On Monday evening, October 2, the Indo-Tibetan Circus & Giant Panda Gypsy Blues Band offered its final performance. And a rather good performance it was. Stimulated by sentiments of finality—in a short while Nearly Normal Jimmy would be taking the band to New York for a recording session and the troupers realized that the circus would probably never be reorganized—each performer uncorked hidden geysers of adrenalin and functiond at the summit of his potential.

Krishnalasa balanced himself on one thumb atop a twenty-five-watt bulb for sixty seconds. (Or was it atop a sixty-watt bulb for twenty-five seconds?) Master Ying swallowed (and disgorged unharmed) six frogs instead of the usual two. The monkey pipers blew until their faces turned black. Jugglers called for sharper blades, taller lampshades, additional marbles. With what clarity Elmer sang the Bhagavad-Gita, the Song Celestial, the ecstasy of the Divine One. Pursued by a gang of drooling amazons, the sugar-breasted Pammie led her yaks and goats to safety through the Tunnel of Hades. (The audience gasped as she braved the fire.) Clowns were stuffed into their suits like sausages. White mice dropped by toy parachutes from the wings of model airplanes. (One mouse broke a leg and was carried off in a tiny ambulance manned by a crew of parakeets.) In the center ring, a collection of paradoxes was exhibited. Déjà vu displays. Infinity chambers. Firecrackers. Chants. Cave paintings. Symbologies. Obscurities. Meditations. Inscrutabilities. Zen Yo-Yos. Kabuki kut-outs. Visions from the Tibetan *Book of the Dead.* Nuclear Phyllis roaring her scooter in and out among the blues chords looking for the peace that passeth all understanding. And so forth.

All this time Amanda lay napping, wrapped in a bulky tapestry. Outside her tipi, a dank October breeze raised goose pimples and flapped flags. The insect yammer of the crowd squirmed through the woven walls. Even into sleep the music followed her: she could hear her husband drumming, drumming as if freed from all the fetters that bind men to life. If she did not visibly respond it was because she was exhausted. Long insistent lines had formed before Amanda's booth that evening, and she had failed no one. Her trances had been crisp and short and accurate—almost staccato machine-gun glimpses of consciousness. And she had dazzled her clients with the data she had dredged from the cards. "I feel like a pressed duck, a squeezed grape," she sighed when it was over.

Now here was Nearly Normal awakening her. He

brought a cucumber sandwich and a half-pint of milk. Good. Food would revive her. The bread slices collapsed like movie-set walls beneath her bite; the mayonnaise squished, the cucumber snapped tartly like the spine of an elf. She held aloft the milk carton and read aloud from it, "Four hundred U.S.P. units Vitamin D added per quart from activated ergosterol." Amanda winced before drinking. "Activated ergosterol? Jimmy, I'm not sure about this activated ergosterol. Do you suppose it could be a euphemism for strontium 90? Maybe it'll make me sterile?"

"That might be something less than a tragedy," said Nearly Normal. He patted her discreetly ballooning belly. "At any rate, the information on milk containers is highly educational. My first concepts of infinity were developed from looking at Pet milk cans when I was a kid. On the label there was a picture of a cow in a can, her big mooey head hanging out of one end of the can—another Pet milk can, naturally—and on the label of *that* can was the same cow in another Pet milk can. And that can also had a cow-in-can design on its label. And those cow cans, one inside the other, just went on, growing progressively smaller, as far as the eye could see. It walloped my little mind."

"They've changed the label," Amanda pointed out.

"Yeah. They have," sighed Jimmy as he left to return to the show. "To Madison Avenue even infinity is expendable."

On Tuesday morning, there was an unseasonal frost. The grass looked as if it had been chewing Tums. Across the antacid residue, Nearly Normal's boots jitterbugged from camp to camp: paychecks to dispense, good-byes to exchange. From camp to camp he trotted through his own breath like a riot cop charging tear gas. His glasses steamed over, his nose was its own gas mask. "Beautiful show last night," he hollered to every performer he saw. "Beautiful." When he ducked into the Ziller tent he found its occupants still abed, although Amanda and Thor were awake playing mommie-baby games in the puffy Christmas of quilts.

Nearly Normal hoped he could convince John Paul to reconsider his refusal to go to New York to record: with Ziller on drums the success of the Giant Panda Gypsy Blues Band album would be assured. But that eye that crawled slowly from beneath the covers, it was not looking for fame and fortune. "Oh, go back to sleep," said Nearly Normal. And the lid fell shut like the trapdoor of a spider.

"Here's your pay," said the manager. "It's a skinny check and I apologize. Unlike some people we know, I think making money can be as creative as anything else and it really brings me down because the circus didn't do better financially."

Amanda bounded from her pallet and took the check. She was naked as a light bulb and Nearly Normal got his first good look at her tattoos. Pregnancy had given them an added dimension. As the dome of the Sistine Chapel had done to Michelangelo's cartoons. For a moment Jimmy forgot his monetary woes.

"A circus is not a department store," said Amanda, sliding (uphill all the way) into a silver satin robe. "Would you like some fresh huckleberries and yogurt?"

"Thanks, I would. Well, at least we didn't lose money. And what's more important, in our own dumb way we injected some Tibetan extract into the American vein."

"Dear Jimmy," Amanda smiled. "You're nearly normal. All that stands between you and Wall Street is Tibet."

"All indeed. I can never forgive John Paul for having been there. Ziller has had his Africa and *my* Tibet. Next to making a million in show biz, my greatest desire is to see Tibet. What a catastrophe! For forty centuries Tibet was the seat of world enlightenment, guardian of the universal secrets, and now when we really need it—are capable of using it—invaded, sealed off, despoiled. No line of communication open. If only we could send them singing telegrams, exchange recipes, subscribe to their newspapers, receive some sign that their wisdom has not been snuffed, receive some signal, as to what the next play should be."

Amanda ceased sprinkling huckleberries into the yogurt bowl and turned her friend over and over like an old coin in the connoisseur fingers of her sight. "So you want a sign, do you?" she asked at last. "Jimmy, my ringmaster, do you think it an accident, a mere coincidence, that LSD became available to the public, was thrust into the consciousness of the West, at precisely the time of the invasion of Tibet?"

Nearly Normal didn't say a word but his eyes throbbed and widened behind the lens of his spectacles and he ran out into the frosty damp and never came back for his breakfast.

"What would you like to see first?" Amanda's father asked his budding twelve-year-old upon their arrival in Paris. "I'd like to visit the brothels," answered Amanda, scarcely looking up from her onion soup. Amanda's papa refused to take his pubescent daughter into the Parisian fleshpots, but he did point them out to her from the window of a taxi. Whereupon the child asked, "Father, if you were in a whorehouse and you couldn't finish, would it be permissable to ask for a bowser bag to take the leftovers home?"

The Japs are to blame. Off the Pacific shore of Washington State the Japanese Current—a mammoth river of tropical water—zooms close by the coast on a southernly turn. Its warmth is released in the form of billows of tepid vapor, which the prevailing winds drive inland. When, a few miles in, the warm vapor bangs head-on into the Olympic Mountain Range, it is abruptly pushed upward and outward, cooling as it rises and condensing into rain. In the emerald area that lies between the Olympics (the coastal range) and the Cascade Range some ninety miles to the east, temperatures are mild and even. But during the autumn and winter months it is not unusual for precipitation to fall on five of every seven days. And when it is not raining, still the gray is pervasive; the sun a little boiled potato in a stew of dirty dumplings; the fire and light and energy of the cosmos trapped somewhere far behind that impenetrable slugbelly sky.

Puget Sound may be the most rained-on body of water on earth. Cold, deep, steep-shored, home to salmon and lipstick-orange starfish, the Sound lies between the Cascades and the Olympics. The Skagit Valley lies between the Cascades and the Sound—sixty miles north of Seattle, an equal distance south of Canada. The Skagit River, which formed the valley, begins up in British Columbia, leaps and splashes southwestward through the high Cascade wilderness, absorbing glaciers and sipping alpine lakes, running two hundred miles in total before all fish-green, driftwood-cluttered and silty, it spreads its double mouth like suckers against the upper body of Puget Sound. Toward the Sound end of the valley, the fields are rich with river silt, the soil ranging from black velvet to a blond sandy loam. Although the area receives little unfiltered sunlight, peas and strawberries grow lustily in Skagit fields, and more than half the world's supply of beet seed and cabbage seed is harvested here. Like Holland, which it in some ways resembles, it supports a thriving bulb industry: in spring its lowland acres vibrate with tulips, iris and daffodils; no bashful hues. At any season, it is a dry duck's dream. The forks of the river are connected by a network of sloughs, bedded with ancient mud and lined with cattail, tules, eelgrass and sedge. The fields, though diked, are often flooded; there are puddles by the hundreds and the roadside ditches could be successfully navigated by midget submarines.

It is a landscape in a minor key. A sketchy panorama where objects, both organic and inorganic, lack well-defined edges and tend to melt together in a silver-green blur. Great islands of craggy rock arch abruptly up out of the flats, and at sunrise and moonrise these outcroppings are frequently tangled in mist. Eagles nest on the island crowns and blue herons flap through the veils from slough to slough. It is a poetic setting, one which suggests inner meanings and invisible connections. The effect is distinctly Chinese. A visitor experiences the feeling that he has been pulled into a Sung dynasty painting, perhaps before the intense wisps of mineral pigment have dried upon the silk. From almost any vantage point, there are expanses of monochrome worthy of the brushes of Mi Fei or Kuo Hsi.

The Skagit Valley, in fact, inspired a school of neo-Chinese painters. In the Forties, Mark Tobey, Morris Graves and their gray-on-gray disciples turned their backs on cubist composition and European color and using the shapes and shades of this misty terrain as a springboard, began to paint the visions of the inner eye. A school of sodden, contemplative poets emerged here, too. Even the original inhabitants were an introspective breed. Unlike the Plains Indians, who enjoyed mobility and open spaces and sunny skies, the Northwest coastal tribes were caught between the dark waters to the west, the heavily forested foothills and towering Cascade peaks to the east; forced by the lavish rains to spend weeks on end confined to their longhouses. Consequently, they turned inward, evolving religious and mythological patterns that are startling in their complexity and intensity, developing an artistic idiom that for aesthetic weight and psychological depth was unequaled among all primitive races. Even today, after the intrusion of neon signs and supermarkets and aircraft industries and sports cars, a hushed but heavy force hangs in the Northwest air: it defies flamboyance, deflates extroversion and muffles the most exultant cry.

Yet one inhabitant of this nebulous and mystic land had had the audacity to establish a Dixie Bar-B-Cue. There is a colony of expatriated North Carolinians up in the timber country around Darrington: perhaps Mom was one of them. Her enterprise had not succeeded, obviously, and a disappointed and homesick Mom may have packed her curing salts and hot sauces and trucked on back to the red clay country where a good barbecue is paid the respect it deserves. At any rate, that aspect of the history of the cafe meant little to Amanda and John Paul Ziller for they were immune to the mystique of Southern pork barbecue. Neither had ever tasted the genuine article. Plucky Purcell had, of course, and he once remarked that "the only meat in the world sweeter, hotter and pinker than Amanda's twat is Carolina barbecue."

Prior to signing a lease for Mom's Little Dixie, Ziller had warned Amanda of the rigors of her new environment. He explained to his bride that there was seldom a thunderstorm

in Skagit country—simply not enough heat—so no matter
whether the influence storms had on her was good or
ultimately evil, she could expect to be free of it as long as
she resided in the Northwest. He told her that there would
be butterflies in summer, but not nearly in the numbers to
which she was accustomed in California and Arizona.
Amanda knew, naturally, that cacti could not endure in these
latitudes. And even their motorcycle would be impractical
during the rainy season that lingered from October to
May. "However," John Paul comforted her, "in those
ferny forests"—he pointed to the alder-thatched Cascade
foothills—"the mushrooms are rising like loaves. Like
hearts they are pulsing and swelling; fungi of many hues,
some shaped like trumpets and some like bells and some
like parasols and others like pricks; with thick meat white
as turkey or yellow as eggs; all reeking of primeval protein;
and some contain bitter juices that make men go crazy and
talk to God."

"Very well," said Amanda. "Mushrooms it will be." And
it was.

"Can you help me, John Paul? If anyone is capable of
solving this riddle it is you." From the tub of scented
bubbles in which she soaked, Amanda extended her hand,
palm up. The inscription had faded somewhat in the two
years since it had so impertinently appeared. Ziller was
forced to squint in order to register its finer details. He
stared at it for a curiously long time. Finally, he said:
"Off the coast of Africa there is a secret radio station.
On a ship. A condemned freighter. Blackened by fire.
Listing to starboard. Flying quarantine flags. It begins trans-
mitting at midnight and until dawn plays the music of
pre-colonial Africa, extremely rare pan-tribal recordings—if
recordings they are: perhaps the sounds are live. Inter-
spersed with this ancient music is commentary of a sort.
In a totally unknown language. I mean it isn't even *related*
to any known human tongue, existing or extinct. Some of

the words are short and grunty, but others are very
stretched-out and angular and sensual—like Modigliani
nudes. Linguistic experts are completely stymied. They
claim the "language" does not follow logical phonetic patterns. Yet thousands of blacks listen devotedly to the broad-
casts, and while they will not say that they comprehend the
commentary, they do not seem baffled by it, either."

Of the five thousand varieties of mushrooms that grow
in the United States, approximately twenty-five hundred
are found in western Washington. "I find those odds
charming," said Amanda, salivating and lacing her boots.

Actually, there was little time for fungi those first few
days at Mom's Little Dixie, although the Zillers did gather
some meadow mushrooms on the golf course at Mount
Vernon and filled another basket in a pasture on the river
road.

The meadow mushroom (*Agaricus campestris* to Madame
Goody) begins life looking like a slightly imperfect Ping-
Pong ball and matures into a skullish white pancake. Its
gills are pink when young, gradually turning chocolate.
Shamefully, it admits to being a first cousin of the
Agaricus bisporus, the mushroom found in the produce section of supermarkets, and of *Agaricus hortensis*, the kind one
buys in tin cans. True fungus fanciers look upon those two
traitors with withering disdain for only that pair among
all the thousands have allowed themselves to be domesti-
cated. The *campestris* has a much more interesting flavor
than the supermarket sellouts, is less dull in color and less
conservative in shape. But it suffers as a result of the

weaklings in its family—its flavor could never inspire the odes or awed burps that the more noble varieties of wild mushrooms command. Still, when sautéed with minced onion in a sour cream sauce and served over rice, it is comfortably close to succulent, as the Zillers would readily attest. Anyway, the *campestris* would have to do for now: Amanda and John Paul hadn't the hours yet to devote to the deep-woods hunt. They were too busy cleaning house.

On the ground floor of Mom's Little Dixie there was an enormous L-shaped dining room defined by an enormous L-shaped counter, a huge kitchen, two fundamental toilets (sexually segregated) and a fair-sized windowless room that may have been used as a pantry. Upstairs (the stairs ascended from the rear of the kitchen), there was an apartment consisting of five spacious rooms and a bath. Out back, in the trees (remember that the cafe sat in a grove on the edge of croplands), there was a garage above which were two rooms that could be used for either storage or quarters.

With pails and mops and brooms and rags and an alchemicus of detergents, scouring powders and waxes (to which well-paid marketing experts had given names such as Pow, Rid, Thrill, and Zap—carefully chosen for their simple violence), Amanda and John Paul set out to clear all those compartments of dirt, dust and debris. Mon Cul was put to work washing windows and although easily distracted and prone to slope, the baboon did get them clean. Even Baby Thor had duties: emptying dustpans and fetching materials. With painting and decorating to follow, the project was destined to take weeks.

At first, Amanda was too occupied to pay much attention to John Paul's detachment; he's an introverted and private man, she thought, and he needs time alone in his head. But the bride, after all, was a female animal and when Ziller's contemplative mood held over into a second day and a third, she began to suspect the worst, wondering if he had turned remorseful about having married her. Eventually, she approached him with her fears, which he dispelled somewhat by balling her on the spot (dust rags beneath her bottom, her head on a mop). Then he confessed that he had been worrying about Plucky Purcell. Not a word had been heard from the Mad Pluck since that memorable morning-after near Sacramento.

"He doesn't strike me as an excessively reliable sort," consoled Amanda. "He's probably followed the charmer's pipes down some remote path of eroticism and simply forgotten all about us." She then admitted that while she was not immune to Purcell's roguish charms, she found him something of a hypocrite: he seems aggressively preoccupied with the wickedness of the American economy, yet he is employed as a logger. And if one is going to pollute one's consciousness with hate, fear and blame, one might as well acknowledge that no single facet of the economic power structure, except for the oil ogre, has so brutally and insensitively pillaged America's natural resources as has the lumber industry. According to Amanda. So there.

Thus, it became incumbent upon Ziller to offer in behalf of L. Westminster "Plucky" Purcell some

BIOGRAPHICAL DATA

I

A career as a public servant became necessary for the youngest Purcell son when other avenues of accomplishment were closed to him as a result of particular indiscretions. Not that he wasn't allowed a second chance. To wit: The United States Navy felt that Plucky had the makings of an officer and a gentleman despite the notoriety that surrounded his Mexican vacation. Despite his silly grin. He was accepted for pilot's training and was graduated from the Pensacola air school, third in his class. Next came advanced training in jets; swifter, more complicated crafts which he flew with his by now customary aplomb. But fate lay in wait for Plucky in the shape of raisin bread.

What irritated Ensign Purcell most gruffly about the navy was the hour which it deemed imperative for its junior pilots to quit their beds. "We are, through the good taste of Congress, legally gentlemen," he argued, "and there are hours, specifically those between midnight and noon, when no proper gentleman would permit himself to be disturbed." Still, Purcell did his duty, arising at five thirty each morning (despite having caroused through most of the soft Florida night) and attending to his toilet prior to visiting the officer's mess for breakfast. Now the mess officer (being, of course, in charge of the officers' mess) had decided, for reasons known only in his most secret and greasy heart, to serve toasted raisin bread each morning. No other kind of bread or biscuit did he provide his guests. Just raisin bread. Toasted. Ensign Purcell complained about this daily, pointing out that only a pervert or a geek would enjoy sweet gummy raisins mucking about in his mouthful of egg, though he said this none too loudly, for all around him the cream of American manhood was chomping away with gusto.

Whatever had initially motivated the mess officer (and it could have been, in fairness, an innocent ploy), sadistic tendencies soon revealed themselves. Mess Officer gleefully ignored Purcell's protests and kept the raisin toast popping.

Came the hour for satisfaction. From the Ship's Service, Purcell purchased a giant family-size tube of Colgate toothpaste. By the light of his desk lamp, he slit the bottom of the tube with a razor blade and patiently extracted is contents. The next evening he spent meticulously refilling the tube with uncolored oleomargarine. He then resealed it. And took it to breakfast. Mess Officer sensed that something was amiss when Purcell cheerfully refused eggs, took a tall stack of toast instead. Raisin bread toast.

Plucky sat at a table in the center of the dining hall and unwrapped his big tube with the Colgate label. Nonchalantly he began squeezing out coils of slick white stuff onto the toast which, piece by piece, he devoured. Conversation in the mess was first paralyzed, then a fierce buzzing commenced. All eyes were on the madman eating toothpaste. Some of Purcell's fellow jet trainees were amused. Most were aghast. The older officers boiled immediately into a stiff-faced huff. Mess Officer observed this and knew that he must act.

MESS OFFICER: Ensign, just what in hell do you think you're doing?

ENSIGN PURCELL: Eating breakfast, sir. The toast is especially palatable this morning. Raisins plump and chewy. (Licks a curlicue of

margarine off a grinning lip. Flashes a
Colgate smile.) Cleans the breath while
it cleans the teeth.

Mess Officer conferred with three lieutenants at a nearby
table. "What can we do?" he asked mournfully. "He's doing
this just to bug me. There's no regulation against eating
toothpaste."

"There's regulations against an officer acting like a gawd-
damned billy goat," said one lieutenant. Call the S.P.'s
and have him arrested. We'll think of something to charge
him with."

As it turned out, Plucky was charged with conduct
unbecoming an officer and was confined to quarters for
thirty days. His sentence weighed on him lightly. Too
lightly for an incorrigible whoremonger, thought Mess Officer, and on the occasion when he was officer of the deck,
he pulled a surprise 11 P.M. inspection of Purcell's room,
fully expecting to find a bar girl or two stashed away in the
ensign's bunk. He found no women. But he did find several
ounces of Acapulco gold, a smokable delicacy for which
Plucky had acquired a taste while south of the border.
Mess Officer's joy in his discovery was tempered, however, by the fact that before he could get to a phone to
report it, he had half a loaf of stale raisin bread stuffed
down his throat.

II

"To a son of the nobility, three fields of endeavor
are open," Plucky reminded himself. "These are: Military, religion and politics. The military has failed me.
There is no public office to which I could realistically
aspire. As for religion, that is a subject which holds a
maximum of fascination for me, but I fear the seminary
gates would be bolted at the earliest signal of my approach."

He sat down upon his duffel bag and with his dishonorable discharge lit a Havana cigar. It was nearly dark
and he was giving up hope of hitching a ride. "There is,
however, one occupation where politics, the military and
religion overlap; which embodies prominent features of all

three." He blew a target of concentric smoke rings, then threw his stogy over a palm tree. Lugged his suitcase and began to trudge. In the general direction of the Pacific Ocean. Despite (or because of) six months in the brig, he was in good condition and prepared, if necessary, to walk all the way. "But," he vowed, "I'm blindfolding myself for eight hundred of those three thousand miles so as to shut out the Middle West."

And on that note of acute discernment and with no small sense of fatalism, Plucky Purcell embarked upon a life of crime.

III

Whether a man is a criminal or a public servant is purely a matter of perspective. Man's peculiarly ambivalent psyche permits him to operate simultaneously according to two opposing codes. There is the code which he professes to live by, and there is the code to whose standards he actually does adhere. The deceit is so ingrained and subtle that most men truly are unaware of it, although to psychologists, philosophers and the like, it is no news at all.

Man is not as good as he thinks he is. (Nor as bad, for that matter, but let's not complicate things.) He has certain needs, demands certain services which in reality are probably healthly and natural, but to which in time's passage and as a result of odd quirks in his ethos, he has ascribed (or allowed his religious leaders—often guilt-warped, psychopathic misfits—to ascribe) negative values. In the queerest of paradoxical metamorphoses, honest desires change into taboos.

To simply "say" that a desire is immoral—or, resorting to even flimsier abstraction, to deem the fulfillment of a desire *illegal*—does not eliminate the desire. It does not eliminate anything except straightforwardness. It creates, in addition to a climate of deception, an underworld into which men "descend" in order to partake of Code B services not permitted under the provisions of Code A. Society hires armed goons to force itself to conform to Code A, but a greater sum of money is spent each year in the surreptitious enjoyment of the services provided by Code B. The underworld persists because society needs it, insists upon it, supports it (at the same time that it denies and persecutes it, of course).

But enough of that. Let's simply say that according to Code A, Plucky Purcell—drug dealer and abortionist's agent—is a criminal. Under the reality of Code B, however, he is dutifully serving the interests of his fellow man.

IV

Although there is probably no such thing as a "typical" citizen of the underworld, Purcell would not conform to any man's conception of the ordinary criminal. For one thing, he doesn't look like a dealer. The genetic system responsible for his physique must have plagiarized openly from the Belvedere Apollo. His face, too, is beautiful, although its classical composition is inclined to crumble when he indulges his goofy grin. Man, Purcell has a grin like the beer barrel polka. A ding-dong daddy grin. A Brooklyn Dodger grin. A grin you could wear to a Polish wedding. His smile walks in in woolly socks and suspenders and asks to borrow the funny papers. You could trap rabbits with it. Teeth line up inside it like cartridges in a Mexican bandit's gunbelt. It is the skunk in his rosebush, the crack in his cathedral.

Purcell's methods are as atypical as his looks. He caters, for example, to an exclusive clientele: his services are available only to artists. Now if Plucky has ever in his life suffered a creative impulse, he either successfully suppressed it or satisfied it under cover of darkness. There are no indications that he is a frustrated artist. Yet, for reasons which his friends have never adequately explored, he attached himself to a wide circle of painters, sculptors, film makers and poets. In fact, among artists on both coasts of America there is hardly a more familiar face. Our most rigorous and challenging geniuses have tasted his dope; their girl friends, models and wives have availed themselves of his medical connections. Moreover, he has been a bodyguard to artists in peril, a baby-sitter for those who did not take advantage of his clinical references and a cherished dinner guest of the great and the obscure. (Although it did not make the papers, a Pulitzer Prize winner once showed up to go his bail.) Did Purcell, convinced of artists' traditional-mythical appetites for sin, and aware, too, of their insulation and intelligence, merely see in the creative minority a safe and steady market for his wares? Or did he recognize that despite the attention paid art today (though actually it is "culture" and not art that draw the light), despite the historically proven importance of the artist to society, artists are still second-class citizens who might need to be served and protected by an agent sensitive to their socio-economic deprivations and emotional demands? Or, is the Mad Pluck genuinely, personally moved by artisthood, its ideas and its works? Well, whatever.

Perhaps the most astonishing characteristic of Plucky's criminal career is the ethics with which he practices it. His fees are more than fair: he seeks to make a living, not a killing. The times are not rare when a girl in trouble without adequate funds has had her surgery bill paid out of Plucky's own pocket. Lest he sound the altruist he is not, however, it should be disclosed that he usually required the girl to share a weekend with him inspecting ceilings in some modest hotel. While he is untainted by monetary greed it cannot be denied that he is a pig for pussy.

There is more to say in Purcell's behalf. He does not escort women to abattoirs—he represents trained physicians who are skilled and compassionate and who wash their hands before and after. As for drugs, he carries a line of the most reliable marijuana and hashish. To a client whom he feels is sound enough to handle it, he also will sell LSD, mescaline, STP, DMT or psilocybin. He does not deal in hard narcotics or amphetamines. He does not tolerate those who do. When he meets pushers of smack and speed, as he does not infrequently in his profession, he attempts to convince them that it is a vile and murderous act to peddle chemicals which can ultimately only destroy their imbibers. If his pleas fail, he batters heads and breaks bones. That makes him unpopular with racketeers and police alike.

Try as they might, neither the Mafia nor the police nor any combination thereof can win the respect of Plucky Purcell. It is possible that Plucky is narrow-minded where mobsters and cops are concerned. Possibly, he does not try to understand the reasons for their boorish manners, their mutual greed, their artless authority. Something in his nature has always been intolerant of authority, especially when it is violently imposed upon those who seem neither to need it nor want it—as is usually the case. Rash boy, his conscience does not even twitch when in his small-fry way he upsets the delicate symbiotic relationship between organized crime and organized crime-prevention. He is insensitive to the losses his prejudices have inflicted upon the international heroin cartel, the embarrassment his interference has caused the police. And as if to add insult to injury, he is always taking part in social protests, marching in demonstrations and otherwise exercising his moral and constitutional rights in a manner that cannot be helpful to the establishment, not the "legal" establishment or the "illegal" one. Thus, with officialdom he is less popular than a tough cut of beef. In fact, Purcell, long before Amanda and John Paul's marriage, had become so hot that he was obliged to spend four to six months each year outside of his chosen profession. During the cooling-off periods he would ship out as a merchant seaman, labor as a cowboy in Texas or Wyoming, enlist as a smoke jumper in Montana, fly crop-dusting duty in California (he has maintained his enthusiasm for flying and is a licensed pilot) or cut timber in the Great Northwest. While he shares Amanda's disdain for tree-exploiters, it is in the big woods that he feels safest. Logging keeps him in top physical shape, and the pure forest air sweetens his brain and his lungs.

"If they really decide to do you in, all the trees in Washington and Oregon can't hide you," a leading painter had warned.

"Oh, man, I'm only a nuisance," Plucky answered. "They won't get their Italian loafers muddy to slap a mosquito." And cranking out his five-pound grin, he grabbed his calked boots and headed for tall timber.

Bravado aside, however, Purcell would have to admit that Ziller's concern for him was not irrational. Amanda, after she had absorbed his background, joined her husband in his unease. Of course, as the reader might have surmised, neither Syndicate exterminator nor super narcotics sleuth reached Purcell in his hard-labor up-country hideaway. It was an event a bit more startling than a rub-out or arrest that curtailed Plucky's customary epistles to his pals. So startling, in fact, that had Ziller an inkling of it he might have been too amazed to have balled his bride on that gray Skagit afternoon, let alone to have proposed the Babylonain slobber magic which they practiced after supper.

No. The author exaggerates. It wasn't as startling as all that.

Amanda went once to a blues club. Her date was Madame Lincoln Rose Goody, who was, as Amanda somewhat innocently discovered, not academic in bed.

All evening, music or no, an old Negro called the Jelly Man passed among the patrons selling from a tray fresh raspberries, sugar, glass jars and little brown spiders.

"Jelly Man," said Amanda, "I can understand the berries and the sugar and the jars. But how did the spiders get in?"

"Under the door," answered the benevolent Jelly Man.

They had two garter snakes and a tsetse fly. And the tsetse fly was not even alive. Hardly a roadside attraction.

They had a baboon, true enough. But under no circumstances would Ziller assign Mon Cul a role in the menagerie. "As long as my friend's body turns on a pivot of crimson buttocks, as long as his eloquent fangs pierce honeydews and melons, as long as he in wisdom and laughter goes on spinning around the sun, he will not be gawked at, gibbered over and goaded by beings less dignified than he."

Ziller's attitude was understood perfectly by Amanda for she had brought her dancing bear to perform with the Indo-Tibetan Circus only to have it choke to death on a handkerchief that some rube in sport tossed into the pen. "But," she answered, "granting that Mon Cul is a remarkable creature, that he is the elder statesman among monkeys, that his marcescent eyelids have opened upon sights and splendors about which the most romantic among us only dream, granting that, do not all wild animals have dignity? Can we justify caging *any* beast, subjecting it to the public gape?"

After some hesitation, John Paul agreed that they could not. He hesitated because he was, after all, a man of the jungle; a man dressed in hides and feathers, a man who had hunted and been hunted in lands where primitive equalities prevail. It was not in Africa (or in India), however, but at the Bronx Zoo that he had been warned of the folly of anthropomorphism. That wolf that paces incessantly in its cage, that panther who sways as if to music behind the metal barricades, we tend to think them unhappy, angry, claustrophobic, in despair because of their confinement, but we're just imposing our own human emotions on animals who are not biologically capable of such feelings. That's what the keeper had said. The soft brown eye-glow of the deer looks sad to us, but that's just the way deer's eyes are built. There are no sad deer, in or out of corrals. Anthropomorphism is a silly deceit. He'd said that, too. Furthermore, he'd claimed that animals are better off in zoos than in their natural habitats. In the wilds, the battle for survival is unrelenting. Hunger follows the animal like a shadow. Thousands of beasts starve each year the world over. What's more, there are predators to escape. And diseases. In the zoo, an animal is safe, well-fed, housed in comfortable temperatures, given medical attention. Why, zoos are almost utopias for the beasts.

It was a good argument, yet John Paul offered it to Amanda with a minimum of conviction, and when she rejected it he concurred. As unrefined and basic as an animal's emotional equipment may be, it is not insensitive to freedom. Somewhere in the archives of crudest instinct is recorded the truth that it is better to be endangered and free than captive and comfortable. In the cage, even in the "environmental parks" which the better zoos are providing for their charges, a creature is out of harmony with the natural rhythms of organ and earth: it must eat foods out of their regular season; soft living erodes its cunning; it becomes confused about mating and often fails to reproduce; an immense FRUSTRATION overtakes it due to its inability to heed instinctual instructions. Were it capable of choice, surely it would prefer to take its chances "out there" against the odds of hunger and hungry. While suffering is no more glamorous—or even necessary—for animal than for man, and while for the being who is at peace with itself survival may be of trivial concern, still there is something kind of noble in the struggle for survival. Whether meaningful or meaningless, the game of life is there to be played—and the animal in his animal way seems to "know" it and the cage is an offense to what his inner animal voice tells him is right and true.

Lubricated by this dialogue, Amanda pushed further. "When a man confines an animal in a cage, he assumes ownership of that animal. But an animal is an individual; it cannot be owned. When a man tries to own an individual, whether that individual be another man, an animal or even a tree, he suffers the psychic consequences of an unnatural act. Have you ever watched visitors at a menagerie or zoo— the fools they make of themselves, the way they leer and snigger and vex and demand entertainment and taunt? A caged beast, like an excess of alcohol, reduces man to his most banal dimensions. And he is only slightly better behaved when observing human inmates of prisons and institutions. A creature, human or otherwise, that has had its freedom compromised has been degraded. In a subconscious reaction that combines guilt, fear, and contempt, the keepers of the caged—even the observers of the caged—are degraded themselves. The cage is a double degrader. Any bar, whether concrete or intangible, that stands between a living thing and its liberty is a communicable perversity, dangerous to the sanity of everyone concerned."

What had gotten into Amanda? She was never moved to pedantry unless . . . She cocked one ear to listen for the telltale thunderclap. But all she heard was Mon Cul shuffling into the room and up to Ziller's side, where he bowed and scraped and grinned apologetically like some creaky old back-porch nigger. Ziller squatted and met the baboon eye to eye, but Mon Cul backed away with an Uncle Tom one-step, opals of spittle popping in the corners of his obsequious smile.

"You Judas creep," scolded Ziller. "You who've lived a life of hedonistic abandon, you would insinuate that I've held you captive? If there is a master in our relationship it is *you* who has owned *me*." The baboon barked uproariously and turned four somersaults. And although Ziller laughed and said, "You'd better watch your manners or you'll end up in Detroit and you know what happens to baboons there," he was mired to his cerebral axle in troubled thoughts.

And over in a corner on a sunflowered pillow, Amanda,

too, was subdued as she remembered the thousands of butterflies she had enveloped in her net. "At least," she thought, "I never once introduced one to chloroform." Her rationalization only shaded the hues of her shame.

It was a hell of a way to start a roadside zoo.

In the absence (perhaps, alas, permanent) of John Paul Ziller, this writer was about an hour ago allowed to look through the missing magician's possessions. After all, the FBI and CIA have rummaged Ziller's and Purcell's belongings so thoroughly there could be little left of intimacy or value. Your correspondent found what he was seeking, however: an English language dictionary. It should be quite useful in the completion of this document and he should have thought of it sooner. Perhaps from here on out the reader will note some improvement in vocabulary, if not in overall what-do-you-call-it.

Already the author has learned that *dawk* is just another word for *dak*, and that *dawt* is Scottish for *daut*. What do you make of that?

"Magnificent!" exclaimed John Paul Ziller, pronouncing the word like he was a Kansas City intellectual describing the Louvre to his sister-in-law who'd called to tell him to bring his vacation slides over some other night because she'd burned the spaghetti sauce and the baby had colic. "Truly wondrous. Appraising it now I feel a bit like Bernard Berenson standing before Michelangelo's 'Temptation,' 'quaffing rare draughts of unadulterated energy' and itching to get his cultivated meathooks on the heroic buttocks of Eve. Though in truth, due to its humility and patience, it's less a Michelangelo than a Renoir: the roundness, the warmth, the rosy delight, the *joie de vivre*, the casual eroticism, the full and robust charm. It is at once a dramatically overflowing embodiment of the life force and an honest monument to the occasional genius of the plebeian palate."

With that blast of language, Ziller stepped back against a fir trunk to gain a slightly more distant perspective on the thirty-foot hot dog.

Amanda was shocked. She had never seen him like this: smiley, ebullient. Not once in the weeks she'd known him, worked and played with him, listened to his drums and flutes and plans, pored over his maps and charts, mingled her beauty and force with his, trapped explosive ribbons of his semen in her various bodily orifices, not once had he replaced his high jungle pride with such easy enthusiasm. It did not displease her, however. She walked to his side and stood with him, the better to admire the object of his excitement: the mighty mammoth king of weenies which he had painted in oils on thirty-four feet of plywood paneling.

"Note how the wrinkles in the bun—it's a steamed-soft bun, of course—fold dynamically, intuiting hidden movement as if they were folds in silks draped about a Renaissance Madonna. The texture of the bun is soft but not rubbery; it has the luster of a prairie moon. The sausage itself possesses a kind of peasant-folk serenity: it lounges in that bun as plump with confidence as a Polack bowling champion snoozing in a backyard hammock on the afternoon before the Greak Lakes regional finals. A simple fellow, the sausage, but the way his gentle contours catch the light and hold it gleaming, one senses something glorious in his spirit. I have molded his bulk—can you sense the physical participation of the artist in the formal objectification of the weenie's presence?—into a continuous volume that consumes vast quantities of space; it is three-dimensional, tactile, larger than life, as rotund and good-natured as Falstaff but not entirely devoid of Hamlet's rank. And what glamour is lent to the scene by the golden cloak of mustard, by the jazzy, jumpy play of flat patterns in the relish. Ahem."

Amanda licked her lips in amazement, more at the verbiage than at the inspiration of it, although it was indeed a hot dog of grand proportions. The panel was thirty-four feet long and nine feet high, the red hot was thirty feet in length and a little less than six feet in height and that weenie was not just loitering there in empty space. She perceived at the left end of the bun a green valley with cornfields and a river and some men in a boat on the river drinking beer and trolling for catfish; and across the river was a stadium with a baseball game in progress, probably a World Series because of all the dignitaries in the stands—political figures, movie stars and their counterparts in crime. In the twenty-four-inch space at the right end of the hot dog there was a brown-yellow plain with just a few thorny trees a-thirsting on it and a pride of lions resting in the stingy shade beneath one of those trees, and far in the distance, too far for the warm lions to bother with, a herd of wildebeests was kicking up dust, and even further in the distance Mt. Kilimanjaro jumped up like God's own sugar-tit, and in a modest encampment at the foot of the peak, E. Hemingway was cleaning his Weatherby 375 magnum (not trusting the native boys to handle such an instrument) and slurping his gin. In some mythic gesture of interracial world solidarity, the frankfurter bridged Africa and America in a manner that no United Nations mission or foreign aid program could hope to equal. It quickened the pulse. And reminded Amanda of John Paul's testimonial of a few days prior in which he professed that the sausage was one of the few achievements of Western technology that he could genuinely respect.

Up above that ambassador hot dog, in the night-blue sky above it, was to Amanda's eyes the most thrilling segment of the whole tableau: a skyful of vanilla stars and pastel planets and rushing comets and constellations (Jupiter was in the house of Gemini) and novae and nebulae and meteors dissolving in spittoons of fire and a tropical moon laid out against a cloud bank like a radioactive oyster on the half shell, and dominating the entire sidereal panorama was Saturn—silver and mysterious mushy omelet of ammonia and ice girded by its sharp gas rings like an avatar egg with a hip-hugger aura. And all this astronomical grandeur merely a backdrop for the mustard-draped shoulders of the cosmic colossal weenie, a sight to put a lump in the throat of the most unambitious Nebraska piglets, bar none.

The hot dog was to be erected on the roof of the roadhouse. Some workmen were coming from Mount Vernon with a crane. In a day or two, as soon as the paint was dry. It would be visible for miles.

The Zillers had reached no decision on the contents of the zoo. They were opposed to cages. Society was opposed to wild animals running loose in restaurants. The proper compromise evaded them. Amanda consulted the *I Ching*. She induced a trance. With no fit results. They had agreed to forget it for a while. In the meantime they could concentrate on what items they would sell in their shop, on what foods they would serve.

Something simple, they both insisted on simplicity. They had no intention of wasting their days cooking and washing dishes for tourist hordes. They shuddered at the thought. "Hot dogs," John Paul had suggested. "Good old-fashioned hot dogs. With steam-softened buns. We'll keep our buns in a steam cabinet the way they did when men were men and the sausage was the backbone of an empire. We'll offer fresh onions, raw or fried. A variety of mustards, catsups and relishes. Bacon, chopped nuts, melted cheese, sauerkraut— optional at additional cost, like whitewalls or power steering. The sausages we will carefully select for size and flavor; 100 per cent meat sausages (a little heavier on the beef than the pork), the best we can buy, the finest offspring of German technical expertise and American ingenuity."

Amanda was not at ease with the prospect of operating a hot dog stand. She was a vegetarian.

Due to the fact that she occasionally consumed milk and milk derivatives, she could not be considered a *strict* vegetarian. "Amanda," purists would scold, "milk is an animal product. How can you drink milk and still consider yourself a vegetarian?" And Amanda would answer, "The label states that this carton contains activated ergosterol. Have you ever heard of a cow that activated ergosterol?" But as vegetarians are a stubborn lot, the argument was never resolved.

At any rate, Amanda protested. "I shan't impose my beliefs on other people," she said, "but my conscience would turn purple were I, a vegetarian, to earn an income selling meat. There are limits to the decency of irony. Why, I'd feel like a Mormon." (Not that Amanda had any particular prejudice against Mormons, but she was a curious young woman, as many persons had established, and it confounded her curiosity that a denomination of nonsmoking teetotalers like the Mormons could justify supporting itself through the operation of supermarkets and drugstores in which alcoholic beverages and tobacco are prominent wares.)

John Paul was untroubled by any undue reverence for meat. "Look," he said, "the world is overrun with animals, great and small, fanged and feathered, all eating one another in happy harmony. Man is the party pooper. He'll eat pig flesh and pretend it's pork. He'll devour a chicken but not a kitten, a turkey but not a Turk. It isn't that he is principled, particularly. In fact, we all gut somebody every day. But it's sneaky, symbolic, unappetizing, ego-supportive, duty to God and country—never with a good pot roast in mind. No cheerful, honest cannibalism. Alas, alas."

Amanda was not much swayed by John Paul's remarks. Incidentally, though, her vegetarian sentiments received a bit of a shake a few months later when Marx Marvelous said to her: "The cow became a sacred symbol to the Hindu because it gave milk and chops and hides. It nourished the babies and kept the old folks warm. Because it provided so many good life-supporting things, it was regarded as an embodiment of the Universal Mother, hence holy. Then it occurred to some monk or other, some abstract scholarly kook, as you would say, that gee, folks, since the cow is holy we maybe shouldn't be eating it and robbing its udder. So now the Hindu has got sacred cows up to here but no more milk and steaks. They starve in plain view of holy herds so big only Hopalong Cassidy could stop them if they took a notion to stampede. The spiritual man's beef against beef is the result of a classic distortion. It's another case of lost origins and inverted values." But that was Marx Marvelous and that came later.

For the present, they worked it out. They had to. While the interior of the cafe was now clean and freshly painted, the exterior had hardly been touched. A warning: the sky bulged like the sooty cheeks of an urban snowman—it hadn't rained yet but it wouldn't be long. The downpour was overdue. Action was required. So, Amanda reluctantly gave her consent to frankfurters and, in concession, John Paul agreed to a ban on dangerous fluids such as coffee and soda pop. For beverages they would serve the juices of fruits and vegetables. Amanda would squeeze them fresh in her automatic juicer. She had fun planning zesty combinations. Apple-papaya juice, for example. Carrot-orange. Spinach-tomato-cucumber. Good health to all! "People will think this a real funny place," said Ziller, "when they can't buy their coffee and Coca-Cola."

It was a funny place anyway. A roadside zoo with no animals. Except two garter snakes and a tsetse fly. And the tsetse fly was not even alive.

A trailer of rain fell for an hour at sunrise, but the afternoon was dry. The hot dog was erected on the roof of the cafe. It looked good. It could be seen for miles.

Ziller's magnificent sausage became a landmark in Skagit County. Directions were given in relation to it. "Turn right a couple hundred yards past the big weenie," some helpful farmer might say. From that time on, Mount Vernon school children would be obliged to compose annual essays on "The Sausage: Its Origin, Its Meaning and Its Cure."

To this day it hovers in plump passivity above the fertile fields. It is a perfect emblem for the people and the land.

A sausage is an image of rest, peace and tranquillity in stark contrast to the destruction and chaos of everyday life.

Consider the peaceful repose of the sausage compared with the aggressiveness and violence of bacon.

"Er, ah, this quite an interesting place you fixing up here." The speaker was Gunnar Hansen, a thirty-fivish pea farmer from down the road a ways.

"Thank you, Mr. Hansen," smiled Amanda.

Gunnar Hansen. Yes. This mystic old Chinese valley (with Dutch undertones) in northwestern America is inhabited almost exclusively by Scandinavians.

"But you folks, your name ain't Kendrick," Farmer Hansen said with uncertainty.

"No," Amanda assured him, "our name is Ziller."

"Well, er, ah, who's this Kendrick?" asked Farmer Hansen, trying to sound jocular through an accent the color of a midwinter suicide. He was nodding his tombstone head at the new neon-bordered sign that stretched across the roadhouse facade just below the great giant sausage: CAPT. KENDRICK MEMORIAL HOT DOG WILDLIFE PRESERVE. That's how the sign read, in letters the height of Jewish ghetto tailors.

"Shame on you, Mr. Hansen," Amanda said. "You don't know your local history."

"Well, I thought I did."

"Captain John Kendrick. You can look him up in *History of the Pacific Northwest* by George W. Fuller. Captain Kendrick was one of the first fur traders and explorers to operate in the Puget Sound region. Came here in 1788. On slim evidence he was reported to be the first white man to navigate the Strait of Juan de Fuca and to circumnavigate Vancouver Island. He did quite a bit of exploring but unfortunately he neglected to leave any records of his discoveries. History has repaid him for that oversight by generally ignoring him. After about five years here, he tired of the Northwest skin trade and set sail for the Sandwich Islands. He arrived on December 12, 1794 and was immediately killed by a shot from a British ship which was saluting him."

"Oh, awful," said Farmer Hansen, with a Nordic insensitivity to irony. He drove away in his truck. Farmer Hansen had five children attending public schools in Mount Vernon and Conway. Perhaps that explains why it is now common belief among Skagit County pupils that Capt. John Kendrick invented the weenie sandwich in 1794.

Amanda climbed to the top of a big spruce tree, the better to absorb the Skagit twilight. She climbed slowly, using only one hand, for with the other arm she cradled her belly much as an avid bowler holds his favorite ball.

The sky was afloat with raw oysters and dead nuns, a grim canopy beneath which flew wild ducks by the dozens. It was a green sunset. The reds, the oranges, the purples which Amanda automatically associated with sunsets had been snuffed out in the soggy cloud pile, and the nearly invisible sun that sank—beyond the fields, sloughs, rock islands and tide flats—into Puget Sound, it looked like an unripe olive photographed through gauze.

From her perch Amanda could watch Baby Thor as he played on the moss near the base of the tree. And she could watch John Paul as he nailed silhouettes of sausages to the newly painted facade of the cafe. The sausages, about two feet in length, had been cut from plywood and covered with diffraction grating, a thin, synthetic, metallic silver material that picks up light and diffracts it so that its shiny surface is constantly rainbowed with moving spectra.

It is amazing, thought Amanda, how John Paul's weenie cutouts succinctly advertise our good common indigenous merchandise while at the same time suggesting the virility fetishes of numerous African tribes. I'm glad that John Paul recognizes that they are images of pleasure not of domination.

Amanda rested quietly in the boughs. Although the mid-October skies were gray, the air remained mild and mellow and she was comfortable in a cactus-colored corduroy jump suit beneath which there was not a thread of hampering underwear. She had devoted the day to arranging furnishings in the upstairs apartment, caring for Thor and baking panfuls of her notorious breads. Now she was due a rest. As she rested, she thought of many things. She thought of Life and said to herself, "It's okay. I want more of it." She thought of Death and said to herself, "If I fall out of this frigging treetop, I'll soon enough learn its secrets."

She thought of the planar fields—some plowed dark brown, others yellow-green with cabbage or broccoli left deliberately to seed—that straightened toward the horizon in every direction, the ones to the east tilting into hills, the ones to the west falling off into the Sound with a slow fuzzy expansiveness, and she said to herself, "Although the surface of our planet is two-thirds water, we call it the Earth. We say we are earthlings, not waterlings. Our blood is closer to seawater than our bones to soil, but that's no matter. The sea is the cradle we all rocked out of, but it's to dust that we go. From the time that water invented us, we began to seek out dirt. The further we separate ourselves from the dirt, the further we separate ourselves from ourselves. Alienation is a disease of the unsoiled."

She thought of the things that lovely young women usually think about when they are relaxing in treetops and unhampered by underwear. And she thought, as she often did at dusk, of the Infinite Goof. Mostly, however, she thought about the dilemma of the roadside zoo. A zoo without animals was no zoo at all.

It was peaceful in the spruce. The breeze about her was buttery; tropical in texture if not in temperature. A Canadian goose flapped over so close she could have reached up and grasped its honk—over the sloughs she'd fly, hanging on to the dark arch of that primordial noise as a subway passenger holds to a strap.

The moments passed. It was very nearly night when she suddenly began to descend the tree, climbing faster than she had moved up it; letting her silken bellyball bounce where it might. "John Paul," she called. "John Paul."

The sausage hammering ceased. Ziller answered: *"Umbatu jigi."* Or was it *"Ombedoo gigi"?* Or *"Ambudu geki"?* It was a Swahili phrase, probably, or Nilo-Hamitic or from a Bantu dialect and Amanda couldn't pronounce it, couldn't spell it and couldn't define it, but her husband always answered with it when she called, so it made sense.

"Insects," yelled Amanda, squirreling down the spruce trunk.

"Insects? In the tree?"

"No. In the zoo."

By this time she had reached the lowest limb and John Paul helped her down onto his shoulders. Her crotch pressed against the back of his neck. She hadn't bathed yet that day although they had made love the night before. She smelled like the leftovers from an Eskimo picnic. He was inflamed. (Didn't someone once say that odor is 80 per cent of love?)

"Insects in the zoo," Amanda repeated.

John Paul took Baby Thor's hand and he walked mother and son toward the back door. "What do you mean?" he asked, interest as faint in his voice as scruples in a letter from a collection agency. She felt his long Egyptian neck arching back against her, forcing the lips of her vagina apart, and she was determined to resist until she could present her new idea. They were in the kitchen now. John Paul was lifting Thor into his high chair, on the tray of which awaited a fat banana. Amanda was still riding John Paul's shoulders.

"An insect zoo," said Amanda. "Insects. The most numerous creatures on earth and perhaps the least understood. They don't require the space for their freedom that animals do. Most of them would be content to range over quite small areas. We could build wondrous cages for them, little palaces and pagodas, labyrinths and landing strips, jewel-like enclosures. Uh. Ummmmm." The pressure against her vulva was unrelenting.

"Am I to ascertain that you are proposing a hexapodium, a roadside attraction of beetles and bugs?" Ziller was walking upstairs. Amanda had to duck to protect her head. Bony Watusi fingers kneaded her thighs.

"Why not? The cricket, the tarantula, the praying mantis, all thrive in captivity and make interesting pets. Many insects live relatively long lives and their upkeep is no problem. Bedbugs have been known . . . Oooops!" John Paul had dumped her onto the mattress. ". . . have been known to live for a year on a single meal. Oh my God."

"I could live for many years on these," said Ziller, nibbling madly.

Amanda's jump suit was unzipped, throat to crotch. Between the parted corduroy her pink belly rose like the mushroom that conquered Hollywood.

"Insects are fascinating. Many of their senses are more highly developed than our own. Our tongues, for example, can't tell the difference between sugar solutions and dissolved saccharine. But bees, wasps and butterflies, while they love sugar water, won't sip a saccharine substitute at all."

Meanwhile, Ziller was doing a bit of tasting himself. Amanda was melting from the glory of it. She felt like the frosting left on the spoon that iced the Cake of the World.

"Insects have hearts and blood circulation systems just as we do. But did you know that it's impossible to take a beetle's pulse?"

Why had she said that? It was irrelevant. She was losing her rationale. John Paul was out of his loincloth. He hovered over her. His rigid member rested against her belly like a hoe handle against a pumpkin. Looking at it, all she could think to say was, "The European cabbage butterfly has the most remarkable coiled proboscis. Gasp!"

Amanda was a stubborn woman. She was determined to have her say. With the mental equivalent of a Dutch boy finger, she tried to plug the hole in the glandular dike from whence her hot juices gushed. "Well, look, don't you think it's a sound idea? We could have an ant farm and a flea circus. Some insect species are so beautiful. The giant rhinoceros beetle, the harlequin bug. And all of them needn't be living. We could exhibit our scarab collection. And my rare mounted moths from South America. And, of course, our tsetse fly which isn't even . . . ALIVE!!" At that moment Ziller had entered her, one-twelfth of a fathom deep. The dike broke, drowning the Dutch boy. And countless wondrous insects of the world.

Amanda shook John Paul awake in the middle of the night. "No," he thought. "It couldn't be. The baby isn't expected for three more months."

His bride was propped on one elbow. He could tell she had just come out of trance: Her face was drawn, her eyes were as lifeless as blotters. A silver candle was burning in her sanctuary—behind the perfumed curtains. Damn. She'd been out of bed. "Civilization is dulling my senses," Ziller mused. "In the jungle nothing could have stirred within a fifty-yard radius without awakening me."

"John Paul," Amanda asked in a soft, tired voice, "are you aware of the animals that are going extinct?"

"Well, er, yes, I suppose I am."

"I don't mean the big beasts of Africa that you miss so much. I'm referring to wildlife right here in this country. Threatened with extinction are: the timber wolf, red wolf, Delmarva Peninsula fox squirrel, grizzly bear, San Joaquin kit fox, Florida panther, Caribbean monk seal, Guadalupe fur seal, key deer, Columbian white-tailed deer, Sonoran pronghorn, Indiana bat, black-footed ferret and Florida sea cow (manatee)."

John Paul jerked with guilt at the mention of "Indiana bat." He suddenly recalled that when Amanda awakened him he had been dreaming of his former wife. They were carrying her out of the Kansas City Opera House, in the middle of Act II of *Die Fledermaus*. Her bat cries were obscuring the mezzo-soprano, drool dripped from her gentle mouth like pearls from the anus of an angel. Ziller shuddered and drew the covers around his shoulders.

"And those are just the mammals," Amanda continued. "There are birds: Hawaiian goose (nene), Aleutian goose, Tule white-fronted goose, laysan duck, Hawaiian duck, Hawaiian dark-rumped petrel, California condor, Florida Everglade kite, Hawaiian hawk (ii), bald eagle, Attawater's greater prairie chicken, masked bobwhite, whooping crane, Yuma clapper rail, Eskimo curlew, Puerto Rican parrot, ivory-billed woodpecker, dusky seaside sparrow, crested honeycreeper (akohekohe), etc., etc.

"That's an irony that Plucky Purcell would adore," added Amanda, sounding a bit brighter. "American economic growth —the cutting of forests, industrial pollution of air and streams, the spread of suburbia—is driving the bald eagle into extinction. And the bald eagle is the very whole and exact traditional symbol of the American Republic. You'd think that a people as hung up on abstractions as ours are would be rather uneasy about the prospects of murdering off its own symbol."

If such conversation was an awkward intruder in the 3 A.M. of his consciousness, John Paul did not let on. Rather, he said, "I read in a natural history book once that eagles are cursed with chronic bad breath. Don't smile. It's a fact. One knows, if one reads magazine ads or watches television, how Americans feel about odors of the head and body. Could that explain their lack of concern over the eagle's demise?"

Life was draining back into Amanda's eyes, as if her pupils had, too, been threatened with extinction only to receive an evolutionary reprieve. "Imagine, a cleanliness-obsessed Puritan society selecting a national symbol with habitual halitosis. But, seriously, John Paul, listen to me. There are reptiles and amphibians going, also: the alligator, blunt-nose leopard lizard, San Francisco garter snake, Santa Cruz long-toed salamander, Texas blind salamander and the black toad."

"And fishes?"

Yes, magi. Fishes: shortnose sturgeon, longjaw cisco, green-back cutthroat trout, Montana West-slope cutthroat trout, Gila trout, Arizona (Apache) trout, desert dace, blue pike, humpback chub, Colorado River squawfish, Devil's Hole pupfish, Owens River pupfish, Gila top minnow, Maryland darter, Clear Creek gambusia . . . you don't want me to list them all?"

"That won't be necessary."

"Well, I thought I'd keep you informed."

"Thank you. You believe there is something to consider here? For our zoo, I mean."

"Possibly. We needn't try to save them all. Couldn't be done. We might concentrate on one species. Like the San Francisco garter snake. The pair we have now, I think they are more the Los Angeles garter snake. But Smokestack Lightning could get us a couple of the San Francisco variety. He's got connections in the snake world. Perhaps they'd mate."

John Paul reached for his bedside drum and made a matrix of sound roll from it with the edge of his right hand and the palm of his left "Rhythm. Creation, evolution, extinction." He hit the drum again. "Rhythm. Birth, growth, death. Rhythm. Creation, evolution, extinction. Extinction is part of the natural rhythm of the universe. Why screw around with God's rhythm section?"

"We already have. The creatures that have gone extinct in the past were gradual victims of natural processes, such as changes in climatology, to which they failed to adapt. But man has *interfered* in the organic, if haphazard, order of things. Through his own greed and indifference—I sound like Plucky again—he is driving dozens of species out of business at a rapid rate."

"Everything happens faster these days. Sometime I will explain to you why that is. In the meantime, how do we know that man's actions, and their seemingly dire results, aren't rhythmic; aren't just another ordained manifestation of the universal ebb and flow?"

"We know because my finer instincts tell me they are not."

"You, yourself, determined that the life-span of an individual butterfly is precisely the right length. By extension, wouldn't that determinant also apply to the life-span of a species?"

Amanda flushed, but not much.

"My magician, if you hope to embarrass me by calling attention to my contradictions, forget it. I was unenlightened enough at one time to believe in the finality of death. I'm not naive enough now to believe in the finality of extinction. Except on a purely formal level. You've been close enough to the source to have learned that beings never really go extinct. Their forms may become obsolete but their essential energies are eternal. The only thing that ever disappears is the *shape* of energy. Long after the visible, recognizable garter snake has vanished, its energy will hang on. [Note: Marx Marvelous, who was later to argue mightily with many of the Zillers' mystic pronouncements, would have to concur with Amanda's foregoing statement for it has scientific basis. As the German biologist Ernst Haeckel established, no particle of living energy is ever extinguished, no particle is ever created anew.] Dinosaurs are still with us in the form of energy. There may be some dinosaur energy in *you*. There is plenty of saber-toothed tiger energy around. And trilobite energy. I ran into some woolly mammoth energy just the other day. So, my sun, what we would be preserving would be merely shapes; containers, as it were, although the containers themselves are composed of energy, are intrinsic and substantial and interwoven communications of energy and do not merely hold it as a jug holds milk. Moreover, the physical appearance of these containers is beautiful; the design, the color, the functions of sensation and movement, the sense action and discernible psychic life. In a way, our zoo of endangered species would be like a museum, but a museum of *full* containers rather than of empty ones as is usually the case. A museum of living shapes that perhaps have outlived their function; therefore a museum outside of time, above time, above death; therefore a poetics."

Ziller put his drum back upon its stand. "Well," he said eventually, "your proposal is certainly a reasonable alternative. Let's sleep on it, as they say." He snuggled down in the covers as Amanda pattered into her sanctuary to blow out the candle. He smiled his wily Bushman smile. "It might be nice being the Nearly Extinct San Francisco Garter Snake Capital of the World," he said.

The postcard was there waiting, marking time, when the Zillers got back from the mountains. With things shaping up at the cafe—Mom's Little Dixie had been transformed inside and out—they were free to invest a cloudy morning in the pursuit of edible and/or visually pleasing fungi. So, they had driven up the river road, singing ancient prehistoric songs of their own invention in order to attract the mushrooms, and on the lower slopes of Mt. Baker, still singing, filled two knapsacks with chanterelles. Driving home, they were tired and let the river do the singing.

The moment they returned, Amanda hurried into the kitchen and poured the mushrooms into the sink: it would take a while to scrub off the dirt and fir needles, and the whole family was awash with hunger. John Paul tarried behind to look in the mailbox.

The postcard was waiting, marking time. It was an old postcard, luridly colored, depicting—in a clumsy, inexact, "touched-up" photographic rendering—a sawmill of certain regional fame. Blurry little workmen in bib overalls had dropped their axes and were lined up on a prize log beside the steaming donkey. They were combed and smiling (we assume) for an insistent cameraman who would reproduce them no larger than gnats. It was a scruffy dog-piss postcard off the postcard rack of broken dreams. The postmark, which could have been Throbbing Wallet, Idaho, or Nouveau Rat's Breath, Minn., was, in fact, Aberdeen, Wash.; the card was addressed to John Paul Ziller:

Dear Ziller,

Guess I missed the circus but I've had a show of my own. Oh boy. What has happened to me the past couple of weeks is so weird even a far-out cat like you wouldn't believe it. So guess I won't bother to go into detail. Pray for me. Love to yr. old lady.

Scoobie doo,
P.P.

The chanterelle mushroom is a ruffled yellow trumpet. Raw, it smells like apricots. Fried in batter, it smells like breaded kidney but tastes like eggs poached in wood-smoke and wine and has the consistency of fowl. Mon Cul preferred them raw. Baby Thor wouldn't eat them at all. Amanda and John Paul, whose ecstatic appetites underscored their animal unanimity with the ways of the world, ate them fried in batter and ate them well.

"Oh my," said John Paul, rubbing his belly.

"Oh my *my*," said Amanda, rubbing hers.

They stretched out on some cushions and had a pipe of hash. For the first time in that pregnancy, Amanda felt motion in her womb. It wasn't the centrally located, coherent movement that a small animal would make were it to turn in its burrow, but a many-places-at-once stirring such as a flight of swallows would make in torpid air.

"What are you smiling at?" asked John Paul.

"The mushrooms have startled the swallows," she said.

Then, after a languid interlude during which Thor and Mon Cul fell asleep, Amanda asked, "What do you make of Plucky's postcard?"

"It will have to do."

"Well, at least he's alive."

"We can assume that."

"And he isn't locked up."

"Presumably, although there's little in his message to warrant such a presumption."

"When do you suppose we'll hear more from him?" Amanda was sliding into a dream as lurid as the tones of Purcell's card.

"I haven't a notion. It could be quite a long time." It wasn't. A letter arrived the following day.

The magician was at work on his magical things. Sprawled upon a pallet of skins, he attended to his maps, charting a course with feathers and inks and wooden calipers. Unlike poor Rand McNally, Ziller was not obliged to limit his cartograms to representations of the earth's familiar surface; no, his maps could and did indulge in languorous luxuriation, in psycho-cosmic ornament that may or may not be helpful to motorists seeking the most convenient route from there to here. If, with appropriate geographical symbols, they indicated the presence of mountain ranges, forests and bodies of water, they seemed also to indicate psychological nuances, regional flavors, genito-urinary reactions and extrasensory phenomena—those "other dimensions" of voyage so well known to the aware traveler. His charts had the look of embellished musical compositions. Perhaps they were. (The London Philharmonic Orchestra will now perform *Map of the Lower Congo* by John Paul Ziller; scale, three-quarters of an inch to the mile.)

Amanda knocked four times before getting his attention. He received her at his sanctuary door. "A letter," she announced, holding it aloft. "A pudgy one. It's postmarked Humptulips, Washington. They've got to be kidding. Do you think it could be from Purcell?"

"What other penman among our acquaintances offends the eye with such nasty scrawls?" asked Ziller, checking the cacography that rampaged across the envelope. They took the missive into the living room and slit it open with an ivory blade:

Dear Ziller (and yummy bride),

Hello. I decided to give you the details after all. I've got to tell somebody and there's no cat I trust more than you (blush). Trust not only to keep my secret but to take it in stride. Dig this:

I am now a monk! That is, I am living in a monastery where the inmates believe me to be one of their own order. Don't laugh, you bastard. This is serious.

This is no ordinary bunch of monks. Oh no. Far from it. They are "Christian," all right, Roman Catholics. But—dig this—they are spies! And killers! Am I getting through to you? Look. I have unwittingly infiltrated a secret order of militant Catholic monks that serves the Vatican as a combination CIA and Green Beret unit.

No, I haven't freaked out. I'm not high on anything. I'm laying it on you straight, baby; the truth if ever I told it, and may Tijuana donkeys eat the man who says that Purcell lies. My desk at the moment is a stump in the woods (which is why my handwriting is more grotesque than usual), and if they should catch me corresponding with you it would be murder in the most awful literal sense of that word.

Guess I'd better start from the beginning, pardon my originality, and tell you how this all came about. It happened so unexpectedly that I've hardly been able to assimilate it myself. The last weekend in September it was, just about a month ago. The circus was performing in Seattle that weekend (I read about the hassle with the city council and the cops, by the way; what an up-tight town that Seattle must be) and I was planning to scoot up to see you guys. The bus developed a bad cough on Friday morning, however, and I admitted it to the VW clinic in Aberdeen; I suspect you are right, Ziller, about the sausage being the ultimate triumph of Germanic technology—God knows I've never had the problems with a weenie that I've had with that bus.

Anyway, I was in a mood to rationalize. "It's just as well," I said to myself. "I'll wait and catch the show in Bellingham at the final performance. Probably be a better party." But there I was, stuck at the bunkhouse some ten miles northwest of town, nothing to read but some old Zane Grey paperbacks and not so much as a faint sniff of snatch (pardon me, Amanda, if you are looking on) in the air. So, on Saturday morning I decide to take a sort of busman's holiday. As if I don't spend enough time in the woods, I decide to hike up a ways into the Olympics, camp overnight, look at the moon, spot some bear or elk, maybe find a bee tree and steal some honey. It's different being alone in the woods, no power saw giving the sky a toothache, no dumb-assed loggers constantly telling me how many miles their Mustangs get to the gallon of gas.

I hitched a ride to Humptulips—there's really such a place! Ziller, what quaint names you Washingtonians bestow upon your villages. Humptulips reminded me that I've always been crazy to do a Dutch girl. You know: wellscrubbed, blonde bangs, china blue eyes, apple cheeks, little cunt that smells like a gouda cheese. She'd have nothing on but wooden shoes and a crushed tulip behind her ear. No kidding. I get an erection every time I pass a gouda cheese in the supermarket. But I digress, and believe me, there's precious little time for digression.

From Humptulips I follow a silver-green finger of valley, hiking eastward toward the Wynoochee River. Eventually the valley peters out and I'm on a deep-rutted logging road, the terrain getting a bit steep and the timber tall and thick and murmuring to me in six dialects of Gothic. It's midafternoon and I haven't gone too far, maybe nine or ten miles from good old Humptuplips, when I spot some mushrooms in the woods to my left. Now I have nibbled the sacred mushroom of Mexico (*that* was a snack I'll be a long time forgetting) and I've sucked up my share of buttons with steak, but I am no mycophile and I wouldn't know an *Agaricus* from an asparagus. But these toadstools fascinate me nonetheless; they look like the kind that little men with green hats sit around on—so, brimming with botanical curiosity, I drop down on my knees for a closer look. Well, have you ever seen a mushroom with five fingers? O, nature is rich and there are strange flora and fauna a-riding on this spaceship of ours. But one of those fingers has a gold ring on it, and even Mother Nature doesn't pull stunts like that.

If you guessed that I had found a human hand you win a Girl Scout cookie. If you guessed that that hand was connected to an arm which in turn was attached to a body, you win a Girl Scout (with a merit badge for dialectics). And if you guessed that that body was dead, congratulations, you win all the Girl Scouts west of the Mississippi. Old Plucky's luck: out for a weekend of contemplation in the deep woods and he finds a corpse in a mushroom patch.

It was a fresh corpse, too. Still warm. There were no signs of violence on it or about it, so I wasn't particularly scared. The cadaver was male, dressed in a wool plaid shirt and khaki hunter's trousers, boots, pair of powerful binoculars hanging about the neck. First thing I do is check for identification. He's not carrying a wallet—has he been robbed, I wonder, and experience a little ding of fear for if he has the culprit could not be far away. But no, he has a wad of bread in his pants pocket, about $300. I'm breathing easier. Then I see a bulge under his shirt and investigating I find some official-looking papers, folded and sealed. Typed on the outside of the packet is the name 'Brother Dallas, F.S.' and that's all, no address. I don't break the seal.

About that time I notice a satchel, a brown leather valise, lying in the moss about four feet from the body. It's locked, but Dead Man has the key in his pocket and in a wink I've got it open. The contents don't exactly set my thyroid to pumping. Men's toilet articles, underwear, dark socks, pair of nondescript black shoes that could have shod any small-time insurance salesman in America. There is a road map of Washington-Oregon and a Catholic prayer book. Aside from that, just one more item: a long, heavy, silken robe as black as blood.

Still no identification. What to do? He is a big cat and I am not about to lug him back to Humptulips. Best thing, I decide, is to skip on back alone and notify the town marshal or the state patrol, although the idea of getting involved with the pigs doesn't have me tittering with delight. I reshoulder my pack and am in the process of splitting when what to my wondering eyes doth appear but a path. It's about thirty feet from me, leading off from the logging road into the woods, and it not only is a well-worn path, it is lined with stones. It has an air of permanence and use, and on a hunch supported by my reluctance to hike to Humptulips for a chat with the heat, I take it. Now, I'm only a short way up that trail when it occurs to me that I am carrying Dead Man's satchel, but, what the hell, I can see no harm in it and that path is luring me on like it's a siren song and I'm the seven seas' horniest sailor.

In a flash—and baby, it *was* a flash—I'm into a huge clearing, and squatting in the center of said clearing, just as cool and calm as Cleopatra on the royal pot, is a fort! Well, anyway it looks like a fort. It's made of logs, with a ten-foot-tall fence of sharpened poles surrounding it, and if the gates had suddenly flung open and John Wayne had led the 9th Regimental U.S. Cavalry out in a thundering charge, I scarcely would have blinked. But Col. John is in Beverly Hills voting the Conservative ticket and the gates are formidably shut and by this time I see a sign that reads "Wildcat Creek Monastery, Catholic Society of the Felicitator, Sorry No Visitors."

Let me set it straight for you. This monastery-fort is

no more than a couple football fields from the logging road, and less than two and a half football fields from where Dead Man is lying, all tuckered out. My steel-trap mind is snapping on connections. Brother Dallas. Black robe. Monastery. Dead Man is affiliated with the monastery. Eureka! I don't have to walk to Humptulips. Here's the logical place to report the cadaver. I'm wondering if they have a lost-and-found department. Anybody here misplace a slightly used monk?

For about five minutes I've been standing at the edge of the clearing, staring at that monastery which is silent except for some low, steady rumbling inside, like that monastery is the world's biggest all-log rustic refrigerator. When suddenly—yipes!—there's a hand on my shoulder, a very much alive hand, a hard hand, and I find myself in between two enormous gentlemen who are standing very close to me but withholding any outward signs of affection: that handhold is no caress. I react instinctively (for experience has taught me 'tis best) and backswing my left arm fast in an arc, a lovely Yokohama chop that knocks the seeds out of the recipient's Adam's apple. As he bends in gurgling pain, I follow through with a rabbit chop to the back of the neck and—thud!—he topples. I whirl to the man on my right, only I don't swing at him because he's holding a cocked .38 Special and it's pointing impolitely at my navel.

For the first time, I notice that the men—the one on the ground and the one putting my vital organs in jeopardy—are attired in blood-black robes. Robes? I glance at my feet for in my impetuous act of self-defense I had hurled Dead Man's satchel to the ground and his robe has spilled out and is curled there in the ferns like the small intestine of a dragon. The gunman stares at the robe, also, and he looks at his buddy whom karate has cut down in his prime, and he says to me in a low chilly voice like he was that log refrigerator talking, "I suppose you are Brother Dallas? Why in Mary's name didn't you identify yourself?"

And yours truly, either because I am a genius of the magnitude of John Paul Ziller, or because hereditary brain syphilis (a common malady among Southern aristocrats) has left me an imbecile of indescribable deficiency, I don't tell the man, "Your Brother Dallas is a bit indisposed and could use any old last rites you happen to have handy." I don't say that; I say, instead, "You startled me. How do you expect a man to identify himself when you creep up on him like that?"

And the gunman says, "I guess you're right, but you aroused suspicion. Why didn't you go directly to the gate and ring the bell as you were instructed? Better let me see your papers."

Do I panic? Yes, I nearly shit little green apples. The good monk isn't pointing the .38 at me any longer but he hasn't put it away, either. My cool doesn't blow, however. I start fumbling around in my pockets, scratching myself wildly like Mon Cul, and I blurt out to him, "Oh my God, they must have fallen out of my shirt back there when I bent over to look at some mushrooms. It's just a little ways down the path. I had 'em just a second ago." I take off my pack and set it down (to help mitigate suspicion) and start back down the trail. "I'll run get them. Won't take a minute."

He's looking at me like I'm Fool of the Year, and he keeps repeating incredulously, "Mushrooms? *Mushrooms?*" He makes a move to accompany me but I say, "You'd better attend to the brother there. He may be seriously hurt." And indeed the poor dude is writhing and moaning in a semiconscious state. So, the big-gun brother he kneels to examine his pal, and old Plucky he zips back down the path; man, his boots were made for walking. Humptulips, I hear you calling. Humptulips never sounded better. Humptulips sounds like it is Papeete, Tahiti, or the French Riviera. O Humptulips, Shimmering Pearl of the Mediterranean! I love thee, Humptulips, even though there is not one Dutch girl in thy whole domain.

Yes, my first impulse is to run for it, and as you know, I am a dedicated follower of impulse. By the time I reach the logging road, however, newer and stronger impulses have eclipsed the initial ones. These secondary impulses do not advise retreat. Quite the contrary. They say "advance." And after a moment's reflection, I realize that I am going to return to that strange silent monastery with its armed monks, that I am going to return there and . . . hold it! Just heard something! Excuse me . . .

Now. I'm back. It was deer. Two doe and a buck. Beautiful things. Wow. Spooked me. In fact, I'm too spooked to continue this narrative. My thought train has been derailed. I've been gone more than an hour so I'd best get back to the monastery. At the first opportunity, I'll write again and extend my tale. Please pardon the raw prose style of this epistle, but there was just no time for literary embellishment. Here's to your health and happiness, chum. Play for peace. And do not try to contact me!!!

> Plucky P.
> The Only White Man the Natives
> Trust.

The afternoon sky looked like a brain. Moist. Gray. Convoluted. A mad-scientist breeze probed at the brain, causing it to bob and quiver as if·it were immersed in a tank of strange liquids. The Skagit Valley was the residue at the bottom of the tank. Toward dusk, the wind flagged, the big brain stiffened (mad doctor's experiment a failure), and ragged ribbons of Chinese mist unfurled in the valley. The blaring cries of ducks and geese and the popping of hunters' guns echoed over the sloughs. During the waning Sung dynasty moments of the day, Ziller cooked up his first batch of sausages. A trial run at the Capt. Kendrick Memorial Hot Dog Wildlife Preserve.

Earlier that day, soon after the arrival of Plucky Purcell's letter, the new steam cabinet had been delivered by the Acme Restaurant Supply Co. of Seattle, and now Ziller was taking it on a shakedown cruise, putting it through its paces, his eyes narrowed in ritualistic test pilot concentration. Like the wife of any good movie test pilot, Amanda ˙waited on the ground, pride in her eyes but worry bending her mouth, and one ear cocked for disaster. (Picture Amanda and Deborah Paget in the kitchen of one or the other's modest little bungalow, drinking cup after cup of coffee and chit-chatting about everything under the sun except the one thing that's really on their minds: their men out there on the frontiers of weenie space. And then the phone rings and they tense up like clothespins, only it's a wrong number and Deborah bursts into tears and pounds her little fists on the formica tabletop, sobbing, "I just can't take it any more, the waiting and the fear. I married Jim because I love him, he's all I have in the world; but he has something else. He's married to the U. S. Air Force and to that gosh almighty hot dog steam cabinet, boo hoo hoo.") But the movie had a happy ending and although Amanda refused to taste a sausage she did eat part of a bun and found it yielding and velvety. John Paul ate two dogs "with everything," as they say, and was pleased.

After the test, they lingered in the downstairs kitchen. Amanda was jiggling Baby Thor on her knee and John Paul was attaching an electrical amplification device to one of his crude clay flutes. The kinetic energy of their thought systems was somewhere else, however: 150 miles south near the hamlet of Humptulips, where it crackled and spit and coursed through one circuit after another in pursuit of the exact position of Plucky Purcell. Amanda's curiosity was almost tangible, a great glowing radio of pique that broadcast from the cavity where the fetus ought to be. One thing was certain, however, they could not intrude. Not only had they been explicitly warned away by Plucky himself, but they were unable to conceive of any immediate circumstances under which their appearance at that forest monastery would have positive results.

"It appears that Purcell has got himself into a ticklish situation," said Ziller, "but it is equally apparent that he must work it out for himself. Actually, we know very little about the true character of his predicament. His aborted letter rather leaves us hanging."

"I hope he *can* work it out," said Amanda, jiggling the child. "For all of his two-fisted heroics and naughty background, there's a kind of, well, *innocence* about him." Jiggle. Jiggle. "At any rate, what are we to make of his story about militant monks who spy and kill? Considering the nature of organized religion in general and considering the history of the Roman Catholic Church in particular, I suppose it should not be surprising. Still, in this day and age it isn't easy to believe such a thing." Jiggle. Jiggle. Jiggle.

"I could not say that it shocks me," said Ziller. "Civilized man's cruelties seldom do. I know very little about the Catholic Church, actually. In Africa I did encounter quite a few Catholic missionaries. They were brave and dedicated humans who worked diligently to alleviate physical suffering among the indigenes. On the other hand, they unwittingly precipitated an awful amount of psychic damage through the superimposition of their dogma upon ancient tribal beliefs. And they seemed abysmally ignorant of the primitive ethos, how rich, how squirmingly musically rich is the savage mind and how deep." Here, Amanda thought John Paul about to reveal something personal concerning his African quest, but instead of continuing his comments he plugged in his flute and blew into it. Whereas it used to go *twoooo twoooo tweeee* rather softly and hollowly, it now went *shatweeeeeee-tweet taa-wow* with shrill blue vibrating edges on it. Could that be considered an improvement? John Paul did not say. He made an adjustment on his amplifier and asked, "You must have had a Catholic education, what were your impressions?"

Ziller knew nothing of Amanda's religious background, but as she was half Irish and half Puerto Rican it was only logical to assume that she had had some intercourse with Roman institutions. "I abandoned formal education in the eighth grade," confessed Amanda. "I must tell you about that sometime. But, yes, I did attend parochial school from the second grade through the fifth. And, of course, I watched many of my little friends 'grow up' (to use a term I detest) under ecclesicastical conditions. My impressions were this:

"There is an insect called the hunting wasp. The female hunts for spiders and other insects and preys on them in an unusual way. She stings them in the large nerve ganglion on the underside of the thorax so that they are not killed but only paralyzed. She then lays an egg on the paralyzed victim (or within its body) and seals the prey up in a nest. When the egg hatches, the wasp larva commences to eat the prey, slowly, gradually, in a highly systemized way. The nonvital tissues and organs are eaten first, so that the paralyzed creature remains alive for a good many days. Eventually, of course, its guest eats away so much of it that it dies. During the whole long process of consumption, the prey cannot move, cry out or resist in any way.

"Now, suppose we view the Church as the hunting wasp, its stinger being represented by the nuns and priests who teach in its schools. And let us view the pupils as the paralyzed prey. The egg that is injected into them is the dogma, which in time must hatch into a larva—personal philosophy or religious attitude. This larva, as that of the wasp, eats away from within, slowly and in a specialized manner, until the victim is destroyed. That is my impression of parochial education."

In a typical Amandan spasm of fair play, she called to John Paul as she went upstairs to bathe the baby, "Public secular education is only a little less thorough in its methods and only a little less deadly in its results."

She continued up the stairs, but Ziller stopped her. "Amanda," he said, "when I was in Ceylon I climbed Adam's Peak, a mountain that is sacred to four world faiths. At the summit there is a five-foot depression in the rock. Buddhists believe it to be the footprint of Buddha; Hindus claim it for their god Shiva; Moslems, for Adam; and local Catholics, for St. Thomas. Geologists at the university in Colombo say it is the result of ancient volcanic action. Who do you suppose is right?"

"All five, of course," said Amanda and she carried the squeaking baby on up the steps.

Ziller smiled. Ziller's smiles are noted for their emery and *misterioso* and this one was no exception. Nevertheless, it was a smile that seemed to say, "I have married well."

Happily for Amanda, whose curiosity was a radio left on all night at full volume and the neighbors complain and the cops come, happily for her only four days passed between the arrival of Purcell's first letter and his second. As did the first, the second epistle arrived with no ceremony. A minor government employee simply slipped it into the Ziller mailbox with a soft dry sound, a scarcely audible rustle of the tail of bureaucracy. John Paul fetched it inside and summoned Amanda. When she had joined him in the parlor, he disemboweled the envelope with a flick of an ivory blade. This is what they read:

Dear z and a (the end and the beginning, eh, folks?),

Hi there. The cat who invented karate was some dude. He did two thousand push-ups a day, pounded tree trunks until his hands were bloody and meditated while sitting under an ice-cold mountain waterfall. Those are the sort of pastimes in which your old pal Plucky is supposed to be engaged—out in the woods alone manifesting the rigors of the karate mystique. Of course, it's all a ruse on my part to enable me to get away from my new companions (I ain't about to punch no tree in the chops), but I am karate-master-in-residence at the Wildcat Creek Monastery and what those mad monks don't know won't hurt them. Out here at my favorite stump, I have the time and privacy to continue my description of this freaky scene of which I am all too much a part, yes yes.

Well, as previously reported, old fast-talking Plucky manages to rap his way out of a potentially grim encounter with a pistol-packing padre and is in the process of setting a world's record for the Humptulips dash when considerations other than personal safety flag his flight. With your permission, I won't bother to articulate those considerations except to remark that they involved things like intrigue, religious fulfillment (ahem) and a simple desire to get my poor bored ass out of the logging business for a while and into some kind of caper.

At least one thing seems obvious, I am thinking: the late Brother Dallas is a newcomer to the Wildcat Creek Monastery—he is expected but not known. He is carrying a map of the area, which indicates he has not been here before, and the two monks of my immediate acquaintance do not know him by sight. He died on his way to the monastery, a mere two hundred yards from it, and the brothers are as yet unaware of his demise. The monk with the gun at least halfway believes that *I* am Brother Dallas, and there is a chance that if he will believe it others inside the monastery will, also. Of course, there is a possibility that someone inside does know B.D. personally, but I'll gamble against that. There are surface implications of something sinister afoot hereabouts and I could be sticking my already rope-burned neck into a noose. But just as likely these implications are the result of coincidences, misinterpretations and general paranoia and probably there is nothing going on behind those unfriendly gates except the usual Catholic hanky-panky and churchly mumbo-jumbo. After all, it is not astonishing that men, even monks, who reside in an isolated semi-wilderness inhabited by cougars, bears, and stray drunk Indians would maintain firearms, although it is a trifle un-usual that a monk who armed himself against the beasts of the hills would choose a .38 Special instead of a more conventional weapon like a shotgun. But that, too, might be explained simply. What my caper will probably amount to is this: I'll sneak backstage at the holy show, experience a weekend of the kind of fun the Great Imposter must have had all of his life, and split the scene in time for work on Monday morning. On the other hand, there is a dead man involved, however innocently, in this business and even if he died of natural causes I have some moral obligation to report his passing—he might have a worried and loving family somewhere. More and worse: suppose I pretend to be Brother Dallas for the weekend, whereupon I confess my true identity and disclose that the real B.D. is dead in the woods—wouldn't I be one hell of a prime suspect in B.D.'s death? Even if I did not reveal B.D.'s rather permanent predicament, which would be damnably unethical, still his body might one day be found. It might be found right in the middle of my masquerade. And then wouldn't Plucky's fat be in the fire? I should nip this irresponsible escapade in the bud and save myself and perhaps a whole lot of honor-able people unnecessary trouble and confusion. But no, by God, there is something screwy going on in that John Wayne monastery; there is, as my old Dixie daddy used to put it, a nigger in the woodpile; something's akimbo if not down-right evil. I can feel it.

All these thoughts are popping like corn in my brainpan, popping very rapidly, it takes only a second or two, while I'm running in place, my knees pumping but my feet ex-periencing no forward acceleration, on that rutty old logging road. Just a few seconds of decisions and indecisions, checks and counterchecks. And then, wham! bam! I flood into action.

First, I run to the dead man and relieve him of his packet of papers, the sealed documents mentioned in my previous letter. Then, I drag the body across the road and down a steep embankment on the opposite side. Just as Richard Brautigan finds a trout stream at the foot of every chapter of his memoirs, I find a trout stream at the foot of the embankment. Oh, I knew it was there. Earlier, as I hiked up the road, my ears had registered the kind of music that usually results when the earth is running about in a fluid condition. Hoping to keep the telltale crows away, I dump the body in the creek in a hole about four feet deep that I luckily (pluckily) find a few yards downstream. I weigh it down with stones. Oooops! Goddam it. I forgot about the three hundred bills. I have to fish that heavy cadaver out of the creek and remove the money from his pocket. Now I know what you are thinking, a pox be on you, you are thinking that Purcell claims to stand in opposition to the whole monetary system, yet he goes to quite a parcel of trouble to latch himself onto three hundred tax-free dollars. But, babies, you know that it is a federal offense to mutilate U.S. currency. And leaving a bankroll to decompose in a trout stream is tantamount to mutilation. Anyway, after the resinking of the U.S.S. Brother Dallas, I dry my hands on my jeans, puff up the hill again, find the path and follow it into the woods at a trot. Less than halfway to the monastery I meet the two monks, one of whom is rubbing his neck, looking kind of dazed, and the other—well, he's glowering and passing a .38 Special from hand to hand. That latter cat worries me. Why can't he, when he gets upset, just run a few laps around the beads like any good priest is supposed to do? I mean, Pat O'Brien used to get red in the face and ball up his fists but this friar fingering his firearms is a bit too much.

"Hello," I say cheerfully. "I found them. That was really careless of me. Ah, but even the saints were not immune to error." I smile beatifically.

The armed monk snatches the papers from me, subjects them to a ridiculously long scrutiny considering that there are only two lines of type on the exterior and that he doesn't break the seal. "Carelessness is a weakness that isn't tolerated in this order," he says in a voice that the average housewife would have to take out of the freezer at two in the afternoon if she wanted it thawed in time for supper. "Ah ha," thinks I, "the Pistol Padre isn't very high in the Wildcat Creek hierarchy; he isn't even authorized to open my papers."

On the way up the path to the monastery, I apologize profusely to the other monk for having laid him low. The blessed wine of Christian forgiveness isn't exactly oozing from the pits of his flesh but he does admit that under similar circumstances he probably would have reacted unpleasantly himself. "Only I'm not as good a chopper as you," he says with begrudged admiration, still massaging his neckbone.

We pick up the satchel, stuff the robe back in it, proceed to the gate and ring the bell. It has a nice tone, properly religious. We are admitted. The gate locks behind us. It does not have a nice tone. It locks with a gray prison clink—*Clink!*—turning an echo and ghastly against the white noise of my central nervous system. That clink tumbles into echoes, first inside of my head and then—tumbling beyond the bitter reaches of consciousness. Jesus, I don't mean to get poetic about it. That's what I get, Ziller, fraternizing with cats like you. I heard this intellectual theatrical dude rapping at a loft party one night in New York and he said that when Nora slammed the door to walk out on her old man in the last scene of *A Doll's House*, that slam reverberated throughout the whole spectrum of Western drama and that it caused taboos to fall in the theater—and in male-female relations—just as a slammed door might cause a picture to fall from a wall; only it was a permanent alteration. Well, when that monastery gate clinks behind me, I feel that it had permanently altered the theater of Plucky Purcell, that my own little short-run drama, my stiff-kneed dance of life, has been transformed. There is a cold lick of finality about it. The monastery gate, rather than a jail door slamming to shut me in, is a landing-craft ramp lowering to let me out, and I have no choice now but to wade ashore on an alien beach where sooner or later I must confront an inhospitable populace. Fear is moist and sticky in my throat, like berries in a plastic sack; but it is a fear more surreal than real, there is even an element of gaiety in it: my brother told me some of the Marines were whistling show tunes when they hit the beaches at Inchon. And why not? The principal difference between an adventurer and a suicide is that the adventurer leaves himself a margin of escape (the narrower the margin the greater the adventure), a margin whose width and length may be determined by unknown factors but whose successful navigation is determined by the measure of the adventurer's nerve and wits. It is always exhilarating to live by one's nerves or toward the summit of one's wits. Such stuff I shamelessly confess to you.

But what, really, is there to fear? Inside the compound the scene is not especially strange. Mainly, there are sterile passage ways off which lead heavy doors, all closed. It is like any monastery I've ever seen in the movies except that instead of adobe or stone it is constructed of wood. As we walk the passageways we pass eight or ten monks and if they don't look like Bing Crosby or Pat O'Brien neither do they look like the Hunchback of Notre Dame. There is less milk and more iron in their eyes than in most priests I've observed; less gravy in their jowls and less booze in their noses. Aside from that, I detect nothing extraordinary about them except their walk. No humble shuffle, no pious servile plod, no prissy strut. They walk with the easy aggressive grace of trained athletes. Among them in the narrow passageways I feel as if I'm back in the stadium tunnel at Duke and I'm nearly expecting one of them to slap me on the ass the way athletic teammates are always slapping each other on the ass (a gesture almost touching in the innocence of its eroticism) and yell, "Let's go get them bastids, Plucky. Come on, man."

Toward the center of the compound, we stop before a door and old Thirty-Eight Special he bams on it. The man who receives us is Father Gutstadt, a monk about fifty years old with the build and physiognomy of a Chicago butcher—and obviously the top cat hereabouts. Father Gutstadt's face is a balloon full of blood, a smooth red bladder with giblets for eyes and for a nose a round, veiny, sugar-cured lump that could have been pruned from the entrails of a bull. The good father is a steaming blood pudding of a man, but crafty; oh, if there is a Hamburg slaughterhouse sprawled over his exterior there is a University of Heidelberg huddled inside.

He does not slobber on his cigar or flick it about, but holds it for long periods a few inches from his mouth while its ash extends to perilous magnitudes. He sips his brandy as if engaged in demanding but pleasurable intellectual exercise. His simplest pronouncements are like excerpts from a lecture on advanced physics. It is not the content of his speech that is so authoritative and confounding but rather the *weight* of it. His words are heavy. His language is dense. While some men's spoken sentences seem constructed of cardboard and canvas, Father Gutstadt's are of brick and steel. When told of my meeting with the two monks, he erupts into jolly Santa Claus ho-hos that roll about the room like boulders. It tickles the hell out of that red old fart that I whopped Brother Boston two hard ones. I guess if I had broken that monk's neck the father would have busted his belly with mirth. He is not so amused, however, at the disclosure of my having temporarily "lost" my papers in the forest. He gives me a discourse on carelessness. It is a short discourse but it weighs about four tons.

With a magnifying glass he checks the seal on my papers. Satisfied, he breaks it and begins to read. Whatever he is reading—man, I wish I knew!—takes a very long time. He pauses every now and then to sip brandy or to puff cigar. Eventually, he separates the papers, placing the majority of them in a drawer of his desk and returning to me what proves to be a passport. "There is every indication that your assignment in Memphis was a complete success," Father Gutstadt says. "Brother Baton Rouge comments at some length on your efficiency. You've distinguished yourself in the eyes of Mary, God and the Church. Good job. Good job." He stands up behind his desk and extends his leg-of-lamb hand. "Welcome to Wildcat Creek Monastery, Brother Dallas. You're now a full-fledged member of the Society of the Felicitator and eventually we shall have some fitting ceremony. In the meanwhile, Brother Boston and Brother Newark will show you to your quarters. Be careful not to startle Brother Dallas, Brother Boston. Ho ho ho." It isn't a laugh, it's a rockslide.

Well, babies, that's the way it happened. In a matter of moments, I'm sitting on my cot in a little cell with a dresser and desk and wash-table, and tatami mats on the wooden floor, and wondering if that shrewd old butcher is playing games with me, if his gizzard eyes saw through my pretensions; but, of course, I know by now that he did not. I have put them on! Yes, yes indeed. I'm in residence at a monastery where through the damnedest maddest insanest most kooky quirk of bat-blind events I am believed to be Brother Dallas the Texas Chopper, recent initiate in the Society of the Felicitator—the blackest band of friars to kill for Christ since the Holy Office of the Middle Ages. On my passport it reveals that Brother D. is thirty-one. Actually, I've just turned thirty. Close enough. The card says B.D. is six foot three and weighs 200 pounds (or about as much as a good belch by Father Gutstadt). I'm six one and weigh 189. But I was standing tall that day and I'm (ahem) no scrawny chicken so the fact that the dimensions are slightly askew hasn't occurred to my new pals. Brother D. is from the South and I have a Southern accent—an authentic one, thank the gods; I'm sure the Father would have spotted a phony drawl. That helped. But the clincher, I imagine, was that B.D. was a karate expert, and right off the bat I had the opportunity to effectively demonstrate my own facility in that honored Oriental art. Then, too, I happened to arrive on the very day that the real Brother Dallas was due, and with proper papers. Imagine! Obviously, destiny is moving me—Purcell, fate's plucky pawn.

To top it off, I get assigned, as part of my chores, to the supply detail. Meaning that once or twice a week a cat named Brother Omaha and I drove the holy jeep into Humptulips and purchase supplies at the general store. (One day not long after I arrived, I got to drive down to Aberdeen to pick up a part for the short-wave transmitter. That was the day I found in my post office box your letter telling of weenies and roadside attractions, and the day I mailed to you a postcard.) We monks are taken at face value in Humptulips, treated with casual unctuosity by that portion of the citizenry that is neither Indian nor drunk and with utter indifference by that larger portion that is decidedly both. The very first grocery run I'm on I sneak an epistle off to the Bavarian Motor Co., in Aberdeen and tell them to place my bus in storage. Another note to the mill tells them I've sailed to a sunny Mediterranean isle to live in a gypsy cave with an expatriate Vassar girl and would they please donate my back pay to the Salvation Army.

Thus, here I am. In tight at the militant monastery. And you are probably saying in unison, "So what, you dumb damn nut?" And maybe I can convince you I'm not a jackass and maybe I cannot, but at the moment it's getting dark out here in the woods and every time a twig snaps, my hair climbs a tree. So the other goodies I have to share with you will have to wait until a later edition.

Meantime, take care, my little friends. Onward the zoo and up the sausage! Brother Dallas bestows bountiful blessings upon you, but please don't write him no grateful regards because if his brothers ever catch him passing notes they'll dig a hole in his head and bury his boots in it.

Love and Kisses,
Plucky P.

"Well," said Amanda, "what do you think?"

"What *is* there to think?" asked Ziller.

"Oh, I don't know. You could think that Plucky Purcell has treated us to an elaborate performance of personal fantasy. Except you know that he's telling the truth. So, you could think that Purcell is on a binge of self-destruction and has deliberately stuck his head into the jaws of the Church, knowing as he must that those jaws do not have rubber teeth. Or, you could think that Purcell had lucked—or plucked—upon a secret so hot it could shake the foundations of Christianity from Humptulips to Rome, and that he's on top of it and he knows he is and that he isn't climbing down until he's ridden it to wherever it's going. Or, you could think that it is an unusual and interesting situation which might eventually prove to have some bearing on our own spheres of activity. You could think that it's our duty to go down to that place and rescue the Mad Pluck before something real bad can occur. You could think that what will happen will happen, according to its divine plan and that we have no right to interfere, but must sit back in our privileged seats and watch it through. Or, you may think, as others have thought before you, that I am a young woman of great curiosity."

Amanda smiled demurely and stooped to pick up a toy that Baby Thor had abandoned on the Persian carpet. As she stooped, she felt the swallows circling inside the dome of her womb.

Ziller said nothing but went to his drums and began to tease them into sound. He beat them and banged them and rattled them and caressed them and evoked from them a substance of duration. He looped a garland of high bright rat-a-tat around the collar of a primitive thud that seemed to thud in chain reaction all the way back to the belly of the beast whose membrane it was that gave life to the empty circle of drum.

"The whole universe is a complex of rhythms," mused Amanda. "We each of us feel a need to identify our bodily rhythms with those of the cosmos. The sea is the grand agency of rhythm. The grain-tops in the wind, the atoms in orbit are rhythmic. The uterus, which is a strong muscular organ, contracts with the birth of the baby—the rhythmic contractions, in fact, are the important motivations for the baby to emerge into the world. Rhythm is how it all begins."

If John Paul's drumming cast no particular luminosity on the question of Plucky and the monks, it did at least give Amanda some insight into the musicality of human behavior. To wit: actions, like sounds, divide the flow of time into beats. The majority of our actions occur regularly, lack dynamism and are unaccentuated. But occasional actions, such as Plucky Purcell's venture into the Wildcat Creek Monastery, are accentuated due to their intensified stress. When an accentuated beat is struck in relation to one or more unaccentuated beats, there arises a rhythmic unit. Rhythm is everything pertaining to the duration of energy. The quality of a man's life depends upon the rhythmic structure he is able to impose upon the input and output of energy. Energy equals mass times the speed of light squared. Einstein understood what Thoreau meant when he spoke of men hearing "different drummers." Thoreau did not say saxophonists or harpsichordists or kazoo players, mind you, but *drummers*. The drummer deals almost exclusively with rhythm, therefore he is an architect of energy. Art is not eternal. Only energy is eternal. The drum is to infinity what the butterfly is to zero.

Amanda was tempted to relate to Ziller her new comprehension of his drumming, but she did not. Instead, she packed some mushroom cookies in an old Kotex box and the family went down to the flats and flew their kites. Once, however, as she dashed through the slough grass, the wind whipping her yellow dress, she yelled to Ziller, "The kite is the simplest geodetic structure just as the drum is the simplest . . . ," and she ran on by and her words were lost in the wind.

The total electrical output of the human body is about one two-thousandth of a volt.

That isn't quite enough juice to light up Broadway, now is it, folks?

Hell, it isn't enough to fry a frankfurter.

No wonder God never bills us for electricity. He wouldn't collect enough to pay for the postage.

Happiness gathered at the roadside zoo. Finishing touches were being applied. Still no animals there, of course. Except for two garter snakes and a tsetse fly so dead it lay encoffined in artificial amber, unable even to decompose. As for the rest of the Capt. Kendrick Memorial Hot Dog Wildlife Preserve, it progressed. Each day another touch or two was added. Applying these touches required usually no more than a twelfth of the day's duration. The remainder of the time could be allotted to redecorating of a more personal

nature. Although both Amanda and John Paul now retreated
for several hours daily to their sanctuaries, the family knot
shrank tighter. Mon Cul had been ill at ease with the
first Mrs. Ziller and she with him ("Darling, I don't want to
sound stuffy or Kansas City bourgeois—after all, it's the
unique difference of your personality that I adore—but taking a baboon along on a wedding trip is somehow, oh I
don't know, John Paul, it just gives me the creeps"), but
with Amanda the learned ape was relaxed to the point
where he scratched her pelt with the solicitude he ordinarily
reserved for his own. Baby Thor took to wearing loincloths
in proud imitation of his new papa. The four of them
played games indoors and out; picked mushrooms and berries,
dug roots and clams, made music, performed their chores,
coaxed the old cafe into further states of wonder and shared
(perhaps) the gleanings of individual investigations into . . .
whatever.

Occasional visitors, mostly strangers, called. Attracted by
the vibrations or alerted by word of mouth. Young men
and women in transit. Moving from California to Canada.
Or vice versa. They smiled a great deal, some carrying
their belongings in tattered guitar cases, some carrying their
heads in bandages. Getting rough out there for the young
and free. They were given a good meal and happy words
for the road.

Adding seasoning to life at the zoo were Purcell's letters,
telling of the wiles of right-wing monks under orders from
the conservative nucleus of the Vatican to protect the Church
against Protestants, tax-minded governments and liberalizing
tendencies. Telling of assassination devices and crafty plots
and narrow escapes. Telling of his monkish longing for pussy.
Letters somewhat unusual in the nature of their information,
letters in a masculine register, letters to be read more than
once. Read with ceremony. Incense and drums. Thus the
days marched across November serenely, almost ecstatically.
And then the rains came.

And then the rains came.

They came down from the hills and up from the Sound.

And it rained a sickness. And it rained a fear. And it rained an odor. And it rained a murder. And it rained dangers and pale eggs of the beast. /

Rain fell on the towns and the fields. It fell on the tractor sheds and the labyrinth of sloughs. Rain fell on toadstools and ferns and bridges. It fell on the head of John Paul Ziller.

Rain poured for days, unceasing. Flooding occurred. The wells filled with reptiles. The basements filled with fossils. Mossy-haired lunatics roamed the dripping peninsulas. Moisture gleamed on the beak of the Raven. Ancient shamans, rained from their homes in dead tree trunks, clacked their clamshell teeth in the drowned doorways of forests. Rain hissed on the Freeway. It hissed at the prows of fishing boats. It ate the old warpaths, spilled the huckleberries, ran in the ditches. Soaking. Spreading. Penetrating.

And it rained an omen. And it rained a poison. And it rained a pigment. And it rained a seizure.

Rain fell on the Chinese islands. It fell on the skull where the crickets live. It fell on the frogs and snails in the gutters. It fell on the giant improbable pacifying vulnerable sausage. It fell against the windows of the hospital where Amanda had been carried, the blood on her legs diluted with rain water.

The rain had nearly obscured her little yelps of pain as she lay in the brush near the mouse burrows. Rain had fallen on the fetus. Prematurely expelled. In the muddy field-grass. Rain had spattered Amanda's unconscious eyes, as it now spattered the windows of the hospital where for eleven days she lay, some days close to dying.

The hospital corridor glistened with quiet. At the reception desk, the nurse—amicable of countenance if bony of physique—looked up from the *Reader's Digest* in which she had been enjoying an article entitled "What Makes a

Good President" by the late Dwight David Eisenhower.
Visiting hours would not begin for another forty minutes,
so the nurse was not expecting a caller. Especially, she was
not expecting a caller such as this one. My God. Most
irregular. A tall, vinegar-colored man with a ball of tumble-
weed for hair; wearing a raincape of python skin, beneath
which was only a . . . *loincloth.*

"Must be some kind of kooky joke," the nurse thought.
"Whatuz he want? How'm I gonna cope with him? How
unlike General Eisenhower he is. Make a piss-poor President?" Her thinking was a trifle shredded.

The man turned out to be polite. Had no thought to
rape and pillage. He was here to see his wife; oh, yeah,
the poor little girl who had the miscarriage. He was aware
that visiting hours had not begun but he had only a moment
to stay as he had left his young son in the care of a
babo—a friend. All the doctors were out to dinner, so the
nurse excused herself and disappeared with practiced indifferent efficiency down one of the white-tiled corridors.
In a few minutes she returned and announced, "Mrs. Ziller
is sleeping. She's very weak. Still on the critical list. I think
it would be better, Mr. Ziller, if you came back tomorrow."
("And for God's sake wear some clothes.") This last statement was made under her bony breath.

"May I please just look in on her?" His voice was tired
but so very cultured and strong. "I'd like to leave these."
He held out a bouquet of fly amanita (*Amanita muscaria*)—
big, robust mushrooms with white warts distributed about
their scarlet caps.

The nurse gulped. "They are poison, aren't they?"

"No. No, they have . . . er . . . abnormal . . . effects
on the nervous system, the brain, but there is no death in
them. Anyway they're for looking, not for munching." He
smiled. "She'll like them very much."

The nurse tried not to fluster. "Well, okay," she said. "Just
leave 'em in that pot you brought them in. But I'll have
to ask the doctor about 'em when he gets back." She led
Ziller through the clean glare and medicinal smell and white-
ness to Amanda's room. "We mustunt disturb 'er," said the
nurse. She cracked the door.

Ziller tiptoed into the gloom. He scooped Amanda's face
up in his vision, weeding out the paleness, the thinness, the

plastic vines running out of her veins and nose, the arms
that lay askew like broken wings. He was afraid to burden
her with a kiss. The magic words he had to say for her he
barely whispered. He left the bowl of blazing mushrooms on
the table at her bedside. And with it, a *haiku* written
on rice paper, stained by the rain:

> *They've built their nests*
> *in the chimneys of my heart:*
> *those swallows that you lost.*

Plucky Purcell says that sooner or later everything boils
down to a matter of a buck. Perhaps Purcell overstates the
case, but few are the lives untouched by considerations of
economics. A financial crisis arose for the Zillers, for example, as a result of Amanda's hospitalization.

In truth, Ziller had brought a tidy little nest egg to the
roadside zoo. He and Amanda had hardly been extravagant-
ly compensated in their employ to Nearly Normal's traveling
Tibetan show (although John Paul was paid union scale),
nor had Ziller grown rich from the sale of his sculptures
(although he had sold a few to collectors of considerable
means). However, his associations with the Hoodoo Meat
Bucket had been quite profitable. Despite the fact that the
band's record album was merchandised under the counter—
no reputable distributor would touch it—and was blacklisted
by broadcasting stations from coast to coast, it become nevertheless a cult totem, an "underground classic," so to speak,
and sold upwards of fifty thousand copies. With monetary
success came an inevitable token of establishment acceptance
—and numerous opportunities for compromise. There had
been an impromptu meeting at the Annex Bar down on
Avenue B. The four musician-heroes quaffing beer and eating
the free peanuts. (In leaner days, Ziller and Mon Cul had
subsisted on Annex peanuts. Protein is where you find it.)

"Look, Ziller," whined Ricki-Tick, the lead guitarist,
"there's two major record companies wants to sign us.

Heavy bread. We don't have to sell out, man. Just tone down the sex trip. Tone down the voodoo trip, the anarchy trip, the trephination trip. Muff the perversities. That's all, man. *Life* magazine wants to do a spread on us."

And Ziller had skewered his fellows with his fierce pyramid eyes and had displayed his smile as if it were a dagger on a pillow. "You gentlemen do what you wish. The pleasures of exile are imperfect, at best. At worst, they rot the liver. Napoleon's hide turned yellow as a buttercup. I leave on the Midnight Special for the town of my birth." And with one last handful of free peanuts, he went away to Africa. But as 90 per cent of the songs in the Meat Bucket repertoire were Ziller compositions, he received a handsome settlement prior to departure.

Travel had been costly. The conversion of Mom's Little Dixie Bar-B-Cue into the Capt. Kendrick Memorial Hot Dog Wildlife Preserve had not been inexpensive. The motorcycle had been traded in on a used but late model Jeep station wagon and quite a few dollars had had to be added to close the deal. Then came Amanda's accident. The sum of the medical bills was staggering. It was Black Friday beneath the colossal weenie.

Now, Amanda's father was probably the most well-to-do overweight Irish immigrant orchid baron in America. As Amanda was his only child, and as he had no wife, alas, he was in an excellent position to alleviate the newlyweds' economic woes. While Papa was not overjoyed with his little one's choice of mate, he gladly would have sent bank notes galloping to her bedside. They would amble up, hats in hand, shaking rain from their green mustaches, and say, in husky voices not the least bit tremulous from the long ride, "Howdy, mam. The bank note brigade. Hallowed protectors of the American way. May we be of service to ye?" Moreover, the Zillers could have touched Nearly Normal for a loan. But if neither of them desired to become dependent upon a relative, the thought of sinking in debt to a friend was even more depressing.

So, Ziller, to whom the telephone was a well-oiled instrument of torture, placed a call to New York City. Heard his hesitant words go limping across the continental span. Heard the twinkle-toe lisp of his dealer come rushing back, oblivious to the hostile stares of cowboys and farmhands as it swished across Iowa and Montana. He endured the pronouncing of his plight into the cold black mouthpiece, endured the lollipop vowels that bunny-hopped into his ear. Endured them. And on the day that Amanda was released by the Mount Vernon clinic, coming home to floral arrangements of cattail and salmon berry branch, to oyster casserole and baby kisses and baboon antics and a favorite tune on the flute, she was told of new wealth in the Ziller domain. She learned that the Non-Vibrating Astrological Dodo Dome Spectacular, formerly on loan to the Whitney Museum, had been sold to an Amsterdam couple for a figure approaching twenty-five thousand dollars. Cheap at the price. The dealer had ladled off a third of those dollars, as dealers do, but a bank draft for the remainder was in the mail.

"There will be a minimum of tourists on this road until spring," John Paul told his bride. "A minimum of connoisseurs searching for old-fashioned red-hots beneath these sour skies and in these hammering rains. We have funds now. Enough. No hassle. The opening of our enterprise can be delayed. We are here in the Northwest Corner; you brightening it, me poking in it—and vice versa, although I have fewer inclinations to brighten than you to poke. The Northwest, albeit on a fairly superficial level, is one of my sources. You spoke of curiosity about the science of origins, or as I would prefer to call it, the science of godward solutions. Well, aside from my personal tinctures—which would only fog the essences in your crucible—there still seem to me to be qualities in this region worthy of our investigation. Mushrooms, for example, and what is left of the aboriginal culture. Perhaps there is even something to be learned from the rains. Therefore, I suggest that we postpone our grand opening until April first. In the ensuing four months let us become intimate with the spaces and speeds and loops and patterns of the Northwest biosphere of which we have voluntarily become a functioning part. That way we may better serve it as it serves us, just as the Wheel People of Anugi serve the circumferences which in turn supply their sacred rotations." He paused. "We shan't neglect our usual interests and private projects, of course."

"Right up my alley," said Amanda quickly. "Pass the oysters. What's the latest word from Plucky Purcell? I love you, John Paul. Have you noticed that the tops of the fly amanita are colored the same brilliant red as Mon Cul's great butt?" Her health was returning in gulps.

The magician's underwear was found early yesterday. Or late the day before. The authorities weren't specific. They assured us, however, that the magician himself would be apprehended within forty-eight hours. What then?

This morning, the agents seemed increasingly sullen. We overheard them discussing the future of the snakes. One of them, we think he was FBI, said, "Let's turn them loose in the woods." But the others, the CIA boys, said, "Mash 'em!" They are planning to kill the snakes. What are their plans for us?

The author realizes that time may be running out. Due to the morbid uncertainty of the situation, it is probably incumbent upon him to spur his Remington into the heart of the matter, to deploy to the front all salient and essential facts under his command. Get the nitty-gritty down on paper while there's still opportunity. And that he shall do, forthwith. If he has been indulgent up to now, if he has subjected you to an excess of background, if he has dallied in the scenery when he should have been upstage center disclaiming, forgive him or chastise him as you will. Just remember that while you may have a stake in this matter—and all of you do—the writer has what seems to him (from his proximity to events) to be a bigger stake. And he has never claimed to be unselfish or heroic.

It must be obvious to you that the author was not a witness to the episodes which he has so far described. They transpired in those elysian days before Marx Marvelous turned up to manage the zoo, before the Corpse appeared and really knocked things on their ears. Therefore, it is important to the author, for personal reasons, to establish in his own mind the prevailing moods, if not the exact sequence of events—that brought Amanda, John Paul and Plucky together in such portentous circumstances. To this end, he had made use of letters, journals and considerable oral accounts.

Amanda insists, although she's not read a sentence of it, that the author is compiling a history. The author knows what she means, of course, but he is not certain he wants that responsibility. Actually, however, there is no cause to recoil from the "historian" tag. Hardly a pure science, history is closer to animal husbandry that it is to mathematics in that it involves selective breeding. The principal difference between the husbandryman and the historian is that the former breeds sheep or cows or such and the latter breeds (assumed) facts. The husbandryman uses his skills to enrich the future, the historian uses his to enrich the past. Both are usually up to their ankles in bullshit.

History is a discipline of aggregate bias. A history may emphasize social events, or cultural or political or economic or scientific or military or agricultural or artistic or philosophical. It may, if it possesses the luxury of voluminousness or the arrogance of superficiality, attempt to place nearly equal emphasis upon each of these aspects, but there is no proof that a general, inclusive history is any more meaningful than a specialized one. If there is anything that the writer has learned from Amanda (and he must confess having learned a measure), it is that the fullness of existence embodies an overwhelmingly intricate balance of defined, ill-defined, undefined, moving, stopping, dancing, falling, singing, coughing, growing, dying, timeless and time-bound molecules—and the spaces in between. So complex is this structure, and so foolishly simple, the historian's tools will not fit it: they either break off and go dumb in the scholar's hands or else pierce right through the material leaving embarrassing rents difficult to mend. Rule One in the manual of cosmic mechanics: a linear wrench will not turn a spiral bolt. Drawing courage from that rule, the author can boast that his approach to history is no worse than any other and probably better than some. And so what?

"And so what?" the writer types, tapping the Remington softly so as not to disturb Amanda. It is sunset now and she has retired to her sanctuary. Dusk and dawn, evidently, are the most advantageous times for trances. Evidently. The poor girl has been in and out of trance a dozen times during the past two days. Her eyes are as flat and lifeless as linoleum cutouts, the skin sags from beneath them like fresh dough dripping from a baker's spoon. And still she's beautiful. She was just in the living room, here, where the author is typing; wearing only blue lace panties and a sheer cotton blouse of the peasant or gypsy variety; not dressed that way in order to arouse the author—as has sometimes been the case—but due to carelessness: her thoughts are elsewhere. All that she has learned in twelve enervating sessions she learned this morning at sunrise when the "voices" informed her that she would soon be receiving a letter. Big deal. Great voices, huh? They did not even say from whom. It could be a letter from Al's Butterfly Shop in Suez soliciting a contribution to *Al's Journal of Lepidoptera,* a monthly magazine. It could be a letter from her Uncle Mick in Pasadena.

Despite her exhaustion, despite her concern over Ziller, over Plucky, over Mon Cul and over, of course, the Corpse—(O Corpse! What terrible schisms will be thy latest legacy?)—Amanda offered to prepare supper for your correspondent before undertaking her twilight trance. (She had just fed Baby Thor his wheat custard and left him to play himself to sleep in his crib.) The author declined. "No," he said, "you mustn't bother. I'll fix myself some hot dogs after a while. What with the zoo closed down the hot dogs are going to spoil anyway. Better to eat them up."

Amanda smiled. "Going to eat sausages, are you?"

"Yes. Might as well. What fitter meal for a condemned man than Ziller's little mythic cylinders of peace?"

"Bon appétit! I've got to go now."

"Will I see you later tonight?"

"If I learn anything in trance I'll report. If not, you'll see me about two o'clock in the morning. I'll come to your room."

What was that? Could it be what the author was thinking? Hoping? Wishing? O thank the gods. Let him sacrifice twelve white doves to Venus. His skin flushed and his hot brain swarmed with delicious fantasies. He suffered such a forceful and abrupt erection that it almost tipped his typewriter off the table.

"Look, now, you don't have to help if you don't want to," said Amanda. "It really isn't fair to expect you to. But I'm going to sneak downstairs late tonight or, rather, early tomorrow morning. And I'm going to free the snakes."

"Well," sighed your correspondent, the conqueror blood draining ignominiously from his penis, "I suppose I might as well risk my life for a bunch of garter snakes as anything else. Soldiers die every day in the service of reptiles. But aren't you forgetting something? What about the flea circus? Aren't you going to liberate the fleas?"

"You're being sarcastic, but the fleas have been provided for. They'll embark from here in a carefully prepared air-mail envelope addressed to a friend who'll see them to safety. As a reward for their faithful service and many exciting performances, they'll be allowed to retire to the back of a pink poodle in Palm Springs."

Amanda kissed the writer lightly on his lips and went off to endure another searching trance. As the writer set about to cook his hot dogs, he found himself thinking again about history. He had agreed to participate in a predawn raid to liberate a pen full of condemned garter snakes. How would a serious historian approach an episode like that? Later tomorrow, he may well help rush an envelope full of trained fleas into political asylum. Would Arnold Toynbee seize that action, would he wring consequence from it? Or would he brush it aside as a bothersome fly on the carcass of greater events?

Look! If Ziller and Purcell are caught, chances are that the Corpse will be found with them. And if the Corpse is identified, as surely it must be, and if that identity is made public (How could such a secret be kept?), then most of the world is in for one hell of a jolt. Perhaps society will roll with the punch or perhaps it will sink to its knees. As you read these lines you may already know how the news was received. At any rate, the wordmen, the explainers, will have to deal with the occurrence. First, the journalists will report it. Then, barring unforeseen reaction, the pundits will analyze it. Eventually, the historians will have their turn; they will shape their various versions of the discovery of the Corpse, Purcell's abduction of it, the Great Dilemma it caused and the final flight with it to . . . wherever it might be out there in the broad American night. But will they, can they—the scholarly historians— reveal what really truly happened? No, the writer is now convinced that he alone can snatch that essence from its wild background and isolate it naked from commotion and myth. And the writer is willing to spill everything. If you dare to listen.

Part III

Part III

An unfamiliar cowboy knocked at the roadhouse one rainy evening in March. He knocked as if in a dream. He was an undistinguished unfamiliar cowboy except that he pulled behind him a chicken in a little blue wagon. The chicken was old and extraordinarily bowlegged.

"Howdy," said the unfamiliar cowboy. "Understand you're planning on opening a roadside zoo."

"I believe that is true," said Amanda.

"In that case," said the unfamiliar cowboy, "you might be interested in buying this here rooster. He's a famous rooster. His name's Big Paint and he was the lead cock in the great coast-to-coast chicken drive of 1969. Led fifty thousand head of hen from Ballard, Washington, to New Jersey. Took 'em four months but they arrived in time for the Miss America contest. Picture it, mam. Fifty thousand chickens a-clucking down the boardwalks of Atlantic City on their way to greet the new Miss America. It was a sight.

"There's some businessmen want Big Paint to lead another drive—from Council Bluffs, Iowa, to Portland, following the old Oregon Trail. But I thought I'd give you a chance at him first."

Amanda purchased the rooster. It was only fair. Some people don't care that chickens have tender feet.

Gonorrhea first came to the planet Earth through the atmosphere as a force of Lord Shiva the Destroyer (*ergo* Creator). It struck down a large populace in a few moments.

Its strength was so great that only those who could withstand severe remedies could be cured once the germ was indrawn by the lungs. (Note: the inbreath is willed, the outbreath is automatic.) In an olden age of evil and corruption, gonorrhea purified the Earth.

The second gonorrhea epidemic had its gradual beginnings in the mid-1960's. Its source is also believed to be divine. (Note: "The second breath of Brahma.") This second gonorrhea germ is considerably more refined than the first (and those weak offshoots of the first that have lingered as vulgar inflammations through the centuries). It is an evolutionary force affecting the reproductive organs of those beings openly susceptible to evolutionary change. Particularly, it has affected (Note: affection) the young—those brilliantly free children who have chosen not to regard love as a discriminatory accolade nor their bodies as exclusive property. If anywhere it has been more prevalent than among the love communities of the United States, it has been among the American soldiers and their native girl friends in Asiatic countries (Note: "trans-cultural pollination"—the fabled blending of East and West).

Public health officials and military doctors lead the war against gonorrhea. They are being thrashed. All "cures" are temporary. Hardly do the medics discover an effective remedy than the germ learns to resist it. Consequently, the germ grows more and more powerful, and the temporary cures more difficult to develop.

Gonorrhea is altering certain physiochemical mechanisms of a significant portion of younger Earthlings. It is helping to prepare man for his next step up the evolutionary ladder. (Note: the Jehovah's Witnesses also believe gonorrhea to be of divine origin. They, however, take a negative view. They claim that the Christian God bestowed the germ upon mankind as punishment for adultery and fornication, noting that the disease is never contracted by husbands and wives who copulate only with each other.)

The preceding theory of gonorrhea is the work of Duke Elohim Jophaniel Forsteton, professor of magic at the University of the Changes and the Echoes in Timbuktu. It was recently sent to John Paul Ziller, who became one of Professor Forsteton's favorite students when he enrolled at the Timbuktu institution after his initial disappointment with the art schools of Paris. Incidentally, it was while studying in Timbuktu that Ziller first met Mon Cul, a mere infant at the time. The baby baboon was then living with its mother, who served as a handmaiden for an Afro-European noble-woman of rare beauty—but that's another story.

Maybe it doesn't prove anything but the cockroach has been around a good deal longer than gonorrhea. In fact, the cockroach has been on Earth at least 250 million years. It is the most primitive of winged insects and its fossils (found in the rocks of the Upper Carboniferous) are the earliest known. No other creature has lived on this Earth as long as the roach.

That's rather an impressive record for the repulsive little geek. Despite his filthy habits, one must give him his due. Come out from under the drainboard, Mr. Roach. We wish to salute you. Award you a gold pocket watch for your perseverance.

But the cockroach has no thoughts of retirement. Oh, no. Not only has he been on Earth far longer than has man, he may well be here long after we are gone. The common urban roach is a crack-dweller; requiring no light, little food or water and able to synthesize vitamin C, he nests in tiny fissures deep within brick and stone. Consquently, he has excellent protection against radiation. Scientists venture that in the event of an all-out nuclear war, the cockroach might be the only species to survive.

Certainly we are not about to rid ourselves of cockroaches by any means *short* of nuclear bombs. These insects share with gonorrhea an amazing resilience. They rapidly develop immunities to each insecticide invented for their extermination. In roach-plagued cities such as New York, every six months brings another sure-fire roach killer to the market. True enough, the new formula knocks them dead for a while. Then they build up immunity to it and pretty soon all it does is make them high. *Zit zit:* you spray with your $1.98 aerosol can of instant roach death and in a second the dirty little devils are cavorting like a bunch of the boys at a musicians' union picnic. The gas no longer kills them. They seem to like it.

The preceding information about cockroaches was offered by Marx Marvelous in order to show Amanda that she wasn't the only person around Skagit County to know a thing or two about bugs. More to the point, it was offered also as a contrast to Ziller's relation of Professor Forsteton's gonorrhea theory, an account which Marx Marvelous found soaked with superstition and romance.

They were glaring at each other like a couple of feisty sailors, John Paul and Marx Marvelous, when Amanda, her interest quickened by both contributions, added a hypothesis of her own.

"Suppose," said she, "that there is an all-out nuclear war. And suppose that the cockroach, that tough little fellow with the frantic antennae, is the sole survivor among living things. The cockroach would rule the Earth. He would survive because he was fittest, and with that justification he would be master of the world. Quite so. But germs and viruses—many varieties of them, perhaps—also would endure the holocaust. Right, Marx? Right. And if some germs survived, surely gonorrhea would be among them for it is so resilient. Right, John Paul? Right. Now suppose the surviving cockroach, lord of the planet, caught gonorrhea. Could he withstand it? Would gonorrhea fail with this insect where it has triumphed with man? Who would conquer whom? Or would it simply be a case of the immovable object meeting the irresistible force? They might lock in an eternal stalemate, unable to budge one another throughout the whole of time. Years after man, over some childish politico-economic misunderstanding, has obliterated himself and turned the green Earth into a cinder ball, then the *real* battle will begin. Gonorrhea and the cockroach fighting it out for ultimate domination of the universe. Now there's your Armageddon."

One moment, please. The author wishes very quickly to relate something of an immediate nature.

Less than half an hour ago, he and Amanda were summoned down to the dining room by three agents. "What if they overheard our plans to absolve the snakes?" worried the author, who, exhausted from the day's typing, had been preparing for bed. Amanda's thoughts were not apparent. She had recently emerged from trance and her eyes bore a green-apple glaze. One of the agents thought she was on narcotics and threatened to go up and search her room. His companions talked him out of it. They had more important things on their minds.

We were shown a fuzzy wire photo of a VW microbus which the agents claimed had been abandoned in an orange grove west of Orlando, Florida. The bus contained no registration papers, they said, and the license plates had been removed. We were asked if the vehicle belonged to anyone we knew.

"Oh, my, I can't tell the difference between one car and another," Amanda said cheerfully. "Chevrolets, Volkswagens, Lingams—they all look the same to me."

The agents groaned.

"I'm sorry but it doesn't ring any bells," apologized the author, thinking all the while that Ziller and Purcell must have gone by Aberdeen and gotten Plucky's VW out of storage. "Why did you think this bus would have any connection with us?"

"In the rear of the vehicle the government found excrement from a medium-sized primate, possibly a baboon," said one agent.

("Mon Cul, it would seem that a creature of your favored background could have controlled himself," the writer scolded silently.)

"Under the front seat the government found a sardine can wrapped in a page that had been ripped outta a notebook," said another.

"The writing on the page was done by the same hand that wrote the stuff we found in the suitcase near Miami," said Agent No. 3.

Agent No. 1 then solemnly read from a teletype tear sheet the following passage:

"We are in man-eating mirror country. The cannibals sleeping in the flowers are carried away by their dreams, or rather their dreams bring them from far away, just as the mirage brings the lapping waters to our feet, just as the leopard behind us can get our scent but cannot get at us. The blossoms pretend to shake their heads. They shower the natives with pollen. Right in the spot where they are restless. In the morning we will trade beads for our reflections."

"Hmmmm," mused your correspondent. "The style is quite like Joseph Conrad's. I don't recall which work of his it might be from, but then I've forgotten so much since I left the university. Have you ever read *Heart of Darkness?*"

"None of your goddamn business," said Agent No. 1.

"Who could have written anything like that?" wondered Amanda, her startling green eyes widening.

"Your frigging magician, that's who!" accused Agent No. 2.

"Get on up the stairs, you sassy-assed bitch," yelled Agent No. 3.

"You, too, punk," said Agent No. 1, attempting to poke the author in the testicles with the putting iron he always carried. His thrust was slightly off center. The author did not give him a chance to bogey.

"I hope you're aware of the penalties for withholding information from the U.S. government," growled Agent No. 2.

The lawmen gathered at the foot of the stairs so that they could look up Amanda's skirt as we ascended. Boys will be boys.

Amanda squeezed the writer's arm. "Just put it out of your mind," she whispered lovingly.

"I've got to put it out of my mind," he said. "I need a good night's rest so I can be halfway alert when I return to my report in the morning. I'm about to introduce my readers to a very special gentleman."

"Fine," smiled Amanda, "but don't forget our rendezvous at 2 A.M."

"No, I won't forget," promised the author, feeling (shamefully) every bit as lascivious as the federal authorities we had left snarling below us.

We parted without speaking of the Corpse or its attendants, who, no longer shielded by the steel and glass of the bus, no longer protected by the mobility of the bus, must be especially conspicuous and vulnerable wherever they huddle this night, strange quarter-dead, quarter-ape foursome beneath the aggressively public Florida moon.

It was a bird-chirpy morning in early May. Sunshine
elbowed through the stained-glass windows of the Capt.
Kendrick Memorial Hot Dog Wildlife Preserve. Sweet smells
rose stiffly from the fields outside and unfurled above the
cafe like banners. Random notes of cheerfulness sailed
through the air like paper airplanes. One landed in the
steam pot among a logjam of sausages. Ziller brushed it
aside and went on with his cooking. Another crashed into
Amanda's hair. She removed the wreckage tenderly and
deposited it inside her blouse between her sun-warmed tits.
She hummed as she swabbed the L-shaped counter. The
front door was ajar and she could see (across the Freeway)
rhinestones glittering on the rain-swollen wrists of the slough.
Indians of the Northwest used to sprinkle tiny flakes of
mica over their well-greased bodies so that they would
sparkle when they danced in the firelight. This May morning
was such a dance.

Gunnar Hansen, the neighborly pea farmer, came in out
of the dance for a cup of coffee. Sorry. He was served
strawberry-grapefruit juice. Last week it was apple-carrot.
He'll learn.

Farmer Hansen called Amanda over. She thought he was
going to complain about the lack of coffee. No, it wasn't
that. He had something to show her. "Er, I thought you
folks'd be interested in this in the paper. If you ain't already
seen it. I thought you'd find it interesting. Seeing that you
got a baboon, I mean."

He handed Amanda the morning edition of the Seattle
Post-Intelligencer and pointed out a short article on page 3.
The article was headlined in 36-point italic:

MAN TRIES TO STEAL
BABOON AT ZOO HERE

A well-dressed young man tried to remove a baboon
from its cage in Woodland Park Zoo late yesterday
afternoon.

The man used a glass cutter to slice through thick
plate glass on the animal's cage shortly after the zoo
closed for the day. He was attempting to coax the ba-

boon into a large cardboard box when he was spotted by zoo attendants. The attendants held the man until police arrived.

The man, about 25, gave no motive for his actions, but he stated that he wished the baboon no harm. The man, neatly groomed and dressed in a natty checkered suit, carried no identification. He told police that his name was Marx Marvelous, but he would not divulge an address or personal details.

Detective Sgt. Ralph Prosser asked Marx Marvelous if he was named for Karl Marx. Marvelous replied that he was named for Marx Brothers. He is being held in lieu of $1,000 bail.

Zoo officials said the 3-year-old baboon—the only such ape in the zoo's collection—is valued at about $300. They said the animal is ill-tempered and might have given Marvelous some nasty bites had he succeeded in getting it out of its cage.

Amanda zipped through the article once, then reread it more slowly. The second time, she giggled. "Oh yes, Mr. Hansen," she said. "That *is* interesting." She glanced through the kitchen doors at John Paul. "I'd like to show it to my husband, but he's pretty busy at the moment."

"Oh that's all right, Mrs. Ziller. Don't give it back. Keep the whole paper if you want it. I'm through with it. Nothing but bad news in it anyway. Even the Twins lost last night. Nineteen to nothing to Chicago in ten innings. Uff!"

"Thank you very much. We appreciate it." She extended a smile that almost thawed the tundra of the farmer's features. "Sorry about your team. I'll say a Cherokee stickball chant for them and maybe they'll win today."

"You do that, young lady," said Hansen, a bit bemused. He finished his juice and disappeared into the dance.

Not for several hours did Amanda find an opportunity to show the newspaper story to John Paul. The new spring sunshine, the bird chirps, the insect whirrs, the awakening organic gases that streamed from the fields seemed to have aroused in the populace an uncommon hunger for hot dogs. It was the cafe's busiest day since the first week it was open, when Skagit neighbors poured in out of blatant curiosity. It was past three o'clock when Ziller read the article, his fierce gaze nearly shaving the words off the page.

"He's being held in jail in lieu of bail, is he?"

"That is what the newspaper says, John Paul."

"Then I suppose we had best go down and get him out."

Amanda beamed. "I'm glad that's your response," she said.

They locked the roadhouse at five o'clock and set out in aid of the baboon-napper. There was some preliminary concern about what to do with Mon Cul. "What if this well-dressed man has some kind of psychotic fixation about baboons? Rather than just liking them as we do, that is. He may freak out when he sees Mon Cul. God knows what he might do. On the other hand, suppose the man in the natty checkered suit is merely one of a band of international baboon thieves currently operating in the area. If we leave Mon Cul at home he might be abducted before we return." Eventually, it was decided that leaving Mon Cul in his bed in John Paul's sanctuary was a minimal risk. Certainly less chance of hassle than taking him to Seattle. Even if Mr. Marvelous had no naughty fetish, should the Zillers jitterbug into the police station with a baboon on a leash they would no doubt, in the peculiar eyes of the law, be implicating themselves in Marvelous' crime. Good-bye, Mon Cul. Away they drove.

"I've been expecting you," said Marx Marvelous. "What took you so long?"

On the way to Seattle, it had clouded over and begun to rain. "Short spring," observed Ziller without malice. It was really pelting down by the time they reached the city. The Seattle Public Safety Building (jail being considered essential to public safety) sat in the rain without crack or fault. It was clean as a pyramid but lacked a pyramid's grace. Monolithic, without interval or tension, it was an unbroken mass of arrogance and power. Except for one embarrassing intrusion: fear. Each small human, uniformed or more sanely dressed, who entered its doors carried fear into the building as a fly carries disease into the soup.

This fear, plus bureaucratic expedience and general poor taste, had left the interior of the structure depressing indeed. In the elevator, Baby Thor had begun to cry. His sobs had been an indication of things to come. It had taken the Zillers several cruel hours to spring Marx Marvelous. Although he was charged merely with two misdemeanors—"destruction of municipal property" and "attempt to commit larceny"—the neatly groomed Mr. M. had not been considered a prime candidate for bond due to the fact that he possessed neither identification papers nor permanent address. The police desired that he remain their guest. Upon scrutiny of John Paul, the desk sergeant had failed to understand why he was not behind bars as well. Finally, however, with the help of an American Civil Liberties Union attorney and after the signing of numerous incomprehensible documents and after the posting of twice the normal percentage of bail, the sergeant had dispatched a flunky to the cells to procure the mysterious Marx Marvelous.

"I've been expecting you," said Marx Marvelous. "What took you so long?"

He was a pleasant-looking fellow. The newspaper had reported that he was about twenty-five, but the leisurely hours in jail obviously had rested him for he looked a few years younger than that. (Actually, as the Zillers were soon to learn, Marx Marvelous was thirty—about the same age as John Paul and Plucky Purcell.) The *P-I* reporter had been right about the man's grooming: neat. Equally correct concerning his olive-and-rust checkered suit: natty. He was not handsome in the traditional American sense. His face was too soft for that—soft, sensitive, moon-cheeked, shy-smiled, babyish. He was . . . well, let's use the word: cute. Women would probably find him attractive. Amanda did. But for all his apparent sensitivity, there was grit in him, too. His eyes were as full of mischief as Jack the Ripper. He could, it was plain to see, be as ornery as dried bird shit. He had sandy hair and was of medium height and build.

"You were *expecting* us?" asked Amanda. John Paul was giving the man a sample of Egyptian eye power.

"Of course," he spoke with something of a drawl. "You're Amanda, aren't you?" A little self-consciously, he kissed her hand. "That's Baby Thor strapped to your back there. And you are John Paul Ziller. Well, well. I saw an exhibition of your work once. Motorized ostrich eggs. Ummm. Yes. Most remarkable. I have often wondered if those eggs could really fly." He offered his hand. Ziller shook it warily.

"I don't get it. How do you know us? And how were you sure we'd come bail you out?" Amanda's native curiosity was popping its buttons.

"I wasn't sure you would, but I rather expected you to. That's why I'm in this lice bin." His gesture took in his immediate surroundings, and the desk sergeant glowered most dangerously "I went to a great deal of trouble to find you two. Or rather to have you find me."

"You mean," asked Amanda, "that this whole business, this baboon-stealing caper, was a plot to have us meet you?"

"You might say that."

She went giggly. "For God's sake, why?"

"Well, Nearly Normal Jimmy gave me a great deal of information about you, but he neglected to disclose precisely where I might find you. In fact, I don't believe he knew *precisely* where to find you, and he flew off to the Orient before I could ask him for approximate directions. Of course, I knew that you were within a sixty-mile radius of Seattle, but I couldn't, lacking funds and identification, hire a car and scour the countryside. I did inquire about you—to no avail—in the more likely looking taverns and coffeehouses. Either your acquaintances are protecting you well, or you have remained amazingly anonymous."

"We seldom come to the city. So, you're a friend of Nearly Normal's, are you? Wonderful. But why did you want to find us so badly? And who are you, really? What's Nearly Normal doing in the Orient?"

"Let's get out of this dungeon, may we? I'll answer those questions tomorrow at the job interview."

"What job interview?"

"I am applying for a job at your roadside zoo. The position of manager."

There was a funny weight-shifting silence.

"You do need a manager, do you not? Nearly Normal was certain you'd be in need of one by now."

Amanda and John Paul stared at one another. Only that morning they had been discussing the prospects of finding someone to run the roadhouse for them. The operation of the cafe and zoo, as simple as they had arranged it, was comsuming more time and energy than they had anticipated. And the summer tourist season had not really begun.

"We'll discuss everything at the interview. For the moment you must get me to a drugstore. Unless you have some Preparation H in your possession. Four days on a Greyhound bus and twenty-four hours on a cement jail floor have my anal tissues in full bloody blossom. What a plague! You women think you have it bad, having babies. Well, a woman can only give birth once every nine months, but a hemorrhoid sufferer goes through labor every time he goes to the crapper. Come on."

The hemorrhoid sufferer called Marx Marvelous kept a journal. It was nothing at all like the journal of John Paul Ziller. There was not an entry in it which read:

"When following the spoor of the Mirror Eaters it is wise not to tread on their droppings."

Nor was there an entry which read:

"On to the Equator! We can see it from here. It's beginning to sag. Poor foundation, probably. A challenge to future engineers. Tonight we will dine in the equatory, observing the mathematical swarmings of stars as we chew. We will wash out our socks among the swans of the equatory and hang them to dry upon the tusks of the equatory. And if the hand outstretched is the Wild Man's hand, we'll drop our bag of wishes in."

There were no entries such as those. Marx Marvelous was not a magician. He did not travel Africa or India. He had not met the Wild Man nor shared a vision of the Bearded Heart. Still, his journal is not without a smidgen of literary merit, if for no other reason than that it offers some insight into conditions at Skagit County's roadside attraction prior to the arrival of the Corpse. For the temperature and texture afforded by its projection of the period, let the author quote from it moderately as he discharges the next installment of his report.

When I arrived in Seattle, the sun was shining and the sky was blue. In its interior streets, away from its old busy waterfront, Seattle proved to be not unlike any other American city of comparable size. With one exception. Looming over the city, beyond its modern skyline, filling the whole southeastern sector of sky, was an enormously tall, enormously broad snow-frosted volcanic cone of mountain: Rainier. It was big and beautiful enough to be disorienting, to make one gasp, to lift one out of context, to stimulate swoops of fancy. I imagined Mt. Rainier to be an iceberg toward which the crowded city was sailing full speed ahead. At any moment there would be a heavens-splitting crunch. Seattle would go down like the Titanic. I could envision the mayor and his council huddled on the sinking roof of City Hall singing "Near My God to Thee."

The sky was still blue, the sun still beaming when they locked me up. But during my incarceration it had begun to rain. The legendary Seattle rain. It was a thin gray rain; hard and fast and cold. In it, we had to walk four blocks from the Public Safety Building to the Zillers' Jeep—we were at its mercy. As was my custom in such elements I hunkered against the rain, drew my head into my collar, turned my eyes to the street, tensed my footsteps and proceeded in misery. But my hosts, I soon noticed, reacted in quite another way. They strolled calmly and smoothly, their bodies perfectly relaxed. They did not hunch away from the rain but rather glided through it. They directed their faces to it and did not flinch as it drummed their cheeks. They almost reveled in it. Somehow, I found this significant. The Zillers accepted the rain. They were not at odds with it, they did not deny it or combat it; they accepted it and went with it in harmony and ease. I tried it myself. I relaxed my neck and shoulders and turned my gaze into the wet. I let it do to me what it would. Of course, it was not trying to do anything to me. What a silly notion. It was simply falling as rain should, and I a man,

*another phenomenon of nature, was sharing the space in
which it fell. It was much better regarding it that way. I
got no wetter than I would have otherwise, and if I
did not actually enjoy the wetting, at least I was free of
my tension. I could even smile. What I smiled at was
the realiazation that I had been in the Zillers' company less
than fifteen minutes and already their example had altered
my behavior. Surely, I was on the right track.*

It was another roadside attraction. How different from
the hundreds of attractions that line America's highways
(like toys on meandering asphalt shelves) one could not tell
from the preliminary advertising.

ROADSIDE ATTRACTION—2 MI.

*was all the first sign said. The second was slightly more
specific.*

SNAKES ALIVE!

See the Vanishing Reptiles

Serpents on the Brink of Extinction

FOOD   JUICE

1 MI.

*If the third billboard was more elaborate it was primarily
because it was dominated by a drawing of a grotesque
and ominous green-globe-eyed insect.*

KILLER OF MILLIONS!

See the Deadly Tsetse Fly

. FREE   Wildlife Preserve   FREE

Hot Dogs   Film

600 Yards

Although I was not astute enough to notice it at the time, each of the signs had been strategically placed so as not to interfere with an appreciation of the countryside (vegetable fields and waterways and a distant ring of wooded hills and dim purple mountaintops.) This was even true of the fourth sign, which was red and gold and approached the ornate.

FLEA CIRCUS

Live Performing Fleas

Fun for Young and Old

See the Chariot Race
in Miniature

See Ben Hur the Flea

Food & Fruit Juice—300 Yds.

The last sign was a summary of those which preceded it, with one rather esoteric addition.

NEARLY EXTINCT REPTILES!

AFRICA'S WINGED KILLER!

FLEA CIRCUS

The meaning of meaning

FREE   100 YARDS

To the connoisseur of Americana or to the fan of popular culture, perhaps there is a kind of poetry in those signs, typical as they are (except for one annoying allusion to "meaning") of the lurid enticements that beckon with bandaged thumbs all along the tourist trails of this continent. As for me, although I am an analytical man by both instinct and inclination, I find in such roadside ballyhoo precious little food for intellectual mastication. Yet there is a measure of substance in it, I suppose.

There was a time when Americans stayed put. For the majority of them, journeys were short and few. Consequently, their live entertainment came to them. The circus, the carnival, the dog-and-pony show, the wild West extravaganza, the freak show, the medicine wagon, the menagerie, brought to the towns and villages on their muddy itineraries glimpses of worlds which the sedentary folks had never visited; not just ethnic and geographical oddities but the worlds of romance and glamour and adventure and style. As we became urbanized and sophisticated and, above all, mobile—highly, highly mobile—the touring attractions naturally declined. That there is still potency in their imagery, fascination in their naive promise of magic, exotica and unknown quantities, is evident in the proliferation of roadside attractions. Today, the tawdry wonders do not come to us, we go to them.

Stop. Ahead. Five hundred yards. See. Camera bugs welcome. Fur Seal Caves. Rocks of Mystery. Frontier Village. Jungle Land. Reptile Farm (see them milk the diamondbacks). Indian Burial Mounds. Alligator Gardens. Swamp Creatures. Big Game Country. Little Africa. Bibletown. Old West Museum. Wild Animal Ranch (see rare white deer). The smell of gasoline and fatty hamburgers mingles with the shabby odors of half-starved mistreated animals. Milkshake blenders whine and jukeboxes jingle-jangle and toilets flush. Stop. The tourists stop, happy for an excuse to pull off the dangerous hot highways; a place for mommie and the kids to pee, a place to stretch the legs, reload the Kodak, mail postcards, buy cigarettes, drink a Coke, see. See. See something they've never seen before. Gila monster. King cobra. Billy the Kid's shootin' iron. Masturbating monkeys. Humpty Dumpty in papier mache. Or, in the case of the Capt. Kendrick Memorial Hot Dog Wildlife Preserve, a flea circus and the meaning of meaning.

It is a hot dog stand. In all honesty, that is what (and nearly all) it is. A glorified hot dog stand. But the key word here is "glorified." I must admit that for a lowly dispenser of frankfurters, it is an impressive establishment.

A giant hot dog is beached like a whale on the rooftop.

It is made of painted wood and is surrounded by an entourage of painted figures in a painted landscape; by comets and peaks. The big sausage is the first thing one sees. It is visible for a mile around.

The yellow facade of the building—the architecture is in frontier style, including a tall false front—is polka-dotted with flat, silver, metallic weenies that borrow light from the elegant neon sign above and bend it into prismatic ripples. Apart from the luminous optical activity of the weenies, which is enjoyable in itself, the manner in which they are distributed over the rectilinear storefront bespeaks a stringent aesthetic that is fascinating to contemplate. What was the weenie-layer's compositional focus? What theory did he adhere to in arranging his modular elements (for that is what the weenies are) so that they would produce the degree of compositional interplay that they do? They seem almost musical in their arrangement. A symphony of silver sausages.

The windows—in front they are at ground level—are of colored glass: strange florid pictographs in which sausages turn into serpents and serpents turn into Arabic alphabets. Or are they Sanskirt?

The building and its parking lot nestle in a crescent of trees. The trees are fir mostly, although I can detect at least one Sitka spruce, a majestic fellow perhaps two hundred feet tall, spreading its tiers of boughs with weary precision. Protuding—no: gesturing!—from the front corners of the building, and at various angles to them, are plexuses of wooden and steel beams. Perhaps the beams exist to block curious customers from the private spaces in the rear of the roadhouse. Perhaps they are primarily decorative append-ages. At any rate, these dense, dark, sheared or thronged traceries—horizontal totems, as it were—tug from both sides at the central facade, stretching it and extending it. If the edifice is radiant and joyful and contained in its weenie-spattered center, it is ragged and anxious and mysterious at its edges. Of the crisscrossed beams, some of the steel ones are embellished with slender serpentine scrolls of violet neon; some of the wooden ones terminate in carved figure-heads; owls, maidens, hippopotami.

Although it was still raining, and although I was anxious to get to a toilet where I could pump the cooling ointment into my rectum, I nevertheless stood for a while before this curiously glorified hot dog stand and made the observations that I have just recorded. The Zillers stood with me. Eventually, I said to John Paul, "Hmmmm," I said, "I thought you had given up sculpture."

He bared his sharpened teeth as if he were of a mind to bite me, and stalked inside.

I should like to record some initial impressions of the Zillers. Perhaps I shall limit the impressions to physical descriptions for it is too soon to note anything significantly deep concerning their characters. Only if I remain faithful to a reasonably scientific procedure of investigation can I hope to arrive at a lasting interpretation of reality. I keep reminding myself of that fact, but in the secret shadows of my heart I become increasingly unsure of my ability to apply scientific methods to this inquest. Certainly where Amanda is concerned, cold formality is out of the question. Moreover, if I am honest with myself, I might consider the possibility that the time has long since passed (if, indeed, it ever existed) when I was in possession of a genuinely rational disposition. However, I am not altogether sure that that is the case. I have had my moments. On the other hand, were I impeccably objective in my methods (assuming that my motives are above reproach), would I even be present at this ridiculous hot dog stand? And under these circumstances?

Obviously, I am raked by doubts. It is goddamned confusing. But I intend to persevere, so let me get on with it.

How would I describe the Zillers were I a journalist reporting for a popular periodical? How could I describe them to my parents, to my former colleagues at the institute? The adjective that comes most effortlessly to mind is . . . no, no, that isn't fair. Such terms are too strong for Amanda and too mild for John Paul. For that matter, most adjectives in my repertoire are too mild for John Paul. This cowboy-rococo hot dog stand, this work of art masquerading as a

*roadside zoo, is presided over by a man so exotic in dress
and demeanor that even if one were favorably disposed to
him one still could not help but regard him as a poseur, an
actor, a walking artifice. And at this early stage of the game
I cannot pretend to be favorably disposed. Oh, I don't dis-
like Ziller. Not yet. He holds a definite fascination for me.
Quite aside from his Tarzanesque trappings, his grass-hut
head of hair, his loincloth, his leathers and jewels, he conveys
an intensity of being that is impossible to ignore; it blasts
out of his disquietingly immobile eyes in licorice rays, and
no doubt would blast just as mightily were he attired in
banker's garb. He did not acquire his reputation as sculptor
and musician dishonestly, one feels. There is a compelling
conviction that the man is charged with that peculiar facility
that can wring poetry out of the most elusive aspects of
life, although it is questionable if he is capable of giving
that poetry the ring of authenticity.*

*Let me admit it: he is too rich for my blood. Too super-
cool. He comes on like the nihilistic gunfighter hero in one
of those awful Italian westerns; the invulnerable paladin
who shoots down everyone in sight and rides out of town
with a smirk or a yawn.*

*On those rare occasions when he breaks his haughty
silence, his speech is so stilted one would swear he had
written it out and memorized it in advance. He is at least
six and a half feet tall and he seems to delight in deliberately towering over me as if he were some kind of god;
jungle king, RKO Pictures, circa 1941. Of course, he has
spent a lot of time in Africa. And Nearly Normal Jimmy
vows that once when the Indo-Tibetan Circus was short of
provisions, Ziller ran down a deer in the woods and slit its
throat. And the following day he stood on the bank of a
stream and snatched salmon out of the rapids with his bare
hands. The day after that, the sound of his flute coaxed
three pheasants into the cook pot. He backs up his un-
spoken boasts, damn him. What's more, he has just spent
over a hundred dollars and a fair amount of time to get
me, a stranger, out of jail. Maybe he wouldn't have done
it had it not been for Amanda, but he did it. So, I'm
going to give him every chance, I'm going to try to understand him—after all, he is one of the reasons I have taken
my drastic steps of late—and I'm going to try to like him.*

But the truth is, friendship won't be easy with that self-styled Prince of Primitives. Not easy at all.

Amanda, oh that's quite another matter. She was instantly likable, instantly lovable, instantly seductive, instantly the mistress of my marrow, the speeder in my pulse. Even John Paul could not describe Amanda, that is one thing he could not do. Nearly Normal Jimmy once described her as a "religion-unto-herself," and I readily admit that there is something beatific about her gentleness, her poise, her radiant face, the way she seems to float several inches above the ground. However, if she is a saint it was a pope of gypsies who canonized her. My God! What colors she wears. Bangles and bracelets and beads. Rings on each finger, on every toe. Her dark hair appears singed by campfires and she moves always as if to music; her manner mixes action and dream.

Like my own, her cheeks are chubby. Her features are more coarse than classical, but they are soaked with passion and grace. Her eyes shine as seeds in water do. Her mouth has triumphed over her front teeth, which are buckled like a derailed train. Far from distracting from her beauty, her crooked teeth cause her lips to protrude in a perpetual pout. Full and petulant, it is a mouth made for kissing and sucking; it pronounces her vowels as if they were fertility symbols, it sends men sliding helplessly over the arch of her Gene Tierney lisp.

It is futile to go on describing her. I am no poet nor am I clever enough to explain why her teacup breasts are as prurient as those of the most bovine enchantress. Obviously, she has bewitched me (just as Nearly Normal warned she would) and for the moment I hope only that I do not completely lose my head.

As for the Zillers as a couple, as for their manner of existence, a judgment now would not only be premature, it would reveal as much of me as of them. I could guess, of course, what the learned gentlemen at the Institute would say of them. Up to a point, I might concur. I am here no more to praise the Zillers than to bury them. I fear I have much to quarrel with them about. From what I know of their philosophy, it is gummy with romanticism, littered with mystic claptrap. Yet, if I did not believe them to be seminal figures, if I did not sense that today they practice a poetics

*that anticipates tomorrow's science, I scarcely would have
set out with them toward . . . that which claims them for
its own.*

My hosts have bedded me down in their living room
on an accordion of vivid cushions and quilts. Should they
decide to hire me, Amanda said, there are two rooms out
back above the garage that I could furnish as I wish. A
far cry from my stately suite at the Institute, but I await
entry to those chambers with the eagerness of a bride-
groom.

The Zillers retired early to their sleeping quarters. Any
lustful envy that I might have felt for John Paul has been
blown out by the bleeding billows of my butt. Damn these
hemorrhoids! They'll make me old before my time. As I
lie here (on my stomach, of course), I detect laughter and
music in their room. Candlelight is flickering—I can see it
beneath their door—and heady incense is being burned.
(Is their famous baboon in there?) They are playing phonograph records, some wild new jazz. Straining my ears just
now I heard Amanda ask, "John Paul, is it true that Roland
Kirk is the entire Count Basie orchestra in drag?"

That concludes a series of observations from the notebook of Marx Marvelous. The author may quote further from
the Marvelous journal at a later date, or he may not. In
any event, he cautions the reader not to take these entries too seriously. They were transcribed at a time when
Marx Marvelous was a trifle confused concerning both his
mission and his methods, when he was vacillating between
a stuffy academic outlook and one that was frivolous.
Actually, such behavior was an old, old story for the

guy. You see, Marx Marvelous was an exceptional young man, the kind who could easily have left his mark on the world. He had loads of brains, loads of talent, loads of class. But he was tainted by a whimsical ambivalence. Ambivalence hung about his neck like a half-plucked albatross. Ever since he was a whiz-kid eighth-grade physics pupil, Marx had dreamed of becoming a great theoretical scientist on the order of Werner Heisenberg or Einstein. Alas, dream as he did of golden achievement, he could not seem to take it seriously, neither the dreaming nor the doing. That is, he could take it seriously only up to a point, or he could take it seriously one week and the next week he could not.

Simultaneously, he entertained a second set of dreams, dreams the author hesitates to detail lest they shame the dreamer. These other dreams were purple hummers. When they poked their snouts into the dry laboratory of his normal consciousness, Marx would find himself snickering in the middle of Kepler's most exquisite equations and scratching his groin when he should have been scratching his noggin. These dreams stood on pianos and shook hands backwards with Errol Flynn and hot-wired the dreamer's thyroid and drove it to Tijuana with the top down; gassy, sassy, crazy, lazy spectacles that bounced on the belly of his more rational ambitions and desecrated his sober instincts. Such was his second set of dreams. And the conflict had never been resolved. Up to now, the life of Marx Marvelous had been a compromise. He had failed both as a genius and as a rogue.

Marvelous is still young and he has gone through many changes since arriving at the roadside zoo. There is hope for him yet. But his future is not really your interest or concern. Just make what you will of his early impressions of the Ziller phenomenon and let us march on to

THE JOB INTERVIEW

I

The rain did not last through the night. Winter had made one final lunge and expired. Come morning, the sun was blaring and the air was very clear. As he shaved, Marx

Marvelous could see from the bathroom window the saw-
tooth range of Cascade peaks as it jutted up and ran along
behind the foothills on the eastern horizon. The Cascade
Range looked as if it were a portrait gallery devoted exclusively to profiles of Dick Tracy. Here was Dick Tracy's chin
pointed north and there was Dick Tracy's chin pointed
south. There was Dick Tracy's jaw jutting down patroniz-
ingly at Junior and here was Dick Tracy's jaw jutting up
obsequiously toward Diet Smith, and way over there was
Dick Tracy's jaw jutting manfully straight ahead into the
adoring gaze of Tess Trueheart. There was a battery of
Dick Tracy noses sniffing the blue air for clues, and there
was one very large Dick Tracy profile (Mt. Baker) that
was covered all over with slobber and foam, as if Dick Tracy
finally had gone insane from a lifetime of slaughtering de-
formed criminals (Pruneface, Rodent, Ugly Christine).

Breakfast was served on a round oak table in the downstairs kitchen. There was poached salmon in hollandaise
sauce, followed by fresh strawberries in wild honey. Tulips
and daffodils by the dozens were bunched on the table.
Recorded Japanese flute music spiraled down from the upstairs phonograph. Amanda had prepared everything after
completing her morning meditations. After her vagina-
strengthening exercises on the banks of the slough.

Baby Thor and Mon Cul were at table. Marx Marvelous
blinked at the luminescence of the child's gaze; his eyes
were like bare wires. He was both amused and flabbergasted
by the baboon's antics, such as the way it juggled strawberries before devouring them, the way it scratched its
pelt with a fork.

Amanda chatted gaily with her son, tossing an occasional
aside to her husband, to the baboon or to Marx Marvelous.
She jabbered about seashell buddhas and sweet cream rain-
bows and about a proposed trip to the hills to hunt the
morel (which Marvelous gathered was a species of mushroom). In contrast, John Paul said nothing. He sucked up his
breakfast with manners that Marx found nearly as atrocious
as the baboon's. Ziller ate everything with his fingers, including the berries in honey. To Marx, this seemed a dis-
gusting display of contrived primitivism. He was about to
say as much when Ziller suddenly asked, "Mr. Marvelous,

do you think that anything exists between space and the wall?"

It was the kind of question that made Marx Marvelous cringe, that offended him deep down in his bowels. Nevertheless, he was prepared. "Albert Einstein once defined space as 'love.' If that is an accurate definition, then we may conclude that if something could fit between love and its object, then something could fit between space and the wall."

"A pleasing answer, Mr. Marvelous. Amanda, you can continue the interview at your discretion." With that, Ziller excused himself to a far corner of the kitchen where he commenced to unhook strings of sausages with the measured delight of a nymphomaniac plucking fruits from her dream vine.

II

First letting Thor and Mon Cul out in the back grove to play, Amanda took the prospective employee on a tour of the premises. In one sun-splashed end of what had formerly been Mom's dining room, there was a rock pile enclosed by wire mesh. Amanda studied Marx's face to see if he was repulsed by the occupants of the pen. "We take good care of these dears," confided Amanda. "There are fewer than one hundred left alive and we're fortunate to have so many here in our charge."

Marx Marvelous tried to tally the exact number of San Francisco garter snakes in the enclosure, but as they were forever slithering in and out among the rocks, over the rocks and over one another, it was impossible to take a precise census. He guessed there were twelve to fifteen. "They seem pretty frisky to be on the brink of extinction," he said.

The flea circus was housed inside a hollow, lighted table, the top of which was magnifying glass. Marx Marvelous could not conceal fascination. The fleas were *en costume*, some dressed as ballerinas and some as Roman warriors; there was a clown or two and a Persian prince and a cowboy and one flea wore a scarlet chiffon sheath and a yellow wig and looked a little like Jean Harlow. Tiny props were stashed in a corner beneath a miniature canopy. "The fleas are my pride and joy—I trained them and sewed their costumes—but they are also our biggest headache," said Amanda. "They require an attendant almost full time because most of the tourists insist on seeing them perform. I can't say as I blame the tourists, but it's a hardship to keep staging shows. As it is, we schedule a chariot race once an hour on busy days, but folks complain if they have to wait. I don't have time to demonstrate right now, but we put the fleas through their paces by blowing smoke at them. It isn't hard, really. With just a little practice you'll become a good flea trainer, wait and see."

Marx Marvelous laughed out loud. "Me, a flea trainer. What would they say at the Institute?"

"The Institute?" asked Amanda.

"Er, well, yes, I was formerly employed by an institution. The, er, East River Institute to be exact."

The name meant nothing to Amanda. "I hope it was fun for you," she said. She led her guest over to a dramatically lighted alcove in which the amber encapsuled tsetse fly rested upon a satin pillow. It was here, with candlelight reflecting from the green igloo eye facets of the killer insect, that Amanda chose to conduct her portion of the job interview.

"Are you scared of snakes?" First question.

"No, hardly a bit. I used to capture live Maryland copperheads for my zoology class workshop in herpetology."

"Can you make change?" Second question.

"I've had twenty-one hours of college mathematics. I think I could change a dollar. Or even a fiver."

Third question. "Could you, do you suppose, endure selling frankfurters to passing motorists and catering to the whims of summer vacationers?"

"I've been informed by the Institute's resident psychologist that I have a masochistic streak a mile wide. I trust that is of sufficient width to qualify me as a servant of tourists."

"Then I guess that's all I need to know."

"You mean, Amanda, that you would hire me on the basis of your current knowledge of me?"

"Why not? You've met the qualifications. What's more, I like you. You have an honest face." (And an intrusive bulge in your checkered trousers, she thought secretly.) "Besides, I consulted the *I Ching* about you early this morning. I threw the yarrow stalks and got the hexagram Ts'ui or Gathering Together. In the Ts'ui hexagram the Lake image is above the Earth image; the Lake threatens to overflow, signifying that danger is connected with gathering together. However, Ts'ui is, on the whole, a joyful judgment, as it is good fortune for strong people to gather together in devotion. I take that hexagram to mean that despite an element of peril, it will be rewarding for all of us if you gather with us here. Don't you interpret it that way?"

Marx Marvelous frowned like the gargoyle that hated Notre Dame. "I'm afraid I put damn little faith in Chinese superstitions," he said. "I wouldn't hire a shit-picker on the basis of the *I Ching* or whatever that book of magic spells is called, and I wouldn't expect to be hired as manager of your business on that authority either."

Amanda was taken aback. "Oh my," she said. "I had no idea you felt like that. Since you are a friend of Nearly Normal Jimmy's, I assumed you were versed, or at least interested, in . . . that knowledge that lies outside the empirical playpen."

"Like most of our young mystics, when Nearly Normal Jimmy starts talking philosophy he sounds like a cross between Norman Vincent Peale and a fortune cookie. And from what I've heard of your pronouncements, you don't come off much better. Empirical playpen, my ass." Marx Marvelous checked his temper and tried to sugar his frown. "I don't mean to offend you, really I don't. But I'm a scientist —of sorts—and concerned—up to a point—with solving humanity's problems. So I get kinda hot when otherwise intelligent people start handing me answers to these problems that sound like naive mishmashes of yoga, Theosophy, vegetarianism, zen, primitive Christianity, flying saucerism and the Ouija board."

"I haven't handed you anything, Marx Marvelous." She said it pleasantly, even seductively. When she moved, her cupcake breasts bounced in her spangled sleeveless pullover, her mouth was as moist as an orchid. "Solving humanity's problems is not my line of work. However, if you find a conflict in science and mysticism, may I suggest that you do not deny the latter the objectivity you grant the former. Professor Carl Jung was one great scientist who found the *I Ching* to be a time-tested, hard-nosed, fully practical application of the laws of chance. Scientists, I suspect, operate on chance more often than they'd care to have us laymen discover. If you are as honest as I think you are, you will admit to me sooner or later that you play hunches, too."

The prospective zoo manager and weenie salesman shrugged. This was precisely the kind of discussion that he had hoped to avoid or at least to delay. He did not know where to go from here. Except to bed. God, but Amanda was a yummy! Marx imagined that if he kept real still, he could hear sexuality working in her like bees in a hive. On the other hand, the bleating of his hemorrhoids probably would have obscured her sultry buzz.

"Look," he said at last, "I appreciate very much you finding me so readily acceptable. If a three-thousand-year-old Chinese oracle has contributed to your opinion of me, I guess I should be grateful. I do want the job very much and if you are offering it, I accept."

"Marx Marvelous," she said with deliberation, "first tell me this. What kind of scientist are you that you want to sell hot dogs and help run a flea circus? Is there a new branch of science that requires internship in roadside zoos?"

"I'm not interested in just any roadside zoo. I want to work in *this* roadside zoo."

"But why?"

"Oh hell," Marvelous sighed. "I was afraid this interview was going too smoothly. Is my employment dependent upon my reply?"

"No, indeed," Amanda assured him. "As far as I'm concerned, you are hired. You don't have to reply if you don't want to. I'm just curious, that's all. If you really are a professional scientist who had a good job with some institution, why did you come here, why have you sought us out? Yes, I'm curious."

The young scientist in the checkered suit sighed again and let his stare drop from Amanda's eyes to the pleats in her short silk skirt. "Do you mind if I don't muck about in my early background? Oh, it's no big secret, it just isn't significant. I will tell you this, though: my department head at Johns Hopkins University wrote on my doctorate thesis—he rejected it and I never have gotten around to resubmitting it—'Brilliant but frivolous.' That seems to be the opinion of

me in every scientific circle in which I've moved. Needless to
say, I don't concur with that evaluation."

"Needless to say," repeated Amanda.

"Ahem. At any rate, my reputation for whimsy did not
prevent me from getting a number of respectable jobs. A
number of them."

"Were you fired?"

"Not always. Only once, as a matter of fact. No, usually
I quit because I didn't find the work satisfying."

"You dreamed of doing your own research."

"Yes. Yes, damn it. I dreamed of doing my own research."
Marvelous was annoyed that his plight seemed so familiar.

"But you didn't have the money."

"No, I didn't have the money. What is this? Has my
biography been on television?"

"Many times. So, what did you do?"

"Well, I received a strange break. That is, it seemed like
a break at the time. An old acquaintance of mine, an air-
line pilot who flew out of Baltimore, got one of his stew-
ardesses pregnant. He was a married man and she was too
far along for an abortion. So, this pilot made me an offer.
He offered to pay me fifteen thousand dollars to marry his
girl friend. She wanted a husband, she wanted her baby
to have a name. The flier introduced us and we went out
on a date. She was a redhead. Named Nancy. A veritable
gyroscope in bed. I decided to accept the offer. Hell, why
not? With fifteen thou., plus what I had been able to save,
I could move to the country, take two years off to research
my own theories. Within two years, I probably could have
pushed my work far enough along to receive a grant to
finish it. Wow. All that and a glamorous wife and a new
baby. I was really looking forward to settling down." Marx
Marvelous released yet another sigh and shifted his vision
to the tsetse fly that lay in state like the fallen emperor
of a planet unknown to the puny lens of man.

"I gather that your scheme met with some obstacle," said
Amanda, moving across the room to unlatch the front door
of the roadhouse. The zoo was now open for business.

"Nancy and I were married and I quit my job. Rented
a farmhouse on the Eastern Shore and began setting up
a lab. But the pilot never paid off. Not a penny. He signed
up for a transatlantic run and I never caught up with the

son of a bitch. In three months I was back at work and most of my savings were down the tube. As for Nancy, we got along all right. She didn't talk much but she was quite affectionate. Nearly screwed my brains out is what I'm trying to say. Cheerful, too. But as soon as the baby was old enough to travel, she moved out. Let me without a word. The sad part of that was, I'd fallen in love with her, I really had. And that baby girl, why I was as proud of it as if it were my own. Why are you laughing?"

"It's what *you* would call a feminine reaction. You wouldn't appreciate it even if I explained it."

"You're right. Anyway, if you think that part was funny, you'll go into hysterics when you hear what happened next. Nancy divorced me and the judge ruled that I pay alimony and child support. I'm obligated to pay it right now. Eighty bucks a week. Keeps me strapped. That's why I was reduced to subjecting my hemorrhoids to three thousand miles of Greyhound bounce instead of gliding west on a jet. What's more, that's why I changed my name when I dropped out of the Institute. I don't plan on paying any more."

"Changed your name?"

"Why yes. Marx Marvelous is not a legitimate appellation."

"That's a pity. It's a handsome name."

"I'm glad you think so. I like it, too. Do you know how I arrived at it?"

"I haven't the remotest idea."

"When I decided to take an alias, I wanted more than to apply a crust to the worn surface of my real identity. I wanted to make a statement, to *express* something through the unexploited medium of *nom de plume*. Being in a defiant frame of mind, I asked myself what it is that my fellows at the Institute—that, indeed, the average American males of my age and economic stratum—hate most. What do they most loathe? The answer I arrived at was Communism and homosexuality. Communists and homosexuals are the targets of the majority of the normal male's fear-honed barbs. Thus you can see how I in my rebellion selected the given name of 'Marx.' The surname was more difficult. Obviously, I couldn't call myself Marx Homosexual or Marx Queer or even Marx Fag. But I remembered having read in a syndicated newspaper column that the one word no red-blooded he-man would ever ever utter was 'marvelous.' 'Marvelous' is an expression reserved for interior decorators and choreographers and is as taboo in the bleachers, the sales meeting or the pool hall as a rose behind the ear or a velvet snood. So, I embraced that maligned term as if it were a victimized ancestor. And here I am: Marx Marvelous." He paused while red monkey hands of shame tugged at his lids. "Isn't that a disgustingly romantic way for a scientist to behave?"

Amanda, who until Marx's last remark had listened with rapture, looked at him the way an exasperated but tender mother looks at a child who has repeated a clumsy mistake. "Poor Marx Marvelous," she cooed. "You do have a hang-up, don't you? Can't you understand that romanticism is no more an enemy of science than mysticism is? In fact, romanticism and science are good for each other. The scientist keeps the romantic honest and the romantic keeps the scientist human."

"You'll have to convince me of that," said Marvelous stubbornly. But he appeared relieved.

Amanda just shook her head from left to right. "At any rate," she said, "you don't look any the worse for your misfortunes. Your eyes are very calm and humorous." Once more she observed the bulge in his britches. "I find you attractive despite your woes and your wrongheadedness. With John Paul's permission, I'd enjoy getting to know you intimately."

Marx's nervous system was suddenly an amorphous screen upon which was projected a crushingly repetitious series of false starts. He felt himself being lowered into a vat of warm Karo syrup. His mind groped for some word to give his tongue, some direction to assign his hands, but he just kept sinking into the syrup and could respond to Amanda's suggestion is no coherent way. It was Amanda herself who ended the syrupy silence.

"You were hurt by Nancy's desertion and you were dismayed, to say the least, by the financial consequences of your marriage-of-convenience. Yet you apparently didn't commit suicide or have a nervous breakdown or turn into an alcoholic brute. How do you account for your sane survival? Was it science that got you through hard times?"

The subject was changed and Marx Marvelous was unsure whether he was disappointed or relieved. "Well," he an-

swered, "it damn sure wasn't the *I Ching*. I was fortunate
in that when I went back to work after my abortive sab-
batical I found a job that I was suited for. Yes, for the first
time in my career I had employment that utilized my talents
and, for a while at least, offered me some personal satisfaction. I'm talking about the East River Institute of Brain
Power Unlimited."

Amanda, who was now sitting in a modified lotus before
the tsetse fly shrine, said, "I believe you mentioned that
place earlier. What is it?"

"It's a think tank."

"Hmmmm. I've heard the expression but I'm afraid I
don't really know what a think tank is."

"A think tank is an institution of closed learning, a miniature university whose students never come to class. The
'students,' in fact, are giant corporations, government agencies
and foreign heads-of-state. But that doesn't tell you anything, does it? Look, it's this way. Life in the twentieth
century is a great deal more complicated than the daily
newspapers would have us believe, and as technology spreads
in every direction—geometric as well as geographic—existence threatens to grow rapidly more complex. To cope with
the nearly devastating effects of technological growth, government and business—man, himself—must have access to
heavier and heavier loads of information and must be able
to sift and sort that data and apply the best or most relevant
of it to present-day problems and to projections for the future. Luckily, there were a few enlightened men in government and industry, men who didn't accept the Candidean
reality of the newspapers, who became aware some years
ago of this situation. It was these men who stimulated the
creation of think tanks—quiet, secure, scholarly institutions
where resident thinkers of high intelligence, learned back-
grounds and imaginative dispositions might, without commercial restrictions or academic fetters, mull over prospects
in any number of given areas, shape hypothetical developments and recommend corresponding programs and actions.
In this way, failures of planning, obsolete or premature no-
tions of service and muddled or dangerously uninformed reactions to confrontations can possibly be avoided. Think tanks
don't make the major decisions of the Western world but
they advise and counsel those who do. They are terribly

influential when it comes to policy-making in this country and abroad.

"East River Institute in New York was one of the first think tanks and its clients are very big and important. It was exciting working there. What a collection of brains! The guy who runs the place, the director, delights in hiring what he refers to as 'genius kooks,' very brainy thinkers who are too creative or eccentric or temperamental or restless to get along well in industry, government or universities. That's how I got hired, I guess. A Johns Hopkins professor recommended me, even though I don't have my Ph.D., on the grounds that I was 'brilliant but erratic.' Well, maybe he was right. Because it was a job I liked considerably, one that I had aptitude for. Of course, I wasn't one of the big guns there, you understand; I was a junior member of the staff. I performed well, though, and got along fine. Until. Until . . . my last assignment. Then I became confused about . . . a number of issues . . . and due to . . . things . . . on my mind, I decided to leave. That was a few weeks ago."

A couple of truckers had come into the roadhouse, but they retreated when John Paul advised them of the lack of their favorite morning drug: caffeine. They growled over their shoulders as they left, wary as bears. Otherwise, the Capt. Kendrick Memorial etc. Entertained no customers.

"Now we're getting down to the nitty-gritty," said Amanda. "I have the feeling that I'm about to learn what motivated you to forsake your career and seek refuge in our little menagerie. Here, why don't you sit down." She patted the floor beside her exposed mackerel thigh.

In turn, Marx Marvelous patted his backside. "My delicate condition prescribes that I remain standing," he said. "It's really more comfortable this way."

"As you wish," Amanda smiled. She tried to pull down her hem, to smooth it over her thighs, but due to the brevity of her red-and-silver skirt and due to the position in which she sat, it was impossible to conceal her pantied crotch. "Please go on. What was your last assignment?"

"Normally," said Marvelous, "the East River Institute concerns itself with probing relatively specific problems and situations. For example, the State Department and the Defense Department signed a joint contract with us for a study of

Iceland. They wanted to know where Iceland was going in the modern world, whether she would be likely to constitute a threat. Considering her history and her racial character, her current state of economic growth, scientific activity and political ambitions, what should be America's long-range policy in regards to Iceland? In our twice-weekly seminars, where we would pool the results of individual research and think sessions, we dined on fish heads and mead and piped in *rimur* music, that's how immersed in Iceland we were. We even turned the air conditioner up as high as it would go to get the feel of the climate. The assistant director caught a terrible cold and missed ten days. That study was top secret, naturally, and I'm violating security by mentioning it, but what the hell. You see, generally, what kind of projects we undertook?"

"Yes, I see," said Amanda. "It sounds ever so important."

Was Amanda giggling or clearing her sinuses? Marx Marvelous could not tell which.

"It is necessary that man extend his vision beyond the political realities of the present," said Marx, somewhat defensively. "When science can assist him in that, it is its duty. At any rate, to get back to the point, about six or seven months ago the Institute contracted for a study with a markedly different flavor. It happened this way: some troubled governmental bigwig hit upon the idea that the United States was going astray. Surveying our internal turmoil and strife, he concluded (unlike the newspaper mentalities who view our various problems as isolated events) that America's many eruptions of discontent were interconnected and symptomatic of a single pervasive illness. He decided that the U.S. had broken with the Protestant ethic that nurtured it; that we as a nation had 'fallen from grace,' as he put it. He detected political, economic and cultural degeneration. And at back of degeneration he saw a bankruptcy of traditional Christian values.

"Now, although his analysis was none too sophisticated, it was a monument of lucidity compared to the newspaper addicts' fragmented conception of events as separate entities with separate causes, or to the vastly more stupid judgment of those ignoramuses who view every defect in our system as a manifestation of the Communist conspiracy. His viewpoint may have been fuzzy and naive, but at least it was encompassing—and in a nonconspiratorial way. It approached the gates of rational thought. Didn't enter them, mind you, but nevertheless approached.

"This gentleman convinced several other well-placed figures in government of the validity of his critique. Whereupon, under the auspices of the Department of Health, Education and Welfare, the government elected to spend several hundred thousand dollars of tax money to diagnose itself. It asked East River Institute to find out what's wrong with America. Why have traditional values been deflated? Why are we as a people guilt-ridden, anxious and prone to violence? Why is there suspicion that a nation of unprecedented wealth and power is tattering at its edges, coming apart at its seams? Where has flown the Great Speckled Bird of Christianity under whose wings we were once so secure? Why, with all our bombs and churches, are we afraid? What is to blame for the unmistakable evidence of social decay? You're laughing again." This time, there was no doubt.

"Yes. I am," said Amanda. "But don't let that stop you. Continue. Please." One lone, long pubic scroll had sprung loose from its place beneath her panties and unfurled against the creamy field of her thigh like a banderole. Marx Marvelous could not take his eyes off of it. He fancied riding into battle with that curly pennant as his flag. For a moment, the glory of it threatened to curtail his speech. "Please go on," Amanda insisted.

"Umm. Yes. Well, I'm concerned that I'm taking up too much of your time. Shouldn't you be helping John Paul in the kitchen?"

Amanda checked the Puerto Rican clock on the wall, the clock with the crucifix coo-coo and the inlaid slums. "In fifteen or twenty minutes we probably will collect a rush of customers," she predicted. "Then I'll have to take charge of the zoo and maybe help behind the counter. Otherwise, since we serve only hot dogs and juice, there aren't a great deal of preparations to make. So please go on with your story."

"Okay. It was like this. The Institute undertook to learn why the United States was going astray. We considered economic reasons, political reasons and social reasons, but our investigational emphasis was on the religious. Taking our cue from the government official (sorry I can't tell you his name), we sought to learn if a spiritual breakdown might indeed be responsible for America's disunity and commotion. It wasn't an unreasonable hypothesis, you know. After all, an individual who is spiritually secure is not usually an individual who goes to pieces easily. The same might be true of a nation.

"My part in the study consisted largely of field work. Because of my boyish appearance (ahem), I was chosen to do undercover research among the young. I spent, oh, five months or more in the field. I infiltrated church groups and Sunday-school classes; played a lot of bingo, sang in a choir and drank ginger-ale-and-lime-sherbet punch until my bladder bubbled: man, those church socials! Conversely, I also hung around campuses, communes, rock festivals and ghettoes where I danced, sat-in, picketed, smoked a little grass, helped stone a police car and burn three deans and two judges in effigy. Those activities were, in all honesty, more fun than the bingo."

"Shocking, Mr. Marvelous. Absolutely shocking."

"All right, spare me your sarcasm. I thought you might be interested in knowing that it was while running around with a far-out crowd on New York's Lower East Side that I bumped into Nearly Normal Jimmy, whom I had counseled years before when he was in Johns Hopkins' High-School-Students-of-the-Year program. At seventeen, I myself had been named High School Science Student of the Year. As a twenty-four-year-old graduate student, I was a counselor in the program when Nearly Normal was selected High School Business Student of the Year. He was a miracle, that kid. Could have been another J. P. Morgan. Why, later, when he was a sophomore in college, he devised a system where-by his marketing professor was able to earn seventy-five thousand dollars on the stock market. Unfortunately, some crazy damn hermit down there in Arizona fed the kid some weird toadstools and after that he dropped out of school and he's never been the same since. He made a little money in show business, I guess, but the last time I saw Jimmy he was higher than a star. Hardly recognized me. Said he was on his way to the Himalayas to show Tarzan movies to the Dalai Lama. Poor nearsighted bastard. But I guess he isn't the only promising young mind to blow his fuses with drugs. It's a shame, though. That old hermit should have been tarred and feathered."

Amanda sat still as an egg, but if Marx Marvelous thought she was in silent commiseration for the drug-blown Nearly Normal Jimmies of the world, he was mistaken. She was, instead, in revere; revering the memory of Ba Ba, his bat cave, his ropes of mushrooms drying over the fire. *Dear Ba Ba. You were the first one, the very first. O the wonders of Bow Wow Mountain.*

As it became obvious that Amanda was not going to speak, Marvelous wrenched his eyes again from the dark coils of his chosen banner and resumed his account.

"My investigations—on one level, at least—confirmed the findings of my think-tank colleagues. It was painfully apparent, really. The Christian church was in a state of crisis. To avoid that conclusion, you'd have to be deaf, dumb and blind. In a nationwide poll, only 25 per cent declared themselves deeply religious. Maybe half of those who so declared really meant it. Even church attendance, which has never guaranteed religious commitment in the first place, has dropped in this country to an all-time low. Every doctrine and every institution in Christianity is being challenged. Bishops are openly rebelling against papal authority, nuns are walking picket lines, priests are getting married. Many pastors today spend as much time in the streets as in the parsonage. The mild-mannered eunuch who used to gobble fried chicken and shit platitudes is now endorsing strikes, demonstrations and disorders. Theology has become radicalized. Nihilistic intellectuals once bugged the clergy by telling them that God was dead; now the theologians themselves—some of them—are writing the Old Man's obituary. Prayer meetings have turned into existential group therapy sessions, liturgies into rock-and-roll shows. Missionaries are being booted out of Africa and Asia. The churches are being sued to end their right to tax exemption. Half the people who still consider themselves Christians are dissatisfied with the church because it's too big, too impersonal and too commercial: it doesn't penetrate their lives as deeply as it does their pocketbooks. They're impatient because it isn't changing fast enough. The other half are up-tight because it's changed too much already; they long for that old-time religion with its honest emotionalism, with its rarefied if potent myths uncontaminated by the involving rigors of social consciousness." Marx Marvelous paused. "I don't know why I'm running through all this. From just skimming periodicals you would be aware of it."

"Actually," yawned Amanda, "the only periodical I read is *Al's Journal of Lepidoptera*. It's published in Suez and doesn't recognize Christianity."

"Oh," said Marvelous. "Hmmmm? In that case, maybe I've told you something you didn't know, although I don't see how anyone who is half-awake could have missed it. At any rate, all phases of the Institute's investigation, my own included, jibed on that one point: the Christian Establishment, no longer in touch with real life, was quaking and shaking in a crisis situation. Yes, we agreed on that much. After that, however, we moved apart. Specifically, most of my colleagues linked the floundering and chaos in the church with what they believed to be a corresponding deterioration in general ethics. My field work, on the other hand, led me to believe that America's so-called moral breakdown was largely myth. For example, I learned that while the FBI regularly publishes figures showing increases in violent crime, these statistics do not take in account increases in population. The FBI will report something like 'In Los Angeles today there is 22 per cent more violent crime than there was in 1950.' But it neglects to note that population-wise, Los Angeles is almost twice as large as it was in 1950. If you consider population growth in ratio to crime, then crime has actually decreased. Is the FBI willfully distorting the facts? And if so, to what end? I don't know, but I can tell you that I was shocked to learn that a respected government agency would operate that way."

"I don't know either," said Amanda, "but we have a friend named Purcell who would consider your shocked reaction a bit naive." A fresh Puget breeze skidded over the flats and in the front door and worked its way up Amanda's legs. Marx Marvelous imagined that the renegade hair was winnowing. He felt like saluting it. Long may it wave.

"The crime hoax was just one potato in the basket. Among the young people who are supposed to be so wicked, I found a surprising moral strength. Sure, they were somewhat loose in their sexual habits and sure they ingested a lot of drugs—a risky and foolish business—but they were very careful about not hurting other human beings; they practiced—not believed in but *practiced*—a live-and-let-live philosophy of tolerance and tenderness, they adhered to an almost severe code of ethics. Their protests and demonstrations, while they may have gotten out of hand at times, were never mindless acts of rebellion; they were aimed at improving conditions for all mankind. The young radicals weren't seeking personal power or economic gains, they were agitating for a more honest, healthy and democratic society. It wasn't confined to the young, either. Across the nation, people of all ages, people who had grown disenchanted with their churches, people who never had established religious affiliations in the traditional sense, people who had gone so far as to reject the transcendent, these people were engaged in overt acts of moral commitment. For the first time in our history, a significant portion of Americans were actively protesting one of our periodic wars. Some of these pacifists sacrificed a great deal to make their stand. People aren't hungry for spiritual knowledge and guidance? Then how explain the widespread interest in astrology and yoga and those other primitive pastimes that you romantics are fond of reviving whenever the mainstream of religious tradition loses its authority?"

"You may refer to me as a romantic or a mystic as often as you find it helpful," said Amanda, "but please remember that the labels are your own." That is all she said and she said it amiably, but to herself she thought, "This darling Marvelous has eaten at many tables and has not been nourished."

"I apologize if I classify you falsely," said Marx. "I apologize, in fact, for classifying you at all." His apology was halfhearted and he knew it. But he didn't care. He had other things on his mind. "I alerted my fellows at East River to the prevailing paradox: here in the U.S.A., religion was at an all-time low but holiness was at an all-time high; at the most shallow ebb of Christian influence, the search for the ultimate had probably never been more intense. Well, they weighed my report carefully. Such is their discipline. The director promised to give it due consideration when drafting the Institute's final recommendations. But I sensed that it was not destined to receive the emphasis that I was positive it required. No, they were missing the point. Some of the quickest minds in the country, and they were missing the point. They thought we had entered, spiritually speaking, a kind of Dark Age. They couldn't see that it was the beginning of a Golden Age. We had a Reformation by the tail and didn't know it."

Marx was becoming a trifle agitated. He paced the floor as Amanda's big green eyes (a feature she shared with the tsetse fly) followed him curiously.

"I got myself to my suite, where I devoted the next few days to reading and thinking, mainly thinking. Along about that Friday, it hit me full force. I had missed the point, too, although not as widely as my fellows. They, in general, believed that the instinct for religious involvement results from a projection of unconscious materials and processes which, diverse as they might be, are universally common. What had happened in contemporary society, they surmised, was a blunting of this universal instinct by technology, a fogging of our unconscious projections by the ubiquitous paraphernalia of affluence. In an electronic technology, cultural changes occur more rapidly than value systems can accommodate them, and in the resulting confusion technology itself becomes a surrogate religion. Christ, the core symbol of Western religious tradition, is unchanged and unchanging, but we have lost sight of him in the buffeting and confusion and must be trained to recognize the Christ Idea again, albeit in the context of complex Space Age technology rather than a simple agrarian arrangement. That was, in essence, the prevailing consensus at the Institute. As I originally saw it, however, the fault lay not in modern man's blindness but in an outdated church's camouflage. How could contemporary man be expected to recognize the Christ Idea as a viable part of his daily experience when the Christ Idea was mincing around on the fringes of society dressed in those old Sunday-school robes and speaking in that quaint King James English? He was pale, puny, archaic, aloof and though richer than a dozen Rockefellers he always had his hand out. In no meaningful way did he fit into the modern picture. The problem wasn't with man but with his religion. I saw all around me a voracious spiritual hunger, but the paleolithic mush served up by the church was neither nutritious nor appetizing. More significantly, I saw people living matchlessly ethical lives without the guidance of clergy or the comfort of organized doctrine or common symbols. Man was doing as well as could be expected under the circumstances. It was the church that needed overhauling— and fortunately, there was evidence that an overhaul was on the drawing boards. Eventually, I thought, a streamlined, fully electric model will roll off the line and people will flock to it and ride it to salvation. Wasn't I ludicrous?

"My colleagues and I had made the same dumb mistake. Although they took a negative view of our spiritual unrest while my outlook was optimistic, we both had assumed that what was unfolding was a *Christian* drama. We regarded the crisis as a Christian crisis and presumed that whatever religious changes were occurring were occurring within the framework of the Christian system. How wrong we were, how foolishly wrong. Alone in my study on Good Friday, I had an illuminating insight that I recognized instantly as truth. Christianity is dead! Dead. It is not being overhauled, it has been traded in. What is afoot is not the reshaping of the Christian mode but the development of an alternative mode, a superseding mode. We at the Institute had thought in terms of a revolution of faith, but that wasn't it. We had misinterpreted the signs. There was no revolution. There was *evolution*—an infinitely more profound and permanent process. Spiritual evolution. Yes. But not creepy-crawling along at evolution's regular pace: an evolutionary outburst! I had spoken of a neo-Reformation, but that wasn't quite correct. Christianity isn't being reformed. It's being replaced. We are in a transitional period between religions. That's what much of our discord and pain and confusion is about. It doesn't explain all of our turmoil, of course. The changes wrought by our new technology are almost as mind-twisting as those precipitated by spiritual evolution. In fact, technological upheaval and religious upheaval are always inseparable overlays. Major technological breakthroughs, such as the ones in electronics and psychochemistry that have occurred in our era, inevitably alter man's image of himself, of his environment and his deity. Remember Galileo's starry band. Galileo did more than invent the telescope and develop the first laws of nature based on observation and calculation. He personified a fresh wind which swept Western man out of the medieval halls of sanctioned impotency. He was the spark that touched off the heap of combustible philosophical residue that had been accumulating beneath the backstairs of Popery for centuries. The resulting explosion blew a constipated hierarchy right off the golden pot. But I'm digressing. What is happening today is far more overwhelming than a Reformation, even. We are in a state of no-religion prior to the ascent of a new religion. The discernible activity in the modern church, the modern ecumenism, social activism, militancy and debates about the state of God's health are merely the nervous twitchings of a cadaver. The handsome new church buildings, the plush pulpits and wall-to-wall carpets are no more than funeral trappings. It's all over. The Christian faith is dead. Dead. Expired. Kaput. Finished. Moved and left no forwarding address. Bye-bye. Gone, if not forgotten. Dead."

Marvelous was pacing and gesturing, visions of public pennant no longer clouding his purpose. Amanda dared to interrupt. "Your theories seem to have brought you a minimum of joy," she ventured.

"That's true. No joy in them at all. How could there be? In the Baltimore suburb where I was reared, my mother was a ferocious one-woman band for Baptist fundamentalism. Until I was eighteen, I spent every single Sunday in church —bored stiff and scared to admit it. Then, at college, I found most of the intellectually developed people—students and professors—to be atheists. Moreover, they were happily atheists. They delighted in atheism. They seemed to take personal pride in the lack of a Creator. There isn't any God, ha ha ha. Eventually, I also became an atheist. But I damn sure wasn't happy about it. Maybe there is no God, but there ought to be one."

Amanda looked at him so curiously he had to smile. "Well," he said, calmer now, *"somebody* should take the blame for all this crap." His sweeping gesture took in the universe.

"I'll take the blame," Amanda said, "if you'll just get on with your story."

"Okay. Accepting the death of Christianity might have been a trauma for me, but it wasn't the end of the world. After all, religions have died before. Christianity was born and everything that is born must die, philosophical systems no exception. Christianity had waxed long and strong and now its turn had come. No point in lingering at the bier. There was work to do. In the past, when a religion has succumbed, another has always come along to take its place. That would undoubtedly be the case this time, too. Another religion would be forthcoming. But when? Where? And more pointedly, what? Was it already here, milling in our midst, waiting to be unmasked? To that question I decided to apply scientific procedure. Up to now, supposedly objective, nontheological studies of religion have been the priority of the behaviorists—anthropologists, psychologists or sociologists—men still capable of believing in such claptrap as souls—"

"You don't believe in the soul?"

"The soul, to us nonmystics, is an electrochemical manifestation: a synthesis of proteins, a flare of nerve electricity. Nothing more."

"In Burma," said Amanda, "they believe the soul is a butterfly."

Marx Marvelous stared at her. He could forgive her anything. Her lisp unlocked his creed and spilled his discipline. "When I was a boy," he mused, "I had a sheep dog that looked like an English poet. Eyes blue and distant as were Shelley's. One day he disappeared and never came back. My mother said the gypsies stole him. Are you really a gypsy?"

"I am a gypsy in name only," said Amanda. "Just as you are a scientist."

"A scientist in name only? How do you mean?"

"Marx Marvelous, your methods may be entirely compatible with those of our so-called 'advanced' technocracy but as far as I can tell, your goals were shaped by the ancient great purpose of life. Now don't curl your lip, it spoils your good looks. That's better. If you're so up-tight about what I said then answer me this: you decided, didn't you, that religions are natural systems rather than supernatural phenomena, and like all natural systems they adhere to natural laws? If you were to study religions as historical structures, as natural entities, you might establish a set of facts and relations about religions. Right? There might, for example, be equations that could predict the movement of gods with planetary precision. You might invent Marvelous' First Law of Religiodynamics. How would it go? A transformation whose only final result is to transform into dogma ethical behavior extracted from a source which is at the same social temperature throughout is impossible. Or something like that. Now isn't that what you are up to?"

"Your parody of the First Law oversimplifies my concerns and makes them sound trivial. But, in essence, you're correct, I guess. By assembling a logic of religious procedure based upon observed knowledge and accumulated data, it might be possible to predict—and maybe control—the nature of the religion that is to supplant Christianity. With such an assemblage at its disposal, science could save mankind an enormous amount of anguish."

"Ah, the pride of intellect," sighed Amanda. "But you know more about such stuff than I do. I wouldn't have known the famous First Law except that a physics major who was once my lover talked in his sleep. Anyway, what happened to your grandiose enterprise? You must have had a first-rate library at your Institute; contacts, computers, resources, a secluded study. The think tank seems perfect for your project. Why did you run away?"

"There are some thoughts that a think tank is not capable of incubating. I had discovered that the church had become too self-centered to deal with real life, which runs in all directions and runs to extremes. Next, I discovered that the think tank is too comfortable for real thinking, which likewise is a radical, and sometimes dangerous, activity. A think tank is an ideal place to consider the meaning of events, but I was becoming obsessed with something other; I wanted to consider—"

"The meaning of meaning?"

"Oh shit." Marvelous slumped against the totem pole that sprouted adjacent to the altar of the tsetse fly. "I loathe that phrase. It makes me gag."

"Marx Marvelous, are you on a scientific mission or a spiritual quest?"

"What? A scientific mission! No, I don't know. I really don't know. I told you that I've been confused about things. Maybe I'm on both. I'm capable of it. I'm such an ambivalent bastard."

"That's a pity," said Amanda sincerely. "Ambivalence is a bigger nuisance than schizophrenia. When you're schizoid each of your two personalities is blissfully ignorant of the other, but when you're ambivalent each half of you is painfully aware of the conflicting half, and if you aren't careful your whole life can turn into a taffy pull. Anyway, you quit the Institute. You still haven't explained why you turned up here."

"I felt that a monumental event in the annals of the human animal was unfolding, unfolding in *my* lifetime; and while its implications reached into the Institute, as they indeed reached into every cranny of existence, I was possessed by the desire to get closer to developments. A major religion was dead or dying and another was materializing in its stead. The consequences of a religious changeover at this particularly volatile moment in our cultural history are immense. I began to think of it as my duty as a scientist and as a human being; my duty was to get close enough to the vortex, to the medulla of evolutionary outburst so that I could experience it in a direct, tangible way. I craved the ultimate scientific luxury of being simultaneously involved and detached. Now look, Amanda, I realize that you are trying to make me out to be some kind of soulsearcher in scientist's clothing, but you're wasting your time. Science is an active response to the world. Mysticism accepts the world. Mystics scurry about trying to get in harmony with nature. Scientists turn nature to issues which *we* define. Science is resistance, rather than acceptance, and I assure you that it was in a mood of responsible resistance that I set out to encounter the new Messiah."

"Dear Marx Marvelous," said Amanda. "Champion of resistance. Have you forgotten so quickly then how you learned to stop flinching and accept the rain? Oh well. You still haven't revealed why you chose to come here. Of course, you needn't tell if you don't want to."

"I'll tell you straight away. I didn't want to wander around from scene to scene, always arriving at the tail end of things. I didn't have time for fads, cults or false prophets. Frankly, the activities which usually characterize a period of religious transition are quite unappealing to me. No, I decided that since the first substantial, recognizable evidence of the next religion would undoubtedly appear out on the limits of the psychic frontier, my best plan would be to find some compatible person or persons who reside on the psychic frontier and to cast my lot with them and work from there. After hearing about the Zillers from Nearly Normal Jimmy and others—your husband is something of a legend in New York—I decided that you were ideal. A photograph of you, Amanda, shown to me by Jimmy unquestionably influenced my decision. One can't be totally devoted to science, you know."

"Marx Marvelous, you're as nutty as a Mars bar. This is a little roadside attraction sitting out in the rains of isolated Northwest America, enticing passing motorists with a sausage smile. We have sunshine juices for mildewed tummies and exotic exhibitions for jaded eyes. But we do not concern ourselves with religions or sciences. We are ignorant of your psychic frontier. Are you psoitive you are in the right place? What was it Jimmy said to lead you to assume that we hold the key to some . . . some evolutionary religious awakening?"

"I don't know that I can tell you explicitly. As much as anything else, I had a feeling about this place."

"A feeling?" Amanda clapped her hands and squealed. "A hunch! You mean you had a hunch. See what I told you. You confessed at playing at chance earlier than I thought you would. You came here on a kind of hunch and you admit it, don't you?"

"Partially." Marvelous was blushing. "Only partially. You people may be going through the motions of operating a roadside zoo, but I know there are other levels of activity here. I have every reason to suspect that your crazy hot dog stand is a front for doings of a more valuable elevation."

"All right," said Amanda. "We can't fool you. You are too shrewd for us. It's only a matter of time before you expose us so I might as well confess to everything. My husband and I are agents of the great Icelandic conspiracy."

"Joke if you must," said Marvelous. "But I know you are up to something extraordinary here. I know it even if you don't."

Amanda giggled and stood up, her skirt settling like nightfall over the maverick cunt-hair that for a golden moment had flown from the staff of champions. "You really are silly," she said. "Luckily for you, I am found of silliness. What's more, you're cute." She dragged her silvered nails along the seam of his trousers.

Marx had grown rather pale and now he slumped even more awkwardly against the totem pole.

"What's wrong?" asked Amanda.

"I guess I just got too worked up. It's another of my shortcomings as a scientist; I get carried away. Damn it all. I hadn't planned to tell you so much. I had intended to live here as somewhat of a spy. Confessions must be hard on me. Anyway, I feel a bit faint." He was gasping.

Amanda withdrew from her bosom a black silk handkerchief bordered with gold braid. Passing it to Marvelous, she said, "Hold this to your nose."

Marx hadn't expected a girl as healthy as Amanda to carry smelling salts, but he followed her instructions. From the handkerchief there came a subtle waft, an effluvium of sweetness. Even while he sniffed it, however, its perfume became gradually stronger, then musky, then barbarically acrid. He was about to yank the fabric away from his nostrils when yet another odor emerged, this one spicy and primordial. In turn, that fragrance also passed and in its place oozed an aroma of lanolin and leather, a rich animal funk flanked by a mineral smell as dry as ash.

Smiling at Marx's befuddlement, Amanda said, "That handkerchief has been dipped in a jar containing the accumulated odors of twelve years in Tibet. I had planned to send it to Nearly Normal Jimmy, but perhaps he won't be needing it."

Dumfounded, Marvelous said nothing and continued to sniff. He smelled malty vapors and fatty ones, thin olfactory outlines of the mountains and windy whiffs of the snows. Meanwhile, as if fulfilling Amanda's prophecy, several cars had parked out front and their occupants were filing expectantly into the roadhouse. "Enough now," said Amanda, reaching for the square of silk. "The zoo has customers and you have a lot to learn. You'd better follow me about and watch me carefully. Tomorrow we're going to be closed all day for a morel hunt, but on Friday you may have to run the place alone."

Blinking, Marx Marvelous returned the handkerchief, but throughout the day as he helped Amanda wipe tables and counters, as he poured juice, memorized a short lecture on San Francisco garter snakes and learned how to direct fleas in chariot races and ballets, there lingered in his nasal passages certain odors of lotus blossom, yak butter, prayer wheels—and one exceedingly stimulating fragrance which Amanda would identify only as Mom's Tibetan peach pie.

"There are three mental states that interest me," said Amanda, turning the lizard doorknob. "These are: one, amnesia; two, euphoria; three, ecstasy."

She reached into the cabinet and removed a small green bottle of water-lily pollen. "Amnesia is not knowing who one is and wanting desperately to find out. Euphoria is not knowing who one is and not caring. Ecstasy is knowing exactly who one is—and still not caring."

Some readers were probably surprised to learn that Amanda spoke with a lisp. The author would be pleased to describe her lisp for you, although it will not be easy. Marx Marvelous observed that it was a Gene Tierney lisp, but he was wrong. It was slighter than that. Slighter, warmer, pinker, more vulnerable. It was more of a Gloria Grahame lisp. Remember Gloria Grahame in *The Big Heat?* Her gangster boy friend threw a pot of scalding coffee in her face. A noisy episode. Gloria Grahame didn't lisp when she screamed.

If you don't remember Gloria Grahame (or even if you do), maybe you have heard of the Great Blondino. He was the Mozart of the tightrope, the Great Blondino. A child prodigy, Blondino was already a virtuoso of high-rope acrobatics at six. As an adult, he won fame for his repeated crossings of Niagara Falls. In the 1860's he walked a rope over Niagara once on stilts, once with both feet in a sack. He hopped over with a man on his back while fireworks popped in the air about him. Once, he sat down on the rope, hundreds of feet above the roaring cataracts, and cooked and ate an omelet. Throughout his career of perilous performances, he never had a close call or sustained an injury. While walking a safe city sidewalk during a stay in Sydney, Australia, however, Blondino slipped on a banana peel and broke his neck. Picture Amanda's lisp as that banana peel.

Or, let us look at it another way. A Chinese philosopher once taught his pupils the meaning of agression by having them wad up spring blossoms and throw them against a wall. To arrive at an understanding of Amanda's lisp, simply reverse the process.

Among the Haida Indians of the Pacific Northwest, the verb for "making poetry" is the same as the verb "to breathe."

Such tidbits of ethnic lore delighted Amanda, and she vowed that from that time onward she would try to regulate each breath as if she were composing a poem. She was as good as her word, and her new style of breathing added to her warehouse of personal charm.

Once, while breathing an especially strenuous stanza, she sucked in a stinkbug that had been bumbling by. "What a rotten rhyme," she gagged. "I think I'll go back to prose."

Amanda took Marx Marvelous on a tour of the grove out back. There was moss in the grove and fir needles and ferns. There was mud and grass and weeds, but no rocks. There was a tipi, and a wooden table carved to resemble a mushroom. On those rare days when it was not raining, the grove was the Zillers' living room, nursery and dining area. It was here, protected and private, that they entertained their few (and mostly uninvited) guests.

In his checkered suit, now rather soiled, Marvelous strutted about the grove, jaws flapping. "Yes, there is an air of asylum out here," he flapped. "This grove does for my insecurities what Preparation H does for my hemorrhoids: shrinks them without surgery. Brings to mind the grove in ancient Italy where Romulus, shunned by his neighbors after he had slain his brother, established a sanctuary for fugitives, rebels, and aliens—the future citizens of Rome. In honor of the god Consus, kidnaped virgins were borne to the grove to participate in bacchanalian festivals and to observe secret feasts and games. A good time was had by all.

"Of course," he flapped on, skewering Amanda with that blue-eyed barbed-wire glare that he reserved for persons whom he suspected of mystical inclinations, "*you* would prefer to compare it to Jetavana, the grove at Savatthi where the Illustrious Buddha dwelt. No kidnaped virgins for old Buddha, huh? Just mangoes and figs. You are what you eat."

Before Amanda could respond, Marvelous came upon a small chicken pen at the outer edge of the grove. There was in the pen a pavilion under whose roof a solitary rooster stood. "My God," exclaimed Marvelous. "That's the most bowlegged chicken I've ever seen. It's outrageous. Why don't you put it on display in the zoo?"

Amanda shook her head. "No," she said. "He's done a lot of walking. He deserves a rest."

"Why has Mr. Marvelous chosen to join us here at our zoo?" asked John Paul Ziller. The hour was midnight. He closed the book with the savage cover (the journal!?) and lay down beside his naked wife.

"Mr. Marvelous has misplaced something and wants to make sure that we have not found it," Amanda answered. As was her nightly custom in cool climates, she was massaging her lower body with Mother Blacksnake's Sunrise Oil. Her tattoos glistened like a new model of the universe.

"I trust that it was nothing important," muttered John Paul.

"Were it important, he would not have lost it," Amanda said.

Hello, reader. May the author once again intrude upon whatever mood his narrative might have established long enough to report on current events? This is the fifth day that Amanda, Baby Thor and your correspondent have been officially held prisoner. We were surrounded for a day or two prior to that, but it was not until John Paul and Plucky fled five days ago that those of us who remained at the zoo were bluntly notified of our quarantine.

Due to the liberation early this morning of the garter snakes—after warming them into a state of hyperactivity with a heating pad we shooed them one by one out the back door past the dozing guards—the agents are unusually hostile. Their pornographic taunting of Amanda has become increasingly sadistic, and the writer has been assured that only a (temporary?) restraining order from a higher echelon is preventing him from being mauled.

Apparently, however, their orders bid them maintain a reasonable distance, for not since the devastating search of four days ago has an agent set foot upstairs. Thus, unless they spot us at a window, or we venture down to the kitchen for food, we are spared their harassment, although their menacing vectors seem at times to penetrate our walls.

Taking his cue from Amanda, who, in between trances, has spent the day teaching Baby Thor the songs of gypsies and Indians, the author has tried to proceed with his writing, aloof from the threatening forces that encircle him. He has done rather well, too. His Remington has been yapping since breakfast and he has grown to appreciate the beauty of its bark. Just one more day! At the rate he is working that is all it will take to finish this. One more good day like this one. Will they grant it?

The reader may be perplexed to discover that this document is fairly near completion while there yet remains so much to learn. Please do not despair. All pertinent data concerning the Corpse will be imparted ere the author brings his account to term—providing, as he has said, that the authorities grant him one more day at the typewriter minus unpleasant interruption. To those readers who may be also annoyed because this report is somewhat remiss in linear progression and does not scurry at a snappy pace from secondary climax to secondary climax to major climax as is customary in our best books, the writer is less apologetic. He is dealing with real events, which do not always unfold as neatly as even our more objective periodicals would have us believe, and he feels no obligation to entertain you with cheap literary tricks.

For those of you who may have come to these pages in the course of a scholastic assignment and are impatient for information to relay to your professor (who, unless he is a total dolt, has it simmering in his brainpan already), the author suggests that you turn immediately to the end of the book and roust out those facts which seem necessary to your cause. Of course, should you do so, you will grow up half-educated and will likely suffer spiritual and sexual deprivations. But it is your decision.

As we drive up the river road, there are sixty thousand trees which I see but do not touch. Like me, Amanda is confined in the speeding Jeep, but she touches every tree.

Entry—May 10
Notebook of M. Marvelous

****

"The morel is a very wary little mushroom," explained Amanda. "It hides under fallen leaves as if it were willfully avoiding the hunter's pluck. Like many of nature's noblest creatures it is a fugitive kind."

The Jeep, piloted by John Paul, was speeding up the

river road. Amanda had executed rough sketches of the morel. She was showing them to Marx Marvelous.

"As you can see, the cap of the morel is shaped rather like a thimble. A withered thimble. It is pitted, carved with irregular indentations; honeycombed, as it were. The color of the cap ranges from tan to creamy brown to a dishwater gray—colors that echo equally the decaying leaves underfoot and the sodden skies above. The stem is ivory-white, long and hollow. Frequently, you will come upon stems alone and you may wonder where the caps have gone. To the deer, that's where. Morel caps are the deer's spring tonic. They spurn the stems and leave them standing. We are not as particular as the deer."

A short distance from the roadside zoo, they had wheeled east-northeastward off the Freeway and motored for a ways through fields and pastures of stinging green. Past Burlington, trees grew more plentiful and there were bright green bogs in which the skunk cabbage looked like exploding canaries or lemons that had been hammered into sheaves. After leaving the town of Sedro-Woolley (site of Northern State Hospital for the Insane), they began to climb, climbing as if the concentrated pressure of those locked-up crazies was propelling them to loftier altitudes. Higher, higher.

The river was an oxide green and buzzing with silvery silt. If there were fish in it they were well concealed, but occasional steelhead fishermen stood in their flat-bottomed boats, silhouetted in the Skagit mist like mackinawed wraiths. Landward, alders, vine maple and cottonwood thronged down the hillsides to the edge of the road. Where these budding deciduous treelings were mixed with larger, older conifers, there Amanda would point and say, "In April, morels lurked in those groves by the hundreds. The weather is too warm for them now. If we hope to catch morels today, we must go to higher elevations. Even there we won't find many. If we apply ourselves we should get enough for one fine dinner, but this is definitely the last morel hunt of the season."

Marx Marvelous looked over the sketches. He read the morel's botanical name (courtesy of Madame Lincoln Rose Goody): *Morchella esculenta*. He re-examined the drawings. Something dark and ill-defined rustled its arms (or wings or tail) in the hollow behind his heart. He was unconvinced that he wished to dine on these demonic fruits. Morel season could have ended sooner for all he cared. "How can we be sure we aren't picking toadstools?" he asked.

"Specialization is such general tyranny," thought Amanda. "Was it when man initiated the division of labor that he lost contact with the complete reality and began to fragment and go numb? Here we have a scientist, a man who has sacrified this lifetime to the study of the Earth and its workings, and he does not know that 'toadstool' is just another name for mushroom, edible or toxic. How puny his particular knowledge. Still, I suppose it is necessary. Isn't it?" She thought these thoughts to herself as in her mind's eye she ran naked through the woods, hugging trees.

To Marvelous, she said: "If it is poison you are worried about, you had better stay away from supermarket foods with their preservatives and pesticides."

"Oh, I feel totally at ease in supermarkets," said Marvelous lightly.

You would, thought Amanda. Canned peas are not a very potent image. A package of frozen french fries lacks roots that reach into the deep chambers of human consciousness. Ah, but mushrooms! They are standard equipment for sorcerers and poisoners, eh, Marx? Associated in art, literature and folklore with the wicked and exotic, the mushroom has been used since primitive times to represent death—and death's fair sister, sex. Mushrooms have been called "devil's fruit" and "satan's bread." They do not take to domestication. They lurk in the forest, assume skeleton hues and smell of rot and Pan. Our dear scientist obviously is uncomfortable dabbling in the black arts of yore. She thought these thoughts to herself as in her mind's eye she hugged each further tree trunk, bark and lichen flaking off in green-red scrumbles against her breasts.

To Marx Marvelous she said: "Frankly, there is a poisonous species which is sometimes confused with the morel. It is commonly called the brain mushroom (how Madame Goody refers to it I do not know) and its cap is convoluted like the lobes of the organ for which it is named. That is how one distinguishes it from the morel, in fact. It is folded into many convolutions, rather than depressed as is the morel.

If you examine your quarry with this distinction in mind, you cannot possibly make an unpleasant mistake."

"I don't know," said Marvelous, scratching in various places his living statue of natty checks. "Mushrooming sounds to me like a risky proposition."

"A bit like life itself," said Amanda.

* * * * * * * *

Although it hasn't rained for two days, the forests are still sopping. The underfooting is spongy, the tree-moss drips and drips. An eerie sunlight filters through dense tangles of ominously serpentine branches. Shadows are soaked with suggestions of primordial menace and obscure, slinking malignity. White snail shells—some vacant, some stuffed with mucus—are scattered beneath the huckleberry bushes like aquatic curds, and sweating tendrils of ivy choke everything that does not move. In this rank garden of vegetable death, Amanda—more goddess than Hecate herself—rakes the nettles and ferns with her fingers, emitting eeeeeks of minnie mouse surprise whenever she uncovers a treasured fungus. I dread the forest for its universal reminders: it is simultaneously an open womb and an open grave. But Amanda is as at home here as if it were in her own mold that was cast the vast greenfrog jelly of eternity.

Entry—May 10
Notebook of M. Marvelous

* * * * * * * *

"Eeeeek!" squealed Amanda, as underneath a great old shaggy-assed cedar she came upon a morel nearly nine inches tall. Earlier, Amanda had told Marx, "The other popular edible mushrooms grow in the autumn. The morel has springtime all to itself." Well, this morel must have had itself one hell of a spring. It was the largest find of the day, the largest of the season. It was a whopper, a prizewinner, a champ, a box-office bonanza, but destined to be dropped right in the basket with the smaller, less glamorous specimens—no star treatment here at Fungus Studios, sorry.

From another part of the woods John Paul materialized, as magicians will, and gave *ex cathedra* sanction to the prize. Even Baby Thor was impressed. He jumped up and down yelling, "Big one! Big one!" Mon Cul caught the fever and slapped his thighs, bowing in the exaggerated manner that he had learned at the Timbuktu Opera. He acted as if the mammoth morel were his own invention, though in truth he had not picked a single mushroom (after all, he was a famous baboon, not some truffle pig). Marx Marvelous had found only about a dozen morels, but with each discovery the thrill increased and he strutted with scientist pride to demonstrate how he had outwitted nature. They were a happy band of food-gatherers, damp and smeared with humus, but happy with the harvest, happy enough to dance, the five of them. And about that time a sudden wild wind gust roared up the Cascade highlands, sounding like a hillbilly hoot, like a Saturday night wahoo; and the shadows grew more tentacular and the sunlight more nocturnal, and the sky thickened like cornstarch and curdled around the tops of the darkening trees. "Let's get home," they hollered, almost in harmony, and singing and chanting four different mushroom hymns in what appeared to be four different tongues (Ziller, as usual, was silent), they Jeeped it on back to the low country, just ahead of the moon.

* * * * * * * *

We are driving home by a different route, not following the river back but cutting through the mountains on what is known as the Darrington road. This is logging country, as I ascertain by the bark chips strewn on the highway, by the timber trucks snorting around the twilit curves with one last day's load for the mills. Our own vehicle navigates a curve, and suddenly it is as if we have trespassed into the shattered heart of a no-man's land. Suddenly there is no more forest. Every hillside, every ridge is bare except for stumps and slash: a cemetery of forlorn stumps; low-spreading barricades of rain-rotted, sun-bleached slash. We are in the midst of an enormous bone yard, a battleground where armies of creatures bigger than dinosaurs might have fought and died. These murdered hills were for untold centuries green. Deer and bear and cougar and dozens of smaller animals lived here; eagles nested in the tops of the firs. Now, they are barren, devastated, splintered, twisted, silent: not even a magpie sings. They look to be grotesque Golgothas on which have been crucified a thousand Christs. I am no lover of the wilderness; the dark, dank woods hold for me a repertoire of unnamed fears. But if the forest is the product of satanic forces, then those forces have been surpassed by the graspings of man. No devil ever dreamed a landscape more terrible than

Entry—May 10
Notebook of M. Marvelous

****

The barbaric spectacle of the logged-off hills stunned them mute. No one spoke until, stopped at one of Darrington's three traffic lights, they saw a small crowd of lumberjacks and their families lined up before a quonset-hut movie theater, waiting for the show. There were children, some no larger than Thor, licking eskimo pies; friendly gossip ran along the line from wife to unfashionable wife; the big men seemed quiet and shy, maybe tired, maybe beaten down by their role in life, their faces already reddened by the spring sun, their Thom McAn shoes muddy, their jaws shiny with Aqua Velva—the medicine cabinet stink was detectable as far as the Jeep.

"They look to be decent folks," observed Marx Marvelous. "Probably not a guilty conscience among them. Our society *needs* timber and these loggers are merely doing their jobs. They probably believe they're performing a patriotic service, and maybe they are. But I wonder if deep down inside they are completely insensitive to the brutality of their operation. I wonder if those beautiful kids will grow up and repeat the slaughter. That is, if there're any trees left to ravage. I realize, you know, that the logging companies are replanting. But a tree farm is not a forest. Is it?"

The light went green and the Jeep lunged forward. Amanda held Baby Thor tightly in one arm while with her free hand she affectionately fingered morels. Ziller looked over his furred shoulder, first at the logger families in the neoned distance and then at Marx Marvelous. "From little acorns grow the acorn eaters," he said.

****

Morels are ugly in the skillet. The caps look like the scrotums of leprechauns, the stems like the tusks of fetal elephants. Aromatically, the report is more positive. From the pan rises the smell of the whole North Woods stewing in butter. The morels grow friendlier to the nose. But in the mouth, now there is where these dangerous-looking plants really prove themselves. My God, I must confess it: their deliciousness exceeds normal limits of restraint. They taste similar to mealy sweetbreads, to eggplant, to country-style steak, to all three at once. As I munch these delectables, my fearful toadstool prejudices dissolve in a glory of saliva. Perhaps the way to a man's tolerance is through his stomach. Would our relations with China be worse if chow mein were not so popular?

> Entry—May 10
> Notebook of M. Marvelous

****

While the mushrooms fried and the rice boiled, Amanda prepared a salad, humming as she worked, filling the kitchen with an hallucinatory light, a feminine splendor that jolted Marx Marvelous' imaginative faculties and made him aware of seraphic appetites in which he professed not to believe. Soon he was on his fifth glass of chablis.

The Zillers, having long ago discovered alcohol to be a most imperfect drug, sipped their wine slowly and repeatedly refused to have their cups refilled. When it became apparent that they would not help him finish the two bottles he had chilled, Marvelous lifted his glass in their direction and asked, "Do you know what Bertrand Russell said about mystics?"

"I do not," said Amanda, ripping the lettuce as gently as if she feared it might cry "ouch." John Paul continued to let jungle murmurings escape his flute.

"Russell said that there is no difference between those men who eat too little and see Heaven and those who drink too much and see snakes." Marvelous leered sardonically into his wine.

"The difference," said Amanda serenely, "is that one of them sees Heaven and the other sees snakes."

"Howdy again, mam," said the vaguely familiar cowboy. "I see that you've opened your zoo."

"That is true," agreed Amanda. "We have."

"Yep, I figured as much," said the vaguely familiar cowboy, squinting at a *pas de deux* in the fleas' *Swan Lake*. "Seeing as how you don't have a real whole lot of attractions in your show, I thought you might be interested in buying this here dog."

"What dog?" asked Amanda fairly, for there was truly no canine in evidence.

"That's the novelty of him, mam. He's invisible."

Amanda looked about for some sign of doggy activity. "You see," explained the semifamiliar cowboy, "my nephew came back from San Francisco last week a-fixing to go in business for himself. He buried two thousand capsules of that LSD out by the corral. Well, our ol' dog he dug up that acid and ate it all, two thousand doses. Six hundred thousand micrograms. We figgered for sure he was gonna die. But that ol' hound commenced to glow and get ghostly foggy-looking and get harder and harder to see and pretty soon he just disappeared altogether. Entered another dimension, my nephew tells it. Here Cheny, here boy." The vaguely familiar cowboy stooped down and began to pet the air.

Amanda wouldn't give any money for the invisible dog, but she did offer to trade for him four of her wishes and three of her dreams.

This noon we dispatched the fleas.

Hmmmmm. Does it astonish you that the author felt a

trifle odd typing that sentence? For one thing, he felt as if he were stealing a line from *Tropic of Cancer* by Henry Miller. "Last night Boris discovered that he was lousy. I had to shave his armpits and even then the itching did not stop." That's how *Tropic of Cancer* begins. Miller could just as easily have written, "This noon we dispatched the fleas."

Amanda's original plan to airmail the subjects of her flea circus to a friend in Palm Springs fell through for reasons about which the writer is not entirely clear. Nevertheless, she was intent upon mailing the fleas to *someone*, and as it turned out she mailed them to *Al's Journal of Lepidoptera* in one of the prestamped, self-addressed envelopes which Al provided for the posting of Amanda's occasional (more hallucinatory than scholarly) contributions to his magazine. "Dear Al, Please see to my fleas," she wrote on violet stationery in a hand that fluttered as lyrically as a silky swallowtail.

The mailing of the envelope is a story in itself, but your correspondent will keep it brief. For the past five days, all mail incoming to the roadside zoo has been intercepted by federal agents. One of them has met the postman daily and thoroughly examined his delivery before leaving it on the kitchen table for Amanda. Today, Amanda was on hand for the delivery, herself. She floated up to the postman and took the letters (bills, they turned out to be) from his hand before the CIA man knew what she was about. "Give them to me," the agent snapped, moving toward her like the head of a hammer moves toward a tack. "Certainly," said Amanda, and she thrust the envelopes in his face while simultaneously, with her other hand, she passed the flea-o-gram to the mailman. It was a sleight of hand trick older than vaudeville—and cruder. But it worked. While the CIA sleuth was checking the sausage bill for coded messages, the less sinister government employee drove innocently away with the fated envelope.

Even after the success of that hair-raising operation, the author had misgivings. Amanda assured him that the fleas would not be injured on their journey and she is probably correct. If the reader has ever tried to squash one of these evasive insects between his thumb and forefinger, he knows that their armor plating leaves them well nigh unsquashable.

Moreover, fleas can go for weeks without a bloody bite, so providing Al treats them to dinner upon arrival they won't die of hunger. Al's envelope is big and bulky so the little passengers should have sufficient oxygen. Well and good. But the envelope did not go via air, and boat mail to Suez (it's halfway around the world, you know) takes longer than Christmas. It's a hell of a trip for a flock of fleas in a plain brown envelope, particularly fleas conditioned to the excitement of circus life. Should they survive the rigors of travel, they still might die of boredom en route.

"Not likely," said Amanda, pointing out to the writer that the flea has been called "the sexual marvel of the animal kingdom." Tiny he may be, but his libido is larger than a whale's. Proportionately speaking, so is his genital equipment. Among fleas, copulation is frequent and long in duration: an average of three hours per set and up to nine hours if their passions are aroused. "Our small friends will suffer no lack of entertainment on their journey," vowed Amanda.

Bon voyage, you little fuckers.

HOROSCOPE

Jesse James was a Virgo. He became an outlaw out of desperation.

Belle Starr was an Aquarian. She became an outlaw because she was very ugly and it was the only way she could get laid.

Billy the Kid was a Sagittarian. He was an outlaw for the fun of it.

Another Roadside Attraction is also a Sagittarian. But don't jump to any conclusions.

Since Marx Marvelous was interested in religion—and since in a short time he earned the Zillers' trust if not their unqualified respect—they decided to let him in on the secret exploits of Plucky Purcell.

One evening after the zoo had closed, they pressed into his hand a bundle of sloppy letters tied with giraffe skin. "Return these in the morning," they said.

The electric lamp in Marx's garage apartment burned most of the night. It didn't take all night to read the letters, of course, but he had to stop after each epistle to reassemble his nervous system and scrape his mind off the stars.

As the reader has already been exposed to the initial Purcell letters, the author naturally will not reintroduce them. Instead, let him reproduce a slightly later correspondence perused by Marvelous that night.

Dear John Paul, Amanda & Co. (I realize Thor can't read yet, but I'm never sure about Mon Cul),

First off, I want to thank you for the holiday goodies, yum, goddamn, yum. Amanda's pastries justified their reputation —in the mouth, in the belly and in the brain. Had myself a high old time, all alone in my cubicle with fireballs in my eyes and crumbs on my lips, wow-eeee. The package disguise was perfect, too; not one of these suspicious bastards suspected a thing. Who did you get to mail the parcel from Texas for you? Nuclear Phyllis, I'll bet. Too bad she couldn't have come along in the wrappings. I would have saved the cookies for second.

I wish I could honestly say that without your gift I would've had one bad bummer of a Christmas, but, for better or worse, that was not the case. Considering the mood I've been in of late (and my position so remote from relatives and friends), it probably surprises you to learn that I had a trippy Xmas—even when I wasn't zonked on your culinary crazies—but I did. As you know, I've been fed up here at Wildcat Creek. I've been playing this monk game for three months now, and I'm worn out from the strain of it and paradoxically bored from the lack of action, not to mention the lack of nookie, that, too. Yes. Uh-huh. Worse, my disgust has multiplied daily for these conniving Catholic cutthroats. Every day, it seems, I learn of another wormy plot that's being hatched or hear another of these pious pigs bragging about a caper he once pulled. It used to make my blood boil to hear these things, but any more it just depresses me, shuts off my joy like I forgot to pay the bill and the joy company sent these monks around to disconnect my service. Let me list a few items and you'll see what I mean.

[At this point, in an epistolary style that rattles and wobbles like a loose headlamp on a Hell's Angel's hog, Plucky describes in varying degree of detail certain activities of the Society of the Felicitator which he had not previously catalogued. After wrestling with a dilemma that cost him a precious half-hour's writing time, the author has decided to delete Plucky's specific references. That the clandestine Roman Catholic order known as the Society of the Felicitator is a sinister organization engaged in espionage, intimidation and guerrilla warfare has been stated in these pages with sufficient emphasis. Should a reader desire details, or should he have a specific field of interest such as Latin America— where the Felicitate Society plays an adhesive police role in the coalition of the Church and dictatorial regimes—let him look elsewhere. Surely, now that the rosary beads have been spilled, there will be no shortage of anti-Catholic writers willing and anxious to research the Felicitators and expose their practices. That, however, is not the purpose of this report. For all the author knows, the Felicitators may be no more typical of Catholic monks than Bluebeard was typical of French husbands. While the writer has no intention of sidestepping controversial issues, he wants it made oxygen-clear that his document is not biased against any race, religion, creed, or place of natural origin. In the unsullied shadow of the giant propitious weenie, bigotry is out of the question. Only when it is relevant to the story of the Corpse will information unfavorable to a particular faith be imparted. The author aspires to be as gracious toward Rome as was Nearly Normal Jimmy toward Peking when, upon learning of the Chinese rape of Tibet, he said simply, "What do you expect of a race that invented gunpowder and hot mustard?"

And now, as the mid-afternoon gray clings to the Skagit landscape the way the shape of Transylvania clings to outdated maps of Europe, let us return to Plucky Purcell's yuletide epistle.]

Well, when I learned that my next assignment might include assassination, I really went on a bummer. I couldn't take it any more. I had about decided, a week before Xmas, to burn this viper's nest to the ground. There's only eleven monks here now, excluding head butcher Father Gutstadt and me. Rest of them are out spying, compiling portfolios on Father Groppi in Milwaukee and other "bleeding-heart Christians." Those of us left here are evidently considered hardcore hatchet men, we are the eliminators. So, I fancied I'd just set a torch to the place and eliminate the eliminators. I think I could do it at such an hour and in such a way as to catch all the jackals in their dens. I mean why not wipe them out? Their human qualities were wiped out years ago by their Roman manipulators. They're merely robots, programmed to kill. I could get rid of the cream of the Vatican's shock troops, including ex-Nazi Gutstadt, plus some valuable espionage equipment—all with one paper match. Should I do it? Could I do it?

My decision, I believe, would have been an affirmative one, and Xmas Eve would have been my target date, except that that decision was reversed or altered or, at least, postponed by the arrival at Wildcat Creek of some very charming holiday guests.

Sister Hillary, Sister Elizabeth and Brother Bruno were Canadians, members of liberal orders that for some time had been administering to Mexican migrants in California. The three of them had left Calif. on temporary assignment to survey conditions among Indians of the Northwest Coast. They had covered Oregon and the Chinook tribes of lower Washington and were at the Quinault reservation near Humptulips when they were granted furloughs to spend Christmas with their families. Well, to these people, "family" meant other brothers and sisters of the Church. They had heard about the monastery on nearby Wildcat Creek, knew that it was isolated, and decided that it might be a charitable act to come over and spend Christmas with us. They arrived bearing oranges and turkeys and three of the nicest Campbell Soup Kids smiles I'd ever seen. They looked like little black tents in their habits, and I wanted to crawl inside and smoke their smiles in my hookah. No fooling, they were lovely gentle folks. I got scared for them right away. They were the very kind of clergy that the Felicitate Society was out to suppress, the very kind, and they had wandered like giddy flies into this Venus trap and I was worried that they were in actual physical danger. But no, old Gutstadt he knew how to handle the situation, he wasn't going to arouse any suspicions, he welcomed those poor innocents with open arms. How hospitable that old pig sticker was! You'd have thought he was St. Nick himself. He was pooping plum pudding and peeing eggnog. Brought out the best brandy, cigars and wine; and after we got the radio equipment and weapons hidden, we had a merry time.

When I described the sisters and Brother Bruno as innocents, I didn't mean to imply that they were underdone do-gooders. These people had been around, they had been into some heavy trips. They had been cursed and threatened by the landowners in Calif., and Bruno had been beaten up in Mississippi once, and Sister Hillary had been shot at. They had subsisted on bad starchy food and slept on straw beds and endured all sorts of hardships. They were strong people, all three of them, and tough in a very gentle way, and beautiful.

Especially was Sister Hillary beautiful. She was like a certain early-morning image of Ingrid Bergman, photographed forever in the eye of a swan. I would watch her saying her rosary like maybe a beer can watches the ocean saying its surf, and I wanted to tiptoe up to her and kiss her cheek. She was the only woman that I've ever met that I could kiss without copping a feel. Except for my mama and sisters, of course, and I'm not too sure about my sisters.

I came onto Sister Hillary kind of rough her second day here. You see, I've spent a little time in migrant labor camps myself; I've picked the apples and grapes and hops. And I know that every Friday night in those camps there is a bingo game sponsored by the Catholic Church. Those poor impoverished, undernourished, ill-clothed chicano migrants can spend half or more of their week's pay on frigging bingo and have nothing to show for it but some tacky little plaster-of-paris Virgin Mary. I've seen it happen, just ask any fruit tramp. So I got on to Sister Hillary about it, and she acknowledged that it was a questionable practice. She wouldn't let herself speak critically of the Church, but she intimated with tender understatement that there were areas in which the Church was failing the poor, and she got very sad-eyed about it and I could tell that it was hard for her to hold back the tears. I felt so low I would have needed a twelve-foot stepladder to get into a Volkswagen.

Christmas Eve, Father Gutstadt said a midnight mass. I haven't had much experience with such entertainments, but as far as I could tell he did a pretty good job. Except that Gutstadt's Latin was even more dense than his English. His nouns were like cannonballs and his verbs, well it would have taken two men and a boy to carry one. It must have been the heaviest mass on record, a massive mass, if you'll excuse me. It's a wonder we didn't sink through the earth from the weight of it. Afterwards, Sister Hillary and I went outside to look for the Star of the East. It was a mild night and we sat on a log, star-gazing. A piece of moonlight fell through the clouds and hit her wedding band. I remembered then that she was married to Jesus Christ. She was married to a concept of universal love and brotherhood, not intellectually committed to it or emotionally attracted to it, but *married* to it; she lived with it and it fucked her and filled her with itself and she was part of it and one with it, in private and in public, and for it she lived in poverty and worked long hours and wore unbecoming clothing and risked her very life. She was the blushing bride of Love; the wife who sleeps in the bed of Peace and washes its shorts and packs its lunch. Corny and insane, but by damn, *true*. She sat on that mossy log in movie-star radiance, and moonbeams flocked around her like birds around Saint Francis. It was damn near a miracle.

At that moment it became clear to me how my own thinking was distorted. I was filled with hate and disgust for Catholicism, I had progressed from its passive detractor to its active enemy. I dreamed of its fall, I conjured in visions the collapse of its tyranny. But I could not have been thinking of the whole of Catholicism because Sister Hillary was a part of that whole; Sister Hillary and hundreds—thousands —like her. What of them, what of these beings of goodness and courage? The history of the Catholic Church is written on charred pages splashed with gore. It is a history of inquisitions and genocides, of purges and perversions, of ravings and razings. Yes, but through those same bloody pages walk parades of saints playing their celestial radios and sowing their sparkles of love. What of the great enlightened souls zonked out on the Infinite, what of the saints so high on

Divine Energy that they kissed those who censured them
and blessed those who put them to death? What of the
Catholic Christian Buddhas and Roman Hindu Vishnus whose
melted hearts are the true gold of Rome? It occurred to me
that Catholicism is a duality of good and evil, that it is a
microcosm of secular society. One cannot hate society, because within society there are loving and lovable individuals.
Similarly, it wasn't the Church I hated, because the Church
contained the bravery and enlightenment of many individual priests and nuns and saints.

The fact is, what I hated in the Church was what I hated
in society. Namely, authoritarians. Power freaks. Rigid dog-
matists. Those greedy, underloved, undersexed twits who
want to run everything. While the rest of us are busy living
—busy tasting and testing and hugging and kissing and
goofing and growing—they are busy taking over. Soon their
sour tentacles are around everything: our governments, our
economies, our schools, our publications, our arts and our
religious institutions. Men who lust for power, who are addicted to laws and other unhealthy abstractions, who long
to govern and lead and censor and order and reward and
punish; those men are the turds of Moloch, men who don't
know how to love, men who are sickly afraid of death and
therefore are afraid of life: they fear all that is chaotic and
unruly and free-moving and changing—thus, as Amanda has
said, they fear nature and fear life itself, they deny life and
in so doing deny God. They are presidents and governors and
mayors and generals and police officials and chairmen-of-the-
boards. They are crafty cardinals and fat bishops and mean
old monsignor masturbators. They are the most frightened
and most frightening mammals who prowl the planet; love-
less, anal-compulsive control-freak authoritarians, and they
are destroying everything that is wise and beautiful and
free. And the most enormous ironic perversion is how they
destroy in the name of Christ who is peace and God who is
love.

Authority is the most damaging trauma to which the
psyche is subjected between birth and death. Isn't that true,
Amanda? Nobody likes authority. You might object that authoritarians must like it, but they don't, they merely resort to
it in order to avenge themselves on those who have imposed
it on them. From the first moment a fresh new human hears

the command, "Stop that or Daddy spank," his outraged subconscious begins to plot revenge. Often, his revenge is mis-
directed and merely perpetuates the sad old cycle of
authority-rebellion; sometimes it leads to activity that is
characterized as criminal or insane. It was leading me to
destructive behavior, I could see that. It's reactions like mine
that give anarchy a bad name.

So, I made a decision that night in the Xmas moonshine.
I decided that if the Church could produce people like Sister
Hillary and her pals, and if they, however blindly, could
serve the Church, then the Church must still be capable of
being a mighty force for good. Does that make sense? And
if the Church has all this potential magic locked up in its
velvet heart, there must be a way to release it. Here I was,
non-Catholic anti-Catholic Plucky Purcell, cast with the most
extreme extension of the anti-life element of Roman authority. Maybe, just maybe, there was something I could do.
What? Hell, I don't know. But maybe something would turn
up, maybe there would be an unexpected opportunity to
help shift the weight of Catholicism toward Sister Hillary's
side. Maybe I could do something more positive than cre-
mating a dozen treacherous monks. At least it wouldn't hurt
to stick around a while longer and find out. In event of failure, I could always turn back to the torch.

What I'm trying to say, gang, is don't bother to put any
beer on ice. I'm going to be at Wildcat Creek for a few more
months. I may not survive the ordeal, but wouldn't it be a
splendidly compensating irony should randy old Purcell meet
his end as the result of a promise made silently to a virgin
nun?

Thanks again for the cosmic cookies. You will be rewarded.
But in the next life, as is customary among us Christians. Hee
hee. Good luck with your sausages, dead and breathing.

Brother Dallas

****

The next three or four letters were less dramatic. Purcell's
new cause produced nothing immediately tangible. The only
major development at Wildcat Creek was in the way of sexual release. Plucky met a fifteen-year-old Quinault Indian
girl who lived about three miles from the monastery in a

cabin with her alcoholic grandfather. Their subsequent friendship made for some tangy descriptive passages in Plucky's correspondence. Otherwise, there was little more than further cataloguing of the Felicitate Society's nefarious activities. Despite his obvious pleasure in his underage paramour, Purcell grew bored again. Various schemes for escape were outlined.

Purcell's waning enthusiasm was not transferred to Marx Marvelous. Marx remained steadfastly goggle-eyed as he trembled through the nearly illegible chronicles. At the bottom of the pile, stuck to the giraffe skin by the deteriorating mucilage on its flap, he found the thinnest envelope in the bunch. Marvelous anticipated an anticlimax. He was wrong.

Scrawled across a Tootsie Roll wrapper with a marking pencil was the following announcement:

"Just received my new assignment. In ten days I depart for the Vatican to serve as karate instructor to the Swiss Guard."

"You don't eat meat," observed Marx Marvelous. (This was a week after the reading of Purcell's letters and the ambivalent young scientist could at last talk of something else.)

"No, I do not," said Amanda.

"John Paul eats meat."

"That he does. He considers it man's evolutionary duty to devour other species. My husband will never kill anything he is not prepared to eat."

"That's a pretty good practice," admitted Marx Marvelous. "If everyone cultivated that habit there would be fewer murders and no war."

"Or a boom in cannibals," said Amanda. Beneath the big spruce, she and Mon Cul were tossing a fluorescent red rubber football. The baboon's style reminded Marx of a certain pro quarterback he'd seen on television.

"But *you* don't touch meat."

"Oh, I touch meat all the time," said Amanda coyly. She

lowered her lashes and jived her tongue along the brim of her lip.

Marvelous blushed. "You know what I mean."

"Yes," laughed Amanda. "I don't *ingest* meat. Those teachers whom I most admire set that example for me eons ago."

"The cow became a sacred symbol to the Hindu because it gave milk and chops and hides," said Marx Marvelous. And he went on to debunk the spiritual origins of vegetarianism. The author relayed Marx's argument earlier, as the attentive reader surely recalls. Amanda made no immediate response (she glided out past the bowlegged rooster's pen to pull down a pass from Mon Cul), but clearly her vegetarian sentiments suffered a jolt.

At twilight, Amanda went into trance. She returned in time for dinner. "You are right, Marx Marvelous," she announced. "Spiritually, it is as proper to eat an animal as a plant."

"Well, I'll be damned," said Marvelous with a smug chuckle. "You saw the light. Here, you're in for a treat." He passed the platter of sausages.

"No," refused Amanda. "I still shall eat no meat. Carnivorousness may be karmically acceptable but stockyards are not. Besides, when an animal is killed, it is usually in a state of panic or fright. Fright releases in a mammal certain hormones which swamp the blood and penetrate the flesh. When you eat meat, you eat the animal's fear. I want as little fear in my system as possible." She helped herself to the dandelion buds.

Marvelous was exasperated. "But you did say now that spiritually it's all right to eat meat."

"Of course," said Amanda. "At the higher levels of consciousness all things are one anyway. There is no difference between animal, vegetable and mineral. Everything just blends together in energy and light."

Marx Marvelous tried to imagine the sausages in god-state, but though they were as plump and passive as little Buddhas, he could not handle the image. "Pass the mustard," he said.

The June morning, thin and gray, arched over Skagit Valley like a plucked eyebrow. At the mailbox of the Capt. Kendrick Memorial Hot Dog Wildlife Preserve, the postman seemed to linger longer than he did usually. This triggered a faradism of excitement in the roadhouse for whether he expressed it or not, each adult human inhabitant of the Kendrick Memorial was anxiously awaiting word from the Vatican. Plucky Purcell at home with the Pope. A cozy picture.

Ziller, who had been polishing the tsetse fly, was first to the letter box. He returned, alas, with forced nonchalance, bearing only the water bill, the June issue of *Al's Journal of Lepidoptera* and Amanda's current selection from the Animal Cracker of the Month Club.

"Very well, Professor Marvelous," said Amanda, "you have been with us for a month. Have you figured out what mysterious functions John Paul and I are performing here on our 'psychic frontier'?" She asked the question without looking up from the microscope beneath the lens of which she was sewing a tiny suit-of-lights for a matador flea.

"Are you kidding? How could I figure out what you're up to when you're so damned secretive? What an outgoing couple! Sometimes I feel like I'm living with Greta Garbo and Howard Hughes, if you can imagine Howard Hughes marrying Greta Garbo and opening a roadside zoo. You and Ziller disappear into your sanctuaries for hours every day. I hear sounds, smell odors—all very strange, none very revealing."

"You must have *some* ideas about our activities."

"Oh, I do. You bet I do."

"Then tell me one. Please." He adored the way she said "please." It was like listening to an alligator bite into a Hollywood bed.

"Okay, I'll tell you one: freedom. I believe that you people, among other things, are obsessed with recovering a lost model of existence, a total life-style in which there are no boundaries between object and subject, between natural and supernatural, between waking and dreaming. It's involved somehow in a return to a consanguinity of life and art, life and nature, life and religion—a ritualistic, mythic level of living which whole societies once experienced in common. The object of your rituals, I believe, is to break free of the conventions that have chained man to certain cliché images and predictable responses, that have narrowed pitifully—in your opinion, at least—the range of his experience."

Amanda whistled with admiration, although due to her crooked teeth she did not whistle well. It was more of a blow. "O my O my," she blew admiringly. "How do you manage to talk like that in clear weather. For me, it would take the most rambunctious thunderstorm these parts have ever seen. It would play hell with the pea fields. Lightning might strike the big sausage. In which case it wouldn't be worth it, no matter what I said."

Marvelous didn't fully understand. "I don't imagine it storms much in this climate," he noted. "But do you admit there's truth in my observations?" The "but" that crouched like a strange sailor in the doorway of his second sentence did not in any way tie his first remark to his second one. It was a "but" more ornamental than conjunctional.

"A speech as fancy as that one doesn't have to have truth in it," said Amanda, busily sewing. "It's like asking if there's truth in the Imperial Russian Easter eggs." Without looking up from the microscope she could tell Marx was disappointed with her reply, so she added, "I will admit to a lifelong and regular fascination with freedom. Why do you suppose that is?"

"Maybe you're in rapport with William Blake," offered Marvelous. "Blake once wrote, 'I must invent my own systems or else be enslaved by other men's'."

"Not to get your mind back on the Vatican and Christianity," said Amanda (who, as curious as she might be, was nevertheless showing signs of weariness with all this hubbub about religion), "but our friend Plucky Purcell is an admirer of William Blake. Plucky says one *has* to admire a man who for 175 years can get away with rhyming 'eye' and 'symmetry.'"

While awaiting news from the Mad Pluck at the Holy See, Amanda herself had an encounter with the Christian ethos. Let Marx Marvelous tell it.

Through the loosest of verbal agreements, I am now manager of the Zillers' roadside zoo. My duties have not been formally defined, but they consist chiefly of explaining to customers why we serve nothing but hot dogs and juice. I've become quite efficient at preparing our wares and were it not for the troublesome explanations I could refuel a couple dozen tourists in about five minutes. In between slipping weenies into buns—and indulging the Freudian fantasies concomitant to such occupation—I lecture on the attractions of our establishment. My San Franciso garter snake lecture includes a pitch for conservation and is popular with little old ladies; my talk on Glossina palpalis, the African tsetse fly, is fraught with allusions to bloodsucking jaws and headachy natives who drop off into eternal slumbers, although in fairness to scientific findings—and to Amanda's fondness for insects (indeed, for all living things)—I add that the tsetse fly is not poisonous but merely a communicator of infected parasites and that both the prevalence and severity of sleeping sickness have been greatly exaggerated. Despite the anticlimax, the kids enjoy the tsetse fly talk.

I'm not as adept with the fleas as I'd like to be. The chariot races I stage never stay on course. Invariably, they end in embarrassing if not dangerous collisions. I am pleased to report, however, that John Paul has only slightly better results. Amanda alone is capable of harnessing the full strength and concentration of the fleas, of causing them to hop with precision, with poetry, with passion and wit.

The Zillers spend more time downstairs in the zoo-cafe than I had anticipated they might. Any suspicions I harbored that the zoo was merely their source of funds—an economic ploy in which they had little real interest—have evaporated. What now appears fact is that Amanda and John Paul, whatever their private pursuits here, are more than a trace concerned about the tourists who stop by. They deliberately interact with the customers, always—I think

—with a definite goal in mind, although they move with such subtlety, the Zillers, that I could not hope to prove premeditation of any kind. Yet, there they are: John Paul softly playing one of his flutes or drums, condescending to make small talk that gradually metamorphoses into some vigorously curving and folding monologue that embraces in its dark syntax both coasts of Africa (or is it India?): Amanda charming young and old with the tone of her aliveness.

There are times when, for monetary reasons, I would prefer the Zillers remain upstairs or out back in the grove. Their effect on customers is not always positive. In fact, I would estimate that 30 or 35 per cent of the motorists who stop at the Kendrick Memorial retreat shortly thereafter in fear or disgust. They're wearing their long-billed toyo caps and their canvas yachting shoes, they're packing their travelers checks and their Enco maps, they've got their litter bags and their first-aid kits; they are equipped and ready, don't you know, for the caprices of the open road. But oh heavens, they hadn't prepared for that hussy in her gypsy colors, for that tall man with the bone in his nose; not here, not in the gentle croplands of northwestern Washington; how unexpected, how . . . "well, frankly, we wouldn't trust the food in a place like this." One minute Amanda will be chatting informatively about fleas and tsetse flies, and the next (as if she used the habits of insects as parables of human behavior), she will be talking about life and the potentiality of living it. There are men who do not take off and leave their departments in the hands of incompetents for two whole weeks in order to be reminded in some ding-a-ling little roadside dive of the greater possibilities of existence. They stop for coffee and feel cheated if served the meaning of meaning instead.

On the whole, however, the Zillers' impact on our visitors is stimulating if a bit uncommon. Sometimes it is the customer himself who provides the thrust of the exchange. Like, for example, what happened today when a Protestant minister dropped by. As the preacher looked over our snakes (thinking God knows what serpentine thoughts about Eve and her herpetological humdingery in Eden), Amanda floated up and engaged him in conversation. It was five minutes or more before I could get away from the counter, but when I had the chance I moved in close. That was one exchange I did

*not want to miss. A three-dogs-with-everything motorcyclist
(a three-dog knight?) soon arrived so I didn't have long to
linger, but while I was in hearing distance, I recorded the
following dialogue.*

MINISTER: *No, I had no connection with the military forces
in Vietnam. I was a civilian missionary. My wife
and I ministered to the Bahnar tribesmen. The
Bahnar are a primitive people and were not involved politically in the war.*

AMANDA: *How did you enjoy the Bahnar?*

MINISTER: *We weren't there to enjoy them. We were there
to help them. But they were very friendly to
us, if that's what you meant. The Bahnar Vietna-
mese are basically fine, simple folks. Of course
they had some extremely backward ideas.*

AMANDA: *Could you please give me an example?*

MINISTER: *Well, for example, your Bahnar believed that
good souls go live under the earth when they
die and bad souls go live in the sky. You can see
what that implies. They thought Heaven was
down and Hell was up.*

AMANDA: *But you changed all that?*

MINISTER: *Oh, yes. Of course. That's what we were there
for. We taught them it was just the other way
around.*

It was a peekaboo summer. The sun was in and out like
Mickey Rooney. One day the Puget wind would lug mono-
liths of quartz in from the Pacific and leave them lying about
all over the sky. The next day, as if some fastidious crew of
giants had worked through the night, there wouldn't be a
boulder cloud in sight; the atmosphere would be high, wide
and blue; sunlight would salt the turgid old sloughs and the
air would be so warm and still you could hear a woodpecker
for three miles and a squirrel for two. Hear them above the
pea-field tractors, hear them above the Freeway traffic even.

The sunny side was up on the Thursday afternoon that Marx Marvelous squatted (keeping his hemorrhoids safely aloft) beside John Paul Ziller in the parking lot. The Capt. Kendrick Memorial etc. closed every Thursday, and on this day off Ziller had been working on the building. Amanda had wanted to go inner-tubing on the river, but Ziller had asked her to wait a couple of hours while he performed some carpentry that seemed to have less to do with the roadhouse's function than with its identity. The edifice was in a constant state of change. It seemed to lollop and dive through space, to bloom each fortnight into a new experience of extent, color, mass and direction.

Maybe scientists and artists can never fully understand each other's pursuits, thought Marvelous, squatting beside the resting Ziller. The grape-thick spheroids that John Paul had just added to the building seemed to Marvelous to be entirely unnecessary, a waste of energy and material. He pondered them in vain. Would he ever fathom the mind of this man? "John Paul," he asked, "didn't you once do a painting on the inside of a parachute? And then repack the chute? So that the only way anyone could enjoy your painting was to jump out of an airplane and look up at it on the way down? What was the purpose of that?"

Ziller wiped his dark brow with a square of Nigerian cotton. He gazed long across the tidal flats the way an aborigine scans for game. "I wanted to test the art lover's commitment," he answered with unexpected straightforwardness. "It might be desirable for museums and galleries to devise a similar test."

"In that case there would be damn few visitors to museums and galleries," Marx suggested.

"Are you more interested in quantity than quality? In the laboratory, isn't one good catalyst preferable to dozens of substances that produce unsatisfactory reactions or no reactions at all?"

"I can see your point, I guess," said Marx. "Did anyone ever go to the trouble to look at your painting?"

"Oh yes. A young Italian contessa paid me five hundred dollars for the privilege."

"And what was her reaction?"

"I don't know," said Ziller. "The chute failed to open."

The sun sounded its alarm at the two men, the one of

them stroking his chin in befuddlement, the other gazing
toward the distant Chinese outcroppings, a smile sliding across
his face the way a Louisiana black snake slides across a
cemetery lawn. The sun's alarm went off in their brains. In a
matter of minutes, the flesh of Marx Marvelous would pink-
en. Tropic treks had awarded Ziller a quantum of immunity,
but he, too, was completely aware of the beam of heat.

"John Paul, 'source' is a word that people associate with
you. You are forever seeking out your sources." Marx
squinted at the white blur of sun. "Now as you must know,
solar radiation is the basic source of life. The rays of the sun
are converted through photosynthesis into chemical bonds
responsible for producing the carbohydrates and other tissue
components whose energies directly maintain the existence
of both plants and animals. Solar radiation is the source of all
biological energy, and ultimately it is the source of you."

Marvelous paused. Ziller nodded ever so slightly and continued staring into the west.

"You do see what I'm getting at," Marx went on. "If you
persist in returning to your sources, then sooner or later you'll
have to go back to the sun."

Marx meant it more or less as a joke, but Ziller accepted it
at face value. "Yes," he said through his arsenal of teeth.
"Returning to sunlight is an inevitability that I've been reckoning with."

His eyes kept patrolling the horizon, as if he expected
something of great interest to appear there. Something . . .
or someone. Could Ziller, do you suppose, have been antici-
pating the Corpse? No, that couldn't be. Amanda is the
clairvoyant. Besides, the Corpse came from the opposite
direction.

Because he was a fugitive from an alimony decree, Marx
Marvelous was nervous about visiting Mount Vernon and
Seattle. If his friends had any illegal botanical matter on
their persons—as they sometimes did when they went into
town—he was doubly apprehensive. He practically walked

with his head in a swivel. Consequently, he was soon the
recipient of what might be called

AMANDA'S UNIVERSAL ADVICE FOR PARANOICS

"About those men who are following you around and
watching your house at nights: don't be alarmed. Try to think
of them as talent scouts from Hollywood."

"It's here," announced Amanda.

"*Ombedoo gigi?*" said John Paul. "Pardon?" He opened his
eyes with jungle swiftness and rolled over to face his wife.
The date was July 5 and the Zillers had slept quite late, having on the previous day entertained hundreds more customers
than normal and dispensed a record number of hot dogs.

"It has arrived," said Amanda. "I can feel it." She bounced
from bed and was halfway down the stairs, trailing her silver
robe behind her, when she met Marx Marvelous. Had it not
been for the item he was fetching, had it not been for the
charisma of the letter in his paw, Marvelous surely would
have seized her. Seeing her nude for the first time—and
seeing her obvious pleasure at being seen—bronco desire
bucked again in his glands, yippie! Sexuality ringed Amanda
the way a penumbra rings a shadow. She became aware of
his checkered erection in the manner that Salvador Dali
became aware of the rhinoceros horn (calling it "the perfect
logarithmic spiral"). She longed to collar it with her fingers,
but when she reached out for it Marvelous extended the letter and her hand closed on it instead.

In the outer circle of postmark were the words "Città del
Vaticano." The stamp bore the inscription "Poste Vaticane."
The handwriting was the mortal imprint of L. Westminster
"Plucky" Purcell.

Leaving poor Marx Marvelous alone on the steps with his
hard-on, Amanda dashed back to the bedroom. "It *is* here,"
she said. "I knew it had arrived." She tossed the letter onto
the bed. "Read it to me while I dress."

"So, Brother Dallas has contacted us at long last," said Ziller calmly. He slit the envelope with a fingernail and spread its contents on the bedspread before him the way a soothsayer might spread the entrails of a fowl.

"Wait," said Amanda, pulling on her panties. "I'll call Marx Marvelous. You can read it to him as well."

She did. And he did. And this is how it went.

Dear Far-away Friends,

As you no doubt have determined, I am writing from the Vatican. Ho-hum. What can I say? I took one look at this place and surrendered. Just gave up.

What earthly difference could it make whether my ambition was to help destroy the Church or help reform it. Can you imagine an ant trying to decide whether to remodel Chicago or tear it down? It's the same. If only you had been permitted to write and alert me to the delusions I was suffering.

From the air, Vatican City looked like a marble Monopoly set. The Church owned all the property from Boardwalk to Illinois Avenue, had three hotels on every lot, and no matter how often it tossed the dice you just knew it would never land on Go to Jail, it would be forever passing Go and collecting $200. From the air, Vatican City looked also like a street dance to which the libraries of New York and Philadelphia had been exclusively invited, those sooty old neo-classical stone depositories paired off in a dignified promenade, too stiff any more to swing their partners, their voices too hollow with centuries of library hush to manage even the most perfunctory do-si-do. Vatican City looked like a Disneyland for zombies and it looked like a drag.

Later I stood in St. Peter's Square with the enormous old Basilica bell-donging above me and the pageantry breaking in velvet waves around me and somewhere in the jeweled bowels of his castle the Pope reading the Italian edition of the *Wall Street Journal* while eating caviar with a golden fork —and I surrendered. What's the use? A guy might see possibilities of effective action when he is up against a small band of ecclesiastical Nazis at Wildcat Creek Monastery, but here at the home office, well, it's just too big and too wealthy and too entrenched and too powerful. Why bother? Maybe shooting peas at the sun is someone's idea of a fine poetic gesture but it's a bore to me. So the Roman Catholic Church is out to Catholicize the world. What of it? Communism is out to Communize the world and Capitalism is out to Capitalize the world. Let them fight it out among themselves. I've got life to live and I can't be bothered. Now that I think about it, I guess that has been your philosophy all along. Oh well. I'm slow to learn.

At any rate, it's one hell of a grand joke, me being here, me working at the Vatican in an official and privileged position. So I decided I'd just relax and enjoy the joke and play it for all it's worth.

A couple of days after I arrived, however, I did discover something that inspired a final twitch of hope, that proved to me the Church was not entirely invulnerable. It wasn't the court of law or the jail that sits right off St. Peter's Square. Although I didn't realize that the Vatican maintained those institutions, I guess I've associated courts and jails with churches for so long that the presence of them at the Holy See didn't come as any great surprise. No, the real chink in the churchly armor is something else. It's the time clocks. In 1956, forty time clocks were installed in Vatican offices. Today, there are about sixty. The official explanation of the time-control system was that it was "to end late arrivals and early departures by staff members of Vatican bureaus and to regulate absences." The only dudes who are exempt from punching in and out are, according to the handbook, "the Cardinal Secretaries of Congregations, the Episcopal heads of other offices, and the Swiss Guard." (Of course, we Felicitate Brothers are also exempt but then we aren't publicly acknowledged as an existing order.) Now I ask you, when a religion has to make its own priests punch a clock, when it so much as admits that its own oath-bound holy fathers have been sneaking off the job early, coming in late and playing hooky, wouldn't you say that that religion has a soft white underbelly? Can you imagine Jesus punching a clock? If he had, would it have prevented his "early departure"?

They claim their church is built on a rock, but it looks to me like its foundation isn't all that solid. I mean, show me a religion with time clocks and I'll show you a religion that has shot its spiritual wad. Give me a long enough lever and a place to stand and I'll topple it.

["Purcell won't have to topple it," interrupted Marx Marvelous. "It obviously is toppling on its own accord."]

So far, no one has handed me a crowbar or shown me a spot to push, and I'm not really expecting to budge this colossus, but every time I pass one of those clocks I smile with the comforting knowledge that God's biggest billy club has a crack in it.

Things are changing here at the home office and a lot of my brothers are shocked, but I don't know whether the changes are for the better or worse. For one thing, the Pope is toning down the pomp. Not long ago, he ordered cardinals, bishops and monsignors to prune much of the regal splendor from their dress. He threw out red shoes, silver shoe buckles, galerum hats, sashes, tassels, capes and ermine-trimmed cloaks. His instructions also allow the title "monsignor" to be used in addressing a cardinal or bishop instead of "eminence" or "excellency." The result is, things aren't as fancy around here as they used to be. However, they are still far from plain. There is gold everywhere, and silver and precious gems and long limousines and valuable art. They could unload just a third of this treasure and feed every hungry mouth in Europe for the rest of the century. And, you may have noticed, the Pope didn't cut any of the frills from his personal wardrobe.

Couple years back, a papal decree was issued to clean up the roster of venerable saints. More than forty of the dudes were dropped from the liturgical calendar, mostly because they never existed in the first place but were merely the invention of fanatics and souvenir salesmen. Among those that got the ax was St. Christopher, the blessed buddy of cruise-ship casanovas, astronauts and six-day bicycle racers.

Scuttlebutt down in the catacombs is that a lot of powerful Catholics, including those responsible for the Society of the Felicitator, are unhappy about those reforms. However, the word is the Pope had to enact them because criticism of ostentation and hypocrisy in the Church has grown so voracious.

[At this point, Marx Marvelous intruded again to contend that such reforms were desperate last-ditch efforts to revive a dying institution. Amanda, who was pinning violets in her hair, silenced Marx with a special look. Sometimes our scientist friend gets carried away.]

Here I am, scribbling a hundred words a minute about internal problems of the Catholic Church and you guys probably couldn't care less. Sorry if I'm boring you but, you know, ever since the freak accident that turned me into Brother Dallas I've found myself getting hung up on churchly matters. It'll pass. I keep telling myself that it'll pass. Someday I'll be a plucky dope dealer again, ministering to my own stoned flock.

Meanwhile, I'm enjoying a unique position, a job shared by no living soul on this planet. Assuming that you've got at least a peapod of curiosity about it, I'll scribble on.

Up until several years ago, the Vatican maintained four branches of military or police (four *known* branches, that is: don't forget the undercover Felicitators). Three of these corps, the Palatine Guard, the Noble Guard and the Gendarmery were flat out law-and-order bad asses. They protected the security of the Holy See with rifles, revolvers, cannon, machine guns and other tools of the trade. If an appreciable number of Catholics saw anything incongruous about a religious mission bristling with weapons, they pretended that cannon were canon and didn't let on. Until just recently. Then, all of a sudden, the implications of holy police were being discussed so widely that the Pope, to head off further dissent, was forced to make his most drastic reform to date. With a well-timed sweep of his ringed fingers, he disbanded the Palatine Guard, Noble Guard and Gendarmery.

In so doing, he increased the power and presence of the Felicitate Society. Whereas once we were mainly troubleshooters abroad, we now swarm in the shadow of the golden throne itself. The smiling jerk who mixes your chocolate sundae in the Vatican soda shoppe may be a master of poisons, the same 007 who slipped Adlai Stevenson his London heart attack pill. The enthralled tourist you see grinding his movie camera at the Gate of Saint Anne may be photographing potential troublemakers for closed circuit TV. I write "may" because I myself don't really know.

All I know is my own job here, and my job is involved with that military corps that the Pope did not dissolve—the ancient and colorful Swiss Guard. The fifty-six dudes in the

Swiss Guard strut around in pantaloons and leggings of blue, red and yellow; silver breastplates and medieval helmets. They are armed only with fifteenth-century halberds, which are long pole-like weapons with ax blades and spiked points. As you must have gathered, they are mainly a showpiece. Or they *were*. Since all other papal soldiers have been fired, and since the Felicitate Society, however strong its presence, must work in secrecy—not only from the public but from most Vaticanians as well—the burden of defending Vatican City has fallen hard on the fancy shoulders of these overgrown Swiss choirboys.

Now, with dissension so rampant within the Church today, and with outside opposition stronger than it has been in decades, the Pope and his pals are theoretically in unusual danger. (On a visit to Asia last year, the Pope required a security force twelve thousand strong and even then he was almost assassinated in Manila.) The threat of demonstrations of one sort or another is constant. So, it is conceivable that the Swiss Guard will be seeing action soon, even if that action consists only of clearing St. Peter's Square of sit-in protesters. Imagine how messy it would look in the press—and in the eyes of pilgrims and tourists—if these favorite picturesque toy soldiers are forced to go hacking and stabbing with their almost comical Renaissance halberds. It would seem especially nasty if the victims of the poleaxes were nonviolent demonstrators. How much cleaner and quieter it would be if, with a few quick, almost unobtrusive hand motions a Swiss Guardsman could snap a spine or shut tight a throat. Maintain the old decorum with a minimum of blood and fuss. It is toward that end that the Swiss Guard is learning karate. Yours truly is its honorable mentor.

I live in a cell just off the karate training room two levels down in the restricted catacombs. I'm adjacent to the College of Cardinals' private rifle range and directly below the VIP cafeteria where Gurdjieff once shared a pizza with Mary Baker Eddy. Below me, the third-level catacombs are really top secret, but as an agent of Felicitate I have pretty much the run of the place. I can get into areas where even the Swiss Guard is not allowed. While trying not to arouse suspicions, I have been poking around in the various bedrock chambers down here at every opportunity. Following are listed some of my more interesting discoveries.

1. *Erotic Art.* Naturally, I list this first. Drool, drool. There are stacks and stacks of paintings and squads of sculptures salted away down here. Many are in exile from public perception merely because they depict men and women in their birthday suits, but some have come by their banishment more deservingly. There is a magnificent Rembrandt, for example, that portrays a couple balling in a hay field. I sneeze and scratch with vicarious pleasure just to glance at it.

2. *Dead Sea Scrolls.* As I understand it, when the Dead Sea Scrolls were unearthed in the late forties and early fifties, some were purchased by Hebrew University, others by the archbishop of the Syrian Orthodox Church in Jerusalem. The archbishop (a Catholic, natch) later sold his scrolls to Hebrew University (does Hebe U. have a football team or aren't they allowed to play with pigskin?), but evidently not before culling those which might contradict traditional religious beliefs or embarrass Catholic dogma. Moreover, some of the Hebrew U. scrolls were processed at the Vatican Library, where additional editing might have taken place. Hidden in the catacombs, along with other old manuscripts and documents that for one reason or another must be too dangerous for inclusion in the 500,000-volume Vatican Library, are Dead Sea fragments whose contents are a mystery to all but a powerful few. These mysterious documents are guarded day and night by a quartet of blind nuns who know them only by touch.

3. *Pharmaceutical Taboos.* Since Catholic missionaries often were the first white men to have contact with primitive cultures, particularly in Africa and the New World, they were in an excellent position to examine—unhampered by scientific proponents of free inquiry—the folk medicines and drug sacraments employed by various tribes. In the process, they concealed a great deal of pharmaceutical information, and were able in some cases to scare the natives into abandoning use of natural drugs. I have found in the catacomb drug room, samples of peyote, yajé and psilocybic mushrooms along with documents dating from 1510 describing their "demonic" effects, plus countless jars of other blacklisted botanical materials containing God knows what lightning-flavored molecules offering God-knows what incredible insights and flashes, oh baby, my mind sputters to consider it. Also locked up in the chamber of pharmacological subversives are native con-

traception potions, any or all of which might be safer and more effective than the Pill. Medical science knows nothing of them. Guess why they were suppressed.

4. *Easter Island Plaques.* When the first white explorers landed on Easter Island, each of the giant stone heads there had at its base an inscribed plaque that presumably explained the significance of the statue. It is widely documented that French Catholic priests destroyed these plaques —for what reasons we may only surmise—thereby depriving science of the essential keys in the most stupendous of anthropological enigmas. Who knows what an Easter Island plaque might have revealed about the stone heads, the mysterious people who built them, about the origins of man. All of the plaques were not destroyed, however, for there are three or four of them locked up here with totems, fetishes and other primitive knickknacks in a dusty chamber. Wish I could smuggle one out to the experts at the Laboratory of Obsolete Impulses because the alphabet used in inscribing the plaques is totally unfamiliar to me. Except that, come to think of it, it does resemble fairly closely that faint writing on the palm of Amanda's hand.

There are additional catacomb chambers through whose barred doorways I can detect the nasty evil glitter of silver and gold, and there is at least one room that is permanently sealed. I'm going to continue my snooping. Should I come across any startling stashes I'll inform you in my next letter. Meanwhile, pray that my employers don't learn that I'm not Brother Dallas, because that old Vatican jailhouse looks as mean as any I've seen in the dog lands of Mexico.

Oh yes, while I think of it, John Paul, our mutual acquaintance George O. Supper has a studio not far from here. George is the first pop artist to win the *Prix de Rome* and he'll be in Italy all summer. Sunday, I'm going to slip into my civilian spy suit and pay him a call. George should have a lot of gossip about the New York art crowd, and maybe he'll have the grace to direct me to a good whorehouse. Happy zoo-keeping, and don't forget those prayers.

Yrs. in His Holy Name,
Plucky P.

* * * * * * * *

Marx Marvelous was beside himself. Double redheaded wow! Purcell's letter he took as a personal triumph, an academic accolade long overdue. It offered further proof, did it not, that the largest church in Christendom has been stilt-walking over quicksand for ages? Now Marvelous, having been recently engaged in religious research, was, even prior to the reading of Plucky's Wildcat Creek epistles, informed of the black side of churchly history. He was not ignorant of a single purge; no conquest, no Vatican intrigue had escaped his notice. But the comparative trifles that the Mad Pluck exposed seemed so instant, so direct that they excited him as secondary historical sources never could.

The indiscretions itemized by Purcell were, so it seemed to Marvelous, indications of increasing Christian entropy. To wit: Christianity has gradually lost spiritual energy over the centuries, only to replace it with political and economic energy. That imbalance has warped the religious structure and although it has heightened its physical force it has pushed its spiritual potential toward zero. Political and/or economic power create frictional resistance to the natural flow of love. In the case of the Church, such friction has resulted in an engine that has considerable momentum but fails to generate salvation.

Yes, Purcell's findings did a lot to bolster Marx's theory, and awarded the dropout thinker new hopes for the successful projection of future religious systems. On and on, Marvelous jabbered about it, jabbering to John Paul as the magician tied his loincloth, jabbering to Amanda until . . . he noticed the big green tears in her eyes.

Had Purcell's disclosures upset her, poor angel? Had Marx's interpretations, underscoring as they did the decadence of our religious heritage, depressed her? No, it wasn't that. While looking out the bedroom window, Amanda had spotted—just below the southern nub of the giant benevolent weenie—a monarch butterfly, the first she'd seen in a year.

Can we, with a straight face, regard it as an omen?

"I understand," said Marx Marvelous, "that as far as you are concerned the most important thing in life is style."

Amanda sighed. She was being challenged again. Worse, her Wednesday bread-baking was being interrupted. As usual, she forgave the intrusion. "Marx Marvelous is in the process of shedding values," she reasoned, "and as the old values are discarded his mind moves him closer and closer to questions of absolute meaning." She preferred to think that was the case, rather than that Marx Marvelous was simply another intellectual tight-ass smugly ripping at every cosmic curtain to expose the specter of dank feminine (irrational!!!) mysticism that he is certain lurks behind it. She preferred not to link her zoo manager with those *Time* magazine types who regard every transcendental experience as some sort of Halloween prank, but who grow as unctuous as sperm whales when they run into a bishop at a cocktail party.

Speaking on his own account, Marvelous still would admit to no interest in the "meaning of meaning." "Purpose is not a scientific concern," he would insist. "You see those stars up there—there is no reason for me to question their purpose or to speculate on their meaning. The age, position, size, velocity, distance from the Earth and chemical composition is the only information I desire about a star. Any additional data are destined to be vague and hesitating in comparison. When I learn what an object consists of and how it behaves, my curiosity about that object has very largely been satisfied."

Yes, Marx purported himself to be an objective man in an objective environment. He liked to assume that of all the billions of aspects of our total experience, only those aspects that inform us about the quantitative properties of material phenomena are concerned with the "real" world. He did believe, however, that man's (mostly illusory) sense of religion had a material counterpart. It was this belief, and his desire to acquaint himself with the quantitative laws of religious phenomena, that had, in fact, led him to the roadside zoo where, as materialistic as his attitude toward stars might be, he did not hesitate to enter verbatim in his notebook Amanda's assertion, "Stars are merely projections of the human psyche—they are pimples of consciousness—but they are at the same time quite real."

It is possible that Marvelous also recorded Amanda's thoughts on style. "Maybe I'm attracted to style because the notion of content is a very difficult notion for me to comprehend," said she, patting dough into loaves. "When you subtract from an object the qualities it possesses, what do you have left? After you have taken from a star its age, position, size, velocity, distance from Earth and chemical composition, are you left with a hole in the sky—or something other? This lump of dough on the table has the properties of being soft, pliable, white, moist, smooth and cool to the touch. But what is it exactly, what is the thing—the content—that possesses those qualities? It can't be defined. I'm afraid that the notion of content has to be replaced by the notion of style." She paused to brush back a curl, leaving, in the act, a gull of flour on her cheek. "But then I'm just reciting the voices, you know. The way the robot kids recite their catechism, the way a river recites the gradation of its bed, the way a farter recites his starch."

"Amen to that last," said Marx Marvelous, "amen and amen again. It must have occurred to your 'voices' that content places limitations on style, in fact *determines* style. You believe in astrology, you contend that the color-light-magnetic pulsations of celestial bodies affect us to the extent of shaping our basic personalities. I say that's bull hockey because the total electrical output of the human body is about one two-thousandth of a volt, hardly enough force to be acted upon by planetary or stellar magnetism. But whether you favor astrology or a more rational concept such as genetics or behavioristic psychology, you must admit to a certain predetermining of our lives. Content is there before we are even consciously aware of it, it is all we have to work with and what that amounts to is that style is merely an *expression* of content. Tell me I'm right and I'll get out front and get ready to sell those sausages. Say, you're sure lovely with flour on your face. You look like Julia Child of the Spirits."

As she assigned her loaves to their stations in the oven, Amanda once more sighed. "I'm not going to choose between astrology and genetics because I fail to see any contradiction. The influences on the human animal are too complex and too paradoxical to be explained in terms of any one particular branch of knowledge. When I was twelve years old I watched a spider drink water. You think that didn't change my life?"

In the rinsing of her mixing bowl her hands played like a line of dolphins. "Those folks who are concerned with freedom, real freedom—not the freedom to say 'shit' in public or to criticize their leaders or to worship God in the church of their choice, but the freedom to be *free* of languages and leaders and gods—well, they must use style to alter content. If our style is masterful, if it is fluid and at the same time complete, then we can re-create ourselves, or rather, we can re-create the Infinite Goof within us. We can live *on top* of content, float above the predictable responses, social programming and hereditary circuitry, letting the bits of color and electricity and light filter up to us, where we may incorporate them at will into our actions. That's what the voices said. They said that content is what a man harbors but does not parade. And I love a parade."

She nibbled a petal of batter from the curve of her wooden spoon. "By the way, Marx, when you're eating your bread tonight would you mind keeping an alert out for my pre-Columbian rock-crystal skull ring. I do believe I dropped it in the dough."

"I understand that you believe in cellular memory," said Marx Marvelous, "that you think that a record of everything that has ever happened—including the secret most inner workings of the universe—is stored inside each human being's cells; and that under certain conditions you can browse in this cellular depository as in a library."

Oh bother. He was at it again. It was a mild afternoon and the clouds were breaking. The sun, like a winning ace up the gray coat-sleeve of Skagit summer, had been played with a sudden flourish. Amanda sat in the fir needles of the grove, eating a tomato and avocado sandwich, helping to rake in the chips. With some effort, she smiled sweetly at Marx's latest confrontation. The ragged lips of her sandwich smiled with her.

Marx took her silence as an admission of guilt. "I can appreciate how you might have jumped to those conclusions blah blah blah . . . Jung's theory of racial memory and collective unconscious blah blah blah . . . drug-induced rememberings of experiences which you could not possibly have had in this lifetime blah blah blah . . . migratory habits of insects and birds blah blah blah . . . the stories primitive man told around the campfire; myths so complex, so multi-leveled, so insightful and symbolically revealing that no atavistic mind could possibly have made them up blah blah. I frankly cannot explain how human—or animal—intelligence has access to such material. Perhaps a form of memory is indeed involved. But I'll tell you this, Amanda, it is not any so-called cellular memory nor is it a part of the genetic process. Memory is a kind of phenomenon different from the retention of genetic information. Memory is an *electrical* phenomenon. Its impulses can be measured by instruments. The DNA genetic information process, on the other hand, is a *chemical* phenomenon. You need only consider the difference in an electrical reaction and a pure chemical reaction to see what a sloppy analogy you've made. Both the memory bank and DNA retain information, that's true. Both your Jeep and my wristwatch have wheels and mechanical workings. But you can't drive my wristwatch to town blah blah blah . . ."

Amanda just grinned at this wonderful logic. (Her sandwich had nothing left to grin about.) But Nearly Normal Jimmy would not have stood for it. He would have countered Marvelous' cool argument with words of fire. John Paul Ziller and even Plucky Purcell might have argued with him, also, for to Marx's chagrin, Jimmy, who possessed the best instincts of capitalism, Ziller, an ultimate artist, and Purcell, a social activist at heart, all shared that tragic leaning toward the nonobjective and irrational shadows of life.

"Tragic" was Marvelous' word for it. Who would know better than he how tragic it truly was? Hadn't he had to fight his entire adult life against similar impulses? Hell, he could have wallowed in the transcendent, could have broadcast magical visions out of both blue eyeballs if he had weakened and given in to his primitive stirrings. But he held firm. He knew that man's potential on earth, his security and survival, lay in the proper exercise of reason. There were technological solutions to all of life's challenges if only scientific reason was permitted to provide them. It had been impressed upon Marx at the university and in the think tank the importance of resisting regressive cultural tendencies. Resist them he was prepared to do, even though he must suffer some in resistance. The angel of the bizarre he wrestled nightly into submission, though he often lost the first two falls. He wore the stains of the "dream world" as shamefully as a guilty smoker wears the yellow on his digits.

"I understand further," continued Marvelous, "that you believe there is no difference between the external and the internal. Well, not only is there a difference, I'll have you know that it is that difference that makes life possible." He launched into an explanation and, as if in retaliation, the sun card slipped back up the coat-sleeve of sky. On and on he went, blah blah, but when he noticed Amanda singing to a newly found cocoon, he began to suspect that she was paying him no attention. When the cocoon opened and a small butterfly wobbled out, he was sure of it.

There was one thing that might shut Marx Marvelous up, and Amanda realized that she must quit postponing it. Alas, however, she could not bring it off.

"I'm sorry, Marx Marvelous, but I can't fuck you." It was ten o'clock at night. Amanda was dressed in a silken lavender tunic upon which had been embroidered scenes from the biography of the queen who chased butterflies while awaiting death. Amanda stood in the doorway of Marx's garage apartment. Her long lashes twitched, fluttered and jerked again, as if they were a pair of feather dusters being machine-gunned against an igloo; and then they drooped elegantly, tugging her lids half the distance over the curve of her eyeballs. "You undoubtedly believe that I've been leading you on, but the truth is I've discussed it several times with John Paul and we have decided that it would not be wise. You're an attractive man and I'd like to, but it would not be smart."

Marvelous, who wore only the trousers to his checkered

suit, pulled nervously at a hair on his chest. "So," he said with some bitterness, "your liberated husband *does* care if you go to bed with other men." Archimedes, who discovered the principle of the lever, once said, "Give me a place to stand on and I could move the world." Archimedes could have stood on Marx's lower lip.

"No, that is not the case. As long as it's done with honesty and grace, John Paul doesn't mind if I go to bed with other men. Or with other girls, as is sometimes my fancy." Her smile was the pride of Botticelli's cherubs.

"Then why the hell did you get married?"

"What has marriage got to do with it? I married John Paul because I'm knocked out by his style. Because I love him and respect him and enjoy the transformations that take place as a result of our sharing the same dimensions. But, Marx, marriage is not a synonym for monogamy any more than monogamy is a synonym for ideal love. To live lightly on the earth, lovers and families must be more flexible and relaxed. The ritual of sex releases its magic inside or outside the marital bond. I approach that ritual with as much humility as possible and perform it whenever it seems appropriate. As for John Paul and me, a strange spurt of semen is not going to wash our love away."

"Then why do you deny me?" whined Marx. He stared at the floor.

Amanda closed the door and moved closer to him. She kissed his cheek. "Marx," she said tenderly, "you are as sensitive as you are stubborn. And, you're, well, shall we say —terribly impressionable. Also, you tend to be possessive. Those are basic characteristics of Cancerians. I know you have no use for astrology but you can't deny that those are your traits. And neither John Paul nor I feel that you could handle a simple, free relationship with me. No sooner would we begin than you'd be in love with me, which is beautiful except that you'd make it so complex. You'd demand more of me. You'd be possessive and play ego games. You'd be jealous of John Paul. Before long, you would create tension . . . between all three of us. Then where would we be? Friction at the Captain Kendrick. No, I just don't think you're ready."

Marx Marvelous slowly, desperately, sank to his knees. He embraced Amanda's legs. He buried his head in her perfumed tunic, in her crotch. His body shuddered. He sobbed against her pelvis, he whimpered. He clung to her tightly, perhaps ashamed now to let go.

For a while, Amanda stood absolutely still. Then she began to caress his fine sandy strands, her fingers twisting his hair in phantom knots. He relaxed a bit. He kissed her through the fabric. (Amanda, if you're leaving, you'd better leave now!) Gradually, like the falling of leaves or the bursting of buds or the other so gradual as to be nearly imperceptible dramas of nature, she pulled up her tunic and slipped her panties down around her calves. When the parachute of love descended, Marx Marvelous was face to face with her enchanted gypsy snatch.

So quietly did Amanda stand that the whole Skagit Valley, animate and inanimate, from the Cascades to the Sound, seemed on the point of standing quietly with her while he kissed and nibbled her about the groin. His tongue made a few exploratory licks, as if he were a child testing the flavor of a lollipop. She grew impatient and thrust her pubus toward him, and then and then . . . His tongue curled and thrust inside of her, his mouth mashed against her, the tip of his nose glistened with her juices. And then and then and then . . . Into the sucking of her went all the bafflement, all the rage, all the immense crazy consuming speechless frustration of his ineffectual genius. He lapped up the sweet darkness, his tongue drum-rolled against her clitoris, he sucked his way toward the plum of her womb. And then and then and then . . .

Her orgasm spanned a career that began with a delicate shudder and ended nearly two minutes later (his face against her all the while) with an volcanic gypsy moan. At first she came gently, as a moth might; then, losing control, she writhed and wallowed in hot cat spasms of crude delight. He thought she would never stop. She feared she would dissolve. Her nectars wet his neck and her thighs. Her clitoris was a ladyfinger cloud pump—and she groaned with animal dignity as it throbbed. Pumped its fishy billows. Its honey and sparks. It was the greatest of the imperfect ventriloquist acts: when his lips moved, her body sang.

After Amanda's pulsations had subsided, she wiped off Marx's face with the hem of her tunic. She pulled up her panties and hugged him good-bye. He was dizzy and ready

for sleep. He had come, too. And he never wore those
checkered trousers again.

At 3:25 on the afternoon of Thursday, August 6, Marx
Marvelous was busy drowning. The Skagit River closed
around his lungs like a wedding ring. The Skagit River, which
bangs down from the high Cascades, which spills through the
wild hills, which is cold and green and silty and (at this time
of year) teeming with salmon spawn, which flows sullenly
through the croplands as if pouting about the loss of speed,
flowing daily, flowing as it did last year, flowing as it did
when the three painted duck-hunting chiefs of the tribal
Skagit rode upon it in their long canoes, flowing, flowing
fearlessly into the future, flowing forever from beginning to
end; the Skagit River did not give one watery damn that it
was drowning the life of Marx Marvelous, promising (if confused) young scientist who had excelled at Johns Hopkins
University and once owned a natty checkered suit.

At first, Marx Marvelous did not like drowning. The water
in his lungs was heavy and unnatural. He thought of a cake
his father once had baked for his mother's birthday. He felt
as if that cake were in his lungs. But drowning is like anything else. You get used to it.

It was a relief to quit struggling. When he struggled his
lungs felt overheated and rusted out, like the muffler on an
old Ford truck in which he had delivered the *Baltimore Sun*
after he grew too big for his bicycle. That passed. When he
ceased to struggle his lungs ceased to backfire. It was peaceful. Would they publish his dead picture in the *Baltimore
Sun*?

Drowning takes a long time. It is not something one does
in a fast minute. Don't think it is. There is time to think.
There is time to eat a sandwich while drowning. Marx
Marvelous would have enjoyed a grilled ham and cheese.
Hold the pickles.

A light followed Marx Marvelous down to the river bottom. He did not know from whence it came. Perhaps the

fishes are familiar with this light. Marx Marvelous stared into the light. It is possible to drown with one's eyes open, you know. The face of Albert Einstein appeared in the light. Einstein was demonstrating that since motion depends upon the observer no one point can be considered the zero of motion. Einstein's face, baggy beneath the eyes, was very kind. Nevertheless, it made Marx Marvelous nervous. He soon replaced it with the face of Someone We All Know and Love. Marx Marvelous and the face hung in the water as if the river were a museum and they were famous pictures placed opposite one another for contrast. The light dimmed. "Our gallery is closing for the day," thought Marvelous.

One witness who saw John Paul Ziller dive off the Conway (South Fork) bridge said it reminded him of the Tarzan movies when Johnny Weissmuller would dive in to save Jane and Boy from the crocodiles. Two other witnesses agreed. It was the loincloth, they said. The remaining witness, a Swinomish Indian boy, said it reminded him of a movie, too. He did not say which one. "It was sure no movie when he pulled that feller outta the water," admitted the first witness. "His face was purple, solid purple. I thought for sure he was gone. I was surprised when they got him to breathing again. Did you see that girl? Her inner tube overturned, too, but she swam to shore okay. She kept calling, 'Marx, Marx.' Then that hairy guy dove off the bridge. Man, that's a long way down. It was like a movie."

Marx Marvelous regained consciousness. His chest ached. He felt sick. He couldn't hear the music any more. Nor see the light. What for an instant he thought was the light proved to be the great rosy buttocks of Mon Cul baboon. The baboon was bowing to the crowd that had gathered. Each time he bowed his butt ascended like a flaming sun, and when he straightened, the sun set. So the day dawned and ended, dawned and ended, over and over again with only a soft sound in between like Magritte's bowler hat rolling upon a Belgian carpet. Time passed quickly by Mon Cul's rectal reckoning. It was all okay.

Marx Marvelous is going to break the genius machine when he grows up. That's what everyone said. He hasn't, of course. As yet he hasn't put a strain on it. The reader, with his training in psychology (via novels, films, TV, Ann Landers, etc.) knows why.

Our sandy-haired young thinker is desperately searching for something in which to believe. Isn't he? As a child he was too sensitive and too bright to be attracted to his family's Baptist fundamentalism for very long. He turned to science almost as a substitute. How cool it was in comparison, how clean and cogent. But that didn't last. With his understanding of Heisenberg's Uncertainty Principle, he began to realize that every system that science proposed was a product of human imagination and had to be accepted with a faith nearly as blind as the religious beliefs which he had jettisoned. Much scientific truth proved to be as hypothetical as poetic allegory. The relationship of those rod-connected blue and red balls to an actual atomic structure was about the same as the relationship of Christianity to the Fish or the Lamb.

What now, dear Marvelous? A fresh examination of traditional religion found it as deficient in function as in creative energy: the wildest scientific postulates seemed sound (and alive!) in comparison. Paradoxically, his investigations in pure science, in abstract mathematics and theoretical physics, frequently led him into areas of thought which he could only describe as . . . well, say it, Marx: *metaphysical*. How could that be? The mental processes of religion and pure science may be similar, but the ends are different. It is not the purpose of science to make a man feel whole, to produce a kind of exalted happiness.

Why not?

It is a pity that Marx Marvelous should amplify that peculiarly Western quarrel of science and religion. But he was so terribly ambivalent. Thrashing about within him were two of the major and vital quests of the human spirit—the search for fact and the search for value. Why did the facts he pursued prove so impoverished in value, why were the value systems he examined so contrary to fact? Could mysticism help him? Various sources informed him that in the life-system known as mysticism there was a harmonium of fact and value. But Marvelous recoiled from mysticism with immediate distaste. Mysticism was so corny, so adolescent, so cluttered with dusty and discredited modes of thought, so clouded with woolly abstractions. No good. No good. He clung to science as a wino clings to a doorjamb. But the deep division within kept spreading its cheeks.

Compounding the spread was yet another side of his personality, the side that had a tooth for the whimsical and outlandish, the side that rutted in him like a lewd and unpredictable springtime compared to the stolid autumn that had settled upon his more public self. The less said about that side the better. Students of Kepler do not stress his lifelong belief in fairies any more than biographers of Benjamin Franklin dwell upon his illegitimate children, his venereal disease. Pass.

After a few months at the Zillers' roadside zoo, however, our boy betrayed a change. Gradually, Marvelous ceased to challenge his employers on every intellectual ground where he suspected them vulnerable. Slowly, even painfully, he fell in step with the rhythms that prevailed at the zoo. In his notebook he himself described the mood at the zoo as one of "intensity within tranquillity." By that he probably meant that the Zillers generated an atmosphere of rest and harmony through which coursed currents of unnamable excitement as veins run through meat. Marvelous could relax without fear of apathy. If he did not penetrate the mysterious activities that transpired behind the scenes at the roadhouse, he did at least share in the air of adventure that surrounded them. If he did not abandon his own attempts to isolate the psychic ember that would flame into the next religious phase, he did relieve the mission of some of its urgency. Following his tasty liaison with Amanda (how like the wilderness she was flavored) there had been a perceptible easing of strain. He became calmly fatalistic about his desire for her. "I want to roll in the hay with Amanda." "I wish the sun would shine for two days in a row." These remarks he made with equal emphasis. Following his rescue from the river by John Paul, he smiled more often at the magician and the magician at him. The three of them became closer friends. Marx gave his checkered suit to the Salvation Army. He let his hair grow long, although he still shaved each morning upon rising. At his baboon-nap trial in Seattle his lawyers wangled a suspended sentence. He developed a tolerance for wild mushrooms and wild music: morels, chanterelles, shaggy lepiotas; the Hoodoo Meat Bucket, the Beatles, Roland Kirk. His hemorrhoids even disappeared. Ah! Sigh!

By the middle of September Marx was secure enough in his new station in life to risk a small vacation. Sure, why not? Tourist season had petered out. The zoo was in fit condition. Might put things in clearer perspective if he got away for a while. Reportedly, a lot of strange things were erupting down around San Francisco, events with religious undertones that might bear looking into. Besides, though life at the roadside zoo was anything but dull, how long had it been since he'd been out on the town, picked up a broad in a nightclub, drank a double martini on the rocks? *Too* long, you bet. John Paul lent him a musician's card that would get him in free to any number of dives. Amanda gave him a scarab for luck and a wet kiss for the joy that was in it. Mon Cul waved good-bye at the airport, and Baby Thor cried to see him go. Marvelous almost cried himself. But what the hell, he wasn't going away forever. Very soon, he consoled himself, he'd be back at the Capt. Kendrick and things would be as they were before, only better. As it happened, however, that was not quite the case.

When two weeks later he returned to the zoo, Amanda was in bed with Plucky Purcell and Jesus Christ was locked in the pantry.

Part IV

Autumn does not come to the Skagit Valley in sweet-apple chomps, in blasts of blue sky and painted leaves, with crisp football afternoons and squirrel chatter and bourbon and lap robes under a harvest moon. The East and Midwest have their autumns, and the Skagit Valley has another.

October lies on the Skagit like a wet rag on a salad. Trapped beneath low clouds, the valley is damp and green and full of sad memories. The people of the valley have far less to be unhappy about than many who live elsewhere in America, but, still, an aboriginal sadness clings like the dew to their region; their land has a blurry beauty (as if the Creator started to erase it but had second thoughts), it has dignity, fertility and hints of inner meaning—but nothing can seem to make it laugh.

The short summer is finished, it is October again, and Sung dynasty mists swirl across the fields where seed cabbages, like gangrened jack-o'-lanterns, have been left to rot. The ghost-light of old photographs floods the tide flats, the island outcroppings, the salt marshes, the dikes and the sloughs. The frozen-food plants have closed for the season. A trombone of geese slides southward between the overcast and the barns. Upriver, there is a chill in the weeds. Old trucks and tractors rusting among the stumps seem in autumn especially forlorn.

October scenes:

At the dog-bitten Swinomish Indian Center near La Conner, there is a forty-foot totem pole the top figure of which is Franklin Delano Roosevelt. One of the queerer projects of the WPA Roosevelt's Harvard grin is faded and wooden in the reservation mist.

Outside of Concrete, boys have thrown crab apples through

221

the colored glass windows of an abandoned church. Crows carry the bright fragments away to their nests.

On the Freeway south of Mount Vernon, watched over by a hovering sausage, surrounded by a ring of prophecy, an audacious roadside zoo rages against the multiplying green damp chill as if it were a spell cast upon the valley by gypsy friends of the sun. Events transpire within that zoo which must be recorded immediately and correctly if they are to pass into history undeformed. Things rot with a terrible swiftness in the Northwest rains. A century from now, the ruins of the Capt. Kendrick Memorial Hot Dog Wildlife Preserve will offer precious little to reimburse archaeologists for their time. No Dead Sea Scrolls will ever be found in the Skagit Valley. It's now or never for *this* bible.

* * * * * * * * * * * * * * * * * * * *

THE SECOND COMING

* * * * * * * * * * * * * * * * * * * *

The Second Coming did not quite come off as advertised. The heavens opened, sure enough, but only to let a fine pearly rain streak through to spray the valley. Instead of celestial choirs, there were trucks snorting on the Freeway. Instead of Gabriel's trumpet there was John Paul Ziller's flute. Jesus himself showed up disguised as a pop art sculpture, caked with plaster from head to toe. And contrary to advance publicity, he was in no better shape upon his return than he was at his departure. He was, in fact, dead as a boot.

But, reader, do not let this fact escape you: it was him all right. Stretched out in the pantry of the Zillers' roadside zoo was none other than the Son of God, the Son of Man, the Prince of Peace, the Good Shepherd, the Blessed Saviour, the Master, the Messiah, the Light of the World, Our Lord, Jesus Christ, the scandal of history.

"It has recently come to my attention," said Plucky Purcell, "that Charles IV (Charles the Bland) once said that life is a pickle factory. I cannot accept that, as I find it impossible to determine whether life is sweet or sour."

"Perhaps," said Amanda, purring as Purcell nibbled her tattoos, "you would prefer the words of Ba Ba of Bow Wow who claims that life is a fortune cookie in which someone forgot to put the fortune."

And that, reader, pity me, is what I returned to. First off, there was Jesus Christ, the most vertical figure in history, lying (quite horizontal) in the pantry of our roadside attraction. That is, his mummified corpse was lying there, but in the case of Jesus as in the case of no other historical figure, coming upon him dead was even more extraordinary than coming upon him breathing. (What an electric heater perched on the rim of the Bathtub of the World that dead Jesus was!) Secondly, and some readers will find it shocking that I could list this second event in such easy proximity to the first, as if the second were of only slightly less magnitude than the first—secondly, there was Amanda and Plucky in the midst of a marathon embrace, their love-red ears tuned in only to each slish and slurp, oblivious to the fanfare of slamming doors that had accompanied my return to the zoo and oblivious, too, to the blast of silent waves that emanated earth-round from that mummy in the downstairs closet, although Amanda later claimed that she had taken Purcell to bed chiefly to get his mind off the Corpse, the presence of which was shoving him toward nuthood. Speaking of madness, I confess it was a close companion to me, too, those first days back at the roadhouse (some folks might believe it visits me still), but nobody rushed me off to the sack, I'll have you know.

Here, the reader has probably noticed that the author has begun to write in the first person singular, and he may have thought, ah ha, the autobiographical first person singular is always the choice of men in trouble, whereas only those writers who are safely disengaged from their subjects may indulge in third person motifs or that most cowardly of all voices, the first person plural—the pompous and devious editorial *we*. Actually, I have slipped into first person singular on several occasions during the drafting of this report, but always I went back and corrected the oversight. You see, it had been my intention to serve up this report as a strip of lean, rare meat ungarnished by the sauces of my own personality. What has become increasingly apparent, however, is that I am irreversibly enmeshed in the events this document will henceforth describe, so even had I time to restore a third-person treatment to the preceding paragraph (and time is growing precious) it could serve no honorable purpose. It might as well be known here and now that it is I, Marx Marvelous, who is your host and narrator at this most anticipated of all encores, the second appearance of you know who.

Your host and narrator, yes indeed, and I excuse you if you are thinking that of all the persons upon this planet to whom might have fallen the chore of witnessing the Advent (or, more correctly, the prelude to the Advent, for even as I type these words the returned Christ might be revealing himself to the cameras on some strip of Florida sand where heretofore only citrus cuties in bikinis may have posed—and can the shock of world recognition be far behind?), why must it have fallen to this admittedly ambivalent boy scientist to whom the true and powerful workings of language remain a puzzle. No more than an amateur plumber can deny the deepening mess on the bathroom floor can I deny the broken pace of this manuscript, its contradictions, its vagueness, its digressions, its—oh my—its thousand and one shifts in style. As for those stylistic inconsistencies, Amanda told me once that it is the natural state of Cancerians to be easily and tellingly influenced, to let the styles of others rub off on them at will, so if the reader is zodiacally oriented (and I maintain that I am not) perhaps the disclosure that I am Cancer-born will lift me off the hook. Of course, an astrological excuse will never suffice for literary critics or professors of English, but they've no damned business with their snouts in a document like this one anyway.

At any rate, I am indeed impressionable and thus parts of my report turn out written in John Paul Ziller's idiom, parts in Plucky Purcell's idiom and parts in the idiom of the young mistress of the zoo (can you pick out those parts where each holds sway?). And there are times when everybody talks alike and that is like a smart-assed doctor of philosophy candidate at Johns Hopkins U. Oh well. I cannot apologize. Granted the literary atrocities (will I be tried and hung at some future Nuremberg for writers?) still I rejoice that it was I and not some super-journalist with eighty million words on his speedometer who drew the task of describing the apocalypse (it makes me shudder to conceive of *Another Roadside Attraction* as *The Day Christ Came Back*). And I am gleeful, too, that it was I who drew the task instead of a biblical scholar or instead of one of our bright young novelists, even, for although they, any one of them, might have brought to the historic task skills and insights beyond my command, I greatly fear that they would have been so thunderstruck by the presence of Our Lord, dead and plaster-soiled, that they would have neglected the girl; the girl: Amanda.

Once, a famous European dilettante visited Amanda's town. The dilettante lectured to the Davy Crockett Fine Arts and Hot Lemonade Society. It was a warm evening in early summer. Amanda's father, enormously fat in a white linen suit, took his thirteen-year-old daughter to the talk. The lecture was given in the high-school gym. Father and daughter sat in the front row.

Amanda, in a dainty pink organdy dress with a yellow sash, was perhaps the only member of the audience who did not sweat profusely on this cultural pilgrimage.

The dilettante must have noticed for the following day he called upon Amanda's father at his greenhouse and requested permission to paint the young girl's portrait. The father was honored. Amanda posed in a wicker chair, but the dilettante painted her rising from behind a cloud. The picture pleased Amanda. She agreed to go walking the fields with the dilettante to learn more of art and European culture.

The lesson, as it turned out, had a familiar ring. Amanda, girlishly thirsty for knowledge, was not certain she was learning anything new at all. All at once, however, she saw—fluttering forward without flaw along its own organic line—a most magnificent Arizona swallowtail. "All problems of art are solved," she thought, for she had found the "line of beauty" in the bumpy line of moth flight. She sprang to her feet and chased after the butterfly while the dilettante stamped and kicked, and shouted at the insect a term which Amanda could not understand, although knowing the dilettante she was certain it was a phrase of a scholarly nature. In fact, years passed before Amanda learned that "coitus interruptus" was not the scientific name for the swallowtail butterfly.

In the evenings, after the zoo had closed, Amanda liked to sit beside the slough and listen to the frogs. Listening to the frogs was like turning the pages of an expensive coffee-table book on Moorish architecture. Each time she turned a page she was met by another mosaic of stupefying density.

"To hear you tell it," said one of her friends, "you'd think the frogs invented algebra."

"Well," said Amanda, turning the loaded pages, "a pollywog is more than a monowog."

Amanda always brushed her teeth with crushed strawberries. The strawberry pulp whitened her teeth and pinkened her gums.

When death finally sucks her down the drain, as it must suck everyone, Amanda will leave an iridescent ring around the tub.

There were no mail-order catalogues in 1492. Marco Polo's journal was the wish book of Renaissance Europe. Then, Columbus sailed the ocean blue and landed in Sears' basement. Despite all the Indians on the escalator, Columbus' visit came to be known as a "discovery."

The "discovery" of the body of Jesus Christ is also a story of plunder. By all rights, it is Plucky Purcell's story and I wish that he were here to tell it. There is no way that I can articulate that little episode and make it sound credible, the way I could make, say, the discovery of the fourth-demensional spin of electrons sound credible, for the mind that directs my typing fingers, nurtured as it was in the safe, sane laboratories of Johns Hopkins University, is not suited to describing quirks in what I have been taught is a rational world. I damn such quirks and wish them the bad luck I wish yogis and astrologers and others who claim to see things in the sky that I and my telescope cannot. In Purcell's mind, on the other hand, reality rushes by like a wild white river, while quirks, like crocodiles or iguanas, sun themselves in grotesque comfort on the shores. Unfortunately, the Pluck penned no letters concerning his discovery (there just wasn't time for that) from which I might quote, and at the moment he is rather occupied with eluding the dragnets of CIA and FBI, not to mention playing his role in whatever worthy plan the magician might have conceived for the Corpse. So, I myself will assume the responsibility of relating how Jesus was found and—dammit, folks, this time I really mean it—I will do it as quickly and simply as possible. Listen.

As most of you recall, there was a fairly severe geological disturbance in Italy on September 27 of this year. The volcano Vesuvius erupted, killing livestock in its immediate vicinity and causing widespread damage to crops. A small tidal wave wrecked boats in the Neopolitan area. And twenty-five or thirty tremors, most of them mild, were felt up and down the Italian boot. The most severe of the earthquakes, although in terms of death and destruction it could hardly be called a catastrophe, was centered in Vatican City. Surely you remember. Windows were smashed, the facades of some buildings were cracked and in Saint Peter's Square a small section of pavement buckled. On the whole, however, damage was light—above ground. But beneath the Vatican proper, the catacombs took a beating. Vast sections of them were harmed. That much you learned from your newspaper and your TV. There was quite a fuss about it on September 28, remember, but journalism is as fickle as a young actress and by the twenty-ninth it was a story the large papers carried deep in their rear sections and the small papers carried not at all. Who, after all, can sustain interest in damaged catacombs in times like these?

There were a dozen injuries in the Vatican tremor, but no deaths, and the only phase of it that provoked conversation around breakfast tables and water coolers in America was the disclosure that its unruly vibrations had bounced His Holiness out of bed. If the papal posterior was bruised in the bouncing the Vatican did not share with the public that intimacy, and thus the incident quickly slipped beneath the sea of reportable events that lap each evening at the feet of the six o'clock news. The caved-in tunnels, the broken art and artifacts, were subjects which only the Vatican paper and some Catholic magazines examined in any great detail. The primary effects of the Vatican quake could hardly, to repeat myself, be called a catastrophe. The secondary effects were something else again. The world has not yet been informed of those secondary effects.

* * * * * * * * * * * * * * * * * * * *

When the earthquake hit, Plucky Purcell—like the Pope —was dreaming. Nearly Normal Jimmy once advanced the theory that it was impossible for the man who awakens in the morning to know with certainty that he is the same man who went to sleep at night. Nearly Normal became rather obsessed with that notion and as a result developed insomnia. Amanda thought the whole thing was silly. Said she, "What difference does it make *who* you are when you wake up as long as you wake up *somebody*." Like the oft-quoted Chinese philosopher, she would have been content to wake up a butterfly. But Nearly Normal Jimmy rested no easier and finally, on the advice of Ziller, called upon a magi who lived in a pyramid in Illinois and had his psyche tattooed. With a small brand inked into the skin of his mind, he could roam far and wide while sleeping and yet always keep tabs on himself. He had belled the cat of his consciousness, so to speak. However, there was one drawback. From the day he was tattooed, Nearly Normal always had the same dream. The only image that ever came to him in dreaming was the image of his tattoo: a leather armchair of the Tibetan variety. It was an image to which Jimmy was attracted, to be sure, but it made for dull hours a-dreaming.

Purcell never had that problem. Whether he lay on a jail bunk, on a motel mattress soaked with sex or on a monk's stingy cot, he slumbered like an old dog and his dreams were as rich and varied as the total output of Hollywood from *Birth of a Nation* until now. "Colossal" is an adjective that could be applied to Purcell's dreams. "I gotta dream spectaculars," he said, "or someone else will dream them in my place." The Vatican earthquake shook Purcell loose from one level of spectacle and deposited him on another. The air he awoke in was choked with dust and rent with screams. Of the twelve persons who were hurt in the quake, seven acquired their injuries not two hundred feet from where Plucky lay dreaming. That boy has a knack for being in the thick of things.

Panic moved through the catacombs like a compulsive housekeeper, emptying the ashtrays of reason and mopping up the tracks of experience. The catacombs took on an insect quality. Confusion spun in the debris. But while the others who roomed in the catacombs—the several score underground soldiers of the cross—while they tried in panic to make up their minds whether to run for the ground-level exit before or after gathering up their possessions, before or after ministering to their wounded comrades, impulsive Plucky Purcell not only chose an immediate course of action, he made a long-term decision concerning his future as well. It was a decision that was to affect the destiny of the race, although Purcell could not have known that then.

****

In Bokonon, it is written that "peculiar travel suggestions are dancing lessons from God."

One two three and four-ah. One two three and four-ah. Fast and funny were the steps Purcell took down the rumbling corridor. Purcell was not so much running as he was dancing and he was not so much dancing as he was laughing with his feet. *One two three and ha-ha.* He moved not toward the stairs that led to the surface but toward those which led to the next lower level of catacombs. As he moved (hop skip wiggle) through the crumbled stone and fearful echoes, his brainpan sizzled with visions: visions of autumn in New York; visions of San Francisco's doll-faced hills; visions of the wonders of Mexican agriculture; visions of studio doors flung open in welcome; visions of burning herbs and young pussy both in such profusion that his heart sickened and flopped like a musical dove in the odors that the visions brought to his nostrils. Visions of big escape, of throwing off that Catholic curse which for more than a year now had held him in its coils and sent him probing closer and closer to the dark dangerous heart of the One True Church, taunting him with religious riddles until he—once happy-go-lucky hustler —could think of little else but finding some way to cope with an immense and growing world-force that twinkled so tenderly of Heaven and stunk so terribly of Hell. Without consciously intending to, he had hacked into the Roman mysteries as a safari hacks into dense jungle, and he had come down with velvet fevers and been bedeviled by such opulent deliriums that he no longer knew if the evil he saw was actually there or whether his sickness conjured it. Now, like a schizophrenic suddenly made whole, like a harried lover at last emotionally free of the bitch he thought he could not bear to lose, Purcell had awakened from his long Catholic nightmare—shaken from it by an actual seizure of the earth —and the visions that unfolded in his mind were familiar ones of a secular life he could barely wait to resume. Feet laughing beneath him, he approached the treasure vaults. Gold and silver are heavy cargo, but even though he knew he could stuff no more than a few thousand dollars' worth into his belongings, it would get him to America and friends and dope and pussy and . . . However much he plundered it was scant payment for the horrors religion had put him through. He danced over a body. No, it was a toppled statue of a Grecian athlete; its censoring Roman fig leaf had broken away in the fall and now its marble penis pointed at the stars and freedom; dance on, Purcell. *One two three and ha-ha.*

Oh my. Whew! You waltz divinely, Pluck. Just as our hero had anticipated, several of the chambers lay open, their barred doorways bent and sprung or their stone walls reduced to rubble. It took Purcell not many minutes to add substantially to the net worth of his estate. "This is the business the Church should have been about all along," he thought. "Sharing its gold with the poor instead of its condolences." Heavier by a good twenty pounds, he nevertheless executed a graceful pirouette and prepared to make his exit. But his choreographer had altered the pattern.

Looking over his right shoulder, for no sound reason, he noticed that the one catacomb chamber that had been permanently sealed now gaped at its seams. The earthquake had squeezed its foreboding face until it smiled like a manic encyclopedia salesman. In imitation not of Nijinsky but of Ben Hur the flea, Purcell hopped directly into the smile. One last probe in the orifices of the Church, as it were. And, of course, that is how he met the Corpse. With bounds that are not within everyone's power, particularly if their pockets are packed with gold, Plucky—pushed by curiosity or intuition or "peculiar travel suggestions"—bounded right into the mysterious compartment, and through the billowing dust observed the mummified body of the Messiah as it rested atop a jewel-encrusted sarcophagus, wrapped about with dry-rotted linens, as if the Messiah were an immense overcooked weenie in a tattered bun; just lying there touched by nothing but time—and gently by *it*—as if the Messiah had been calmly awaiting Plucky Purcell for these two thousand years.

The question the critical reader must raise at this juncture is: How did Purcell recognize the mummy as Jesus? It is not an easy question. I, myself, being a skeptical man of science, did not hesitate in scraping off a sample of the wood fragments and dirt that clung to the Corpse (beneath its more recent coating of plaster) and airmailing it to the radiocarbon laboratory at Johns Hopkins for dating. My friend at the lab found the specimen unsuitable for really exact carbon-14 dating, but was able to approximate its age as from fifteen hundred to three thousand years. Probably, that finding helped support my conviction of the body's identity, but to tell the truth, I was convinced without it. In fact, from the moment I focused vision upon the Corpse I knew that it was who it was. Plucky must have known instantly, too. It looked, to be sure, nothing like the milky portraits we had been shown in Sunday school, looked hardly at all like the handsome gentleman with the Aryan profile and the five-hundred-watt glow who effulged at us from calendars in Protestant parlors all over Dixie. It was short, as swarthy and oily as a Greek olive, and its face was overshadowed by a nose that arched and hooked like the beak of an enlarged buzzard. Yet it was inexplicably familiar. Although dead and withered, the Corpse was animated by the absolute. When one stared at it, one's pupils jangled like alarm clocks that had been set long ago to go off at this moment. Logic was not necessarily suspended nor common sense ignored. This simply, positively was not the body of an ordinary man. In its befouled stupor, it incited awe and marvel. Those of us who spent time with it experienced at least some of the tremendous power it must have held when it walked Galilee. Doubt collapsed in a racket of revelation, and we, most of us, paid homage to the pitiful Hebrew mummy as if it were a living saint.

The chamber in which the Christ was hidden was small and dirty and apparently had not been opened in several centuries. However, the gems embedded in the tomb and the golden candelabra that bristled in the corners suggested that it had once been a shrine of highest (if secret) rank. Perhaps medieval popes had awakened after midnight to traipse in purple splendor down to that deepest catacomb where they conducted clandestine masses for none but the most privileged princes of the Church. Then, one year long ago, it had been decided that the secret was just too hot and the risk too great, so the Holy Office sealed off the remains of its precious figurehead, sealed them off even from itself. Maybe one curious prelate or another had looked in on them, had paid respects, but it seems doubtful if even a pope had peeked at the illustrious body in recent times. Of course, they knew it was there. Or did they? And if they knew, *who* knew? Those are telling questions which we will deal with a little later. For the moment, let us appreciate the discovery: Purcell had chanced (danced) upon the Lamb of God, dead and helpless in Vatican concealment, and he had realized, furthermore, who it was whom he had found; and as stunned as he may have been, and as temporarily ignorant of the full apocalyptic implications of stealing the body as he may have been, he did not tarry, faint or fret but immediately scooped up the mummy tenderly in his arms and prepared to bear it into man's modern world.

****

No sooner did Plucky spring from the tomb than he became aware of an influx into the catacombs. Up until then, the voices and footsteps had all been moving in the other direction, as the bleeding and confused and the scared made their way to ground level. Now, in the quake's buzzing aftermath, investigating squads and files of guards were cautiously exploring the tunnels. They were still well above Purcell, but there was no way he might avoid meeting them in his ascent. What's this? A person coming? Damn the luck! He hadn't gotten twenty feet with his prize before somebody had spotted him. It was like being tackled at the line of scrimmage, a frustrating failure anytime, but especially when Jesus is one's football. The figure, however, approached without seeing. Well, what do you know? It was one of the blind nuns who stand watch over the forbidden library. The tremor had played havoc with her collection of scrolls and left her in a daze all the more confusing because she was sightless.

"Forgive me, sister."

Plucky administered to her the most painless knockout in his karate repertoire. Like a rag penguin, she folded at his feet.

Have you ever tried to undress a nun when you were in a hurry? It was maddening—all the tiny black buttons, the stubborn hooks—but he at last disrobed her and clothed the Corpse in her habit. The nun he wrapped in the Corpse's rotten linens and deposited upon the sarcophagus. There he left her, but in case it has crossed your mind to wonder, as some of the purest people have wondered before you, what the good sister wore beneath her habit, let me remind you that Plucky Purcell is a Southern gentleman and while the air he exudes may by some moral standards be excessively sulphurous, he would never ever be guilty of embarrassing or insulting a lady. What, if anything, the knocked-out nun wore closest to her private parts is a secret Purcell is prepared to protect to his grave.

Crashing like a moose calf through the cranberry bogs of its first winter, Plucky crashed through catacomb earthquake debris, his natural running grace blunted by the Corpse in his arms and the heavy gold doodads in the inner pockets of his robe. He made it to the first staircase with no opposition save his excess baggage and the rubble underfoot, but at the head of the stairs, on the second level, he ran into a party of soldiers.

If I have given the impression that the Vatican was a bit casual in its concern for the treasures in its catacombs, you must keep in mind that while the combined contents of those few rooms of gold and silver and gems and art might be worth say, oh, a hundred million dollars, it is but a bubble in the Church's bucket of wealth. The Vatican owns stocks and bonds valued at about seven billion dollars. It is the largest single stockholder in the world. The Vatican also owns property—secular as well as churchly—valued at many billions. It is the largest single real-estate owner in the world. The baubles hidden in the catacombs are artifacts left over from an age when such hardware was the trappings of power. In these times, they are clumsily anachronistic, almost embarrassing. Sooner or later, they will be converted into more efficient tender. Meanwhile, however, they may be slighted but they have not been forgotten. As soon as the quake had subsided, the Pope or one of his senior aides ordered the Swiss Guard into the catacombs to secure the valuables and restore order.

The Swiss Guard filed into the dusty depths, armed not with quaint halberds but with the latest automatic weapons supplied free by the Catholic munitions makers of America and Germany. Thus armed, it met Purcell as he lurched up the stone staircase from his rendezvous with Christ.

Plucky was breathing hard. His breaths rolled through the squad of soldiers like the waves of a second quake. The ocean of his breathing collapsed around the showy soldiers the way the ocean of fame collapsed around the gums of Judy Garland.

"I've got a sister here," gasped Purcell, trusting that the well-educated captain of the guards understood English. "Must get her to a doctor."

"Let me see her," ordered the haughty officer, his English as perfect as a snowflake. "Perhaps she needs first aid."

"No, no," stammered Plucky. "She isn't seriously hurt. I think she's just fainted. Got to get her up in the fresh air."

The captain recognized upon Purcell the black robe of Felicitate. Uninformed as he was about the exact nature of the Society of the Felicitator, he knew that it occupied a special place of favor with the Holy Father, perhaps a more special place than his own command. He hesitated, and as is written in *Poor Richard's*, "He who hesitates will never stop Plucky Purcell." Our hero danced around the soldiers and plunged toward the next stairwell as if it were the Georgia Tech goal line. He was not pursued.

St. Peter's Square was a chaos of searchlights, police cars, fire engines, ambulances, utility trucks, Church officials of high and low standing and emergency personnel of all sorts. At that time, the rumor that His Holiness had suffered grave injury had not yet been denied officially, and the fate of their Pope concerned the policemen to the point where they were emotionally unable to bring any kind of order to the scene in the square. Nobody detained Purcell as he rushed through the milling throngs, though many were the great Italian clucks of pity as bystanders witnessed the limp "nun" in his arms. Plucky hurried to an ambulance parked at the edge of the square and pulled open its rear doors.

"*Spitale!*" he shouted, having somehow during his Roman stay learned the Italian for "hospital."

"*Devo trovare un dottore,*" explained the driver.

"*Io sono un dottore,*" Purcell lied. "*Spitale! Presto!*"

On the way to the hospital, the ambulance was frequently detained by traffic jams as thousands of Italians, their eyes wide for spiritual experience, poured into Vatican City from throughout Rome. When finally he screeched up to the emergency door of the hospital, the driver found his ambulance empty. *Mamma mia.* The monk, the poor sister! Where? The driver fell to his knees and crossed himself.

After bailing out of the ambulance, Plucky had bailed out

of his robe (he wore jeans and sweat shirt beneath it). He wrapped the Corpse in it so that the Corpse no longer looked like a nun. Several pieces of gold fell out on the sidewalk. Plucky left them for the whores and hurried on. He made his way to the studio of George O. Supper, the American pop artist famed for his plaster-of-paris sculptures of anonymous men.

"Now, George O., buddy, what I've got here is an unusual request. I've had the good fortune to get my meat hooks on an Egyptian mummy. A king, I think it was, a great pharaoh. Rather valuable. It's all perfectly legal, George O., it's legally mine—"

"Bullshit," said Supper.

". . . excepting that I'm not allowed to take it out of Italy. Now what I'm asking you to do is—"

"I *know* what you're asking. Let me think about it for a few days."

"George! Tonight. Remember when you came to me with that little Long Island deb? I didn't ask to think it over. She could've had triplets by the time I thought it over."

Sighing, Supper helped Plucky carry the Corpse into his plastercasting room. "Purcell, if this mummy is full of drugs . . ."

"Word of honor, George O. You can examine it if you wish."

"Okay. Okay. I'm sleepy."

"I've got to ship this out on an early morning flight. I'll build a crate while you plaster. Do you have any of those shipping tags that say 'Work of Art'?"

Goaded by his old friend, Supper worked feverishly. Beginning at the feet, the Corpse turned slowly into a ghostly bland every-man or non-man or anti-man, depending upon one's frame of reference: a white blob of a figure, so empty of humanity that the viewers of the figure would have thrust upon them the startling option to fill in the vacancy, to draw in character, to color the blandness from the palette of their own experience. It would be a typical Supper poker-faced marshmallow monolith; not so much a man as a hole in the air where a man had stood seconds before being vaporized. Man disappearing, man reduced to a silent white shadow of his species. As Supper built this latest testimony to the existential impermanence and insignificance of John Doe, he felt queerly moved. No living model had ever affected him that way. Some strange kind of peaceful power seemed to surge from the mummy. By the time he began to plaster the face, Supper's hands were trembling. He felt himself in touch with what he imagined were the ancient forces of Egypt.

"Funny," he said with little amusement. "It *looks* Jewish."

It is midmorning. A few minutes ago I took my coffee break. I am speaking figuratively, of course. There's not a drop of coffee in this place and there never has been. As a matter of fact, we are also out of juice. On my coffee break (ha ha) I had a hot dog and a glass of tap water. There are plenty of damn hot dogs, all right. And water, too. Last night, the rains started.

Amanda, as pale as the raindrops but in good spirits, joined me on my coffee break. She sipped her water from an Apache bowl. No hot dog. You know, her vegetarianism no longer annoys me. If she doesn't want her belly to be a graveyard for dead animals, I can appreciate her view. *Her* belly is for the living, not the dead.

But this weenie business I could never understand. I enjoy a good hot dog, myself, but let's face it, it is not an elite cut of meat. They grind up hog hearts in weenies, and cow muscles and chicken fat and the diaphragms of sheep and the esophagi of goats. Of all the meats with which a vegetarian might be reluctantly associated, surely the sausage is among the least respectable. Yet, Amanda had chosen John Paul as her husband and John Paul had chosen the sausage as his trade. Strange bedfellows.

"It's not as strange as all that," said Amanda. She sipped her water from a clay bowl with mythological designs. The rain stormed against the former roadside zoo (I say "former" because the place has been stripped of its serpents and its fleas) like trolls splashing swamp water on a sight-seeing bus. "The hot dog is not so much a food as it is an institution. President Roosevelt fed hot dogs to the king and queen of England when they visited here in 1939. Babe Ruth ate noth-

ing but hot dogs and soda pop for twenty years. Hot dogs are
found wherever Boy Scouts get together. It is hot dogs the
packers have in mind when they boast that they use everything but the squeal. It's not what hot dogs are made of but
what they symbolize. The hot dog is the pillar of democracy,
the pride of the Yankees, the boneless eagle of free enterprise."

Well, I couldn't refute that. Come to think of it, it is typical
of John Paul Ziller that he would choose to work his African
magic through the medium of one of America's most beloved
institutions. Ziller has turned the weenie into a wand.

It was most agreeable sitting with Amanda. In the mustard
pot, I traced the legend of her beauty. Amanda smiled and
touched my hand. Life lifted its heavy wheels. I forgot about
the task at the typewriter upstairs. I forgot about the rain.
But just then two of the agents burst in, shielding their
weapons from the wet. They gave us greedy patriotic looks.
"Hey," they yelled. "Fix us a bunch of them dogs."

Ben Franklin to the contrary, one cannot take a stitch in
time. No, not even to save nine. If only it were possible to
stitch time, to pull it up tight, to hold it back. You see, I have
reason to believe that today is my last at the typewriter. The
agents are supremely confident that Ziller and friends will be
apprehended at any hour. Suppose they are right? I do not
know what that will mean in terms of my fate or Amanda's.
But I strongly suspect that have I not concluded this report
by tomorrow morning, it will be involuntarily curtailed. Doom
rides my typewriter carriage like a fat lady on a rubber
horse.

I pine for time because had I more of it I could more
successfully metamorphose my vigil with the roadside zoo's
quaint realities so that other men might appreciate as well as
I the setting and circumstance across which Christ's body
continued its silent journey.

If I write no further of Amanda's attempts to train butterflies to unfold dinner napkins (two insects to a napkin, of

course), or of the maps with which Ziller traced his origins back to the sun, I'm sure I shall be forgiven. On the other hand, there are facts of daily life at the zoo to which the reader is entitled.

I should like, for example, to tell more of Baby Thor. Forgive me, Thor, if you are grown, a schoolboy, reading this document either on assignment or out of natural curiosity concerning the historic event to which you, a yard-child of less than four, were privy much as little Anastasia was privy to the annihilation of Russian royalty; forgive me if I have neglected you in my chronicles. You were a joy to us always. Ah, the flash upon your eyes. Your eyes summed up for me my studies in science. Your eyes reminded me of experiments in wave physics, of exercises in galactic mechanics. Your eyes reminded me of a dozen different chemical reactions, particularly those which, if not carefully controlled, threaten to blow up the laboratory.

Thor, your stepfather had (perhaps I should use the present tense, for Ziller has extraordinary resources and he may well have survived his present pickle) a special feeling for light. He felt that since energy was the only permanent "thing" in the universe, it was the most (if not only) significant "thing." And although he had great respect for sound, he believed that the highest form of energy is light. He seldom used color in his art because he had a theory that color was a disease that afflicted light, a parasite that lived off of light and destroyed its purity. He was disturbed by the fact that 400 trillion waves of deep red light enter the human eye every second. What happens to light after it has been absorbed by the eye is a question that has intrigued many scientists. Ziller's attitude was, "To hell with what happens to the light. What happens to the *color?*" In an effort to control "color pollution," he had trained his pupils to remain stationary for long periods of time. Ziller spoke of light as if it were applicable to living tissue—and since, ultimately, living tissue is a product of solar radiation, he was not entirely mistaken. "But, John Paul," I cautioned him once, "the temperature of living tissue is much too low to produce the kind of energy that is necessary for radiation. We speak metaphorically of girls having glowing complexions, but flesh is never an actual source of light." And Amanda said, "How about fireflies?" Your mommy certainly knew her bugs.

"Well," I blushed, "that's true, fireflies make light and some worms glimmer and some toadstools, but living tissue is never, never energetic enough to stand a chance of combining with 'activation' energies such as sunlight." Then, Thor, your stepfather gently interrupted the game you were playing with Mon Cul baboon and led you up to me so that I could look into your eyes.

Thor, I can't forget your eyes, but neither can I forget your happy heart. I do not know the identity of your true father (your mother is more stingy with her gossip than with her love), but in your almost omnipotent cheerfulness you were every giggle Amanda's child.

Had I time, I also would like to write more of the people who stopped in at the zoo. Gunnar Hansen was typical of the surprisingly sophisticated farmers and fishermen who live in Washington's Skagit Valley: the broad-mindedness and general awareness of the sweet-tempered Skagit folk have made the area a refuge for artists from the generally more provincial metropolis of Seattle. La Conner, a picturesque wooden village built out over the Swinomish Slough, has been an important art colony for forty years. Paintings and poems have sprung from the misty valley in an abundance nearly equal to the salmon, strawberries and peas. It was not until Boeing Aircraft built, in the mid-sixties, a factory on the valley's edge that prejudice and reaction was smuggled into Skagit country, a part of the baggage of technicians and engineers. On those occasions when the sheriff's office or the state patrol were called to investigate the goings-on at that "weirdo hot dog zoo," invariably it was a newcomer to the valley, some clear-eyed, tight-lipped little wing-tank designer, who was behind the call. Farmer Hansen, although he was mystified by certain elements of the zoo's character (as, in truth, was I), always approached the giant weenie with robust respect. You, Farmer Hansen—and your peers who fish these jade waters, who till this Chinese brushstroke landscape and make it sprout with vegetables and flowers—I salute you. I do not know to what extent your lives are full, or how passionately enlightenment has touched you, but in your rare rural tolerance for eccentric people and new ideas, you have singed the damp air with your honor.

Among the other regulars at the zoo was Salvadore Gladstone Tex, the cowboy who eventually became so familiar we were obliged to learn his name. I recall a mild evening in July. The sky was bent double by a heavy bar of moon-soaked clouds. The cowboy (Salvadore Gladstone Tex) knocked at the roadside zoo. He knocked as if shaking a tambourine. His horse, Jewish Mother, was left to graze in the parking lot. Slim pickings. "Howdy mam," the cowboy said to Amanda. "I noticed that you haven't added no more attractions to your zoo." "That's correct," said Amanda. "We're standing pat." "Well," said the cowboy, "I thought you might be of persuasion to buy this here watermelon." He held the melon in his arms as if it were an infant. "Oh," said Amanda. "I'll bet it's one you grew yourself." "I grow lots of watermelons, mam. This one's different. It talks." Amanda listened politely. She overheard the melon say something like ". . . according to Plan Q . . ." The watermelon had a high, squeaky voice. "I was just meandering through the melon patch when I heard it carrying on. There were three or four melons right snug together and I had to listen real close to find out which one was doing the talkin'. It's this one, all right. To tell the truth"—his voice assumed a confidential tone—"I think it's the space people. They're trying to contact us through watermelons." Amanda listened again. The watermelon said something like, "Driver, a sizable reward for you if you reach the station in time for the express." High. Squeaky. "Hmmmmm," said Amanda. Was the cowboy throwing his voice? She gave him (Mr. Tex) a two-dollar deposit and told him that if she was satisfied she would pay the rest on Saturday. She thumped the melon. At least it was ripe. While Amanda was upstairs giving Thor his bath, John Paul came home from the woods. He had been drumming, jungle style. He was tired and in need of refreshment. He sat at the kitchen table and devoured the melon. Amanda couldn't hear him with the water running. And that was the end of that. Except the next morning at his bowel movement, John Paul swore the first turd said, "Hello."

Were I trying to compose the Great American Novel instead of factually documenting a particular event, I would draw my characters not from the Zillers (as worthy as they may be and as much as I've come to care for them) nor from the likes of Salvadore Gladstone Tex, nor even from the young long-haired itinerants who, by the scores, called at the Capt. Kendrick Memorial Hot Dog Wildlife Preserve as if it were a stopping-off place on a vast socio-religious pilgrimage; no, my subjects would be selected from among the tourists and vacationers—the ordinary clerks and machinists and salesmen, their wives and kids—for just as the zoo could not have thrived without their patronage, the nation itself is wedded to their aggressive mediocrity (they are in the stuff of America as the corn is in the pudding), and it is upon their reaction to the discovery of Christ's body that the future of Western civilization may well rest: whether the revelation of the Corpse will expedite an evolved golden era free of religious superstition, false hopes and crippling guilts or whether it will plunge humanity into a horrible dark age of helplessness and despair, is entirely up to them. Already they sense (as, in a more articulate and less fearful manner, do the young itinerants) that something is amiss in mankind's motor, that enormous changes are swelling on every horizon—and they are skittish. Just observing them at the zoo, munching frankfurters and gathering amusement from the pretty painted fleas tilting their chariots on the sharp turns of the track, I accumulated fair insights into the national mood, and were some perceptive writer to follow them back to their beauty shoppes in Salt Lake City, their barbecue furnaces in Moline, their TV dens in Riverside, Massillon and Fargo, they might be looked through as living microscopes, magnifying in ignorance both the dangerous germs and precious bacteria that advance upon the organs of our race. But that is not my assignment. I simply haven't time for that.

Surely, the reader can understand my hurry. Outside my door are armed agents who delight in reminding me that prison—or worse—awaits me as soon as the magician and the athlete are nabbed with their precious booty in whatever Florida cypress grove they cringe. That, however, is not the only reason why I escalate the drafting of my report. These past few days of constant sitting at the Remington have succeeded in aggravating old rectal troubles. It is said that Napoleon suffered most of his life from similar afflictions, and in fact, may have lost his battle with Wellington due to an acute attack of hemorrhoids. If hemorrhoids could cost Napoleon his Waterloo, what toll might they take on your diligent correspondent? Amanda's butterfly songs do not altogether cheer me as I sit in the smoking wreckage of my second largest, if not second loveliest, orifice.

Jesus crossed the Atlantic on Trans World Airlines Flight No. 115. Despite rumors of his ascension, it was probably the longest trip he ever took.

I write "probably" because there are parties who would have us believe that Jesus got around. Pardon me, but I reject out of hand the notion that the Messiah spent his "missing years" on another planet. I believe that the flying saucer was Jesus' customary mode of transportation no more than I believe that Mon Cul knows an English word that rhymes with orange. There is no limit to the nonsense some people expect you to swallow.

I have heard that Jesus went to India for his missing years. Not likely. Just because, by Hindu and Buddhist standards, his "radical" teachings were old hat does not prove he went to India to formulate them. Jesus read a lot. His favorite subject, next to Jewish culture (he would have been attracted but not sympathetic to *Portnoy's Complaint*), was philosophy. Moreover, his hometown was just off the Great Road that connected the Roman world with the Far East, and caravans were often camped beneath Nazareth hill. An inquisitive young man could pick up a lot of philosophy around a caravan campfire. On the other hand, there is no reason why, at least once, he could not have gone up the Great Road to India himself. If you were Jesus and had missing years to kill, where would *you* go?

Nearly Normal Jimmy is of the opinion that Jesus took his missing years and went to Tibet. Without blinking a lash, Nearly Normal Jimmy will tell you that Jesus spent the prime years of his life on a lamasery prayer rug, charging his spiritual batteries for the work ahead. Nearly Normal Jimmy believes all things enlightened originated in Tibet. Adolf Hitler was of the same persuasion. I'm not kidding, its a fact. Hitler had a mystical streak as wide as the Rhine. Hitler believed the Aryans a super-race and his anthropologists traced the roots of Aryan stock to Tibet. Hitler went all out for Tibetan friendship. In 1939, there were more high lamas in Berlin than any place in the world outside of Lhasa. Nearly Normal Adolf.

Any way you look at it, Jesus was covering new territory. Rome to Seattle. Inside a plaster cast. Inside a wooden crate. Inside the freight belly of TWA Flight 115. The Atlantic Ocean lay beneath him like a frozen sky. And then the land. At the exact moment that his plane crossed over Newfoundland, an elderly St. John's lady, known for her visions of the Virgin, had an epileptic fit.

George O. Supper, taking Jesus to the air freight terminal, almost had a fit himself. His anxiety was unwarranted, however. He had shipped to New York or London at least a dozen of his plaster figures, and the customs officials were used to them by now. (Accustomed to them, I might say if I were of a mind to pun.) At 5 A.M., after a night of tremors, the customs men welcomed something to joke about. They deserved their laughs. They were men of the Italian tradition. Their culture had produced Michelangelo, Giotto, Leonardo, Botticelli, Raphael and Titian, to name but a few old masters. Who could blame them for poking fun at those crude plaster ghosts the Yankee Supper insured so heavily and labeled "Works of Art." The customs men were laughing so hard they failed to notice that on the Yankee's latest pale, lumpy and baseless "sculpture" the plaster was not yet dry. Nor did they pay particular attention to the fact that this last Supper (gulp!) was addressed not to a museum or gallery but to a "memorial hot dog wildlife preserve." Crazy Americans, anyway.

Plucky Purcell boarded the Jet Liner and sat down by the only unescorted female passenger on the flight. Her beauty was moderate, but Plucky needed her voice, her scents, to ease his nerves. He had been up all night—building the shipping crate, locating a fence to buy his gold. In the pizza-colored dawn, the implications of his body snatch were coming home to him. A shudder slid down his athletic backbone like a moon-mad snake down an alcoholic's watch chain. He turned to the young woman passenger. He gave her his cement-mixer grin. The plane cleared the field and she fell immediately to sleep.

For the time being, Purcell wasn't terribly worried. He

had analyzed the situation and drawn temporary comfort from his reasoning. (A tender "good morning" from his fellow passenger would have helped, but he would get along without it.) Only a few very powerful officials in the Church would know of the existence of the Corpse, he reasoned. It had been a night of chaos. Possibly, they did not know as yet that that most dangerous of skeletons had been liberated from Rome's closet. Even if they had discovered the theft, they would be limited as to steps they might take for recovery. Obviously, they would not be able to spread a general alarm. They would be afraid to alert the Italian police. Oh, if he, the Mad Pluck, were under suspicion, they might ask the help of secular authorities in tracking him down, but in the confusion of the moment they would not have settled on a suspect. Sooner or later, he would be their target and their agents would sniff for his trail, no question of that. But that was a day or two away. Meanwhile, he would have made it to the roadside zoo. He and his cargo. And then . . . ? Plucky lit a cigar. The stewardess ordered him to extinguish it. He snarled at her. "A woman is not always a woman, but a good cigar is a horse of a different feather," he growled.

Somewhere over the sea, over a pod of whales or a school of anchovy or some flotsam or some other confetti of the sea, the girl beside him awakened. Purcell could tell she had been dreaming, much as he and the Pope had been dreaming only nine hours earlier. "I just had a geographical dream," the girl said in a voice nearly as soundless as the jet. When he pressed her for details (before she turned to the window), she said, "It was a geographical dream. You know, one to file with your *National Geographics.*"

That was the week for coming out of dreams, trailing clouds of glory.

There is a time in the life of every little girl when she wants to grow up to be a nurse. There may be a time, too, when she wants to be a movie star or a cowgirl, but those fantasies quickly pass, while the nurse fantasy may linger—with intermittent cowgirl and movie star flashes—from kindergarten through the first years of high school. She will nurse her dolls for broken limbs or sawdust hemorrhages, scolding them when they fall out of bed or do not eat their mud-puddle soup. She will daydream of caring for real little babies and of giving aid and comfort to whole hospitals full of nice men like her daddy. The archetypal mother goddess, the ancient image of woman as nature's healer and restorer, stirs early in the breast of the female child. The experience of playing "doctor" with the little boys in the neighborhood in no way diminishes her ambition (O the pre-pubic thrill of the backyard enema!).

Amanda, an exception to the rule, never aspired to be a nurse. She mended the wings of dragonflies and in other ways fulfilled her duties as guardian of the life process, but there was a minimum of charm for her in the notion of wearing starched uniforms and performing mundane chores under orders from ill-tempered spinsters. Amanda did not want to be a movie star or a cowgirl, either.

"What are you going to be when you get big?" her father asked.

Amanda, in an orange sunsuit, had tired of chasing moths and was studying the peculiar afternoon shadow projected across the countryside by Bow Wow Mountain. "There is no name for what I'm going to be when I get big," she answered.

On the Rand McNally Atlas map of the world, the United States of America is colored pale lime. I assume it was an arbitrary choice of color. Not symbolic and certainly not realistic. As anyone who has flown cross-country well knows, the U.S.A. is greenish brown.

There may be patches of gray, yellow and blue, some solid chartreuses and some solid chocolates; but generally America, from the altitude of an airliner, is a light brown flecked, smeared or mottled with various shades of dull green. That color scheme is maintained from East Coast to West Coast, an admirable if monotonous consistency. One of the few places where the scheme is altered, where it really breaks down and becomes a color experience of a different order, is in the area of northwestern Washington. After hours of flight above lackluster greenish brown, a Seattle-bound plane will eventually cross the Cascade Mountain Range and suddenly find itself gliding over the open throat of an emerald. The scene below is moist and brilliant; a light, bright, pervasive green at once so misty and so vivid that one suffers the illusion that one has come at last to the only region of our nation that is truly green, the place where green turns Zen cartwheels in celebration of the death of brown.

Jesus spent most of his days in brown. Jesus walked on stony places and thin soil. Jesus climbed gaunt hills and naked mounds. Jesus slept in austere deserts and in towns made entirely of clay. Jesus was a child of the scorpionlands, a poet of the dun flanks of Galilee. The Mideast sun had baked brown into his eyes so thoroughly that not even the lush Plain of Gennesaret could relieve his thirsty vision. Now, thanks to Plucky Purcell, Jesus of the ultimate thorny brown was landing amidst the ultimate melting green. It is unfortunate that Jesus was not aware of his new surroundings. It would be interesting to observe what effects such a nebulous, green landscape would have upon the teachings of such a stark, brown philosopher.

As far as Purcell could determine, there were no Catholic agents waiting at Seattle-Tacoma Airport. He rode the limousine to the Olympic Hotel in downtown Seattle, took a taxi to a service station that rented U-Drive trucks, leased a van, drove back to the airport (stopping for a Big Mac burger and a root beer), picked up the destined crate and headed north on Interstate 5. It was about 4 P.M. when his tired eyes caught sight of the giant weenie. "There's the giant weenie," he said aloud. There was no response from the crate.

Having come finally to the Ziller's fabled roadhouse, Plucky threw himself through the door with an abandon that would have broken the joints of the gods. He traded his exhaustion and anxiety for a bouquet of surprise. "The message sent on the wind" (as the Tibetans call telepathy) had failed to advise Amanda of Purcell's visit, although since moving to the roadhouse she had known that momentous meetings were to transpire there. There was hugging and laughter and poetic exchanges and passings of the hashish pipe. Baby Thor climbed aboard Plucky's broad shoulders, and Mon Cul, bitten by the festive mood, executed a series of the most amazing somersaults. A toasty joy set the zoo aglow as the old friends savored reunion. But then there came the business of the Corpse. . . .

They opened the crate in the pantry. As John Paul, using his sculptor's tools, peeled the plaster from the mummy, Plucky paced. Ziller had never seen him nervous. Tremulous knees seemed incongruous on such a healthy specimen of manhood. Purcell, however, could recall other moments of knee flutter. First game on the Duke varsity. Opening kick-off. The ball seemed to float for hours in the tobacco-yellow Carolina September, hovering against the Indian summer blue sky like a sausage with gland trouble hovering over a meadow of hungry hobbits, lolling toward his end of the field with no more movement than a sailboat in a Dufy watercolor, tumbling finally toward his waiting embrace like a suicidal actress falling in slow motion at the climax of a French film, end over end in lazy lyrical descent while every eye in the bourbon-bathed stadium focused upon the much-heralded sophomore sensation; and eleven angry men, none smaller than himself, thundered toward him at one hundred times the speed of the buoyant football. A muted whump as the pigskin settled in his arms. Squeezed it harder than he had ever squeezed any hot-pants cheerleader in his daddy's old Pontiac. A leap down the field. Five yards. Fifteen. Then the nauseating crush. The breath flew out of him as wildly as if a buffalo in a rocking chair had suddenly rocked back on his lungs. Hit the ground so hard beads of blood rolled out of both nostrils. The crowd moaned with him, and together they, Plucky and the thousands, felt the tension evaporate in the mellow air.

"You, er, *know* who this is, don't you?"

"Yes," said Amanda slowly. "I think I do."

John Paul's head bobbed slightly in a cautious jungle nod.

Baby Thor and Mon Cul had fallen asleep. The last Beatles record had finished playing twenty minutes earlier and the phonograph had shut itself off. In silence, the three of them stood in the pantry and stared at the withered body.

"Well, what are we going to do with him?"

Ziller would say nothing. From his loincloth he pulled a small bamboo flute. He sat at the Messiah's feet and played very softly. The notes could not be heard outside the room.

Plucky turned to Amanda. "What are we going to do with him?" he repeated.

Amanda swabbed plaster dust from Jesus' forehead with a sponge. Her gaze was drenched with tenderness. "I think he deserves a decent burial," she said.

There are several ways of looking at an FBI agent. One of these ways is over a tsetse fly. Our tsetse fly was moored in a cube of amber, its thin wings frozen in single-minded elegance, its hairy legs straddling eternity. Not a bad way to be preserved, I thought—and then, still looking at the agent over the tsetse fly, I recalled the shabby remains of Our Lord.

A couple of days after Jesus arrived at the zoo, Amanda gave him a bath in a tub of Mr. Bubble and anointed him with oil of the prune. That helped a lot. When John Paul ran away with the mummy, moreover, he dressed it in Plucky Purcell's $250 pinstripe velvet-collared rock-and-roll suit, hacking inches off pant legs and coat sleeves with his hunting knife to get a fit. No matter how moldily he may for centuries have lain, the Messiah has gone to the apocalypse in style

From my perspective, the FBI agent's head rose above the coffin of the tsetse fly like a North Atlantic moon rising above a barge of lemon Jell-O. It was a cold moon whose light made lovers shiver and change their minds. The agent, as I saw him over the tsetse fly, was swinging his customary putting iron. He swung with bland concentration. If the agent had wanted to smile at his imaginary golf ball, neither Amanda nor I would have stopped him. But he swung with bland concentration. Perhaps he could not bridge the gap between the real club and the illusionary ball. Perhaps if he were on the links with the turf beneath his feet and a buddy to share his sport and no roadside distractions in his life, he would have gathered some mirth in his swing. He was, after all, a man still in his prime, not without dignity, not without a cleft chin for which any aspiring young actor would have paid dearly at the Cleft Chin Makers to the Stars.

The agent, as I saw him over the tsetse fly, looked as if he were someone's father. No doubt he was. The tone of his voice, in fact, was fatherly as he, contrary to orders, began to converse with Amanda in the kitchen.

"I can't understand you young people. I mean I just can't understand you. I guess you've just had it too easy, we've spoiled you 'til you're soft and rotten."

"How do you mean?" asked Amanda. She was boiling wheat custard for Thor's lunch.

"The way you show no responsibility . . ."

"Responsibility to *what?*" inquired Amanda.

"Why, to our democratic way of life, to our tax-supported institutions . . ."

"To individual human animals," Amanda ventured.

"Ours is a government of laws, not of men," the agent proclaimed.

"Maybe that's the problem."

"What do you mean, problem? You don't know what you're talking about. Our laws are sacred."

"Aren't our people sacred?"

"Until a law is removed legally from the statute books, it must be obeyed blindly by everybody if we want to continue to live in a democratic society and not slide back into anarchy. We've got to have laws and retribution. Ever since we crawled out of caves, retribution has followed wrongdoing as the night the day. When retribution ceases to follow evil, then the fabric of civilization begins to unravel."

Amanda stirred the custard. "If we've always had retribution, how do you know what happens when we don't have it?" she asked.

The agent scoffed. "You people. You people in this, this *weirdo* place." He gestured toward the front room, but did not see me behind the shrine of the tsetse fly, resting my hemorrhoids. "You people, that fucking magician, I don't know all it is you've got yourselves into. But you wouldn't be in this mess with your government and with the Church if somebody had raised you with a little guts, if somebody had put the fear of God in you."

"You're talking about the fear of authority."

"Authority. Damn right. You never learned to respect authority."

"In order to be respected, authority has got to be respectable." Amanda whipped the custard with a wooden spoon.

"Oh? Our duly constituted authority isn't respectable enough for you."

"The only authority I respect is that one that causes butterflies to fly south in fall and north in springtime."

"You mean God?"

"Not necessarily."

"You can't possibly question authority," said the agent, ignoring the implications of her last remark. "Who are you to question it. You don't remember the war against fascist aggression back in the forties, when America defended herself against Hitler, you weren't even born. Young lady, I risked my life in order that you could have freedom and education and all the good things of our society; the *authorities* of this nation saved it as a free and decent place for you to live in, but you don't remember that, do you? I risked my life . . ."

"You risked your life, but what else have you ever risked? Have you ever risked disapproval? Have you ever risked economic security? Have you ever risked a belief? I see nothing particularly courageous in risking one's life. So you lose it, you go to your hero's heaven and everything is milk and honey 'til the end of time. Right? You get your reward and suffer no earthly consequences. That's not courage. Real courage is risking something you have to keep on living with, real courage is risking something that might force you to rethink your thoughts and suffer change and stretch consciousness. Real courage is risking one's clichés."

The agent was thoughtful for a moment. Then he spewed, "What the hell do you know? Who are you, one infantile weirdo girl, to make those charges? What crap! What nerve! The United States of America is and always has been the greatest country on Earth."

"The United States of America is less than two hundred years old. There were great civilizations in India and China for four thousand years. Tibet was in a state of advanced enlightenment six thousand years ago." Amanda talked quietly. She loathed arguments. They were small-scale wars. "Here," she said. "Have some of this warm custard. There's plenty for all of us."

Amanda offered a Haida bowl brimming with custard. The custard steamed and soaked up milk. The custard did its work silently. It made a pleasing contrast to the cool Northwest rain that drummed its countless fingers on the woods and fields outside. That bowl of custard was something you could depend on; something domestic and secure. It would not run off to sea with Jack London or follow a shaman into his hut. That custard was tractable and responsible enough to suit any authority. And its warm diplomacy could conceivably heal ruptures between opposing philosophies. But the mention of China had been too much for the agent. China? Too much! Scorning the custard, he stalked out the back door, putting iron in hand, whirling around in the wet grove to yell, "I'm an American and proud of it!"

Amanda gently closed the door behind him. "I'm a human animal and prepared to accept the consequences," she said.

There are several ways of looking at a lovely young woman tasting custard. One of these ways is over a tsetse fly.

****

It is approximately 11 A.M. now but the rain is coming down like high noon. The sky is as gruff as a Chinese waiter. It keeps slamming silverware against the horizon. The sloughs look like spilled tea. Amanda, in a gypsy ensemble as gay as the day is dour, is standing by my table talking about the incident with the agent downstairs.

"Actually," she was saying, "he was rather fatherly."

"Yes, I believe he wants to like you. But the political gulf is too wide for him to cross."

"I don't know a thing about politics."

"That's *all* he knows. He's completely power-oriented."

"He's a symbol junkie."

"A what?"

"A symbol junkie. People like him—that is, the majority —are strung out on symbols. They're so addicted that they prefer abstract symbols to the concrete things which symbols represent. It's much easier to cope with the abstract than with the concrete; there's no direct, personal involvement —and you can keep an abstract idea steady in your mind whereas real things are usually in a state of flux and always changing. It's safer to play around with a man's wife than with his clichés."

Her logic is so simple that I am afraid to trust it. Yet, I want to keep her talking at all costs. "Give me an example," I say, zeroing in on her nipples which, like revolutionary raspberries, are storming the walls of her shawl.

"Laws are the most obvious example. Laws are abstractions. Laws symbolize ethical arts, proper behavior toward other human animals. Laws have no moral content, they merely symbolize *conduct* that does. These symbol junkies are always yelling about how we've got to respect the law, but you never hear one of them say anything about respecting fellow beings. If we respected each other, if we respected animals and if we respected the land, then we could dispense with laws and cut the middleman out of morality. Here in Washington State the government has a slogan, you may have noticed it, 'Drive Legally.' If this were a concrete, realistic (as opposed to a civilized) society, the bumper stickers would not say 'Drive Legally' but 'Drive Lovingly.' "

"What can we do about the symbol addicts?"

"Do about them? Marx, you do react to things in a peculiar way. Why, for goodness sake, should we do *anything* about them?"

I protest, but it is too late. She is leaving the room, going to her sanctuary (with its scents of Bow Wow scenery), going to try another trance, perhaps. And as she disappears behind the perfumed curtains, I hear her say once more: "I don't know a thing about politics."

For once, Amanda did not get her way. Had Plucky and John Paul consented, the lot of them would have left the next morning for the Southwest and lain Jesus to rest on Bow Wow Mountain.

"I thought about that little knoll overlooking the place where the Skagit north fork enters the Sound. You know, the one with the patch of *Amanita muscaria* and the mossy rock that looks like Walt Whitman's imagination. But that isn't right. Too much rain. Too much chlorophyll. He wouldn't be comfortable there. If we can't take him back to Nazareth, then Bow Wow is the spot for him. He'd feel at home on Bow Wow Mountain."

Sometimes one got the idea that Amanda thought Bow Wow Mountain was the center of the universe. But she didn't have her way. A rapid burial was not quite what Purcell had in mind for his treasure. And Ziller offered no opinion, he just kept blowing his flute.

Amanda and Plucky tried to talk it out, but Plucky was barely coherent and his voice took a turn toward the shrill. He clearly was experiencing nervous exhaustion. His sudden escape from the Church after a year of cloistered karate; the aftershock of his apocalyptic theft; the harried, sleepless night—these were taking their toll. It was touching to see so robust a man on the verge of hysteria.

"You'd better get some rest," Amanda said.

"Rest, hell, I can't rest." It wasn't like the Mad Pluck. He had snoozed in a station house swarming with hostile cops following the police riots in Chicago. Now, perched on an alchemist's stool, he lay his head against Amanda's shoulder. "What kind of mess have I gotten us into?" he moaned.

Amanda slipped her hand into the front of Purcell's jeans. Her arm, bracelets and all, slid down inside his shorts. Her fingers closed with exquisite gentleness around the twin pods of his testicles. She lifted them lightly and let them nest, like the eggs of a rare songbird, in the spoon of her palm. The bird stirred on its nest. The weight upon her hand gradually increased. Her fingers worked their way out to the blunt end of a corona that was ballooning and throbbing like an inflatable tomato.

"Well," said Amanda, "at least *part* of you is unbowed by Christian travails."

Plucky grinned sheepishly. His big aristocratic face, which minutes before could have been mistaken for Hamlet's mirror, cracked with a lopsided pool-hall leer.

"John Paul," Amanda said, throttling the tomato, "I'm going to take Plucky up and rock him to sleep."

Ziller nodded. He motioned with his eyes that they should use Marx Marvelous' apartment above the garage. As for himself, he continued to sit at the feet of the Christ, fluting single notes into the confines of the pantry as if he were feeding the fish in a pond.

Amanda and Plucky left by the kitchen door. When more than twelve hours later, I, in innocence, returned from vacation, she was still rocking him to sleep in my bed. If the sound I overheard was a lullaby, it was news to Brahms.

This next chapter begins with the image of a Greyhound bus streaking through a rural valley in the American West. That image is, in my humble estimation, an excellent one with which to begin a chapter (unless one is writing an epic of the Civil War) and I am gratified to have an opportunity to use it. Amanda came in just now to borrow a match for the lighting of incense and candles. I told her about the image with which this chapter begins.

"Good," she said.

"I think that's an excellent beginning image," I said.

"It's fine," agreed Amanda. "You sure you haven't seen the wooden matches?"

"It's just about as good a beginning image as anyone could come up with," I said. I was feeling cocky about my bus and my valley.

Amanda stopped searching for the matches and looked me over. "Yes, Marx," she said. "One could begin a chapter with an image of feats performed by fairies or an image

of immunity from certain disasters or an image of the moon-
stone and its properties or an image of Don Ambrosio's pact
with the Devil or an image of Chinese court dogs in moments of leisure or an image of the origins of virginity or
an image of an owl flying in an open window and perching
on Picasso's easel or an image of the unexplained appearance of gypsies in Europe in the fifteenth century or an
image of what J. H. Fabre in *The Life of the Caterpillar*
called the 'Great Peacock evening.' But you have chosen to
begin with a bus and a valley and that is wonderful. Now,
where are the fucking matches, dear? I've got my trance
to attend to."

This next chapter begins with the image of a Greyhound
bus streaking through a rural valley in the American West.
The bus is rolling toward Canada. It is the Seattle-Vancouver
express. Not many passengers on this bus are noticing the
huge flocks of ducks that are flying over the bus, flying
from the mountains visible miles to the right of the bus
and flying toward the salt marshes and inlets miles to the
left (and just out of sight) of the bus. Yet the passengers
on this bus are interesting if for no other reason than they,
like all who travel by Greyhound, believe—for the duration
of the trip, at least—in their own immortality.

Among the passengers on this bus—and, for the moment,
believing strongly in his immortality—is a mild-mannered
though slightly disreputable-looking young man who is trying to con the driver into making an unscheduled stop. The
driver had agreed earlier to let him off in Mount Vernon,
which was not a scheduled stop, either, but there is a
Greyhound depot there and they could get away with stopping for a second, but now the young man is saying, "That
roadside attraction about a mile up the road, the one
with the giant enormous weenie, that would be perfect."

The driver at last consents. With an irritated stomp of
the air brakes, he whooooozzzzeeeees to an unsteady halt

in the parking lot of the zoo and, of course, it is I, alias Marx Marvelous, who jumps out.

According to my calculations, the day was Thursday. Sure enough, the zoo was closed. I walked around back, barely squeezing my suitcase between the trees and the grotesque ends of the ever-changing horizontal totems that protrude from the corners of the building. "Oooff," I said, squeezing through. For a second, I was face to face with a horrible gargoyle bulldog. A string of sausages dangled from the fierce trap of his jaws. In his eyes were purple-red stones that Ziller had brought back from Africa. Or was it India? Carved drool dropped from the bulldog's lips and glistened on the flanks of the sausages. "This is where you live and work?" I asked myself incredulously.

I went directly to my quarters above the garage. The door was unlocked, but I had turned the knob only half-way when from my bedroom I detected the unmistakable grunts of love. I withdrew my hand. The grunts turned into giggles and the giggles into groans. "Hmmmmmm," I said. I started down the stairs. Then I thought, "That's *my* bedroom." I whirled back to the door and again I grasped the knob. The groans had turned into slobbers. My grip collapsed and fell from the handle. I resumed my descent. On the way downstairs, my brain chug-a-lugged a quart of Tabasco and wiped its lips with a saw.

In the kitchen, John Paul sat with Thor and Mon Cul, sharing an early lunch. Ziller had made cream of banana soup and they, the three of them, were dunking their doughnuts in it and lapping it from clay bowls. Ziller and his stepson were dressed in loincloths. Mon Cul, in between laps and dunks, would climb on the table and twirl from the light fixture, much as the broads in Ringling Bros. circus twirl from ropes while the band plays "I'm in Love with the Girl in the Moon." "This is the place where I work and live?" I inquired of myself once more.

The boy and the baboon waved wildly when I entered, slamming the door behind me. John Paul arched his mustache in welcome. Well, I *assumed* it was welcome. He offered me soup but was not surprised when I declined. He was aware of how red was my brain. "Relax," he said. "The Mad Pluck has returned from his Catholic odyssey and is even now enjoying the deserts of the prodigal."

Purcell was here! That made me feel better. But not much. Finding no other spirits, I poured myself a tumbler of wine vinegar, cursing the Italian who brought the grape to such ignoble end. I joined the rowdy trio at table and told Ziller a bit about my trip. In California, I had encountered an organization known as Frontiers of Science. Its members were scientists and interested laymen who had become concerned with the ultimate meaning of their lives and their work. For them, the line between the subject and the object was vanishing. Their creed was this statement by Heisenberg: "The scientist can no longer contemplate and investigate nature objectively but submits it to human questioning and ever links it to the destiny of man." Heeding the advice of Einstein and Oppenheimer, they were beginning to put their vast knowledge to a more inspired use than weapon-making and extraterrestrial one-upmanship. Their research in pure science had taken them beyond science into the realm of the personal, the poetic, the mystical . . . the occult. One of them explained in my presence why physicist Murray Gell-Mann calls his theory of mathematical symmetry among particles in space "the eightfold path." Another took me to a lecture on *Western Biology and the Tibetan Book of the Dead* in which the speaker accounted how advanced biologists have found karma and its corollary of reincarnation genetically reasonable.

John Paul could understand why I was attracted to Frontiers of Science. For the first time, I had found colleagues with interests somewhat similar to mine. I write "somewhat" because I still regarded 95 per cent of mysticism as a crock of crap. At the same time, however, I was convinced that science had a critical role to play in the religion of the future. For the winter, Frontiers of Science had leased a rundown resort hotel in the hills above Stockton. Its members were sponsoring three months of seminars and research. I told John Paul that I was considering joining them there. I didn't tell him that I was also considering *not* joining them. It was difficult to admit even to myself how much I had missed Amanda on my holiday. And I was still stubbornly, injustifiably of the opinion that something of consequence might transpire at the roadside zoo.

Something of consequence, indeed.

"You are back just in time," said Ziller. He gave me the

oddest look I have ever seen on a man's face. Perhaps it was the look of a wry warlock who, immediately prior to being burned at the stake, has requested wool socks to keep his feet warm. Then he took me to the pantry where he unfastened a brand new padlock and introduced me to Jesus.

By the time I Jeeped back from Mount Vernon, where I had mailed (via air, special delivery) a Corpse scraping to the radiocarbon dating lab, Amanda and Plucky Purcell were on their feet. Hoorah for them. Hoorah and hooray. I trusted that Mr. Purcell was adequately rested. I trusted that he had gotten his eight hours, as they say. He looked fit enough.

It was my first glimpse of Mr. Purcell. I thought, begrudgingly, that he resembled the actor Paul Newman, except that Purcell's cheekbones were higher than Newman's and his nose more aristocratic. Then he smiled. His smile was not like Paul Newman's. His smile was not aristocratic. His smile was like a splash of ham gravy on a Statue of Liberty necktie.

Amanda hugged me and kissed my cheek. Big deal. I said nothing. Outside, the mallards owned the sky. They traveled in high, vibrating lines. In frame houses all over Skagit County, men in tee shirts and house jeans sat calmly cleaning their shotguns. The continuum between the men and the ducks was eloquent.

After a while, I shoved my jealousy aside. If Ziller was unperturbed, and he seemed to be, why should it torment me? There were more important things at hand. Oh, such important things! I suggested that we gather around the oak table and pool our thoughts about this mummy we had on our hands. The moment I ceased trying to conceal my excitement, it gushed forth in geysers. Wow! Hell yes! Let's get at that mummy!

"No," said Amanda firmly. "Not today."

I couldn't believe my ears. Not today?

We were to have a cooling-off period, she explained. A time for adjustment. A ceremony. Things of moment must begin with ritual. It was the cadence of the ages. The following day the zoo would remain closed. We would meet all day, if necessary, and discuss the Corpse. For the present, however, we would prepare ourselves. At sundown, the ritual would begin.

"Look," I said, trying to speak evenly, "if that mummified body is who you contend it is, we have locked in our pantry a bigger firecracker than the hydrogen bomb. Do you have any idea how serious the repercussions might be? If that body is who you say it is, then every hyena in Christendom will be breathing down our collars by this time tomorrow. We could be murdered in our sleep."

"I don't think so," objected Plucky. "Oh, the high hyenas will be stirred up, all right. They've probably got every monk in the Felicitate Society assigned to the case right now. And they can use whatever resources they want of the CIA and the FBI. The CIA and the FBI have been sucking the Pope's shoes for decades, and that's a fact. But, you see, Marx, they will be working within some strict limitations. It's my guess that less than a dozen men in the whole world know of the existence of the . . . of the Corpse. And those dudes are all behind-the-scenes honchos at the Vatican. They can't tell the agents *what* it is they are looking for, or *why* they are after me. You dig? They can only order them to locate me. Okay. As shrewd as they may be, and as many resources as they can make use of, they still are going to have a tough time tracing me to this zoo. It'll take them a few days, maybe even a few weeks. Meanwhile, I've got some capers I want to pull with that Corpse. I didn't go to the risk of ripping it off just to have the Romans snatch it back. You're right, Marvelous, we've got us a megaton of celestial blasting powder lying in there in that pantry, and what use we put it to could change a lot of things for a lot of people for a lot of time. And we've got to reach an agreement on it pretty quick. But even so, I think we have time to prepare ourselves, as Amanda says."

Plucky lit a cigar and settled down on a pile of cushions, as if to give notice that he was ready for whatever ritual the setting sun might bring.

Amanda was pleased. "Tonight we shall feast," she said, "and tomorrow we shall fast."

"Fuck a duck," I grumbled, meaning no offense to the mallards overhead.

Amanda had said that we were to feast and as sure as Big Paint's rooster legs fit around a volleyball, feast we did. Amanda picked the Skagit Valley up by its damp green heels and shook its whole stash of goodies out onto our table. She shook out a silver salmon, big as a baby, baked with a sour cream glaze. There were fresh oysters, both steamed and raw. Late broccoli in a hot sauce with overt sadistic tendencies. Corn on the cob. Burdock tubers. Cattail roots. Biscuits baked from cattail pollen. Four varieties of wild fungus: chanterelles, meadow mushrooms, lepiota and king boletus. Cow parsnip (the stems were peeled and eaten raw like celery). Roasted lady-fern stalks. Creamed onions. Lichen soup. Pine nuts. Wild honey. Starfish eggs. Pumpkin pudding. Apples. Pears. And so forth and so on, all of the food having been gathered by the Zillers free of charge, as is still possible in Skagit country despite the toxic cement encroachment of industrial horrors.

"You people sure eat some queer things," I said.

"We have great knowledge of such things," said Amanda.

We washed dinner down with gulps of wine, as Jesus and his buddies would have done, and afterward the hash pipe circled the table, pausing to poke its stem into each set of lips as a thirsty hummingbird might insert its bill into every bloom in a lei of orchids. Having many of the common prejudices, I had never been entirely at ease with "drugs," but on that occasion the rich smoke worked its teases in my blood, its tiny wings fluttering to the rhythm of vegetable voodoo. "Must look into the botanical background of substance known as hashish," I jotted in my journal, writing by the light of candles that grew incessantly jewel-like even as protean wafts of incense approached my snout like platters of ripe fruits borne on the backs of

Nubian pages. My spine curled around a caravan cushion like the methodical lash of a slave whip, and after that trick, I really milked the Arabian imagery for all it was worth. "Take a letter to Kublai Khan," I said to Mon Cul, pretending that the baboon was my secretary. Instead, the creature showed me the deepest scarlet of his posterior as he rose to dance with Plucky Purcell.

Everyone enjoyed the ballet, though it was more obscene than graceful, and Baby Thor (decorated with berry juice for the occasion) followed it with a kiddie dance of his own. We laughed until we feared we'd wake the ducks snoozing out in the sloughs. Yet, through the ha-ha and the horseplay, the vibrations from the pantry continued to make themselves felt—don't think we, one of us, really forgot our Man in there. We were aware of his presence every minute, but, in his favor, he didn't put a damper on the evening: in fact, the mammoth secret of him contributed an odd topping of elation to the feast. And more than that, it just felt *good* having him about.

If the hash pipe played a part in the benevolence, well, let it be. After all, the hashish and the Christ were from the same neck of the woods. Wonder what other surprises that Middle East has got up its ancient crescent sleeve?

For comfort's sake, the party might have adjourned to the living room upstairs, but I guess nobody wanted to get too far away from the pantry. Rather, we pushed back from the table dreamily, as lazy boaters might push away from dock, and drifted on the choppy black eddies of saxophone flash flood that the Roland Kirk recordings sent gurgling and breaking and spraying down the steps, turning the staircase into a furious ebony waterfall. In Timbuktu, there is a university run by magicians indifferent to education. If Kirk was not playing excerpts from that school's curriculum, then why was the baboon mooning at his braided codpiece with such obvious nostalgia, and why was John Paul Ziller slowly gathering about him his family of painted drums?

The night was taking a turn toward the primitive, as if to prepare ourselves for the Christ we must shift our attention to the Devil and see what insights *he* might offer. The red-assed ape scratched his hide, Ziller scratched his drums, the distant Kirk saxophone had a sudden bowel movement of the most primordial chords, and the scorching, popping, spitting charisma of the bogey man seemed all about us. In white Western civilized fear, I looked to the pantry, but the vibrations that flowed through its walls were serene and seemed to say, "Relax. It's all in the family."

On that hairy note, Amanda, in a skimpy dress of woven cornstalks and wearing more than the usual inventory of beads, bracelets, rings, bells, amulets and ribbons—and golden flakes embedded in her makeup—stood up before us and changed the game. Hamstrung by hashish and hoodoo, I was in no condition to record her words, but, in effect, she told us that it was story time. Like the Indians who had lived on this spot at the time of Christ, like the gypsy chieftains around their private fires, we were to take turns entertaining and edifying one another with tales appropriate to the occasion.

Ah, that's more like it, I thought, for that other business was giving me goose bumps where no bumps ought to be. My connection to the material world was like the bond of the dancer with his partner, and I didn't cotton to no dark formless shapes from the stag line of the Irrational cutting in. So to speak. Do you?

"I'll go first," volunteered Amanda, and that delighted me further for although she was forever singing to things and at things, I could not recall her ever having told a formal yarn. On cue, the phonograph shut off, Ziller rolled his drums, and we sat back and waited for Amanda's lisp, pretty as a pink snail, to crawl into our hearing.

AMANDA'S STORY

In the garden known as Eden, our mythological sweethearts went too far. Tempted into unnatural positions by the Trickster, they aroused the censors who promptly shut them down. Management threw in a curse to boot, and that primal curse declared that the earth, because of man's funky nature, would thereafter bring forth thorns and thistles.

As it came to pass, thistles grew almost everywhere. Wherever thistles grow, however, there is found the thistle butterfly—the "painted lady" or *Pyrameis cardui*, as our academic friends are in the habit of calling it. All over

Europe, all over North America, in Africa—save for the dense jungles of the Congo—throughout South America, in far-off Australia, and on many islands of the sea this beautiful butterfly is found. At some seasons it is scarce, but then again there are times when it fairly swarms, every thistletop having one of the gaily colored creatures squatting on its head, and among the thorny slums of the leaves being found the webs which the caterpillar weaves.

Once, on Bow Wow Mountain, having followed some butterflies into a thistle patch much as young scholars follow Great Truths into a university, I held a thistle crown to my ear, expecting, as a result of having read that awful Tennyson in Eighth Grade Lit., to hear the inner workings of the cosmos. It pricked.

You might say that after that, I was anti-thistle curse. But the butterflies continued to come and go, back and forth, like phone calls between Adam's and Eve's lawyers and the censorship board. Hoping to settle out of court.

* * * * * * * * * * * * * * * * * * * *

"Amanda, how'd you like another cup of wine?"

"Oh, no thanks, Marx. No more for me."

"How about you, Plucky?"

"Sure, man. Fill 'er up."

John Paul had taken Amanda's place at the front of the kitchen. Evidently, he was offering to tell his story next. That was okay with me. That was sure okay. I hadn't a word in mind. Accompanying himself on a small barrel drum suspended in archaic fashion from his neck, Ziller began, in a voice negroid but glossy, to recite from his African diary.

JOHN PAUL ZILLER'S STORY

The road to Boboville runs through the backyard of a fetish. Here they chain clouds to bamboo poles and keep the winds shut up in pots of terra-cotta.

We stop in order to cool our blisters and to make discreet inquiries concerning the elements. The sun is of particular interest.

Maidens pass among us selling bubbles that they have

trapped in their pubic hair while bathing in the river. Imitating Dr. Schweitzer, they take my temperature. And bring me another.

The art of tying the rain in three knots is explained to us by a shaman. Perhaps intentionally, he leaves out two essential steps in the process.

As the sun sinks lower and lower in the greasy green Congo, the maidens play the game of cat's cradle in order to catch it in the meshes of string and so prevent its disappearance. Darkness is a long time coming. We offer a carton of Chesterfields for the secret, but the high priest smokes filter tips only.

Soon, campfires are lighting up the equator like rubies in the belt of a heavyweight champion. Rattles hiss in black fists. Pig fat stews in the cookpot. Magic sticks are removed from the clay holes where they have spent the day. The chanting grows so loud it causes our hammocks to pitch and toss, as if we were aboard a ship. In order to dilute the noise and to disperse the smoke from the barbecue, a gentle breeze is released from a jar. It plays on the bare breasts of the dancing maidens and ripples the potent beverage our hosts have served in cups made from inverted toadstools. It ruffles the fur of the sacrifice.

The curtain of jungle parts to let in a party of missionaries anxious for a weather report. They are on their way to an organ concert in Schweitzer's amphitheater and are concerned that it doesn't monsoon. The missionaries are shocked by the degree to which paganism has permeated meteorology. They pass out picture postcards showing how Jesus calmed the storm on Galilee, and read papers on such subjects as the Great Flood and the parting of the Red Sea.

By morning, the whole tribe is converted to Christianity. The maidens, in one-piece Catalina swimsuits, are being sprinkled on the riverbank, and shamans are sheepishly singing "Rock of Ages" as the collection plate fills to overflowing with jewels and nuggets formerly used in their profession.

Thus, we continue on to Boboville with no further knowledge about the sun other than that it is classified among the yellow dwarf stars: a vast sphere of hot gas orbiting the Milky Way while converting four million tons of matter into energy every second in accordance with Einstein's basic formula, $e = mc$ squared.

****

Ziller closed with a cavalry charge of polyrhythms. As loud as it was, the drum did not awaken Baby Thor or Mon Cul, who, arm in arm, had fallen asleep in a corner. Amanda covered the sleeping pals with a quilt. As she did so, she signaled to me that I should be the next to tell a tale.

Well, all right. Ziller's reference to Professor Einstein had given me an idea. I would tell a story about science. After all, science was what I knew best. But I wouldn't discuss the Apollo space program or my own experiments concerning the properties of the crushed state of ions. No, I would talk about "strangeness numbers" and the "absolute elsewhere," recent concepts of sufficient poetic sparkle to hold the interest of this group. A splendid solution. When I went to the front of the room, however, the hashish and the wine (I guess it was) took over and my mind dumped another load entirely.

MARX MARVELOUS' STORY

My Baltimore childhood was made out of bricks. Bricks. And more bricks. Here in the Pacific Northwest, they build everything out of timber. Back in Baltimore, it was brick. Boyhood vistas of brick row houses lined up along brick streets. Brick sunsets, brick picnics, brick newspapers delivered on frosty brick mornings. Everything the color of bacon and dried blood: brick. I lived in brick homes, went to brick schools, bought Snicker bars in brick candy stores, watched Gene Autry rout the bad guys in brick movie theaters, and played lacrosse on brick playfields behind brick walls. Only the churches were wooden. The Protestant churches, that is. The first church I attended, the one out in Chesapeake Hills, was white frame and so was the one the family attended when we moved closer into town. Come to think of it, I don't recall ever seeing a brick Protestant church in Maryland, although I'm sure there must be some. Everything else was brick, but the churches were usually wooden. As if brick was okay for secular things but when he got down to salvation, a Baltimore Protestant needed wood around him. The Catholics didn't make those distinctions; praying or profiteering, they took brick.

There was a brick tavern on the Baltimore waterfront called the Big B. B for Baltimore. Maybe B for brick. It should of been D for Dizzy Dean. They worshiped Dizzy Dean in that tavern, even though he pitched for the St. Louis Cardinals and never played in Baltimore. The Big B tavern was a shrine to Dizzy Dean. The bartender had purchased Dean's old strikeouts and melted them down and made candles. The day Dizzy pitched and won both games of a doubleheader was encased in a corner of that tavern with fresh cornflowers at its head and feet and applause draped around it like bunting.

When he was a young man, my father spent a lot of time in the Big B. He drank Red Top ale and cracked the great delicious Chesapeake crabs or slurped the great delicious Chesapeake oysters—depending on the season—and talked with the Big B regulars about Dizzy Dean. It was a happy thing, although sometimes it got drunk and mournful and throbbed like Dizzy Dean's foot when he got it broken by a line drive to the mound.

Marriage to my mother ended my dad's Big B career just as that line drive to the mound ended Dizzy Dean's pitching career. My mother thought alcohol in any form was the sperm of Satan, and although I doubt if Dad ever truly shared her sentiments, he went along with them. Just hitched his water wagon to the shooting star of her faith.

You see, my mother was a stampede of fundamentalist religion. The Baptist faith was her shield and her sword. She outfitted herself in it and stormed into life, defying anyone or anything to oppose her. In her righteousness, she was invincible, and we never for a moment forgot it. When her nose wasn't in the Bible or her Sunday-school-lesson magazine, it was in the air in pious defiance. God was on *her* side, you bet. She spoke of her Master, Jesus, as if she and he were as cozy as bugs. And the way she talked about the Reverend Billy Graham, well it made me as ashamed for my father as if he were an actual cuckold.

For Mother, it was simple. You either believed the King James Version of the Bible, word for word, cover to cover,

or you didn't. If you did, you were one of God's chosen
ones and owned your fair share of stock in eternity. If
you didn't, you were "lost." My dad didn't want to be lost,
any more than anybody else, so he went along with Mother's
bag, often defending it in his own quiet way, but I had
the sneaky notion that he would rather have spent an hour
in the Big B with Dizzy Dean than an eternity in Paradise
with Norman Vincent Peale.

As for me, I was spooked by the whole scene. Its om-
nipotence overwhelmed me and made me feel inadequate,
guilty and uncomfortable. I didn't reject my Baptist training or, for that matter, even question it. But I longed for
relief, wishing that just once I could open my box of Self
out of range of God's blue eyes. The constant invasion
of my privacy brought me down.

In the summer of my thirteenth year, shortly after I
(with vague misgivings) had been baptized in the Potomac
River, I learned that Einstein was an atheist. My mother
herself had told me that Einstein was the smartest man
in the world, and now, sitting in my tiny alcove room
overlooking the evening streets of Baltimore, I read in a
magazine that Einstein not only had not been "saved," but
he didn't even believe in God. My dad, home late from
the hardware store, called me to supper. And called me
again. But I sat looking out the window thinking bewilder-
ing new thoughts—while Baltimore frowned from brick to
brick.

From that day on, each little intellectual step I took was
a giant stride away from Christian dogma. Yet, stretch and
pull as I might, I couldn't snap the emotional bonds. Intellectually, I soared high and free, but my emotions remained anchored in Baptist bedrock. Even today, I cannot
claim that I have snipped the ties. In college, after a night
of drinking and discussion, I would lie on my cot—head
humid from the booze and voice box raw from the rough
winds of debate—and wish that I had the simple faith of
my parents to bolster me. Tonight, here at the zoo, I wish
it still. Is that man's fate: to spend his closest hours to
truth longing for a lie?

* * * * * * * * * * * * * * * * * * * *

I caught myself staring first at the pantry, as if my confession had been a kind of prayer that the Man inside might act upon, and then at my three companions to see if my confession had spattered pitch on their bright mood. From my friends I received only the polite nods and smiles that had acknowledged the first two stories. From the pantry there was neither sign nor sound. I sat down.

Purcell ambled up and took my place. He chomped his stogy and began to drawl.

PLUCKY PURCELL'S STORY

I used to be enamored of a chick so mean that if she had been a kangaroo she would've sewn up her pouch. She had two husbands, one a Protestant chaplain with the boys in Vietnam and the other a cop who had accidentally sprayed himself with his own can of Mace and was in a V.A. hospital trying to get his 20/20 vision back. She collected checks from both of 'em and she had her door nailed shut from the inside and wouldn't open it for nobody. I had to crawl in through a small hole in the laundry room floor. Just behind the drier.

You may be wondering why someone of my background was attracted to a woman of such low character? And what she taught me about the power of positive thinking? Well, it was—

Knock! Knock! Knock!

There came a heavy and authoritative rapping at the front of the zoo.

Knock! Knock! Knock!

Again, a most violent and official knuckling. Plucky staggered back a few steps and nearly swallowed his cigar. I spilled wine all over my knees and froze in place. Even unflappable Amanda turned pale as a petal.

Only John Paul had his senses about him. Within seconds, he had moved from the rear of the kitchen into the dining-room-and-zoo-proper, sailing in long silent strides like a cat of the veldt, yanking his dagger from his loincloth as he moved. He sprang so quietly and quickly I honestly was unaware of his movement until I suddenly saw him crouched by the front door, blade in hand, ready to strike.

Plucky was the next to thaw. As three ominous knocks

echoed once more through the roadhouse, he regained composure and ran to the pantry, where he checked the lock. When he was satisfied that the small room was secure, he stationed himself by its single entrance, poised like a guru of Oriental brawling, his muscular hands and feet prepared to hold off a platoon of commandos should one foolishly undertake to assault his position.

Next, Amanda came unfrozen. She rushed agilely about the kitchen blowing out candles. The roadhouse fell into blackness. Trembling, I stood and braced myself, for what I did not know.

The scent of peril was so thick in the zoo that it snatched Mon Cul from his sleep. However, the baboon contributed no foolishness. Instinctively wise in the ways of the hunted, he merely growled very low in his throat and readied himself for fight or flight without betraying his whereabouts. In the front room, we could hear the garter snakes stirring in their pen. Perhaps the fleas, too, sensed danger, but, of course, we had no way of gauging their reaction.

Baby Thor slept peacefully. In the dark, I could make out Amanda standing over him as a tigress stands over a threatened cub. Something cold had invaded the roadhouse, like a wave unbound by ocean. We entertained our separate fears and listened to the urgent roar of blood.

Knock! Knock! Knock!

On our psyches if not on the door, it left the imprint of the gestapo glove.

When at last Ziller flung the door open, my heart fell like one of those sets of false teeth that periodically are dropped off the Golden Gate Bridge. The figure silhouetted in the doorway was in uniform. Why did I find the attire of our visitor less than assuring? Hadn't I been taught that the policeman was my friend? At least there was only one of them, as far as I could tell. Would he go for his gun—or what?

"Special delivery for Ziller. Mr. and Mrs. Ziller."

John Paul accepted the letter and returned to the kitchen far less hastily than he had left it. Amanda switched on the lights. To hell with candles.

"Aren't we a pretty pack of paranoiacs?" said Purcell. I didn't share his embarrassment. Considering what we had to hide, I didn't find our shyness a bit misplaced.

We heard the mailman drive away. Then, as Plucky and I finished off the wine straight from the bottle, John Paul used his dagger to slice the envelope. It bore a blue stamp with a picture of a hooded cobra on it and a postmark that read New Delhi, India. Due to the jitters of the moment, I neglected to obtain a copy of the letter or to successfully memorize its contents. However, if the reader will trust me, I am certain that I can accurately summarize the message.

The author of the letter was a young woman serving with the Peace Corps in India. She was writing on behalf of Nearly Normal Jimmy. Jimmy could not attend to the correspondence personally, as he was otherwise occupied. He sent his love.

Disappointment, it seems, had marred Nearly Normal's sojourn among the Tibetan refugees in New Delhi. He had failed to receive an audience with the Dalai Lama, who had taken to reading *Time* magazine and *Reader's Digest* and had publicly expressed doubts concerning his own divinity. The god-king drove around in a Nash Rambler and talked about a trip to Europe or America to learn more of the West. In the papers, he spoke of investing his followers' funds in Swiss securities. Among his aides at Tibet House, the conversation was not of *tumo* or *Myanghdas* or the coil of birth and death or the Thousand-spoked Wheel of the Good Word of Buddha, but of politics, economics and international diplomacy. It appeared that a whole new sphere of interest had opened up for the theocrats. "They've discovered the Mickey Mouse *bardo*," Jimmy complained bitterly. "Contrary to the old saw, you cannot only take the lama out of Tibet, you can also take Tibet out of the lama."

So, on October 2, a disillusioned and desperate Nearly Normal Jimmy did what no white man had done in two decades, and few ever. He crashed across the most forbidden frontier on Earth.

Jimmy, O Jimmy! Son of Arizona's most successful insurance salesman. Born with a silver policy in his mouth. Honor student, class president and voted "most likely." Admitted to U. of Arizona at age sixteen on full scholarship. Precocious wizardling of finance. Wall Street gritting its paper teeth in anticipation of his onslaught. Weekend house guest of the Goldwater clan. Despite bulldog nose and acute myopia, Southwest debutante's delight. Jimmy. Who, on his palomino with expensive saddle, followed Amanda's motorcycle up the Bow Wow trail—and learned a different arithmetic. Jimmy, Jimmy.

The Peace Corps girl had watched him go. Crossing the prohibited mountains by the shine of midnight moon. Darting like a jack rabbit through the Himalayan ice, cowboy boots kicking up stones and churning snow, footsteps flying in cataract against the crusted banks of the river bed, glasses fogged, giggling madly, long red hair flapping in the thin air at the rooftop of the planet. Jimmy! Defying Communist machine-gunners and forty centuries of esoteria, arcane fancies dancing in his head, he sprinted furiously toward the fabled holy city of Lhasa . . . clutching under arm as if it were the jewel in the lotus, a rattling tin canister containing four reels of *Tarzan's Triumph*. Nearly Normal Jimmy. Barrel-assing toward Buddhahood. *Om mani padme hum*. Yippie!

We awoke the next morning to the sound of distant guns. Perhaps more than one of us imagined, as we toppled out of dreams, that the armies of the Vatican were advancing across the pea fields. For sure, *I* leaped to the window and searched the horizon for gaudy standards, for frenzied Latin temperaments, for canteen wagons crammed with pasta and peppercorns.

Of course, it was merely the opening of the duck season that had aroused us. Hunters' skiffs plied the river and the sloughs. Men and boys under red hats tramped the marsh-meadows and the low dikes that delineate the cattail-and-sedge-lined pockets of backwater. From my window, the red hats looked like polkadots that had escaped from a bandanna and run to the marshes in an effort to elude the bloodhounds. There was not a mallard in sight.

Unencumbered by breakfast, the four of us gathered in the pantry. Thor had been fed and left to play in the kitchen. The toy he selected that morning was a wooden duck. I suggest that we consider it a coincidence. Mon Cul had been assigned to guard duty outside the pantry door. As scouts and sentries, baboons are reputedly better than Indians, although a cowboy-and-baboon movie is too much for us to expect from television.

The Corpse lay on the butcher's table right where we had left it. It looked like something that had been dragged out of the storeroom in an Egyptian flophouse. Nevertheless, it had a presence. Nothing you could offer me, not even two weeks with Amanda in a honeymoon resort, could persuade me to say that it had an "aura." Aura schmaura. But it had *something*. An intensity of being that went beyond psychological suggestion or wishful thinking. If the Christ in life had had, as the cliché goes, "leadership written all over his face," then death had been a bum eraser.

John Paul Ziller sat at the head of the Corpse. Tall, thin, dark, gaunt and bushy. He wore low on his hips a sun-brilliant white loincloth, from the waistband of which protruded a dagger and a flute. His long neck was ringed by a collar of monkey fur, and teeth that some witch-dentist had plucked from a reptile.

At the feet of Our Lord, closest to the exit, sat Plucky Purcell. Husky, handsome, Aryan, forehead broad and manly beneath tight curly hair that was receding at a gallop. An occasional grin upset his fine features like linoleum yanked from under the feet of an emperor. He was dressed in logger's pants and a faded sweatshirt that bore the legend "Tijuana Jail."

On the right hand of Jesus was Amanda. Fat-cheeked, pouty-mouthed, paganized, poised, vulnerable and regal, the full sweet funk of womanhood rising like steam from her open pores. Her green eyes shone like Renaissance icons. She wore a pound of jewelry, a peasant blouse, and a skirt of many colors in the lap of which she folded her hands as might a pious nun.

Yours truly sat at the left side of Christ. I had previously recommended that we approach the problem of him much as the problem might be approached in a think tank, and since no one else had a better plan, we concurred. As I was the only person here familiar with a think tank's operation, I was elected to officiate at the proceedings. Fair enough.

"To begin with," I said, facing my three friends and the mummy from Rome, "to begin with, Plucky has assured me that we have a minimum of three days to attack our problem. Considering the nature of the problem, that is far from adequate time, but we must do with what we have. Ahem. Today, I thought we could engage in some elementary group discussion about the, eh, matter, while tomorrow each of us will remain alone to read and ponder and to think out a solution as best he can. The third day, we shall meet together here in the pantry again for deep and conclusive discussion. At the end of the third day—that will be Sunday night—we must come to a final decision as to what is to be done about the . . . Corpse." (Note: from that time on we seldom referred to our guest other than as "the Corpse.") "Is everyone agreed?"

Ziller nodded inscrutably, Amanda nodded coyly and Purcell said, "That's okay by me, man. Let's get into it."

"Well, then. I suppose the logical point of departure is to ask ourselves if our Corpse is really whom we suspect it is. Could such a thing be possible?"

"You know how I feel about it," said Plucky. "Even if your radiocarbon dating report comes back that the dude died in 1918, I'll still believe he's who I believe he is and not the Unknown Soldier Goes Italian."

Amanda giggled. "Why couldn't it be possible?" she asked.

"While I was in Mount Vernon yesterday, I picked up a copy of *Jesus* by Charles Guignebert at the public library. Let me read you this passage."

"My goodness, Marx," exclaimed Amanda.

"What?"

"I don't know. I mean you're just so *efficient.*"

Not knowing if she was complimenting me or putting me down, I opened the hefty book and commenced to read aloud: " 'There are many serious contradictions in the Gospel accounts of the Resurrection. It is evident that the one statement that they have in common—*the tomb in which Jesus was placed the night of his death was found empty the next morning*—has been amplified by various (after the fact) details intended to explain how it took place, and which, because they vary so greatly in the different accounts, are all suspect. Suspect at the least of not corresponding to any memory and of arising from apologetic considerations.'

"Let me read another short passage: 'Much ingenuity has been wasted in an attempt to establish the probability of the removal of the body either by the Jews who had commanded the crucifixion; or by Joseph of Arimathaea, the rich believer who, having provisionally deposited the body in the tomb near Calvary, would come and remove it in order to give it a final burial elsewhere; or by some of the women; or by some disciple without the knowledge of the others. The eviction of the body by the owner of the tomb has also been suggested; or that Jesus was only apparently dead, and that, having fallen into a comatose state, he might have been awakened by the chill of the tomb, escaped, and taken refuge with the Essenes sect, or elsewhere, and survived forty days or more.' "

"I'll bet the women did it," said Amanda. "I'll bet they took him out of the tomb and cared for him and gave him a decent burial in some little garden somewhere. That's what *I* would have done."

For the moment, I ignored her.

"Professor Guignebert goes on to personally testify—in a more pessimistic vein—that the whole story of the empty tomb was a myth. He says, 'The truth is that we do not know, and the disciples knew no better than we, where the body of Jesus had been thrown after it had been removed from the cross, probably by the executioners. It is more likely to have been cast into the *pit for the executed* than laid in a new tomb.' "

I closed the book. "So much for that. The conclusion we can draw from the scholars is that nobody really knows what happened to the body. There is no historical proof and not even any biblical agreement as to what was done with the body. So, if we don't accept the story that Jesus ascended into the heavens, either assisted by flying saucers or under his own steam—and I for one don't believe that anybody, Jesus, Buddha, Captain Marvel or anybody else, ever went skydiving in reverse—then we can entertain the idea that somebody might have snatched the body, hidden it, and later whisked it out of the country. Paul or Peter might have had reason to harbor the body, and they could have smuggled it into Rome even more easily than Plucky smuggled it out. Or some other early Christian could have taken it abroad for safekeeping any time during the forty years that elapsed between the crucifixion and the destruction of Jerusalem. In fact, that is the more likely explanation since, as the body is mummified, it probably lay for a long while in a hot, dry climate: Palestine instead of Italy. I'm not saying that is what happened, mind you, or even that it is probably. But we can rest on the knowledge that it is possible."

Purcell squinted his eyes and rubbed his expansive brow with his fist. "Marvelous, my man, I don't want to cool your trip, *but* . . . all you've said is academic bullshit. It doesn't matter one damn bit how the Corpse got to the Vatican. Dig? All that matters is that I found it there. It might be interesting to study the background; yeah, it might be a real groovy subject to write papers on and lecture about someday. But save that for your old age, man. Right now, we've got a much hotter item on our agenda." He tapped the Corpse on its kneecap, respectfully but gingerly. "This here is the body of Jesus Christ. I found it. We've got it. Some real shook-up folks are gonna come looking for it. What are we gonna do with it? That's the question, and everything else is academic."

Very, very much I longed to dispute Purcell's assertions. I wanted to deny that there was more than the wispiest circumstantial evidence that our mummy had been the man celebrated as Christ. But when I touched the wrinkled victim and felt the centuries of distance between us throb with light, the margin of rational disbelief slimmed before my eyes and protest died in my throat the way sleepy-lagoon wallpaper dies in the hall of a cheap hotel.

* * * * * * * * * * * * * * * * * * * *

Nobody could blame Purcell for being impatient. What a relief it would have been if we could have reached a speedy decision! But although Plucky's surge through life may have been crass and physical, he had never been a dummy. Moreover, in the course of his odd extralegal relationships with poets and artists, he had acquired a broad if uneven education. He recognized what an awesome responsibility we had, we who must decide the fate of Christ's body—and, perhaps, in so doing, the fate of Christianity and the fate of the Western world. Yes! It could come to that! And in the secret brothel of his heart, Plucky knew that before we reached a decision on this matter we must establish a foundation for that decision. So, begrudgingly, he allowed me to persist in my think-tank approach, although in deference to his impatience I sacrificed a large measure of thoroughness.

In the main room, the Puerto Rican wall clock sounded the hour of 8:50 (it was always ten minutes behind). There was a slight rustling in the snake pen. Who knew how the fleas were enjoying their holiday? As for the tsetse fly, it was as self-contained in its lonely house of permanent preservation as was the Corpse who was laid out on the table before us like a banquet at a Rotary Club for ghouls.

"Assuming," said I, "that the Corpse is who we suspect it to be, the next question is: what are the implications of it having been concealed by the Roman Catholic Church? Plucky believes that only a tiny handful of Vatican officials know about the Corpse. Right, Plucky?"

"Yeah. I'm sure of it. Just a few administrators in the Holy Office would know about it. The information would have passed down from generation to generation by a very select hierarchy of hard-nosed fascists. Otherwise, you know, it would of leaked out long before now. As for the general run of cardinals and bishops and monsignori, some are good, kind, loving holy men and lots are psychopathic, ambitious, egotistical power freaks as ugly as any that work the street corners of Hell. But good or bad, they—being human—couldn't carry on without their faith. Why, those jackals in the Felicitate Society have a sincere belief in Jesus and Mary, even though their duties are a mockery of everything Christ is supposed to have stood for. No, I'm sure that only a handful of big operators are in on the concealment. Maybe even the popes aren't always in on it. I doubt if Pope John XXIII was. On the other hand, Pius XII was just the type to have been a party to it. This current cat, I don't know about him. Say, Amanda, is it against the rules of the fast for me to light up a stogy?"

"Well, no, I suppose not. Go ahead."

"Okay," I said, grimacing at the unmoving fish to which Plucky applied the heat of his match, "if only a tiny band of high-echelon conspirators have been aware through the ages that Jesus was not alive and well in Heaven but stone-cold dead in the basement of the Vatican, what has been their motives; what are the implications of the concealment? Look, folks, *the Resurrection is the foundation of Christianity.* It's the mainstay. You might say that without the fact of the Resurrection, the Christian religion is just an empty charade. Maybe it ought not to be that way, since immortal or not, Jesus taught a lot of wonderful things to help man lead an ethical and humane life, but that's the way it is." I opened the New Testament I had purchased in Mount Vernon the afternoon before. "Let me read you this in Paul's own words. It's First Corinthians 20:14: 'And if Christ be not risen, then is our preaching in vain, and your faith is also in vain.'

"There you have it. Whether or not the idea of the Resurrection is relevant to the true meaning of Christ, it has been essential to the foundation, development and expansion of the Christian Church. Right? Now, if certain key Catholic administrators have been aware all along that there *was* no Resurrection . . ."

"Then the Church is the biggest can of worms in human history," said Purcell through a ghost-sheet of smoke.

"Maybe. Maybe and maybe not. Depends on the motives."

"Why is that, Marx?" asked Amanda. Although she had contributed little to the discussion so far, Amanda remained curious and alert. Ziller, on the other hand, seemed content to stare moodily at the Corpse, studying it from all angles as fellow magicians had studied Houdini's butterpat-in-an-empty-cafeteria trick.

Before I could answer, Purcell butted in. "There's a sound possibility, chums, that the highest spiritual authority in human history" (Plucky was growing enamored of that phrase "in human history") "has never been concerned with matters of the spirit at all. Not the top dogs, anyway. There's the possibility that it has always been a secular organization masquerading as a religion. The fact is, and it is a *fact,* the Catholic Church has never had but one single ultimate goal: the total mental, physical and spiritual domination of every being on this globe. Every move the Church has made throughout its existence has been to further that goal. Despite periodic lapses in taste, such as the Inquisition and the various purges and conquests, it's been crafty and subtle in moving on its goal. Crafty and subtle—and *successful*, considering that there are 650 million Catholics in the world today, and that the Church is the richest corporation in the world and one of the most powerful political forces. Today, the Church is more apt to use censorship and economic boycott and political pressures to get what it wants—it has learned the lesson of more civilized conquerors—but it's still working day and night for totalitarian Earth domination. You'd better believe it. If that big old bulldozer of conquest was operating in the interests of Jesus and Mary and God—as incongruous as that might be—it wouldn't be half so scary. But now that we know that *they* know that their Christ was not divine and that their most essential dogma is only a con job, well, what are we to think but that the Church is, at its highest level, a super-duper fascist conspiracy that uses the Jesus hype just to control people and manipulate them?"

Purcell's speech sent a shiver up my spine like an electric eel shinnying up an icicle.

"As much as I'd prefer to deny it, Plucky, your contention is a definite possibility."

"Why would you prefer to deny it?" inquired Amanda. Her hands were still folded in her lap.

"Why? Because, dear, if the high authority of the Vatican has never believed in Jesus but has only used Christianity as a front for political and economic tyranny, then . . . well, it's just too depressing to dwell on. Even its critics have seen Catholicism as a moral, if misguided, force. But if it has been consciously secular all along, if it has been immoral in its liver and its bones, then it represents an evil so frigging huge and dark and deep that it makes the human spirit seem puny and gullible: too vulnerable to cherish. It makes the struggle of living seem a sick joke."

"Oh, Marx," Amanda sighed. "You're so melodramatic. So what if it's this way or that way? When I was in convent school I used to stare out the windows at the clouds. I used to chase butterflies in the Mother Superior's flower patch. Those clouds and those butterflies, they didn't know secular from religious—and they didn't care."

"I'm neither a cloud nor a butterfly," I snapped.

"We're all the same as clouds and butterflies. We just pretend to be something different."

My next remarks I addressed to Purcell. "Your contention is a possibility, but there is, fortunately, another possibility. Myabe the Vatican bosses have been more enlightened than we suspect. Maybe they have always known that Christ's life was an example for the living and not a sky-pie promise for the dead. Maybe those few hardy leaders have been cognizant of that and could accept it; but simultaneously, they have been aware that the mass of Western man could *not* accept it. So they have conspired to *protect* mankind from that heady knowledge, to protect him from it until that time when evolution has molded him into a stronger creature, one unafraid to face dying without the illusion of a Disneyland beyond the grave. Maybe their concealment has been a humane act of the most noble proportions."

Plucky munched his cigar and furrowed his virile brow. "It could be, Marvelous. It could be. It wouldn't alter the general situation much—but I like to think that it could be."

"I wish this pantry had a window in it," said Amanda.

She was probably daydreaming of clouds.

* * * * * * * * * * * * * * * * * * * *

An erratic clock kept track of our arguments. It ticked with a Puerto Rican accent. In the clock's ticking I heard Carmen Miranda dancing. Did you know that after Carmen Miranda's death her estate was sold at auction? Andy Warhol went to the auction and purchased Carmen Miranda's old shoes. Carmen Miranda had extremely tiny feet. Her shoes were about a size 1. Or smaller. If there is a shoe size minus 1, then that is what Carmen Miranda wore. The heels of her shoes, however, were very high, so that her shoes were as tall at the heel as they were long overall. Carmen Miranda must have felt as if she were always walking downhill. Anyway, Andy Warhol has her shoes now. A diamond-like hush has overtaken Carmen Miranda's dancing feet. Only their echo is preserved in the Latin ballroom of our wall clock.

"So, Plucky," said I, "we've got those two possibilities as far as motives go, but as you say, it's academic because it's impossible for us to verify it one way or the other. However, and this hits a little closer to home, no matter which motive is correct, the authorities responsible for the concealment are going to be pretty frantic about getting the Corpse back. Right?"

"Right you are, dad. They'll want it back or they'll want it destroyed. Either way would probably suit them. The one thing they cannot afford is to have the concealment become public knowledge. Especially at a time like this."

"What's so special about this time?" Amanda wanted to know.

"Hell's bells, Amanda, didn't you read my letter? The Church is in trouble, the biggest trouble it's been in since the split in the sixteenth century. I explained all that to you. I made quite a study of it and bored you shitless with it in my letters. If you remember, I raved about how the whole Catholic setup is isolated, defensive, antiquated and authoritarian and how it's in a state of crisis. The all-powerful position of the Pope has been weakened with millions of Catholics disobeying his prissy old virginal order that they can't fuck without making babies—Catholic babies. Priests and nuns and monks in various parts of the world are rebelling openly against their so-called 'superiors' over a whole shooting gallery of questions—like civil rights, war, celibacy, poverty, repressive dogma, superstitious doctrines and fascist politics. Man, there's revolt on a hundred different fronts over a dozen different issues. Not long before I bugged out, there was violence in St. Peter's Square. It was the night before the world synod of bishops opened, and the liberal and conservative Catholics were fist-fighting right under the Pope's window. It was a 'prayer vigil' for poverty, a subject the Church has always had a minimum of interest in, and it turned into a free-for-all. Man, it took every microgram of will power in my little pink body to keep out of it. Wow, I'm telling you my palms were sweating."

"I can imagine," I said. "Amanda, I've talked to you, too, about the deep division in the Church. About how the slaves are throwing off their chains, to coin a phrase, and how the Church is coming apart at the seams."

Amanda nodded. "Yes, I remember. It's delightful, isn't it? All that howling for freedom. But I guess I don't think about it much."

"Well, now's the time to start thinking about it, baby love," I said. "Because like it or not, you're directly involved."

"He's not putting you on," confirmed Plucky. "With the Church so shook by internal revolution it's more defensive than ever. Now, of all times, it simply couldn't afford the scandal of a *corpus delecti*." Again he tapped the mummy on its shrunken knees.

Amanda puckered her eminently puckerable lips. "You guys have only talked about the poor Catholics," she said. "Where do the dear Protestants fit into this?"

I took it upon myself to explain. "As I see it, the fundamental difference between the Catholic Church and the Protestant churches is that the Catholic Church is a tightly organized, international power whereas the Protestant churches are a fragmented, unorganized, largely impotent, national power. There are plentiful differences in dogma, of course, but as our pal Plucky is fond of saying, that's academic. Basically, the two churches are bound together much more intimately than most Christians think. Should the Roman Church fall, the Protestant churches won't rush in and fill the void. They will fall soon afterward. The Catholic express and the Protestant choo-choo are rolling on the same rails, and if the bridge washes out, both are destined for the gulch. In the long run, Protestants stand to lose as much from the mortality of Jesus as do the Catholics. We can't expect any support from them. Except maybe the Unitarians. They'll embrace any heresy, I understand."

Purcell abruptly rose to his feet. A funeral plumage of concern arrived as if by messenger in his blue eyes. "Look here, you all," he said, "it's possible that we here in this pantry stand between the Church and its survival. Do you dig what that means? They'll stop at nothing to prevent us from blowing the whistle on this Corpse. If they get to us before we make it public—if that's what we're gonna do—they won't hesitate to kill us. Every one of us, including Thor. I brought this dead Jesus here into your house without an invitation—and I've put your lives in danger. It's grim, man. The sensible thing for me to do would be to take the Corpse and bug out. I could hole up with it in a motel or somewhere until I—or we—decide what to do with it."

"Oh, Plucky," said Amanda in the voice that her lisp made seductive even when her thoughts were far from sex, "we wouldn't think of it. You just don't want us to have any fun."

John Paul gave Purcell a look that could be counted as a vote of confidence. As for me, I checked on Mon Cul to ascertain that he was not dozing on the job. I heard an assassination in each muffled blast of duck-hunter's shotgun. I heard a rendezvous with alien triggermen in each approach of vehicle on the Freeway. I heard the spike heels of Carmen Miranda dancing toward me in the dimension of the dead, intent upon avenging this smear on her Catholic girlhood, cha cha cha.

****

At this moment, that demented clock is still ticking in the depopulated zoo downstairs. I can't hear it up here in the living room where I am typing, but I can feel it. As artificial as the notion of "passing" time may be, its pressures are very real. Each unheard tick gouges me in the back, as if time were a menopausal lady wanting to call her sister in Cleveland and I'm on the pay phone trying to talk a sweetheart out of suicide. "Shortage of time" makes it impossible for me to register verbatim our discussion in the pantry that October Friday, or to relay to you each piece of behavior or nuance of mood. I am forced, in fact, to skip over a great deal of dialogue—but you mustn't feel shortchanged, for it probably wouldn't interest you anyway. Not that it is my mission to interest you. When writing a novel, an author includes only that information that might interest his audience, but when compiling an historical document, as I am doing, it is the author's obligation to record what happened, whether it is interesting or not. Time, however, is giving you a break.

It was late afternoon when we got down to the nitty-gritty. By then, Purcell and I, unaccustomed to the rigors of fast, were producing uncontrollable sounds in our intestinal chambers. Plucky's stomach would growl with a bravura, grandiose passion; and then my stomach would growl just a bit weaker, a shade lighter, as if Plucky's stomach growl was the work of an Old Master and mine a modern copy made by a conniving forger or a graduate student at the art institute. If the reader is inclined toward realism, he may remind himself during the following passages of dialogue that two privileged bellies were whining, gurgling and rumbling—point and counterpoint—throughout.

· "Why don't we quit beating around the bush?" demanded Purcell. "We've been yapping for nine hours if you can believe that crazy clock: it sounds like it learned to tell time in a Cuban whorehouse. I feel like I've had a crash course in Christian history from 40,000 B.C. to twenty minutes ago, you know what I mean? I'm not knocking it, but what I'd really like to learn is what you all think we should do with the Corpse. I'd like to put the question to you. We don't have to reach a final decision until Sunday night if that's how the think-tank game is played, but I'd sure enjoy hearing what you folks feel we should do with . . . it . . . him." Plucky looked from face to face.

Ziller obviously was not going to speak. He continued to watch the Corpse as a cat watches a mousehole.

"Decent burial on the slopes of Bow Wow," offered Amanda. "Appropriate ritual, then peace at last. The blue sky to keep him company, the winds, the waters, the clouds, butterflies, trees, stones, mushrooms, animals, the wild old ways. Ba Ba leaving no path in the grasses when he brings him flowers on special mornings." She sat with her hands in her lap, appearing as calm as when we began our session nearly nine hours before.

"I can't say that I accept Amanda's sentiments, altruistic as they may be," said your correspondent. "But at the moment, I don't have an alternative. I just haven't settled on any scheme worthy of sharing yet. What about you, Pluck? Apparently you've had your mind set all along. What do *you* want to do with the Corpse?"

Purcell sprang upright in his wooden chair. His eyes burned like the snout of his most recent cigar. Yes, he had a plan all right. "Here's what I wanna do with him. Blow him up on page 1! Illuminate his mug on channels 0 through 99! Plaster his wrinkles on the cover of *Life!* Bounce his kisser off Telstar satellite! Newsmen from all nations here asking questions! Press corps deserts Washington and Cape

Kennedy and moves into Skagit County! Movie cameras churning, flash bulbs zapping, microphones crackling, tape recorders spinning their nosy spools; the roadside zoo struck by media lightning! Pundits arriving by private helicopter! Sulzberger rushing out to call the Pope for a personal denial, then using his prestige to get back to the head of the line for another peek in the pantry! Columnists, editors, commentators, prize-winning photographers camping in the parking lot! And don't forget the underground papers—the *East Village Other*, the *Barb*, the *Rolling Stone*—having their turn! Fill every page, every screen with him from here to Katmandu; South Pole melting from the heat of the news wires, drums carrying the story down the Congo and up the Amazon, total World Ear-Eye glued to the final and ultimate death of him!" Pluck paused for the effect that was in it. "That's what I wanna do with the Corpse."

"Pardon me, but I get the impression that you don't wish to keep this thing a secret. You want to drop the Corpse on society like a bomb. Why? What would be the purpose of that?" It was my voice that was asking. In the background, my belly had a few questions of its own.

"The purpose isn't hard to figure out. There's more than one purpose, for that matter, and none of 'em are hard to figure out. The first purpose is to get some honesty back in the game, to restore an element of truth to life. Man has been living a lie since the very beginning of the Judaeo-Christian era. The lie has warped our science and our philosophy and our economy and our social institutions and our simplest day-to-day existence: our sex and our play. Man doesn't stand a chance of discovering—or *re*discovering, as Amanda might prefer—who he is or where he fits into the cosmic picture, the natural Ma Nature scheme of things, as long as he's numbed and diverted by the easy Christian escapist superstition. I don't know what the ultimate truth is—hell, I don't even know whether life is sweet or sour" (Plucky grinned at Amanda and, coyly, she smiled back) "but I do know that you can't find truth if you start with a false premise, and Western tradition, the best and the worst of it, has always moved from the false premise of Christian divinity. This Corpse here could destroy the lie and let man begin over again on a note of realism. That's the first purpose."

The athlete-turned-outlaw cleared his throat. Or was it his stomach? "Purpose number two," he said, "is the jolt it'll give the establishment. Man oh man, it'll be a bodacious blow to authority."

"You mean the authority of the Church?"

"No, man, I mean authority, period. Secular authority has made the mistake of tying itself too closely to Christianity. Actually, the whole Judaeo-Christian setup is authoritarian; it's a feudal system with God—the king, the big boss—at the top. It's the ideal religious organization for control freaks, reward-and-punishment perverts and power mongers. No wonder it has succeeded so spectacularly."

"In the *old* religion there were no bosses," said Amanda. Her little observation was lost on me.

"No," agreed Plucky, "and there're no bosses in nature, either. But Christianity isn't based on nature, it's based on a political model. As far back as the Emperor Constantine, the authoritarians spotted Christianity as the perfect front, and they've been using poor old Jesus ever since—using him to bolster their business, to sanction their armies and to generally yoke and manipulate the people. Napoleon had the grace to coldcock the Holy Roman Empire, but look at those so-called Christian-Democratic parties currently in power all over Europe: whenever a Christian-Democrat takes office, you know that the Vatican has recaptured another hunk of territory. Both American government and American business—if there's any difference any more—are rolled in Christian rhetoric like a chicken leg is rolled in flour."

The reference to the leg of the hen caused his abdomen to bellow with deprivation. A bit less dramatically, mine followed suit.

"It's pretty ironic," Purcell went on, "because as I understand it, Jesus was a freedom-fighting radical who scorned authority—he booted bankers in the ass and made fools of high priests. However—*however*—he may have the last laugh yet. Because authority has chosen to identify itself with Christ—or rather with the Christian lie about Christ—and now *we* have the means to explode that myth. All authority, from the Holy See to the White House to the Pentagon to the cop on the beat is gonna suffer as a result. Man, we just might bust things wide open!"

Plucky was laughing and pounding the table, causing the Corpse to bounce up and down like the Kraft meatball dinner that fell out of love with gravity.

I shook my head in dismay. "Plucky," I said solemnly, "I don't want to accuse you of taking this matter too lightly, because I realize that you are quite serious about your reasons for exposing the Corpse. Moreover, they aren't altogether bad reasons. There's a lot of moral idealism in the first purpose that you outlined and a lot of, well, poetic justice in the second. But in the end I have to reject them both, reject the idea of the super press conference, because, Plucky, I think you are overlooking the very grave consequences of such an act."

The grin slid off Purcell's face like an ill pigeon slides off the equestrian statue of Ralph Williams in Los Angeles. As he lit another cigar, he motioned for me to proceed.

"Correct me if I'm wrong: you would use the Corpse to kill off Christianity, a religion which is, at best, a distortion of the teachings of Christ, and, at worst, is an authoritarian system that limits man's liberty and represses the human spirit."

"Yeah, man, that's pretty close to the way I feel."

"Well, to begin with, Pluck, Christianity is dying of its own accord. Its most vital energies are already dead. We are living in a period of vast philosophical and psychological upheaval, a rare era of evolutionary outburst precipitated by a combination of technological breakthroughs, as I explained it to Amanda. And when we come out of this period of change—providing that the tension and trauma of it doesn't lead us to destroy ourselves—we will find that many of the old mores and attitudes and doctrines will have been unrecognizably altered or eliminated altogether. One of the casualties of our present upheaval will unquestionably be Christianity. It is simply too ineffectual (on a spiritual level) and too contradictory (on an intellectual level) to survive. So, in forcing the knowledge of the unresurrected Christ on the public you would only succeed in abruptly, crudely hastening a death already taking place by natural processes. It would be like shooting a terminal cancer patient with a bazooka.'"

"So much the better," said Purcell. "Why drag it out? Anything we can do to speed up the end of those old authoritarian, antilife ways, why we should feel a duty to do it. Hell, man, that's why I got into dealing drugs. I wasn't just selling a product for a fancy profit, I was selling people a new look at the inside of their heads, laying a lot of powerful energy on them that they could use to open up new dimensions to their existence. I was trying to help change things. For the better. That's part of my trip."

"You're a utopianist, that's what you are. A wild-eyed utopianist, aren't you? Well, let me tell you just what kind of utopia you'll bring about by thrusting this mummified Jesus on the world. Thoreau once wrote that most 'men lead lives of quiet desperation.' And that's a damn accurate summation. Most people are lonely and most people are scared. They may not show it, but they are. Their faith in Christ is all that most people have in this civilized Western world. Because even if they aren't practicing Christians— and the majority of them probably aren't any more—they still believe in the Christian God. And in times of stress, such as death or serious illness or self-doubt or frustration, they turn to their faith in God. It's all that gives them the will to persist. The ultimate function of religious belief is the destruction of death. It helps man to conquer his fear of dying and his dread of what may lie beyond. If he learns that Jesus died—and *stayed dead*— then what solace is there for him? Most people will conclude, I'm afraid, that if Jesus doesn't live then God doesn't live. And if God doesn't live, what's left for them? See what I mean?

"We're caught in a time of demoralization as it is, due to the changes we're undergoing. Man is already losing hope. His world is in a mess and he's running out of options for saving it. Think what the mortality of Jesus will do to him. Your plan would shove mankind into a century of the darkest desperation and hopelessness. People would panic. They'd flip out. There'd be waves of suicides. Retired folks would eat their sleeping tablets, dentists would break down at their drills, salesmen would cancel their calls, secretaries would stare blankly at their typewriters, mothers would wander off and desert their children, insane asylums would be standing room only, crime would carry away the countryside, there'd be blood in every gutter, cold gloom on every face. It would shatter the stability of society."

"Aw, Marvelous, you're overdramatizing it. Sure, it'd freak out some people. The old and the rigid and the weak. And that wouldn't be pretty, but hell, it's necessary if we're going to get the species to evolving in a sane direction. Evolution always takes casualties. Besides, there'd be loads of people who'd get with it and dig it. The mortality of Christ could mean a fresh start for Western man. All the bullshit cleared off the boards and a spanking new, pure, honest beginning to find out who and what we really are and where we stand as regards the universe and the forces that we've nicknamed 'God.' The young would go for it. They'd eat it up. The young and the creative would welcome such a chance and they'd pitch right in and build a more liberated, joyful, realistic culture. What's this horse crap about a 'stable society'? You've gotta be kidding. Nature isn't stable. Life isn't stable. Stability is unnatural. The only stable society is the police state. You can have a free society or you can have a stable society. You can't have both. Take your choice. As for me, I'll choose a free, organic society over a rigid, artificial society any day. If people are so weak that they have to have the Heaven crutch to keep 'em from fear and death, well, maybe fear and death is what they need. And if they're so unethical that it takes the Jesus lie to keep 'em from going crazy in the streets, robbing each other and doing each other in, well then fuck 'em, man; let 'em go crazy because crime and insanity may be what they deserve."

My belly did two rolls and a spin. A ripple of notes twisted and squirted up my digestive tract as if my digestive tract were a horn and that black guy, that Roland Kirk, was on the other end. I squeezed myself around the middle and choked off Roland Kirk in mid-solo. If I don't eat soon there's going to be trouble with the musicians union, I thought.

"Remember Sister Elizabeth and Sister Hillary?" I asked Purcell. "They said marriage vows to Christ. How do you think this unresurrected Jesus is going to affect them? How's it going to affect the other brave nuns and priests you met during your year with the Church? Is death and fear what they deserve, Plucky? What about your parents and your brother and your sisters, they're good Episcopalians, aren't they? Do they deserve to suddenly have their most vital beliefs kicked in? What about my parents, my momma and daddy? They're fine people, they've always done the best they could for me and everyone else they knew. They're kind and generous, *feeling* human beings. Religion is all my mother has in this world. Because she has given herself heart and soul to a doctrine that's largely myth, does that mean we have the right to destroy that doctrine for her? After all, that doctrine includes principles of the highest ethical degree. She's lived a better life because of her Christian standards, despite the falseness of their accompanying lore. What difference does it make if the Gospel is mostly a lie? It's an engrossing story and the words of its hero are excellent words to live by, even today. My code of ethics—and yours, too, if you'll admit it—grew directly out of Christianity. Don't we owe it anything? Do we have the right to pollute our wellspring of morality? Do we have the right to destroy my mother? A million other mothers?

Plucky could not answer right away. He was silent and brooding. Even his stomach hushed. Plucky's mood was a boardinghouse the night the cook fixed liver and onions; it was five below outdoors and the TV was on the blink. Eventually, he said, "I've got nothing against Jesus. It wasn't his fault that all this killing and cheating has been done in his name. He was one of the greatest dudes who ever was. You know what I dig about him? He lived what he preached. He taught by example. He went all the way and there was no compromise and no hypocrisy. And he not only was against authority, he was against private property, too. Anybody who opposes authority and property is sweet in my heart. Jesus? Hell, I *love* the cat."

"Yes, Pluck," I said, "we know that. We realize it isn't Christ or his original teachings that have you riled."

"No, it isn't. It's what he's come to stand for that pisses me. It's the perversions and the tyranny and the lies. What I can't understand about you, Marvelous, is how you can defend the lies just because some good has come out of 'em. And you're supposed to be a scientist. I thought scientists insited on facts—regardless of the consequences."

It was my turn to brood. Before I could articulate a reply, Purcell spoke again.

"You said yourself that the world's in a mess and we're running out of options. We have radical problems and radical problems demand radical solutions. Our leaders aren't gonna solve our problems, that's obvious. It was leaders, the good ones right along with the bad, who got us into this mess to begin with. And not one of 'em has vision enough or guts enough to push a program radical enough to get us out of the mess. That's why my plan for exposing the Corpse seems so important. It's radical as all hell, and it's gonna hurt a lot of technically innocent people and all that, but it's the *one* solution that might work. It could jolt society so hard that it'd be forced to try a whole new approach to life. It could free us from our authorities and free us from our superstitions that keep us in the Dark Ages even though our technology is putting us on the moon. To me, it's the only way out. I honestly don't think it was an accident that I found the Corpse. I'm starting to think that I was *supposed* to find it, that it's part of a divine plan to rescue the human race. And if some of the species has to be destroyed in order to save the species as a whole, well, that's the way evolution has always worked. But if you all don't want to help me with my plan, if you're afraid to accept the responsibility, if you just wanna stick the Corpse in the ground and forget about it . . ."

"I've never intimated that I wanted to stick the Corpse in the ground," I objected.

"That's right. You don't know *what* you want to do with it."

"Yes, I do. I do now. You've given me an idea. I have a plan by which we may be able to use the Corpse to improve human conditions without ripping the entire social fabric to shreds in the process."

Purcell looked skeptical. "What's that?" he asked.

"Simply this. We reveal the Corpse only to certain key figures in world government. We let the Pope know we have it, if he doesn't know already. We let the President of the U.S. know, and a few other powerful authorities. And we make sure that they are cognizant of the full consequences of the Corpse becoming public knowledge. Right? Then we make demands. We demand of the Pope, for example, that he rescind the papal encyclical banning artificial contraception. That would go a long way toward solving the population problem. We demand of the President that he withdraw all

U.S. troops from foreign soil, and that he scrap provocative defense systems. And we demand of the Pope, again, that he issue an encyclical excommunicating any individual who serves in the armed forces of any nation. That would help to take care of the war and aggression problem. We demand Congress shut down Detroit until it agrees to produce electric automobiles exclusively. Think of how that would help the pollution and ecology problem. Are you getting the picture? We demand that the authorities themselves overhaul society and start making it healthier and happier. Or else. Or else we make public the mortality of Jesus and break up the ball game."

Plucky roared. "Blackmail! Marvelous, you sneaky bastard, you're a blackmailer. Aren't you ashamed? I'm surprised at you, I really am. You're suggesting that we blackmail the President and the Pope." Purcell shook from the laughter the way a rosebush would shake beneath a dodo seduction. The pantry was draped in extinct feathers. "It might work. I don't know. We'd have to devise a foolproof scheme so that they couldn't just kill us and end the threat. We'd have to sit down like we were Leonardo da Vinci inventing the parachute and polish every little detail and make it foolproof. It'd be one bodacious bitch of a caper to pull off— but it might work. At least we should think about it." He slapped his thigh. The dodos were at it again.

The clock struck (if you could call it that) 6:50. We had been cooped up in the pantry for ten hours. Baby Thor was fretting for attention. Mon Cul was complaining about the length of his shift (in the wilds a baboon sentry is relieved after five hours). I was hungry, tired and damn near suffocated by cigar smoke. Purcell and I had at last reached an area of relative agreement. It seemed the appropriate moment to adjourn the meeting, and I was about to do so when Amanda motioned that she wished to speak. "By all means," I said, for she had said little that day and I was anxious for her opinions.

"I was on a butterfly hike through Mexico," began Amanda, "when I was offered a ride by a young American and his elderly grandmother. The young man taught school in Ohio. He lived with his grandmother who was over eighty. He wanted to travel in Mexico during summer vacation, but there was no one to look after Granny. Besides, the schoolteacher earned a small salary. The grandmother had all the money. So he took her along.

"For several days I rode with them. It was extremely hot. One day about noon, the grandmother had a stroke and died. We were in the desert, miles from any settlement. What to do? Well, we put the grandmother in my sleeping bag and zipped it up all around. Then we tied her to the top of the car. On we drove. Followed by vultures.

"Toward dusk we came to a fair-sized town. Our throats were parched, so we stopped at a cantina for cold beer. When we came outside, we found that the car had been stolen. Sleeping bag, grandmother and all.

"The schoolteacher and I stayed in the town for a week. We bribed the police daily. But our possessions were never recovered. Even today, there is a missing Ohio school-teacher's car somewhere in Mexico. A missing sleeping bag. A missing grandmother. Perhaps she is still tied on the top of the car."

"That's an interesting story," I admitted, "but I fail to see how it relates to—"

"I haven't finished. The schoolteacher and I became lovers. We rented an adobe house with the grandmother's money and lived like Mexicans. Every morning I got up and made tortillas. While I worked, the schoolteacher sat in the shade in his undershorts and read aloud to me from books. I did not care for his taste in literature, which ran toward the clas-sical and the morbid, but it made him happy to read to me so I did not object.

"One morning he read me a story by a pessimistic Russian. It was about a man who wished to test the intelligence of religious believers, so he began to practice asceticism and to utter ersatz profundities. He quickly attracted thousands of disciples to whom he preached his made-up doctrines. They proclaimed him a saint. Then one day, to show his fol-lowers how easily they'd been duped, he announced that all he had taught them was nonsense. Unable to live without their belief, they stoned him to death and went right on believing."

Amanda got up to leave.

"I get the point," I said.

"I get it, too," said Plucky Purcell.

Had our negotiations been in vain?

Would society regard the Corpse as a hoax?
Would Jesus fail to save mankind in death as he had in life?
Would we get our butts shot off?
Where could we go from here?

****

Darkness had fallen. The duck hunters had long since left the waterways. Green-scented clouds obscured the moon.

I followed Amanda upstairs to watch her give Thor his bath. It excited me when she scrubbed his private parts.

Despite Amanda's intimation that our hopes for the Corpse were futile and our fears for it without foundation, I believed that the first pantry session had been beneficial. It had put the situation into frontal perspective, had established guidelines for further discussion and had disentangled some of the strands. That Plucky and I had done 99 per cent of the talking caused me neither surprise nor dismay. The Zillers had been engaged on their own levels of selfhood, levels perhaps more absolute than ours. In time, they would speak. Or act. I remained convinced of their special wisdom, and I was confident that they would make a substantial contribution to whatever solution was reached concerning the mummy. Deadline was still two days away. I was prepared to wait.

Baby Thor giggled when Amanda soaped his balls. His tiny penis grew erect in her slippery hands. "Jesus was nailed to the cross," said Amanda. She said it matter-of-factly.

"That's how the story goes," I said. "So what?"

"The cross is a tree, and the tree is a phallus. There's something in that, Marx." She examined Thor's member as if it were a crucifix. I imagined it on a chain about her neck. (Don't flinch, Thor, I was only kidding.)

"If there's something in it, it's too obscure for me. Can you explain?"

"Jesus was a Jew. Judaism was a father religion. Christianity also grew into a father religion. But the *old* religion was a mother religion. We've had two thousand years of penis power."

"Is that bad?"

"It isn't a question of bad or good. It never is. But when

the phallus is separated from the womb, when the father is separated from the mother, when culture is separated from nature, when the spirit is separated from the flesh . . . then life is out of balance and the people become frustrated and violent."

"Well, the past two thousand years have been frustrated and violent, all right. What you're saying is that Jesus came into a naturally balanced world and threw it out of line."

"All I'm saying is, tomorrow when you are alone thinking about Jesus, open your window. Don't sit there in your stuffy room, all full of books and no air. Open your windows to the fir needles and the ducks and the fields and the river. That way your approach will be more unified and your conclusions more exact."

Her remarks sounded, on the surface of them, straightforward enough, yet there was something elusive about them, a meaning or pretended meaning which my mind's fist could not close around. I suspected the meaning had as much to do with Amanda as with Christ. However, she would say no more and I'd learned not to pump her, so I thanked her and made my way to my quarters.

In the cool black of the grove I stood and stretched. It had been a long day. A day like no other. And it was just the beginning.

Upstairs in the Zillers' bedroom, lights went on. I found myself smiling. "Soon you'll show me your secrets," I said to the figures silhouetted against the drapes. "The Corpse will see to that."

Then I slipped into the garage, where I had stashed four raw weenies and a pint of beet juice.

John Paul Ziller is six and a half feet tall and wears a bone in his nose. He is seldom mistaken for anyone else. The agents can't understand why he has not been nabbed. Neither can I. For the law enforcers have made fine advances in their art. Technology has served them as dutifully as it has served industry. With laboratories, computers, chemical formulae, vast electronic communications networks, college-trained triggermen and millions of informers at its disposal, should law enforcement fail to locate and apprehend a jungle-bred magician, a notorious athlete-outlaw, a ninety-pound baboon and the body of Christ—all traveling together in one convenient package—then it must reconcile itself to a failure of the magnitude of the collapse of Ford or the inability of Standard Oil to turn a profit.

With all my meat and blood and breath, I am rooting for the success of the magician's trick. But the noise of hope is not a racket in my heart.

Meanwhile, Amanda goes about her business. Which is? Which is, if I am honest, what this report is all about. Which is, at the moment, the perfection of the techniques of trance. She falls effortlessly into the trance state now, turning on the "voices" with no more difficulty than turning on the eleven o'clock news. But she always gets the same advice: "Expect a letter."

Therefore, Amanda is awaiting a letter. I am not. How could a letter reach us here? I've explained how the agents intercept our mail. Besides, would John Paul be such a ninny as to reveal his whereabouts to the Post Office? Ridiculous idea, a letter. All that is delivered to the roadhouse these days is rain. Air mail, special delivery, by the bagsful. How did so much rain get our address?

On Saturday morning, Salvadore Gladstone Tex banged at the door of the zoo. The cowboy may have had something valuable to sell, but nobody answered his knock. Later, Farmer Hansen came by, read our sign and departed. The sign said: *Closed Until Monday.* Since the Jeep was parked out front, Hansen probably wondered what was going on in here. He might have wondered if we were ill. Who could guess what Salvadore Gladstone Tex might have wondered. He galloped away on Jewish Mother, feeding his snot to the wind.

I remained alone in my quarters that Saturday, Amanda

and John Paul spent the day in their respective sanctuaries, and Purcell, providing he abided by the rules, spent it in the kitchen where he had spread his bedroll close to the pantry door. This was the day when we were to put all our energies into thinking about the Corpse.

The weather was chilly and misty, so I neglected to open my window. Honestly, I didn't see how that could make any difference.

Approximately two thousand years ago, a pellet of wisdom dropped into the fetid, heavy, squirming, gasping, bloody, bug-eyed, breast-beating, anguished, wrathful, greasy and inflamed world of Jewish-Oriental culture as a pearl might drop into a pail of sweat. CUT!

His name was Yeshua ben Miriam, but history came to know him as Christ or Jesus. Sorry, sir, your face is familiar but just can't recall your name. CUT!

After a career as a maker of wooden farming implements, Yeshua (or Jesus) was moved to become an itinerant rabbi and kicked up a local fuss with his fanatical adherence to a philosophy of brotherly love. His strength of character was incomparable, yet he was not the least bit original in his thought. In fact, he had only one real insight during his life (and even that one was commonplace in India and Tibet). When he came to understand that the Kingdom of Heaven is *within*, he lit up like a Christmas tree and illuminated Western civilization for twenty centuries. They nailed him up but they couldn't unplug him. CUT!

On a Michigan funny farm there are three inmates, each of whom believes he is Jesus Christ. They are all correct, of course, but when they learned the secret—that everyone is divine if only he knows he is divine—they became confused and behaved in a manner that led them to the looney bin. Their culture hadn't prepared them for divine revelation. It hadn't even encouraged them to ask the only important question—"Who am I?"—let alone taught them to give the only logical reply. So when these three lower-middle-class working stiffs stumbled onto self-knowledge, they translated it into the absurd vision of the Sunday-school Superman, then wondered why they got locked up. Tough titty, boys. We prefer our God to be as singular as he is distant. CUT!

A prophet in the Jewish tradition, Jesus had little truck with Gentiles. ("I was sent only to the lost sheep of the house of Israel." Matthew 15:24.) On at least one occasion he referred to Gentiles as dogs. He saw his mission as helping to bring about the fulfillment of Jewish aspirations—and that mission ended in a grotesque fiasco. He differed from the mainstream of Jewish thinking only in that he believed in loving one's enemies. A radical difference, to be sure, but he would have been appalled by the suggestion of a Gentile religion being founded in his name. He never intended to sponsor a church, let alone an Inquisition. CUT!

JESUS: Hey, Dad.
GOD: Yes, son?
JESUS: Western civilization followed me home this morning. Can I keep it?
GOD: Certainly not, boy. And put it down this minute. You don't know where it's been.

CUT!

The clown is a creature of chaos. His appearance is an affront to our sense of dignity, his actions a mockery of our sense of order. The clown (freedom) is always being chased by the policeman (authority). Clowns are funny precisely because their shy hopes lead invariably to brief flings of (exhilarating?) disorder followed by crushing retaliation from the status quo. It delights us to watch a careless clown break taboos; it thrills us vicariously to watch him run wild and free; it reassures us to see him slapped down and order restored. After all, we can condone liberty only up to a point. Consider Jesus as a ragged, nonconforming clown—laughed at, persecuted and despised—playing out the dumb show of his crucifixion against the responsible pretensions of authority. CUT!

"Jesus, it's me, you know, the friendly with-it priest who puts your transcendental rap into the groovy idiom of the cool kids on the corner. Hey! Are you running with me, Jesus?"

"Boy, I'm running with you, passing with you and kicking with you. And you're still losing." CUT!

For God so loved the world that he gave his only begotten son that we might not perish but have everlasting ... CUT!

Jesus, there is practically no historic evidence of your existence. Jesus, the Gospel is mostly Greek myth, literary embellishments and publicity releases. Jesus, we know so little about you. Jesus, is it your absence that makes our hearts grow fonder? Jesus, we don't have you, we have abstractions the Church has woven around your name. Jesus, you are a mystery. All mysteries, however mundane, have the stink of God about them. Jesus, is that your game? CUT!

When Jesus overturned the bankers' tables and kicked the capitalists out of the temple, he momentarily succumbed to the temptation to indulge in violent revolution in the cause of freedom. He did not persist in this behavior. Although he remained a rebel, Jesus was to support a revolution in consciousness rather than a violent overthrow of corrupt establishment. For his trouble, he was hung up on spikes. Would his fate have been different had he persisted in militant opposition? For his refusal to pursue political goals, Jesus lost popular support—and gained a legacy. CUT!

Over the strong red soil of Galilee he sailed like a boat. Picture him sailing past the feasts at which the men dance to melancholy music. Sailing through the olive orchards, through the vineyards where black grapes pout like moons. Sailing across the viaduct that spans Cheesemakers' Valley. Sailing up and down the slopes of ripening wheat. Sailing around the harp-shaped Lake of Galilee. Sailing through the heat, through the barking of dogs and the sawing of grasshoppers, through the herds of cud-chewing camels whose burdens bear scents of Eastern spices, through the crumbling villages where at dusk flitting bats frighten the women at the wells. And always, as he sailed, spouting his madness to his astonished disciples; his mad, extremist, unstructured, nonlinear, poetic babble of forgiveness and love. CUT!

* *

Think-tankwise, it was not a good day for me. I approached the image of Jesus from various and unlikely directions, as the director of East River Institute would have had me do, but I had trouble concentrating on any single aspect for more than a minute or two. I lost sight of my best ideas as one loses sight of a friend in a crowd, my mind roamed in un-mentionable directions, and on a half-dozen occasions I must confess that I dozed off.

Toward nightfall—and without recalling that Amanda had advised me to do so—I raised a window, hoping that a spurt of fresh air would clear my cerebrum. I reclined on my bed and permitted the dank but feathery Skagit atmosphere to wash over me. Its shadowy body and its fir-odored volume of ancient vapors descended upon me and, with salty quivers, activated forgotten imprints into vivid experience.

Jesus was sitting on a rock in the desert, meditating and reading the Law, when Tarzan came riding up on a goat. Tarzan was munching nutmeg seeds and playing the har-monica. "Hi, Jesus," he yelled.

Jesus jumped like he was stung by a scorpion. "You startled me," he stammered. "I thought at first you were Pan."

Tarzan chuckled. "I can understand why that put you up-tight. When you were born, the cry went through the world, 'Great Pan is dead.' But as you can plainly see, I'm hairy all over like an ape. Pan was a shaggy beast from the waist down. Above his belly button he was a lot like you."

A shudder vibrated Jesus' emaciated frame. "Like me?" he asked. "No, you must be mistaken. Say, what's that you're eating?"

"Nutmeg seeds," said Tarzan, grinning. "Here, I'll lay some on you."

"Oh, no thanks," said Jesus. "I'm fasting." Saliva welled up in his mouth. He pressed his lips together forcefully, but one solitary trickle broke over the flaky pink dam and dripped in an artless pattern into his beard. "Besides, nutmeg seeds: aren't they a narcotic?"

"Well, they'll make you high, if that's what you mean. Why else do you think I'm gumming them when I've got dates, doves and a crock of lamb stew in my saddle bag? If you ask me, you could *use* a little something to get you off."

At the mention of lamb stew, Jesus lost control of his lake of spittle. Now he wiped his chin with a dusty sleeve, embarrassment coloring his dark cheeks as the rosy-fingered dawn colors so many passages of Homer. "No, no," he said emphatically. "John the Baptist turned me on with mandrake root once. It was a rewarding experience, but never again." He shielded his eyes against the radiant memory of his visions. "Now, I'm what you might call *naturally* stoned."

Tarzan, who had climbed off his goat, smiled and said, "Good for you." He sat down beside Jesus and mouthed his harmonica. A jungle blues. "You gotta blow a C-vamp to get a G sound on one of these," he said. He did it.

Obviously distracted, Jesus interrupted. "What did you mean when you said that Pan was a lot like me?"

"Only from the waist up," corrected Tarzan. "Above the waist Pan was a highly spiritual dude. He sang and played sweeter than the larks; and his face was as full of joy as a sunny meadow in spring. There was a lot of love in that crazy rascal, just as there's a lot in you. Of course, he had horns, you know. And cloven hooves. Good golly, Miss Molly, how those woolly legs of his could dance! But he stunk, Pan did. In rutting season you could smell him a mile away. And he'd take on anything. He would've screwed this nanny goat if he couldn't find a nymph." Tarzan laughed and ran the scale on his harmonica.

Jesus didn't appreciate the references to carnal knowledge. He made an attempt to get his mind back on the Law. But wherever his formidable intellect voyaged on the roiling sea of Hebrew instruction, it drew the image of Pan like a dory behind it. Finally, he shoved Moses aside and asked, "But you say he was a lot like me."

"I said that, didn't I, man? I said he was like you, but different, too. Pan was the god of woodlands and pastures, the deity of flocks and shepherds. He was into a wilderness thing but he was also into a music thing. He was half man and half animal. Always laughing at his own shaggy tail. Pan represented the union between nature and culture, between flesh and spirit. Union, man. That's why we old-timers hated to see him go."

The newsboys of paranoia hawked their guilty papers in

Jesus' eyes. They were the same shrill urchins who would be hawking when Jesus would predict his disciples' betrayal and denial; when, in his next-to-last words, he would accuse God of forsaking him. "Are you blaming me?" he asked. His stare was as cold and nervous as a mousetrap.

By this time, Tarzan was pretty loaded. He didn't want any unpleasantness. "All I know is what I read in the papers," he said. He waved his harmonica to and fro so that it twinkled in the sunlight. "Do you have a favorite tune?"

"I like anything with soul in it," Jesus replied. "But not now. Tell me, Tarzan, what did my birth have to do with Pan's demise?"

"Jesus, old buddy, I'm not any Jewish intellectual and I can't engage you in no fancy theological arguments such as you're used to in the temples. But if you promise, Scout's honor, not to come on to me with a thick discussion, I'll tell you what I know."

"You have my word," said Jesus. He squinted in the agreed direction of Paradise, whereupon he noticed for the first time that an angel was hovering over them, executing lazy white loop-the-loops against the raw desert sky. "That angel will report everything it hears," thought Jesus. "I'd better mind my P's and Q's."

Tarzan spotted the angel, too, but paid it little attention. The last time he had eaten nutmeg seeds he had seen a whole dovecote of them. One had landed on his head and pissed down his back.

"In the old days," Tarzan began, "folks were more concrete. I mean they didn't have much truck with abstractions and spiritualism. They knew that when a body decomposed, it made the crops grow. They could see with their own eyes that manure helped the plants along, too. And they didn't need Adelle Davis to figure out that eating plants helped them grow and sustained their own lives. So they picked up that there were connective links between blood and shit and vegetation. Between animal and vegetable and man. When they sacrificed an animal to the corn crop, it was a concession to the obvious relation between death and fertility. What could be less mystical? Sure, it was hoked up with ceremony, but a little show biz is good for anyone's morale. We were linked to vegetation. Nothing in the vegetable world succumbs. It simply drops away and then returns. Energy is never destroyed. We planted our dead the way we planted our seeds. After a period of rest, the energy of corpse or seed returned in one form or another. From death came more life. We loved the earth because of the joy and good times and peace of mind to be had in loving it. We didn't have to be 'saved' from it. We never plotted escapes to Heaven. We weren't afraid of death because we adhered to nature—and its cycles. In nature we observed that death is an inseparable part of life. It was only when some men— the original tribes of Judah—quit tilling the soil and became alienated from vegetation cycles that they lost faith in the material resurrection of the body. They planted their dead bull or their dead ewe and they didn't notice anything sprout from the grave: no new bull, no new sheep. So they became alarmed, forgot the lesson of vegetation, and in desperation developed the concept of *spiritual* rebirth.

"The idea of a spiritual—invisible—being was the result of the new and unnatural fear of death. And the idea of a *Supreme* Spiritual Being is the result of becoming alienated from the workings of nature: when man could no longer observe the solid, material processes of life, and identify with them, he had to invent God in order to explain how life happened and why death happened."

"Now just a minute," snapped Jesus.

"Maybe I should run along," said Tarzan, sticking his harmonica into the myrrh-stained Arab silk that girded his loins.

"No," said Jesus. "If you have more to say, then out with it. Where does Pan fit into this blasphemy? And I?"

"If you're sure you want to hear it. Confidentially, you look a bit under the weather to me, pal. You could use a pound of steak and some fries."

"Do continue," sputtered Jesus through his drool.

"The point is, J.C., we had a unified outlook on life. We even figured out, in our funky way, how the sun and moon and stars fit in to the process. We didn't draw distinctions between the generative activity of seeds and the procreative cycles of animals. We observed that growth and change were essential to everything in life, and since we dug life, when it came time to satisfy our inner needs we naturally enough based our religion on the transformations of nature. We were direct about it. Went right to the source. The power to grow and transform was not attributed to abstract spirits—to a magnified ego extension in the sky—but was present in the fecundity of nature. We worshiped the reproductive organs of plants and animals. 'Cause that's where the life force lies."

Jesus kicked a pebble with the worn toe of his sandal. "I've heard of the phallic and vegetation cults," he said. "Not very sophisticated. My father expects more of man than a primitive adoration of his carnal nature. He must rise above . . ."

"Rise to what, Jesus? To abstractions? And alienation? Your scroll there, your book of Genesis, says that in the beginning was the Word. The simplest savage could see that in the beginning was the orgasm. Life is reproduced from life, while resurrection—the regeneration of seeds, the return in the spring of the leaves that fell in the autumn—is of matter, not of spirit. Unsophisticated? Maybe it's unsophisticated to venerate mountains and regard rivers as sacred, but as long as man thinks of his natural environment as holy, then he's gonna respect it and not sell it out or foul it up. Unsophisticated? Hell, it's going to take science a couple of thousand more years to determine that life originated when a cupful of seawater containing molecules of ammonia was trapped in a pocket in a shore rock where it was abnormally heated by ultraviolet light from the sun. But we pagans have always sensed that man's roots were inorganic. That's why we had respect even for stones."

Jesus looked up sheepishly from the pebbles he'd been kicking. "But you hadn't been saved," he protested.

"Didn't need to be," said Tarzan. "Wasn't of any use to us."

"Well, in the old days the female archetype was the central religious figure. Man had the power of creation, but it was in women that we observed the unfolding of the life cycle: reproduction, death and rebirth. So we celebrated the sensuality of God the Mother. Agriculture is umbilically tied to the Great Belly. Whereas the domestication of animals, a later pursuit, is more of a phallic activity—it was a step away from God the Mother and a step toward God the Father. But a harmonious balance was maintained. And Pan personified that balance. He kept things unified, him with his beautiful music and his long red erection.

"But when you came along, well, the way I hear it is your coming represented the triumph of God the Father over God the Mother, the victory of the Judaic God *of* spirit over the old God *in* flesh. Your birth-cry signaled the end of paganism, and the final separation of man from nature. From now on, culture will dominate nature, the phallus will dominate the womb, permanence will dominate change, and the fear of death will dominate everything.

"Pardon me, Jesus, 'cause I know you're a courageous and loving soul. You mean well. But from where I swing, it looks like two thousand miles of bad road."

Jesus looked to the heavens for guidance, but he saw only the angel, hanging in front of their parley the way a sign hangs in front of a TV repair shop. "Then that explains why you have withdrawn into your private nirvana," he said at last.

"You might say that," said Tarzan, standing up to stretch. "Why beat my head against a penis abstraction? And you, what are you doing out here in this snaky wilderness, frying your butt on a hot rock?"

"I'm preparing myself for my mission."

"Which is . . . ?"

"To change the world."

Tarzan slapped his side so hard he bent his harmonica. "The world is perpetually changing," he roared. "It doesn't do much else *but* change. It changes from season to season, from night to day, from ice to tropics. It changed from a pocketful of cosmic dust into the complicated ball of goof and glory it is today. It's changing every celestial second with no help whatsoever. Why do you want to stick *your* nose into it?"

"The peoples of the world have become wicked and evil," Jesus said gravely. "I believe, in all modesty, that I can eradicate their evil."

"Evil is what makes good possible," said Tarzan, hoping that he didn't sound too trite. "Good and evil have to coexist in order for the world to survive. The peoples haven't become evil, they've lost their balance and become confused about what they really are."

He jumped on the back of his goat and gave it a smack. "I'm afraid, Jesus baby, that you're gonna confuse them all the more."

The jungle yogi started to ride off, but Jesus leaped up and grabbed the goat by its tail. "Whoa, now, whoa," he called

in his rich olive-green baritone. The animal stopped and
Tarzan looked Jesus in the eye, but Jesus had difficulty ar-
ticulating the activity in his brain. "If you think carnally then
you are carnal, but if you think spiritually then you are
spirit." He just blurted it out, but it didn't sound too bad,
and the odor of the goat obscured any desire he might have
had to develop his idea more comprehensively.

Tarzan rattled the nanny's rib cage with his heels and she
bolted out of the prophet's grasp. "Any law against thinking
both ways?" he asked. He began to ride toward the south.

"You're either for me or against me," yelled Jesus.

"Well, adios then. I've got to beat it on back to the Congo.
Jane promised to lay out a luau when I returned. Been gone
two weeks now, a-riding over the good earth and a-playing
for anybody who'd listen. Bet Jane's as horny as a box of
rabbits. Git along, nanny!"

The goat galloped off in comic-strip puffs of dust. Jesus
returned to his rock and shooed an entwined pair of butterflies off of the Law. His heart felt like the stage on which
some Greeks had acted a messy tragedy. So occupied was
he with swabbing the boards that several minutes passed before he thought to look after the angel. When his eyes found
it, it was flapping erratically in the high, dry air, first soar-
ing after the disappearing strains of Tarzan's harmonica and
then returning to hover over Jesus, back and forth, again and
again, as if it did not wish the two to part—as if it did not
know whom to follow.

On Sunday morning, I overslept. The day was rumpled
and dreary. It looked like Edgar Allan Poe's pajamas.

Oddly elated, I hurried through the back door of the roadhouse. The session had not begun. he pantry was locked.
Purcell sat on the floor playing checkers with Mon Cul. "The
baboon cheats," he complained. I did not hear the other side
of the story.

"How was your Saturday?" Plucky asked, and promptly lost
a king.

"Weird. Full of strange visions, stupors, dreams. I felt like I was tangled in witchcraft."

"Probably fallout from Amanda's trance," said Plucky. He watched the baboon move in for the kill. A banana that the wily human drew suddenly from his pocket kept it from happening.

I inquired as to the whereabouts of Amanda and John Paul, only to learn that they had hiked across the fields to the foothills to gather mushrooms and herbs. It appeared that the fast had been called off. Amanda had spent half of Saturday in trance, and upon awakening professed a complete lack of interest in the Corpse. "No more father figures," she had proclaimed. "The world has had enough father figures. I wanted to give him a lovely burial but no one would have it. Now I wash my hands of him. No more father figures." She didn't wish to participate in further discussion.

For unclear reasons I was not surprised. "What about Ziller?" I asked. "He's watched that mummy like a hawk. He must be interested."

Plucky moved two checkers simultaneously. The baboon didn't seem to notice the excess. "You know what interests John Paul most about Jesus? That he was called the *light* of the world."

"But that's just a metaphor," I protested.

"To an artist a metaphor is as real as a dollar," said the Pluck. Mon Cul moved three checkers so rapidly that his opponent saw him move only two. Even with one move recalled, the game was won. And while the victor howled, Purcell and I adjourned to the pantry.

How nice it would be for you, reader, if the two men hunched over Jesus' body were famous philosophers or theologians. How exciting if one were Eric Hoffer and the other Jean-Paul Sartre. Or if one were Reinhold Niebuhr and the other Alan Watts. Or if one were Pierre Teilhard de Chardin and the other old what's-his-name. Then you'd get your money's worth, by golly. There'd be dialogue that would ring in the ear of the world.

As it is, however, it was just Plucky Purcell and I who met to negotiate the Corpse's future that Sunday. And as it turned out, we didn't have a lot to say.

We agreed that Amanda was probably correct when she intimated that most Christians would persist in their beliefs even if confronted with the lifeless body of their Saviour. The majority would dismiss the news as "preposterous" and nothing could change their minds. The Vatican could simply issue an outraged denial. The U.S. government would follow suit. The press would call down the wrath of the ink gods. And we at the roadside zoo, upon whose unprepared shoulders fell this monstrous burden, would be widely despised as the perpetrators of an especially noxious hoax. We might be imprisoned. Or murdered. Or committed to institutions where shock treatments and heavy tranquilizers would leave us as burned out as the unfortunate rabbi who lay on our table.

On the other hand, we agreed that a portion of the population would be severely affected. Maybe a portion of sufficient size (considering the trouble the Church was in already) to demolish what was left of national and Christian unity. Most significantly, the young would believe us. I was positive of it. And the young were increasing in number and influence. . . .

Any way you sliced it, it amounted to a furor in the making, perhaps a furor of unprecedented scope and consequence. We agreed on that. Where we disagreed was on the necessity of the furor. I wished to avoid it. Plucky looked forward to it the way King Kong looked forward to a date with Fay Wray.

If our initial arguments were animated by a frenzy of social (and personal) concern, an epidemic of silence soon broke out in the pantry. It was as if the tsetse fly had escaped its translucent depository and stilled us with its lullaby bite.

For hours we sat saying nothing. The only sound in the zoo was the gimp-legged rhumba of the wall clock. And an occasional checker flung by an impatient sentry against the kitchen wall. Purcell grew bored with sitting. The ruby claws of my hemorrhoids began to rustle. So we dissolved the think tank and went out to welcome the Zillers home from harvest.

You might say that it was intermission at the Second Coming. A break for a Coke, a cigarette, some chit-chat. Then back to the final act, which, if you could believe the program notes, was scheduled to go on forever.

The zoo reopened on Monday. Considering the season, traffic was heavy. We served sausages to a hundred or more customers, all of whom, children included, looked like undercover investigators to me.

As a result of the four-day layoff, the fleas were rusty and undisciplined. Their chariot races ended in helter-skelter collisions; on the ski jump some fleas went down backwards and others not at all; the prima ballerina—our most lovely insect —danced Joffrey's *Astarte* with one slipper missing and turned it into a fiasco: luckily our tourists were not connoisseurs of ballet.

By the close of business, I was a walking greenhouse of neurotic flora. Here a rare potted tic, there a twitch in full petal, everywhere exotic tropical wrinkles digging their anxious roots into the humus of my flesh. Even Purcell jerked nervously when Amanda suggested after supper that we Jeep over to Anacortes and take in the drive-in movie.

The Pluck and I argued mightily against it, but the Zillers insisted that entertainment was what Plucky and I needed. They made it sound as if the trip to the movies was all on our account. And they would do no less than bring the Corpse along.

Jesus was wrapped in one of Smokestack Lightning's Apache blankets and propped upright in the backseat between Plucky and me. "If the police should stop us for a narcotics check," said Amanda, "we'll say that the Corpse has consumed excessive firewater and that we're driving him back to the La Conner reservation." Beautiful logic. Back to the reservation by way of a drive-in show. And what if the police should decide they want to deliver the "Indian" themselves?

As it was, it cost us an extra dollar to get Christ into a performance which for him was some centuries late.

I can scarcely recall the films we saw. One was entitled *Return of the Squirrel Bride* and was about taxidermists and reincarnation. Amanda giggled a lot and Purcell commented that one reason aborigines have keen eyesight is because they never watch movies or television. "Well, what are we doing here?" I asked. "Movies are made of light," John Paul reminded us and he leaned toward the screen amidst a fluster of popcorn. In the second feature a boy named Chuck brought his girl friend home late from the prom. The father was furious. Especially when the girl missed her next period. As it turned out, it was only nerves that made her miss. I sympathized completely.

We drove out during the happy ending.

For me, the true happy ending was when Ziller's whopper weenie appeared in the distant sky. Bathed in neon, the steamed sausage rode the misty horizon as the soft side of man's nature sometimes rides over the raw hamburger of his depravity.

We pulled into the parking lot just in time to see two large male figures run from the roadhouse and vanish in the shadows of the pea fields.

After an uneasy night during which every dream was a bad one, I labored out of bed early Tuesday morning and drove to a telephone booth at a Chevron station on the outskirts of Mount Vernon. There I called the lab at Johns Hopkins and secured the results of the radiocarbon test. If I am not mistaken, I have already shared these with the reader.

The zoo looked peaceful enough upon my return. A trio of elderly ladies—widows perhaps—sat at the counter sipping juice. They were on their way to Victoria, B.C., to tour the gardens. At least that is what I gathered, for Amanda was conversing with them about the Butchart chrysanthemums. She was telling them that the Japanese consider the chrysanthemum a gastronomical delicacy. "Cannibals," exclaimed one lady beneath her breath.

Over by the snake pen, where I did not notice him at first browsed a massive middle-aged man with a face as crimson as Mon Cul's behind. He aroused my suspicion, but who didn't: those old ladies could have had swords in their knitting bags. Poison gas. Napalm. As I passed through the door into the kitchen the man boomed, "Waitress! Two more wieners, please. These gorgeous reptiles give me an appetite."

His voice was like a steel dog barking bricks.

I have never heard the voice before but I knew instantly to whom it belonged. Forty Hell's Angels roared up my colon. Parked their bikes in my diaphragm. Swaggered into my esophagus, ordered beer from my larynx and began shoving my tongue around.

Purcell was hiding behind the kitchen door. I could tell from his expression that he knew. Father Gutstadt had found himself a roadside attraction.

****

Father Gutstadt hung around the main room for a half-hour longer. He munched up four or five more hot dogs and asked morbid questions about the feeding habits of the snakes. Amanda treated him cheerfully. And eventually he went away. From an upstairs window I watched his Buick station wagon—a vehicle favored by nuns in the archdiocese of Seattle—proceed in the direction of Mount Vernon. He had made no overt attempt to pry into affairs at the zoo. However ...

The remainder of the day was a jittery blur. Visitors, including Farmer Hansen and his oldest boy, were in and out with regularity, prohibiting a closure of the zoo or discussion between the four of us human adults who lived there. While the Zillers attended to business, Purcell and I huddled in their flat. Around four in the afternoon, we noticed an armed man in a skiff on the slough directly across the Freeway. He pretended to be after ducks, but we determined his target was in actuality the roadhouse. No local duck hunter would assume a post so close to the highway.

From the bathroom window we then observed two men

working at a tractor, as if repairing it, in the field to the rear of our building. "They're closing in," said Plucky. "We're being surrounded."

At dinner, where only Amanda and Mon Cul consumed their mushroom soup with gusto, Purcell outlined a plan to bolt with the Corpse to the studios of Channel 5, Seattle's liberal TV station. I proposed to go out and confront the men who were spying on us, demand to speak with their leader, and offer to return the Corpse if certain concessions were made in Washington and Rome. Amanda thought we were both courting unnecessary risk. John Paul suggested that we wait another twenty-four hours before action of any kind. When asked to justify the delay, he uttered an African (or was it Indian?) proverb which, in its atavistic convolutions, made so little sense I cannot remember it.

Nothing was resolved. At one moment the zoo seemed like a place under siege, and the next it seemed, well, as "normal" as it had ever been.

Amanda brewed herb tea that had a calming effect, and then went up to sing Thor to sleep. Ziller took up watch at his sanctuary window and assigned Mon Cul a station at the front door of the roadhouse. Purcell was to remain close to the pantry and I was to retire to my quarters above the garage where I would have the most favorable view of the eastern perimeter: our flank. When I requested a weapon, John Paul gave me a blowgun. "Just don't inhale," he warned. Thanks, pal.

Deciding that a second cup of the tranquilizing tea might prevent me from boring myself to death with spontaneous imitations of popular earthquakes, I lingered a while in the kitchen. Plucky and I fell to talking. He told me about growing up in rural Virginia, about fast cars and moonshine and free-for-alls after football games, about fishing in the Shenandoah and about the bitterness that sometimes tinged his relatives' reminiscences of the days when they had been landed gentry. He talked about his lifelong weakness for women. And about drugs and abortions and how, in dealing in them, he honestly was trying to do some good in life—to minister in areas where the more respectable humanists would not venture. He reiterated his theory that in our culture everything sooner or later boils down to a matter of a buck. But he expressed a desire to learn something about science from me. He said he realized that his knowledge of religion, politics, economics, art, philosophy and so on was fragmentary, and that he supposed someday he should make another stab at formal education, although he wasn't sure it would make him any happier. He quoted some lines from his friend Sund the poet to the effect that "it's surprising how many people are laughing once you get away from universities and stop reading newspapers." Then he laughed himself.

I told him that he should at least devote some time to reflecting on the year he had spent as a monk of the Church, as that was an unusual educational experience in itself.

"Yeah, man," he said, "I'd sure dig holing up in a cabin somewhere to sort and sift it for a few months. And I'll do it, too. If I get out of this mess with any fuzz on my balls."

We parted warmly.

Not remembering which end of the blowgun was which, and as afraid to pick up one of the poison darts as I would have been afraid to goose a hornet, I put the crude weapon aside and crouched unarmed at my rear window. Every fifteen minutes or so the harvest moon would bleed through the tourniquet of cloud cover that conspired to squeeze every droplet of pictorial sentiment out of the Skagit landscape in order that a more refined Chinese mood might brush the countryside. In the aloof washes of moonlight no form seemed to stir. After what felt like thirty hours of uneventful scrutiny, I dropped asleep, awakening in the dishwater light of dawn with my head on the window ledge. I was as stiff as the drainpipe that gargled embalming fluid.

A ragged round of calisthenics set my blood to circulating again. Then, after ascertaining that the coast was clear, I hobbled across the dewy grove to the roadhouse. In the kitchen I found Amanda scalding the teapot. She wore a look of intense curiosity and little else. Just a pair of panties, as a matter of fact. The blood which I had just managed to set flowing only with great effort and with a sluggish and insubordinate lack of cooperation, now surged into my penis with such merry abandon that it caused it to stand on end.

I wondered what Amanda was doing up at such an early hour—but I needn't wonder long. The pantry was unlocked. And I could see in the dawn light that the Corpse was gone.

I feared the worst, but Amanda assured me that there had been no invasion while I slept. It was an inside job. John Paul and Plucky had fled with the Corpse. Mon Cul, too. They had all disappeared in the middle of the night.

"Well, I'll be damned," I said. "I'll be double damned."

Clues—and Amanda's noted intuition—led us to believe that the abduction was Ziller's idea. With the baboon's aid, he had attempted to steal away with the Corpse, but despite his jungle stealth, Plucky had caught him in the act and insisted on joining the caper. Of course, it was possible that Purcell had been in on it all along.

Perhaps Ziller had removed the Corpse in order to protect his wife, Baby Thor and me. Perhaps he had decided to dispose of it. Perhaps he and Plucky planned to expose it in some sensational or novel way. Perhaps he was going to display it in New York, where the art world had been clamoring for his comeback. I recalled his exhibition of ace-of-hearts magnetism and clockwork duckbills three seasons ago.

We could only guess why the body had been removed. And to where.

All we knew was that Christ Jesus was loose on the planet again; Jesus the mysterious powerhouse of the spirit, who having been betrayed once by a kiss and then by a religion, seemed destined to suffer less from his pagan opposites than from those kindred forces of righteousness who claimed to love him best. Ah, but he had a different set of disciples with him this time. Maybe they would stand him in better stead.

I felt a strong urge to pray, an equally strong urge to rip Amanda's panties off and make love to her on the floor, and a third urge that insisted that I leave the Capt. Kendrick Memorial Hot Dog Wildlife Preserve as swiftly as possible. But then there came a thunderous pounding at both the back door and the front, and I realized, like the president of the Amos 'n' Andy fan club, that my desires had become obsolete.

As with an odd mixture of subtlety and brute arrogance, the agents went about their business of search-and-interrogation, it became apparent that they were ignorant of the Corpse. They knew that occupants of the roadside zoo had been in possession of a piece of property on which the Vatican State placed highest premium, and on which hinged issues of international moment. They understood that it was of great concern to the United States government that the culprits be apprehended and the property returned to the Holy See. They understood that matters of national security and prestige were at stake. But—*but*—they had not been briefed as to the nature of the property at large. Nor were they likely to be. Therefore, the raid upon, and subsequent occupation of, the roadside zoo had its delicate side.

For example, though Amanda and I were questioned maliciously and at length, all questions concerned the whereabouts and intentions of Ziller and Purcell. Not once did the agents refer directly to the Roman "property," and if it appeared that one of us was about to discuss it, they scrupulously changed the subject. (I teased them unmercifully, but Amanda refused to be unkind.)

They knew John Paul and Plucky had flown, the missing "property" with them. I gathered that our boys had clobbered an agent during their flight and had left him bound and gagged in the slough grass. When he was discovered at daybreak, he reported the escape. I gathered, further, that Father Gutstadt and the Felicitate monks had then taken up pursuit, anxious as they were that the Corpse should never be revealed, not even to their federal friends, and that cooperating FBI and CIA men had been left behind to guard Amanda and me and to seek information regarding the destination of the fugitives. The Felicitators were obviously calling the shots, and they had ordered their secular counterparts to steer clear of the issue of the "property."

The zoo, particularly John Paul's sanctuary, was ransacked thoroughly. The agents had a huge amount of data on the fugitives, which is not surprising considering that Purcell had for some while been on the government's long list of undesirables, and that Ziller, as a result of his musical and artistic activities, was a mythic figure in certain circles of Americana. Ziller, especially, seemed to intrigue the agents, almost to obsess them; they referred to him darkly by his chosen title, "magician," and regarded his very existence as a threat of an almost personal nature. On the other hand, they knew virtually nothing about Amanda and me, although they fingerprinted us and vowed that our pasts would not remain a secret long.

The zoo was closed and locked while throughout the day and night the agents searched and questioned. The following day, fresh orders must have arrived, for our captors moved their gear into my garage quarters (I am not permitted to leave the roadhouse) and from then on have not actively fraternized with us, although they have concocted schemes both crude and ingenious to continue their intimidation and harassment.

So (whew!) that brings the reader up to date. I had prayed (to whom I'm not sure) for one more day of writing, and now that day is ending and this report is current. I'm going to give my hemorrhoids a rest, if you don't mind. I'm going to soak my hemorrhoids in a tub of warm tap water, exactly as Lord Byron soaked his in the peacock surf of the Aegean Sea. And I shall not return to the typewriter until there is a break in developments here—or in the Sunshine State of Florida, where I understand a new class of celebrities are vacationing this year.

Well, I'm back. My Remington and I were parted less than four hours, during which time the letter arrived: the letter from John Paul Ziller about which Amanda's "voices" had prophesied. In reality, it was not a letter, nor was Ziller the author of it. Moreover, it did not "arrive" in any usual sense. Nevertheless, the "voices" were accurate enough to merit our respect if not our total trust. The circumstances of the contact were so:

The Puerto Rican timepiece, the one with the inlaid carnivals and overpopulated face, is what is known as a ninety-day clock. That is, it is designed to require rewinding every ninety days. This particular clock, however—due, no doubt, to its Latin temperament—invariably runs down after seventy-seven days. It, in fact, begins dragging its heels after seventy-five. Thus, when seventy-six days have passed, Amanda takes up its key, which is shaped like a bishop's gaudy staff, and tightens its springs. Today was the day of the winding ritual.

When Amanda reached behind the wall clock to grasp its key, she accidentally caressed the smooth cheek of a paper envelope. Retrieved, the envelope proved to be addressed to her in John Paul's handwriting (who else writes with a tailfeather plucked from a rosy spoonbill, so that each character penned seems to wade knee-deep in the very ink that nurtured it?). Lest an agent glimpse it, Amanda secreted the envelope in her small but aggressively feminine bosom, and hurried it upstairs. There, she ripped it open and removed its sole contents: a clipping snipped from a Seattle newspaper of some weeks past.

BABOONS ARE SPACE AGE MAN'S BEST FRIEND

TAMPA, Fla.—(AP)—When America's gigantic solar balloon lifts off from nearby Palm Castle Naval Air Station later this month, the "crew" of the significant atmospheric probe will consist of five baboons, animals that in the Space Age seem destined to replace the faithful dog as man's best friend.

An African native once told a British naturalist, "Baboons can talk but they won't do it in front of white men for fear you will put them to work." The ape's silence has been in vain, for man is putting baboons to work in large numbers and in a variety of fields.

In South Africa, baboons have been used for centuries as goatherds and shepherds, and a few human mothers have entrusted their children to the care of baboon babysitters. Recently, baboons upon whom frontal lobotomies have been performed to curb the surly tendencies the apes sometimes develop as they grow older, were employed as golf caddies, tractor drivers and as redcaps in South African rail and bus depots. (Tipping presumably is no problem, although conceivably a baboon porter might perform more diligently if rewarded with a banana or a fresh ear of corn.)

Baboons also have been used in testing auto safety devices at Holloman Air Force Base in New Mexico and by workers in Detroit. The Ford Motor Company's auto-testing site in Birmingham, Mich., was picketed by animal-lovers a few years ago as a result of publicity arising from the use of baboons as passengers in crash cars there.

By far the most extensive use of baboons has been by the medical profession. Baboons by the hundreds are being used in medical experiments in South Africa. The long-faced apes are paving the way toward conquest of the problems involved in transplanting organs from one human to another, medical men say.

Baboons are common in South Africa's mountains, and research centers buy them for 10 rands, or $14. The same animals cost $200 in the United States.

"The only primate available in unlimited numbers is the baboon. Gorillas and chimpanzees are almost extinct," says Prof. J. J. van Zyl of Stellenbosch University.

Baboons are also the most intelligent of all monkeys. They are almost manlike in their social organization. They can count, reason within limits, and use mechanical gadgets.

The availability of baboons contributed to Dr. Christiaan Barnard's pioneer heart operations. Dogs, used in other countries, were not nearly so satisfactory, scientists say.

More than 250 baboon-to-baboon kidney transplants have been done at Karl Bremer Hospital in Cape Town. A Bremer spokesman said they "accumulated a vast amount of data on the physiology of the baboon and his blood types, which are the same as human blood types."

Dr. Barnard has suggested that baboons be used as living storage units for human organs. Organs would be transplanted as they became available into the animals and later implanted in human recipients as needed.

"There is a chance that we will be able to store hearts in baboons for several days," he explained.

Whatever the baboon's past or future contributions to medical science, his most dramatic moment will come in mid-October when five specially trained baboons will ride to the outer edge of the earth's gravitation field in a transparent gondola suspended from the largest balloon ever built.

The purpose of the flight is to test effects of solar radiation. The latest Icarus XC experiment will be the most thorough thus conducted, spokesmen at the Florida test site claim. The baboon crew will be wired to instruments designed to measure their reactions to what

will undoubtedly be the strongest blast of direct sunlight ever experienced by a living creature.

The Icarus baboons have been trained to operate
closed-circuit TV transmitters and other devices to aid
man in his quest for knowledge of the sun.

While the heat-resistant plastic from which the gondola is constructed will act as a partial shield, it will
not protect the baboons once they near the outer limits
of the atmosphere, Palm Castle researchers say. The
latest crop of baboon heroes will not survive their space
adventure.

"The baboon launch, was it today?" Amanda asked. She
struck a match and held it to the clipping.

"No, I don't think so," I said. "I overheard something about
it on the agents' radio and I think the announcer said it
would be tomorrow. Yes, I'm sure of it; it's tomorrow morning."

The clipping burned quickly, as newsprint does. Amanda
said nothing. Her lower lip quivered simply and nobly as if it
were an insect wing held in the strands of a web.

"Do you want to try to do anything about it?" I asked. I
should have known better.

Convinced that nothing need be done, she took her tears
to bed, leaving me to drum upon my machine just as outdoors in the Skagit darkness the rain is drumming upon the
great sausage, the whopper hot dog that is shaped, I note
suddenly, like a zeppelin, a balloon.

The fear of death is the beginning of slavery, Amanda has
said. If she is right, then I was enslaved at an early age. It
started with a little prayer my mother helped me memorize
when I was four or five.

Now I lay me down to sleep,
I pray thee, Lord, my soul to keep.
If I should die before I wake,
I pray thee, Lord, my soul to take.

If I should die before I wake. Until I learned that macabre
line it had never occurred to me that one morning I might
not get up to play. The thought of death creeping into the
covers with me shaded my young soul and marked me with
an existential dread that has lingered, embellished through
the years, into manhood. How many other Christian children
have lost their purchase on life and liberty while on their
bunny-suit knees repeating the chilling words of that nursery-
room plea for immortality? I wonder.

This morning I awoke as I have awakened each morning
since learning that terrible prayer twenty-five years ago:
relieved, and a little surprised, to be alive. If the feeling
was particularly keen today, surely the reader understands
why.

For the first time in days, I had no typing to do, so I
spent the morning with Amanda. She was sorrowful but entertaining. She showed me seven ways to peel an orange,
each method more elaborate and aesthetic than the last.
Amanda has amazing information about the orange, but she
does not know an English word to rhyme with it. Only Mon
Cul knows that. And he's not telling.

Often the things that pop out of my typewriter regale me,
especially when I am trying to say something else and in a
different way only to have a kind of metamorphosis take
place during the act of typing and—whammo!—a concept I
hadn't counted on is strutting its vaudeville on the page. But
like love and art, you can't force it to happen. For example,
out of that business about fear and oranges I had hoped
would gel a profound preamble to the news I am about to
relate. It didn't work, obviously, so let me get down to it and
tell it straight and without fanfare, just the way it happened.

About an hour ago, about 2 P.M., an agent came upstairs.
It was the moon-headed, cleft-chinned agent with whom
Amanda had argued. There was a quality very close to
civility in his manner. Perhaps he felt sorry for us or perhaps
he was simply overwhelmed by the turn of events. Maybe it
was a combination of the two. At any rate, he handed

Amanda a long sheet of thin white paper, stamped "Top Secret," and motioned that he did not object to me reading over her shoulder. This is what we read:

Informal statement by Commander Newport W. Pleet, USN, Director of the joint civilian-military solar research program at Palm Castle Naval Air Station near Tampa, Fla.

At approximately 0345 hours (3:45 A.M.) Wednesday, Oct. 21, a party of persons unknown released from its moorage an Icarus XC high-altitude research balloon and ascended with it. A man believed to be connected with the theft was shot on the ground by guards as he attempted to escape.

The balloon was filled with helium in preparation for an 0700 lift-off which would have taken five baboons to what we call the outer "edge" of the earth's atmosphere (while the actual atmosphere extends many times higher, 99 per cent of the matter making up the atmosphere is confined to within 20 miles of the earth's surface) in an experiment to measure effects of solar radiation on living tissue. The experiment, which was also to have photographed the oxygen spectrum and the sun's corona, was to have been one in a continuing series originating at the Palm Castle site to probe the upper atmosphere for information needed for space flights and manned space stations.

The Icarus XC, when fully inflated, is 1,020 feet in height. More than 15 acres of polyethylene film reinforced with dacron fibers were used in its construction. It supported a transparent gondola of heat-resistant plastic resins, 22 feet in length and elliptically shaped. The gondola contained measuring devices and life-supporting equipment of various types. The entire apparatus was valued at approximately $980,000.

The Icarus XC series is not classified and most of the information obtained is to be shared with other nations including, presumably, the Soviet Union. Nevertheless, stringent security was in effect. Visitors are not allowed beyond the gates of Palm Castle Naval Air Station without a pass. Additional permission is required to enter the test site vicinity. Ten naval enlisted men armed with carbines stood watch at strategic posts near the balloon pad this morning.

We now believe the thieves entered the main gate with stolen passes. At least one naval officer, Ensign Goober Clooney, was robbed of his wallet in the men's room of a

Tampa cocktail lounge late Tuesday night. Ensign Clooney's identification papers were found on the person of the man shot by guards. In addition, an automobile belonging to a Navy enlisted man and bearing a sticker which permitted it to enter the test area was stolen during the night. It was abandoned on base a quarter of a mile from the balloon pad.

Three guards were knocked unconscious by the thieves as they made their way to the balloon. The Palm Castle sick bay reports that the men were struck on their necks, presumably by some sort of karate blows. Even with three guards indisposed, the thieves must have worked with incredible stealth to unmoor the balloon and enter its gondola.

The balloon was 100 feet in the air before the remaining guards noticed it had been launched. Initially, they thought it had been released accidentally, but hasty investigation proved the moorage lines to have been cut. At least four guards testified that they saw a man or men moving about in the gondola as it ascended.

I was telephoned at the BOQ and reached the test site at 0410 hours. By then the balloon had entered the overcast and was not visible to the eye, although it was easily fixed by radar. We attempted to contact the Icarus XC by radio but received no response except for what seemed like laughter and the sound of a flute.

In the Icarus system we are able to control altitude of flights by a feeding device that can increase or decrease the balloon's helium supply. That device was not operative this morning. Other equipment was functioning properly.

By 0435 hours, the balloon had obtained an altitude of 12,000 feet. Air-to-air rescue of the abductors seemed unlikely. The gondola was fogged with condensation, and the observation plane that I had ordered aloft had little to report. I considered, at that time, requesting fighter interceptors to shoot down the Icarus XC, if for no other reason than that appeared to be the only way we might learn who was aboard and why.

While I awaited permission for an air attack, the slain man was brought to the control building. He had been shot three times in the back by guards at the outer perimeter of the test area at approximately 0350 hours. Security personnel reported that he was running and ignored commands to halt. He proved a difficult target and eluded 20 to 25 rounds before being hit. In addition to Ensign Clooney's wallet, the man carried papers identifying him as L. Westminster Purcell III.

Purcell is a former football star at Duke University who created some scandal about eleven years ago when he absconded with his coach's wife. He is said to have later engaged in criminal activities. As a naval officer prior to dishonorable discharge, he underwent jet pilot's training at Palm Castle. If the man is indeed Purcell, he would have had firsthand knowledge of the base. That might partly explain the success of the theft.

Among the dead man's effects was a note scrawled on the inner side of a cigar pack. It was blood-soaked and much of it was obscured. However, I recorded the following paragraph:

". . . I have reached the conclusion that the Second Coming would have no real impact on our society. It would simply be absorbed and exploited by our economic system (even I was tempted to use the C. as a springboard to wealth and power). Our society gives its economy priority over health, love, truth, beauty, sex and salvation; over life itself. Whatsoever is given precedence over life will *take* precedence over life, and will end in eliminating life. Since economics, at its most abstract level, *is* the religion of our people, no noneconomic happening, not even one as potentially spectacular as the Second Coming, can radically alter the souls of our people. Therefore, I have temporarily abandoned my dream in order to help fulfill the dream of Z. Meanwhile, Marx, I can only hope with all my baggy heart, that the white magic of A.—and of others like her—will in time ace out the black magic of . . ." (rest illegible).

These are the words of an atheistic Communist or of a madman. In my opinion, he was both.

At any rate, permission to shoot down the Icarus XC was granted at 0500 hours by Admiral Stacy Horowitz, Commander, Third Naval District. Shortly after our interceptors were airborne, however, the order was rescinded by the White House. No explanation was offered. Our aircraft were called back and I was ordered to let the balloon proceed without interference. I was ordered further to desist from radio or television contact with the balloon. Later, personnel of the Central Intelligence Agency dismantled our transmitters.

At this time, the Icarus XC is at approximately 70,000 feet. It will travel to well over twice that altitude. The gondola, fully pressurized, is equipped with a self-contained oxygen supply; enough oxygen is aboard to keep three persons alive for a week. However, the illicit passengers will not live for a week. They will perish after less than 24 hours from the effects of solar radiation. Acute dehydration will reduce their bodies to almost nothingness and they will decompose at an accelerated rate. By the time next month when the balloon begins to lose altitude and subsequently to disintegrate, only their bones will remain, and should the balloon stay aloft long enough, even the bones will turn to dust. The gondola will be nearly as empty as if it never contained life at all.

Investigation of the theft is not in my province. I have been informed by the White House that I am to consider the case closed. In closing, however, I must confess to being particularly puzzled by one aspect of the event. In our control building we have quartered five baboons. They were not to be placed in the solar gondola until 0630 hours today. Indeed, they are in sight of me at this moment. All five of them. Yet, before our transmitters were disconnected this morning someone aboard the Icarus XC briefly switched on the TV monitor—and for about 60 seconds my colleagues and I gazed into the grinning face of a baboon. Gentlemen, make of it what you will, but there is an unauthorized baboon aboard that fated balloon.

In some superstitious mouse-gnawed wine-stained gold-braided inner sanctum of the Vatican, a half-dozen elegant and elderly cardinals are being addressed by a black-robed churchman of undetermined rank.

"Yes, your Eminences, the results are irreversible. No one could alter the balloon's flight now, even if he so desired."

"Save for God himself," a cardinal interjects.

"Really, Luigi," says another, "we can rule out divine intervention, don't you think?"

A third prelate, the oldest and most elegant of the lot, has been kneading his puffy right fist in his puffy left palm. "Why?" he asks no one in particular. "Why, why, why, why, why, why, why? Why did such a peculiar thing happen?"

"God goes about his business in mysterious ways," says one cardinal. The elder gives him a puffy glare that seems to say, "Don't hand me *that* old rubbish."

"Maybe we have ourselves to blame," ventures the youngest prelate present. "We have harbored a skeleton in our closet—so to speak—for far too long. Maybe we should inquire of ourselves if there are not other skeletons here—I speak figuratively, now—that might disturb the moods and philosophies of the world were they disclosed."

"I am unsure of the implications of your remarks, Vasco," says the elder, "but I trust you had no intention of leaving the range of allowable discussion. We cannot oblige ourselves to the secular world without harm."

"Oh, I agree, Father. I only meant that for the Church's protection . . ."

"Yes, yes. Quite, quite. But my mind is absorbed now with the balloon ascent and not with the follies that preceded or the precautions that must follow."

The figure in the black robe clears his throat. "Ahem. These people who were involved in this episode are beyond the power of human understanding, Father. They represent a fringe of modern liberalism that is wholly demented. But if you would like, I will file with you a complete report on the persona and their actions so that you might search for your own conclusions therein."

By various methods, the cardinals indicate that they would indeed like a detailed report. The air in the chamber is like the sculptured exhaust of a marble Cadillac parked overtime in an invalid's bedroom.

"Meanwhile," says the elder, "there is no chance that . . ."

"No chance at all, your Eminence," the black-robed man assures. "By this time tomorrow there will be nothing left of the, er, body. Or of that magician and his monkey. They will literally have vanished into thin air."

Kneading his puffy right fist in his puffy left palm, the elder cardinal goes to the window to look at the heavens, only there is no window in the chamber and he is faced with a tedious wall of ancient age. The marble Cadillac spins its wheels, grinding the invalid's bifocals into the rug.

Shortly thereafter, blue-and-white jersey No. 69 was retired by the Duke University football squad, and never again on a brassy autumn afternoon in Durham will you see that number flashing in the soft-cider bee-fuzz Carolina sunshine. The Mexican Federation of Marijuana Growers would have sent a nice wreath had they known. Had they known that Plucky Purcell had fallen, three hoarse slugs in his champion physique, his vulgar grin outlined in blood; dead at age thirty without ever having decided whether life was sour or sweet.

This case could be made for Plucky Purcell: that he was another victim of Christ/Authority. The same could not be said of John Paul Ziller. Ziller's moves were calculated in full consciousness. He was nobody's victim, maybe not even his own.

Ziller had always operated at that junction where the archaic path of nature and necromancy crosses the superhighway of technology and culture. As he lived, so he died, as they say. A man in between Heaven and Earth.

In mastering the science of origins (excuse me, the science of Godward solutions), Ziller carried the quest to its most personal extreme. Clear-eyed and confident, he returned——literally—to energy, dissolving in the pure essence that spawned all life.

Even as I type these words, John Paul Ziller, the baboon with the firebug buttocks and Jesus the Christ of Nazareth are melting together into sunlight.

Part V

Rain fell on Skagit Valley.

It fell in sweeps and it fell in drones. It fell in unending cascades of cheap Zen jewelry. It fell on the dikes. It fell on the firs. It fell on the downcast necks of the mallards.

And it rained a fever. And it rained a silence. And it rained a sacrifice. And it rained a miracle. And it rained sorceries and saturnine eyes of the totem.

Rain drenched the chilly green tidelands. The river swelled. The sloughs fermented. Vapors rose from black stumps on the hillsides. Spirit canoes paddled in the mists of the islands. Legends were washed from desecrated burial grounds. (The Skagit Indians, too, have a tradition of a Great Flood. The flood, they say, caused a big change in the world. Another big change is yet to occur. The world will change again. The Skagit don't know when. "When we can converse with the animals, we will know the change is half-way here. When we can converse with the forest, we will know the change has come.") Water spilled off the roofs and the rain hats. It took on the colors of neon and head lamps. It glistened on the claws of nightime animals.

And it rained a screaming. And it rained a rawness. And it rained a plasma. And it rained a disorder.

The rain erased the prints of the sasquatch. It beat the last withered fruit from the orchard trees. It soaked the knotted fans who gathered to watch high-school boys play football in the mud. It hammered the steamed-up windshields of lover's lane Chevvies, hammered the larger windshields of hunters' pickups, hammered, upriver, the still larger windshields of logging trucks. And it hammered the windowpane through which I gazed at the Freeway reflection of Ziller's huge innocent weenie, finding in its gentle repose precious few parallels with my own condition.

"You know," I said to Amanda, "this whole awful business might be easier to endure if we were on a sunny Mexican beach instead of drowning under a Northwest waterfall." I gestured in the direction of the weather.

"The last time I was on a Mexican beach, some guy stole my transistor radio," sighed Amanda.

"Why, that's a dirty shame," I sympathized.

"Oh, it was all right," she said. "He took the radio but he left the music."

The postman always rings twice, I think the expression goes. An FBI agent visited us yesterday in midafternoon; the dreadful circumstances of that visit I have dutifully reported. Just after dusk last night he appeared again at the head of the stairs.

"Hey, buddy," he yelled at me, causing me to drop the orange I was peeling (via method no. 5). "You're gonna be leaving here tomorrow. Just thought I'd clue you in. We'll be staying downstairs tonight, so don't you try any funny stuff."

When I attempted to assure him that I had no funny stuff in mind, his putting iron took a juicy whack at my orange—which had had the poor judgment to roll right up to his black shoes—and he growled, "Don't get smart with me, mac. You'd just better be thankful it was me who came up to tell you and not somebody else. Some of the boys are itching to get their hands on you."

He turned to Amanda, who had walked over to wipe up the orange pulp, and said in a kinder tone, "I don't know when you and the kid will be leaving. But the government is taking over this property, so be prepared." Having deposited those dollops of cheer, he returned downstairs.

I could have spent the night wondering what they are going to do with me. I could have fantasied all possible punishments and executions and then, as I tossed in my bed, I could have wondered what I would do even should they take me to Seattle and turn me loose with a warning. By neither reputation nor inclination am I still a scientist. And even if I were, what role will there be for scientists, for men of culture, in this new world that the Indians prophesied and the Zillers advertised? (For some centuries now we have been in charge of things and I had thought that we would cast the man of the future in our own image, but now I must ask myself: Is a day breaking when we will be at the bid and call of persons who scorn our progressive values, who nonchalantly commandeer our special skills, products and services in order to expedite a kind of pagan magic?) I could have spent long gruesome hours worrying about my future and worrying whether *I had* a future—but I didn't. For shortly after Baby Thor had been tucked in his sleeping skins, Amanda called to me from her sanctuary, and I was permitted behind the perfumed curtains at last.

Opulent Persian weavings smoldered on the floor, and there was a festoonery of incense burners and candelabra. Everything else, however, seemed to have come from the wild.

In one corner, a tabletop was laid out with seashells. There were purples and whelks, rice shells and harp shells, marsh snails and pond snails, periwinkles and egg ribbons, agate shells and ear shells, razor clams and sand clams, helicinas and wentletraps, turban shells and moon shells, keyhole limpets and abalones, staircase shells and fig shells, South Pacific mollusks known as "wine jars" because they are so capacious, and, of course, the famous giant conch shell valued as a long-playing record of the ocean. Beside these were the ornate armors of sea cucumbers, urchins, anemone and starfish from the gelid waters of Puget Sound. And beside these, tubes and castles of coral, some encrusted with polyps. And next to these, a snailery: bubbles of air rising in its water showed that all was well. Snails coiled like confectionery watch springs among the leaves and stems of floating plants; and clams, too, lived quietly in the aquarium, traveling about when they felt like it, plowing with extended foot through the gravel.

Arranged along the windowsills, where they could best satisfy their appetites for sunshine, were rows of cacti. There was a Christmas cactus and a prickly pear and a fishhook cactus and a purple hedgehog cactus and a night-blooming cereus, and several chollas with barbaric spikes and others whose spines I dreaded and whose names I did not know. They looked none too healthy, although that was to be expected in this cloudy climate. Amanda's cacti strained their rough ribs toward the very sun that was eating her husband. But, of course, I said nothing of that.

Hanging from the walls by various means were the vacant nests of countless birds. There was, among the many, a hammock-shaped nest of the golden oriole, an igloo-shaped nest of some jungle specimen, a grass-at-all-angles nest of the ouzel, an eagle's nest spacious enough for Thor to hide in, and yes, a cuckoo's nest, which is to say the nest of any other bird the cuckoo finds handy. If one goose had flown over it, he had dropped no leaflets nor any other explanation of why he did not fly east or west like his peers.

In among the nests were cones of the pine, the Douglas fir, the redwood, the sequoia, the spruce and the hemlock. There were limbs to which types of acorns were attached. There were pieces of driftwood, fossilized roots and dried leaves. Cattails protruded from a ceramic urn. The cattails looked like a promotional display for Ziller's sausages. I thought of the happy lunches when I would eat two "with everything."

Ferns (as if there weren't enough outdoors) grew in earthen pots. Philodendrons also grew, and jade plants and carrots and soybeans and avocado saplings and plants of the notorious family *cannabis* (had she no speck of fear for the law?). Iron containers, some rusted and barnacled, were stuffed to overflowing with dried grasses and grains. Next to them were heavy rocks which served as hillsides and plateaus for miniature Gothic cities of lichen. Dried fungi were present in some abundance (a single wavering ray of candlelight saluted the still-red tops of the ominous *Amanita muscaria*), and between pages of clear glass were pressed wild flowers of these varieties and more: trillium, buttercup, violet, daisy, crocus, creeping Jennie, narcissus, foxglove, scarlet pimpernel (looking not a fraction as erotic as its name suggests), rhododendron, edelweiss and lily of the valley.

Scarabs lay about everywhere, as did the iridescent shells of Siamese beetles nearly five inches long. And, naturally, butterflies: butterflies and moths of so many kinds that it would take a more patient correspondent than I to attempt to list them all, let alone to describe the gentle colors with which their docile wings were powdered. Let me emphasize that Amanda never killed butterflies herself, nor did she encourage others to do so. But she was not so pure as to refuse the tropical collections that her father brought back from orchid-buying trips, or the mounted specimens sent to her by Al of Suez and her male admirers at the National Institute of Flying Creatures, Department of Fluttering and Frittering.

In the midst of this assemblage of flora and fauna (I did not even mention the tiny chests and carved boxes crammed with stones, seeds, teeth and pollens), Amanda had sat daily —meditating, chanting, caressing, performing rituals and otherwise laying hold on the primitive values that had once allowed man to view the world and his experience in it as a sacred whole. Here, her green eyes looked into the heart of the wild. And saw her Self looking back.

Last night she was crouched on the carpet, completely naked, her femininity agape. Apparently, she had quite recently given herself one of her homemade gooseberry douches, for her pubic hair was slick and damp, rising to a froth-edged peak like a stylized ocean wave in a Japanese woodblock print. I thought of Hokusai and Hiroshige.

Her lisp, as pink and nacrous as the inner part of any shell, called me closer. I went without hesitation, but stopped in my tracks when I was near enough to see what she was doing. Two finite black dots were moving on her body, just below her right breast. They were Rock and Natalie, her favorite fleas! Unknown to me, she had held this pair back, sparing them the rigors of exile. Visitors to the roadside zoo will remember Rock as the flea with the pasha mustache who refused to learn any of the regular circus routines, preferring to satirize or improvise upon the performances of his fellows. Natalie, well, she had a zest for roller skating and was a bit of a vamp. Funny, but in all my months at the zoo, I had neither seen the fleas dine nor questioned their gastronomical practices. I had assumed that they were fed a

formula of some sort and that, perhaps, on high feast days
they were allowed to entertain themselves at the veins of
Mon Cul. Last evening, however, I learned that only fleas
who gorge on human blood are hale and hearty enough for
circus work. The Zillers had had the pleasure of flea company regularly at dinner.

(They never scratched. But, of course, with employer-
employee relations what they are, they didn't dare to.)

"Marx," said Amanda, "I entered a semi-trance a short
while ago and received a telepathic communication from
Nearly Normal Jimmy. He screens *Tarzan's Triumph* every
night for the Chinese officers and is contemplating opening
a chain of motion-picture theaters in Lhasa. Wants me to
send him a print of *Yellow Submarine* with the Beatles. Says
it will restore things to normal in Tibet. What do you think
of that?"

What could I think?

I waited until the fleas were full of her. And then I took
my turn.

In accordance with his theory that man is nothing but
slowed-down light, John Paul Ziller had seen fit to accelerate.
"I haven't lost him," explained Amanda, "because each time
I sit in the sunshine he will envelop me and tickle me with
his warm reminders. He was the drumbeat in my past and he
is the heat in my future."

Ah, but there was rain in her present. Rain and Marx
Marvelous.

Sometime during the night of squish and bliss, however, I
had the ill manners to think again of the morrow. And the
morrow after. "Amanda," I asked, "if the universe is ultimately meaningless, as you say—big and beautiful but meaningless—then why go on living? Why not commit suicide?"

"Suicide has no class," she answered. "It's bad form."

"Oh yeah, that's right. The most important thing is style."

"Style, Marx."

"Right. I forgot."

"Don't forget."

"I promise. But, seriously, if life has no meaning—"

"To say it has no meaning is not to say it has no value."

"But to say it's all meaningless. Isn't that a cop-out?"

"Maybe. But it seems to me that the *real* cop-out is to say that the universe has meaning but that we 'mere mortals' are incapable of ever knowing that meaning. Mystery is part of nature's style, that's all. It's the Infinite Goof. It's meaning that is of no meaning. That paradox is the key to the meaning of meaning. To look for meaning—or the lack of it—in things is a game played by beings of limited consciousness. Behind everything in life is a process that is *beyond* meaning. Not beyond understanding, mind you, but beyond meaning. Mmmmmmmmmmmmmm. It still feels good when you touch me like that. Like *that!*"

Back to squish and bliss. (Amanda snuffing out the incense, for as someone once said, smell is 80 per cent.)

I had more questions later. I asked them in desperation and she turned them aside with charm. But the last thing I remembered hearing, except for the gurgling of the snailery and the rain on the roof, before I took a slippery slide into sleep was her whispered lisp in my ear, "Nothing to lose, Marx, and nothing to gain. Nothing to lose and nothing to gain. A man can be as free and happy as he wants to be because there's nothing to lose and nothing to gain."

It is dawn now. The perfumed curtains have been removed and from where I sit typing I can look directly into Amanda's sanctuary. She is packing. Her face is flushed with that passionate serenity that is evidently known only by those who live outside of man's laws and according to nature's.

In my own head an odd new joy is crowing.

Amanda has just informed me that she is pregnant again. At first I thought she meant by me. I realize that it has only been a few hours, but after all, she is clairvoyant. But, no, alas, it wasn't I. Presumably, it was the magician. Although it may have been Plucky Purcell. Or one of the wayfaring black men who stopped off at the roadside attraction. Who knows?

She is placing her belongings in an old wicker suitcase. Many possessions will be left behind. Without regret, I imagine. She has just laid in some folded panties. And some butterflies.

She is not packing as would one who was off to an institution or an execution. Or who was returning to the family hearth. She packs like one who is about to run away with the whirlwind of life. She just put in some gypsy toe-bells. And the tsetse fly.

As it has for days, a language of rain babbles against the windows. It sounds fresh and right to me now.

Oh oh. From below, they just called my name. Not "Marx Marvelous," but my *real* name. The bastards! On top of everything else, there will be alimony to face.

They call again. I recognize the voice. The voice thumps up the stairs one word at a time, as if the words were lead basketballs dribbled by a rusty robot. It is Father Gutstadt calling. "Get your things together," says his geological boom. "You've got five minutes."

I already have my things together. So I will add a few last words to this report. Amanda is starting to come toward me now. Coming to kiss me good-bye. In her face I notice a terrible beauty. Like the terrible beauty of nature itself. It reveals to me two facts. One: she loves me deeply. Two: she is completely indifferent as to whether she ever sees me again.

Looking past her to her suitcase, I ascertain that it is not yet full. Good. For she has promised to leave room in it for this manuscript.

Reader! Let this be a signal to you. If this manuscript has survived, it will mean that Amanda has survived.

And if AMANDA is ALIVE . . .

And JESUS is DEAD . . . .

. . . .

. . . .

Pine Cones on the Tent,

It's a cold, clear morning; the sun has come over the canyon wall, but you're still dozing around, when something hits the tent. Open the flap and the sun's in your face; the world is ready.

Let Amanda be your pine cone.

About the Author

TOM ROBBINS was a student of art and religion, later worked as a copy editor and an art critic before "dropping out" to write fiction. Born in North Carolina and reared in Virginia, he now lives in a tiny fishing village north of Seattle.